THE LOVER

Laura Wilson

WINDSOR
PARAGON

First published 2004
by
Orion
This Large Print edition published 2004
by
BBC Audiobooks Ltd by arrangement with
The Orion Publishing Group Ltd

ISBN 1 4056 1015 8   (Windsor Hardcover)
ISBN 1 4056 2010 2   (Paragon Softcover)

British Library Cataloguing in Publication Data available

Printed and bound in Great Britain by
Antony Rowe Ltd., Chippenham, Wiltshire

THE LOVER

It is the autumn of 1940, and London is in the grip of the Blitz. An unidentified female corpse is discovered in an alleyway in Soho—the fourth to have been found in a matter of weeks. The women —all prostitutes—have been horribly mutilated.

Rene is a Soho prostitute with a young son to support. For her each night on the streets is a terrifying ordeal as the killer begins to pick off her friends. Lucy is a young office worker living with her family in Clapham, her head full of romantic notions of how love ought to be. Jim is a fighter pilot, handsome and much admired for his heroism in battle. The killer instinct makes him perfectly suited to the daily challenge he faces above the skies of southern England, but the strain is beginning to tell.

In ordinary circumstances, their paths might never have crossed, but in war-town London, anything can happen. One night a bomb falls, with terrifying consequences for them all . . .

PROLOGUE

SATURDAY 19TH OCTOBER 1940
Soho, London

The alley was pitch dark. The two men, hats and overcoats wreathed in a post-pub fug of cigarettes and beer, lurched along the broken pavement, leaning on each other for support.

'I said to her,' slurred George, 'I said, "You want to stop thinking of what you'll look like blown to pieces, that's what you want to do." I said, "You go down the shelter if you want. I'm not getting out of bed for bleeding Hitler." I said to her, "You've got too much imagination, that's your trouble."'

Bob belched. 'Shouldn't have had that last.'

'There's no talking to her,' said the other. 'Ever since they copped it three doors down, she's been that bad with her nerves . . .'

'They're bastards, that's what they are . . . Do you know something?'

'No, what?'

'I can't see a bloody thing.'

'Nor me.'

They stood together, swaying and peering hopelessly into the black void.

'Got a torch?' asked Bob.

'Can't get the batteries. Shop's had nothing for two weeks and there's sod-all chance elsewhere.'

'Oh, well . . .' Bob stepped forward. 'Long as we don't walk into a wall.'

'No bloody walls left, after the last few nights. I heard a good one yesterday, did I tell you? There's

1

three blokes, all in the pub, they've had a few—'

'—Like us—'

'Well, they make this . . . pledge . . . when they get home, each man, whatever his wife tells him, he's got to do it. The one that doesn't, he's got to buy the drinks. So off they go, and the next day, they meet up. The first man says, "Well, I did it." He says, "I've got home, and I'm a bit . . . you know . . . I piss in the sink, and the wife says, 'That's right, piss all over the place.' So I do—the table, the chairs, the curtains, the rugs—"'

'Steady!' George's foot slipped, and he cannoned into Bob, who grabbed his arm.

'Whoa! Sorry, mate. Bit slithery round here.'

'It's you, you daft berk, you've had a skinful.'

'No, it's the ground. Something down here, slippery . . . So then the next man, he says, "I did it, too—I've got home, and I'm the same, so I go to light a cigarette and I drop the match on the rug. And my wife, she says, 'That's right, burn the bloody house down.' So I do. The whole lot, up in smoke." Then the third man, he's a bit quiet, so they say, "Well, what about you?" And the third man, he says, "Well, I've gone home, and the wife's in bed, and I fancy a bit of the other, so I put my hand between her legs, and she says, "Cut it out, Sid . . ."''

'Cut it out! Cut it out . . . Steady the Buffs, for Christ's sake, or we'll both go over.'

'It's a good one, though. Blimey, this pavement . . .'

'Just a bit of rubbish. One of the shops.'

'Aren't any shops. Not down here.'

'Yes there are . . . aren't there?' They halted again. The darkness was impenetrable, like a

2

barrier. 'Christ, where are we?'

'We're bleeding lost is where we are.'

'Amazing . . .' Bob sighed. 'We could be anywhere. Anywhere at all.'

'Well, we've made a balls of this, all right. I'll be the one who cops it tonight, I'm telling you. I promised Edna I'd be home before the next lot.'

'You got a match?'

'What?'

'A match. There *is* something down here, an' all . . . Ta.' There was a scraping sound, followed by a brief flare of light.

'Watch it! You nearly had my eye with that. What's down there?'

'Dunno. Butcher round here, is there?'

'Not down this way, there isn't.'

'Well, somebody's been and dropped their supper. Liver, by the looks of it.' Bob staggered backwards as his companion bumped against him and slid down onto the pavement. There was a wet, slapping noise. 'Sounds like my dog licking its bits . . . You all right?'

'Christ, it's . . . Oh, *Christ* . . . My hand, my hand in it, Jesus, oh Jesus . . .'

'What are you talking about, your hand?' said the other, impatiently. 'You've come a cropper on a sandbag, that's all.'

'Sandbags . . . don't . . . wear . . . nylons . . . God, I'm going to—'

'Here, not on my shoes, you bastard! You finished, are you?' Bob bent down and felt for his companion in the darkness, gagging at the stink of vomited ale. His fingertips brushed over something viscous and then felt thick material—wet, soaking—a coat pooled out over the grimy stones.

3

His hand travelled along its length and he felt the bony lump of a hip, the slope of a thigh—chilly, doughy skin—and then the top of a stocking. 'Sorry, love. Thought you was a sandbag. It's just my pal, he's—'

Footsteps. The man turned and saw a dim pool of torchlight moving towards them, dark shoes and uniform trousers behind it.

'You the warden?'

'Yes. What's going on?'

'You tell us, mate. Woman here fallen down. My pal tripped over her.' He took a couple of steps towards the light and said in a low voice, 'I think she must have had a few herself.'

The warden sniffed. 'Dear oh dear. Let's get some light on the subject.' Watching the little beam from the warden's torch skip over the stones, Bob had a sudden image of his children playing hopscotch in the road, of grubby knees, flashes of knicker and bunched, bouncing hair, extinguished in a gasp as the light caught the edge of a puddle of dark fluid, thick and shining. The warden stopped. 'Blimey!'

'That's blood, that is.'

'Blimey,' repeated the warden. 'Blimey O'Reilly.' His torch played across the pavement, and stopped. In the centre of the pool of light lay a bloodstained metal claw. 'Tin-opener,' he said, flatly.

The men kept silent as the torch beam moved again, this time catching the hem of a blue coat with a pinkish tangle of bulging, glistening flesh that seemed to be slithering out from beneath it.

Bob clutched the warden's arm. 'What's that?'

'I don't know.'

The light fell on the woman's open palm, and

4

beside it, a little piece of blue cloth, folded over like an envelope.

The warden drew in his breath. 'My God . . .'

'What is it, mate? What you seen?'

'Never you mind,' said the warden, sharply. 'Just stay back.'

The beam followed the greyish-pink flesh of a leg to a knee, streaked with blood and dirt, a nylon stocking rucked round an ankle, a high-heeled shoe lying on its side, and then traced its way across the blue coat to reveal a bloody mass of dark, clotted hair and a scarf, and then, incongruously, a fringe of shining, chestnut-brown curls and the clean, pale edge of a profile, the skin white and lustrous in the torchlight, the eyes closed and the expression almost passionate.

Greta Garbo, thought Bob, suddenly, before his eyes followed the beam down to— 'Oh, Jesus *Christ*.' He took a step back. 'Her neck—her throat—he's cut her throat—he's carved her up . . . with a *tin-opener* . . .' He staggered over to the opposite wall and sat down, his head in his hands.

George shuffled towards him on all fours and collapsed across his shins. He blurted, 'It's him again, isn't it? He really cut it out this time, didn't he?' then raised his head and vomited again.

The warden ignored them both. He turned off his torch and, standing quite upright beside the body, he took off his helmet and clasped it against his chest. 'No,' he whispered into the darkness. 'It can't be . . .'

FIVE WEEKS EARLIER—SATURDAY 14TH SEPTEMBER
Essex

'Are you going to let me walk you home?' he asked.

'Why would you want to do that?' As if she didn't know the answer! He was keen on her, anyone could see that.

'So I can kiss you goodnight.'

'Ooh . . .' She leant back against the bar—you couldn't agree too quickly, that would look fast—but her elbow hit the edge and the jolt spilt some of her drink. She looked down at her arm, which didn't quite seem to belong to her, then edged carefully to one side. There was a puddle on the wood, and she didn't want her sleeve in it. She put her glass down and looked at him again, hoping he hadn't noticed the upset. 'I'm not sure about that,' she said.

'Which? Walking you home or kissing you?'

She giggled. 'Oh . . . *you* . . .' Someone jostled her from behind, and she toppled forwards against his chest.

'Careful,' he said, and put a hand under her elbow to steady her. 'Time to go, I think.'

Suddenly, she thought so too. Time to go. She felt uneasy—tired, and, well . . . *peculiar*. She glanced round the pub. Nothing seemed straight, somehow, not the packed bodies of airmen and girls, the heads and shoulders wreathed in cigarette smoke under the low, dark beams, the jangle of the piano, the clatter of pewter mugs, the singing and the laughter. She'd wanted to be part of it so badly, to be grown-up, but now . . . now she just wanted to

6

go home.

Her friend Mona was nowhere to be seen. They were supposed to be going to the pictures, and—cross your heart and hope to die—that's where they *were* going, until the car filled with blue uniforms had come barrelling up the road. Mona had whispered, 'Pilots,' in an awed voice, and they'd stood back to wave. Then, miraculously, the car had pulled up in a cloud of dust, the window was wound down, and they'd found themselves gazing at three—three!—of these handsome, glamorous heroes, and even Mona, who was seventeen and had been to London and knew just about everything, couldn't think of a thing to say.

'Come on girls, jump in!' That was all it took. They'd exchanged glances—too good to be true—propped their bicycles against a tree, and rushed to open the door. She'd kept quiet and let Mona make the introductions, and tried not to notice—or to look as if she noticed—the warmth and pressure of the man's leg against hers in the crowded back seat. She clenched her buttocks to try and shrink herself a bit, but it didn't make any difference: the pressure was still there, and anyway, the car kept jolting them together. Mona accepted a cigarette, so she had to have one too, or risk being thought unsophisticated. It had made her cough a bit, but she'd managed it all right. Then she'd watched, impressed, as Mona had opened her compact with a flick of her wrist and re-done her lipstick—perfectly, in spite of the bumps—and wondered if her own make-up, applied by Mona behind the apple tree in the garden, was still in place.

Then Mona had thrown back her head and laughed and tossed her hair, so she'd done the

7

same. The pilots had laughed right along with them, and they'd roared down the road in the sunset and everything was lovely. And then the best one, the handsomest, and, she was sure, the bravest—any girl would have welcomed his attentions—had chosen her when they'd reached the pub. Not Mona, who couldn't keep the envy out of her eyes, but *her*. He singled her out, bought her a drink—drinks—and chatted to her. He'd said how nice it was to talk to a girl who wasn't in uniform, and how pretty her eyes were, and after a while he'd started telling her private, important things, like about his sister who'd been ill but was terribly brave and never complained, and how much he missed the poor kid and how he looked forward to her letters, and then he'd apologised for boring her and she'd just gaped at him—well, she hoped she hadn't actually gaped, because that was rude, but that's what it felt like—but she was so delighted to be there with all of them—with *him*—and the whole thing was just . . . *heaven*.

All the same, she wished she were better at talking to him. She could chatter for hours at home, but here, with him, she couldn't think of anything to say that wouldn't sound foolish, or . . . She'd thought it would help, having the drink, but it hadn't. It just tasted funny and after three of them everything started to blur—things and words. Only his face seemed still and clear, held in a sort of glow. He was *so* handsome, with his bright blue eyes, tanned face and corn-coloured hair. I wish I knew his name, she thought. She'd missed it in the car. Awkward, and watching Mona for cues, she hadn't taken it in, and she couldn't ask him now.

It would be dark outside. She didn't want to walk

by herself—she wasn't even sure she *could* walk by herself—but the thought of trying to find Mona in the crush, of disengaging her from a flirtation and of being told, afterwards, that she was a spoilsport or, worse, 'just a kid', was disheartening. In any case, what better way to prove she wasn't than to leave with an airman—a pilot, no less! As long as he left her at the end of the road, of course. Impressing Mona was one thing, but if her mother were to see her coming back with a *man*, she'd never hear the last of it. But she could take care of that when the time came. As for the goodnight kiss, well, the book she'd got said you had to leave them wanting more—it hadn't quite put it that way, but that was what it meant. In any case, you couldn't just let a man kiss you, or goodness knows what he'd think. And she'd be seeing him again, wouldn't she? Surely she would. Imagine: a pilot! Woozily, she pictured her friends' faces when she told them. Jealous and greedy at the same time. She grinned to herself.

'You're smiling,' he said.

'It's just . . . nice. That's all. Talking to you.'

'I think I've done most of the talking,' he said.

'Listening, then. Nice listening. To you.'

She let him turn her round and steer her towards the door of the pub. It banged behind them, and suddenly they were alone in the darkness. 'Whoo!' she said. 'Fresh air.'

'Over here,' he said. She took a few tipsy steps into the lane. The ground was uneven. *She* was uneven. She heard the pub door open again, and turned her head. Mistake. Now everything was uneven. She had to get home.

He took her arm and guided her towards the

9

wall of the pub. 'Lean against this for a minute. You'll be fine.'

She could feel the roughness of the bricks through the back of her frock. 'I've had such a nice time,' she said, 'such a lovely time. But—'

'Just stay still. You'll be all right.'

'My torch . . .' she fumbled in her pocket. He put his hand on top of hers and took it out again.

'You don't need that,' he said. 'Not now.'

'No,' she said, 'I want it.'

'Leave it.' He crowded in on her, pinning her to the wall.

'You're squashing me—'

'You're all right,' he muttered. 'You'll be all right.'

This wasn't how it was supposed to happen, she thought, muzzily. This was all wrong. 'No . . .' she squirmed and raised her arms to push him away, but he grabbed hold of them, both wrists in one hand. Then he bent slightly, she felt the other hand push up her skirt, and then his knee was between her legs, prising them apart.

'Don't do that,' she whimpered. 'Please . . .'

'You'll be all right.' His voice was thick now, urgent, and his hand was inside the leg of her knickers, touching . . .

'No!'

'Sorry, sorry,' he muttered. The hand was withdrawn.

She wrenched her own hands free and straightened up, smoothing her skirt, looking down, away, anywhere but at him. 'Go away.'

'It's all right,' he said, and raised his hands to her face. She tried to sidestep but lost her balance and went over on one ankle. The world seemed to tilt

10

and spin, then he pulled her arm and jerked her upright, pushing himself against her, and before she could move his hands were at her throat. She tried to beat him away but it was no good, and her head was pounding, bursting . . .

Just as suddenly, he let go. She slumped to her knees, choking and gasping, doubled over, and felt his breath as he bent towards her. She flinched away from him, but he grabbed one of her wrists. 'Here, take this, take it,' and pushed something into her palm. Then she heard him back away, scuffing gravel, and he turned and ran off towards the road, while she coughed and coughed and tried to get her breath.

When the racking and heaving eased up, leaving a dull pain in her neck and chest, her first thought was, they mustn't find me on my hands and knees. She scrambled upright, using the wall for support, glad of the darkness.

Footsteps. She cringed against the wall. Was he coming back? He couldn't be . . . *couldn't* . . . No, there was a torch. He didn't have a torch—he'd said they didn't need . . . but that didn't mean he didn't have one himself, did it? Oh, God, please . . . Her stomach churned and her legs felt as if they might give out at any minute. She put her hands over her face, hunched over, and slid down against the bricks, barely registering as her dress hitched, then ripped, on something sticking out. More footsteps, the torch swung in her direction, lighting the ground in front of her, and then— *A man's voice.* She opened her mouth, but no sound came out. She should make a run for it, do something, anything . . . Why doesn't someone come and help me? Please, she begged, silently. *Please . . .*

11

'H-hello?'

It wasn't him. She knew it straight away. The voice was different. Lighter. More boyish. Hesitant.

'Hello? Is anyone there?'

She tried to force some words out, but nothing came, only the panting of breath.

'I thought I heard—'

'Yes,' she gasped. 'Yes. I'm here.'

The torch swung towards her, blinding her. 'N-no. Don't.'

'Sorry. I didn't mean to frighten you. You don't look . . . are you all right?'

'Yes, fine.' Why had she said that? Of course she wasn't all right. 'I'm fine,' she repeated. 'Just tripped over, that's all. Wretched blackout.' She managed a little laugh.

'May I help you up?'

'No, really.' Blue uniform. Air force. Black hair. Pale face. She couldn't see properly. Not one of those from the car, or he'd recognise her—wouldn't he?

'Holden-Browne. Guy Holden-Browne.'

A hand in front of her face. Her head jerked back involuntarily, banging against the wall. She blinked. The hand was still there. She took it, and it . . . shook. Up and down. He's shaking my hand, she thought, astonished. 'Oh,' she said. 'Megan.' Then, automatically, 'My mother's Welsh.' Then, in a blurt, 'AndIthinkI'mgoingtobesick.'

He stepped away while she turned her head and vomited, and when she turned back, he was holding out a handkerchief, neatly folded. 'Take it,' he said. 'Please.'

'Thank you.'

When she'd wiped her face, he said, 'Do you

12

think . . . I mean . . . couldn't you stand up?'

'I . . . Yes. I think so.'

Upright again, she held out the handkerchief, but he didn't take it. 'You needn't worry about that,' he said.

Mortified—of course he wouldn't want it back, not with *that* on it—she balled it up and stuffed it in her pocket. 'Sorry. I . . . I'll wash it for you.'

'No, it's fine. Keep it. Or throw it away, if you like.'

'I'm sorry,' she repeated.

It was awful. She wished he'd go away. She wished never to see him, or any of them, ever again. She wished she were home. She wished she were dead, or anywhere except where she was. His kindness made it worse, far worse.

'Look,' he said. 'You can't go home on your own, not when you're . . . you're . . . not well. I'll take you.'

'No, honestly, I—'

'It's all right, really. I won't . . . you know.' He sounded embarrassed. 'You'll be quite safe. Please let me help you.'

'Well, all right, then.'

She didn't take out her torch. One was enough, and besides, she didn't want any more light. The night was quiet, and they walked together, without touching or speaking, except for her brief directions. The vomiting and the cool air had sobered her; now all that remained was the bad taste in her mouth, the pain in her neck and chest, the memory and the horrible, mounting embarrassment of what he'd seen, what he must be thinking. By the time they reached the end of her road, her shame was overwhelming.

13

'I'm fine now,' she said, grateful that he kept his torch low, and she couldn't see his face. 'It's only just down there.'

'Are you sure? Just . . . you did seem very frightened, back there.'

'Really,' she said, impatiently. 'It's fine.'

'Well, if you're sure. You'd better take my torch.'

'No, I've got one.' She brought it out of her pocket and switched it on.

'Well, goodnight, then.'

'Yes. Goodnight.'

The kitchen door was ajar. She paused in the passageway long enough to call out, 'I'm going straight up, Mum.'

'You stopping in your room?'

'Yes. I'm really tired. I'll come down if there's planes.'

She sat in front of the scarred wooden desk that served as her dressing table and examined herself in the mirror: the remains of make-up on the blotchy face, hair half down, the marks, red and livid, on her neck. She clutched a hand to her chest. The brooch, Mum's green brooch that she'd filched from her bedroom: it was gone. Must have fallen off when . . . She fingered the place where she'd pinned it. No—there was a small rip in the material. As if it had been torn off. As if he'd pulled it off her dress when . . . But that was stupid. Why would he?

It wasn't an expensive one, only Woolworth's, but Mum was bound to notice. She'd have to say it had fallen off at the pictures. She stood up and took off the dress. The skirt was filthy, and there was a long rip down the back. She could say she'd had an accident with the bicycle. Fallen off. Damn.

They'd left the bikes in the lane. She'd have to go back and get hers in the morning. She could say that was when she lost the brooch, too. Say she'd gone back to the place and looked, but it wasn't there. The handkerchief, though: she'd have to get rid of it. She pulled it out of the pocket, and something else—paper—came along with it and fluttered onto the rug. A pound note.

How . . . ? Then she remembered: the man, he'd put something in her hand. She sat down again, in front of the mirror, and stared at herself.

He'd tried to kill her. Then he'd given her a pound. For the brooch? She could buy another one now, a replacement, so she wouldn't have to lie about that, at least. But the bicycle, first thing—she mustn't forget.

He'd given her a pound.

That other pilot, who'd walked her home . . . she hadn't said thank you. Rude, when he'd helped her like that. Too late now, she'd never see him again. Hoped she wouldn't, anyway.

He'd tried to have his way with her, then he'd tried to kill her. *He'd tried to kill her.*

She knew she'd never be able to tell anyone. Her reflection, with its dull eyes and smudged, forbidden lipstick, confirmed what her mother would think: it was her fault. She inspected her hands—grazed and dirty—and picked a bit of grit out of her knee. She'd asked for it, hadn't she?

He'd tried to kill her, and it was her fault.

MONDAY 16TH SEPTEMBER
RAF Hornchurch, Essex

Flying Officer Jim Rushton

Look up. Blue, blue sky. Light breeze. It's a perfect day for flying, and here we are all sprawled on armchairs, baking in full kit.

Look down. Scuffed grass beside the trench. You can see the earth. Feet in flying boots, parachute harnesses dangling. Metal catches the sun. Funny how you always notice details, *before* . . .

Look out, over the airfield. Airmen filling in craters by the runway. The grass is still dotted with red flags marking unexploded bombs from the last few raids. Huts—what's left of them—hangars. I remember filling the sandbags when we first came here, making pens to protect the Spitfires. After we came back from France. It seems like years ago. Teddy Norton was still here then, and Stuffy—I was at RAF College with him—Felix Marshall . . . Bimbo Tanner . . . All gone, now.

Let's see. What's in the paper? *The Queen's private apartments were badly damaged when Buckingham Palace was bombed again yesterday.* Won't be too many more nice days like this one. It'll be cold, soon. We'll have to wait inside . . . whoever's left, that is. *The RAF had one of its greatest days in smashing the mass attacks on London. Thirty of our machines were lost, but ten pilots are safe.*

I see Corky and Mathy are still arguing about tactics. Funny to see those two together—Corky's almost taller sitting down than standing up, and Mathy's over six feet, far too tall for a fighter pilot. God knows how he ended up inside a Spitfire. Davy with his rugger nose and ruddy cheeks, reading a book. He looks calm enough, but he hasn't turned a page for at least twenty minutes. Czeslaw staring up at the sky. Lined face—he's older than the rest of us, like most of the Poles: twenty-seven. Flint's asleep—must be dreaming about flying because his eyebrows are wiggling up and down. Balchin's next to him. He's dozing, too, cap tipped over his eyes, arm dangling down by his side, hand very white. That's how it'll look when he's dead—unless he's burnt, of course. There's Ginger Mannin off to the latrine, again. *Miss Air Force is a blonde and only 18 years old . . . the Boys in Sky Blue like 'em young!*

The newspaper is plunged into shade now and I can't see the picture. A bulky shape—Flight Lieutenant Webster, the adjutant—is blocking out the sun.

'*Adj . . .*'

'Sorry.' He moves round to stand behind me and jabs at the paper with his pipe. 'She's a bit of all right, isn't she?'

I shrug. 'I suppose so.'

Balchin pushes back his cap and blinks at him. 'How's . . . you know?'

'Tinker?' offers Mathy.

'That's not his name . . . Taylor, wasn't it?'

Davy looks up from his paper and says, helpfully, 'Soldier?'

'Shut up, Davy,' says Corky.

'Sailor, then.'

'Shut *up*,' says Corky. 'He means *Tucker*, Adj.'

17

'*Do* I mean Tucker?' asks Davy, in mock surprise.

'Yes, you do. Take no notice of him, Adj.'

'Not fair,' says Davy. 'I can't help it if they all look alike.'

I can't remember what Tucker looked like, either. Must have been his first scrap—he only arrived two days ago. Webster hasn't said anything, but he must have shaken his head because Balchin squints at him for a moment, then grunts and pulls his cap back over his face. *Pictured on the right is a Dornier crashing in flames . . .* Bimbo Tanner in the hospital, with his melted face, eyelids gone . . . Webster's saying something.

'What?'

'I said, you're on five-minute stand-by.'

Ginger returns, doing up his fly, sees Webster, and says, 'How's Whatsisname, Adj?'

'Bought it. Where've you been?'

'Putting rouge on his nipples,' says Davy. 'All for your delight, Adj.'

Webster frowns, but doesn't reply.

'What's wrong with that, anyway?' Ginger nods at the field telephone.

'Buggered.'

'This whole airfield's buggered,' says Davy, irritably. 'Craters everywhere, no bloody huts left, place crawling with dead WAAFs.'

I picture a dying Miss Air Force crawling on all fours at the bottom of a trench, dishevelled head hanging down, hair full of dust, skirt hiked up round her hips.

Davy looks at me. 'I don't know what you've got to grin about, Goldilocks,' he says.

'It can't be,' I say.

'What can't be what?'

'The airfield. It can't be *crawling* with them. Not if they're dead.'

'Jesus, Goldilocks . . . *Stiff* with dead WAAFs, then.' Davy returns to his paper and Webster fiddles with his pipe.

After a moment, Mathy says, 'Are they sending a replacement, Adj?'

'If you can call him that.' Webster shakes his head. 'Six hours on Spits.'

Davy sighs. 'Another bloody public school boy, no doubt. Must be a factory somewhere, turning out replacements. Hope he's better than Tucker.'

'This one's called Sinclair,' says Webster. 'Gervase.'

'Gervase, eh?' says Davy. 'He can keep Holden-Hyphen-Browne company. We don't want him.'

Flint opens his eyes. 'Well, you've got him. And you're going to take him up this afternoon, show him the ropes.'

Oh, well . . . what else is in here? *Messages of the Stars . . . Leave the petty things for others to worry about. Get out of the rut and do not hesitate to try something new.*

Try something new. I'd forgotten about Saturday until I found the brooch in my pocket. Must have belonged to that kid in the pub: no other reason it could be there. I don't know how it got in my pocket; don't remember taking it. Might as well keep it, though. I can always find some girl who'll want it. Give it a story, make it special. They like that sort of thing. Like that yarn I told about my sister—ought to use that line again. Makes me laugh, how they lap it up. Anyone that stupid deserves to be lied to. But that was a queer thing—

19

one minute I wanted to throttle the life out of the silly little bitch, the next minute, I'd lost interest.

When I saw that girl in the car putting on lipstick I wanted to take it from her and do it myself, scrub it all over her mouth. She was pretty full of herself, that one. I should have chosen her—that would have wiped the smile off her face pretty quick. Wouldn't have been so pleased with herself after that, would she? But I thought the younger one would be better. It all started when I saw the girl using the cosmetics; I knew I wouldn't be able to settle until I'd . . . But then, out there with the other one, I knew I wouldn't be able to do anything. Didn't like her struggling like that.

Waste of time. Not cheap, either—had to hand over a quid to keep her quiet. I thought that flying had put me off all that other business. I hadn't so much as noticed a girl in months, then suddenly that happened. That stupid bint in the car, I'd have settled her all right. *Do not hesitate to try something new*, that's what the paper said. Can't be local, though, and WAAFs are definitely off limits. Too risky.

Bloody fool thing to do. Running low on funds, as well. I shut my eyes. A torso rears up in front of me: loose, pale breasts, pooling out to the sides. You could pull them away and they'd stretch like lumps of dough.

Hear a rustle of paper under my nose and the first thing I see are the sagging, dun-coloured dugs of Corky's Mae West as he bends down to snatch the *Daily Mirror* off my lap. *'I'm so thankful that at last I've found a powder that's non-detectable, says Lady Cecilia Smiley,'* he reads in a falsetto voice. 'I just hate detectable powder, don't you?'

'Can't abide it,' says Mathy, 'frightful stuff.'

'Pond's face powder matches my skin colouring so perfectly that it might have—'

The scramble klaxon sounds, and it all falls away as if it had never existed, which, in a way, it hasn't, because compared to this, nothing is real. It's like being lost in a maze, and suddenly finding that all the hedges are flattened and the view is clear. Nothing between you and what you're about to do.

I have spent my life waiting for this. Right from the first time—I was ten years old, and the plane was an old Avro from one of those flying circuses that used to go up and down the country. I thought it was the most beautiful thing I'd ever seen, and I knew, straight away, that more than I'd ever wanted anything, I wanted to *fly*. The Avro was a rickety old crate, but I couldn't take my eyes off it: the canvas and wires, the propeller, the struts, all seemed to glow with a special light. I loved everything about it, even the way it smelled. I stood there so long that eventually the pilot said he'd take me up for a ten-minute flip, even though I had no money to pay for it. I'll never forget how it felt, the moment of leaving the ground and soaring through the air, up and away from all the people, watching them get smaller and smaller and knowing that I was free, no longer bound to the earth, to my family, to insignificant things. For the first time in my life, the world was marching to my drum.

When I got out of the plane, a boy I knew a little, from school, came up to me. He stood staring, and then he put his hand out and touched me, lightly, on the chest. He didn't say anything, but I knew he wanted to see if I was changed in some way, transformed, from having been up in the sky. It was the first—I think the *only*—time in my life I'd really wanted to talk to anyone. I could see the excitement in his face—a reflection, I suppose, of my own—and I wanted to tell him how wonderful it was, but I couldn't put it into words. You can't, really, not the joy of it, the extraordinary fact of being in the air. Oh, there was the glamour and all the rest of it, and I'd read *Biggles* and thought it was jolly exciting, but that was at second-hand. This was real, a pure, sharp, *true* sensation, and it was the first time in my life I'd experienced anything like it. Anything else one did was dull by comparison, blunted—a meaningless, domestic fog of home and school.

I remember running away from the boy and into the next field and throwing myself down in the long grass so that I was hidden by the hedge. I knew then that I didn't need to talk to anyone about it, all I needed to do was to close my eyes and re-live, over and over again, the sheer wonder of it. That was the best day of my life, and from that time on, I read everything about aeroplanes that I could find. I used to dream about them, too—or, at least, dream about flying. For some reason, there was never an actual aeroplane in the dream, just me, alone in the air, sitting in an invisible machine, but knowing it was there, and I could fly it, and being proud of that, and happy. Powerful, knowing that nothing could touch me. And every time I dreamed it, I'd wake up with a sense of rightness, a certainty I'd never known before. I'd always felt that I was different from other people, but now I knew the feeling was special—something to be proud of, not ashamed. They didn't know what I knew. Only pilots knew, and I swore to myself that some day, I'd be one of them. I felt as if I was being kept in mothballs until then—nothing had a meaning, or a point.

I'll never forget my first solo flight in a Spitfire. The first time up there on my own. She was frustrating at first, flying herself, leaving me behind—laughing at me, almost—daring me to control her, and for a moment I thought I couldn't, I'd flunked it, but then there was a second, lengthened into a minute, then five, ten, when I was her master. More than that: I was part of the plane. Don't know how I could have thought she was too small—she's perfect. No vices: she's all you could wish for. Exactly right.

It was a relief when the war started—finally, the chance to do what I'd been training for, although it was pretty dull at first. Because there can be no better feeling in the world: mind and body attuned to the job, entirely self-reliant. No yesterday, no tomorrow, nobody else, just the perfect clarity of each moment.

In the sky, everything is possible: I know that even if I die tomorrow—*today*—I shall have lived more than the people on the ground.

We start to run across the airfield, towards the planes.

MONDAY 16TH SEPTEMBER
Clapham, London

Lucy

They started at ten past eight tonight. We filled the
buckets and turned off the gas and came down here
to get settled—if you can call it that—and I'm in
my usual place under the kitchen table. Not the
most comfortable way to spend the night, but it's
better than being under the stairs with Mums. She's
in a deckchair and my sister Minnie is beside her
on the cushions from the settee. She's got her head
in the cupboard and her feet stuck out in the
passage, where Dad is sure to trip over them when
he comes in from the garden. I wish he wouldn't go
out there because Mums gets so nervous and she
keeps getting up and calling out to him to come in,
but he pretends he can't hear her. Or maybe he
really can't hear—they're making enough racket
tonight. We're luckier than a lot of people, living
here, but it's definitely getting worse. Dad says it's
because of Clapham Junction—the Germans want
to demolish our railways, if they can, and it's a big
station.

When Mums isn't calling out for Dad, she's
fussing over the Anderson shelter. 'We should have
had it the first time when they offered. I told you,
Billy, I said this would happen . . .' I'm positive she
didn't say anything of the sort, but of course that's
all changed now the bombing's started and the
builder's saying he can't do anything for six weeks
because the military have taken all the materials

and he can only get a pound's worth each month. Or something. Mums goes on and on, and I've got so fed up with it that I don't listen any more.

She's been bad since it started, but recently . . . I went to Bourne & Hollingsworth last week, at lunchtime, and bought a sweater. When I showed her, she said, 'What did you buy that for? It's bad luck.' She meant, because it's green. To be honest, it was more than I could afford, but I thought, if I live it'll be a bargain, and if I die, I'll die broke, won't I? When I said this to Minnie she put her hand up to her mouth, and said, 'Oh, *don't.*' I told Mums I was going upstairs to put it on, and when I came back she said, 'Anyhow, it doesn't suit you.' Charming! Anyway, I don't think the house is more likely to be hit because I'm wearing a green sweater. The Germans don't know that, do they? I pointed this out, but it didn't make any difference. She's always been one for finding fault. Minnie doesn't seem to come in for it so much, but I've never been able to do anything right: if I'm talking, I'm either fibbing or showing off; if I'm quiet, I must be sulking, and so on and so on . . . But then I have always preferred Dad to her. He's much easier to talk to, and doesn't criticise all the time. I try not to make it plain, but I suppose it must be— she certainly thinks that Minnie loves her much more than I do, I know that. In any case, I'm trying not to mind it too much, because we're all tired, and that makes everyone irritable. But it's all right for Mums—Dad's a full-time warden now, and Minnie and I have to go off to work in the morning. She can stop in bed and have a nap, if she likes.

I've been thinking about Frank today, a lot. I do enjoy our time together, and I like talking to him, even though he makes me feel an awful idiot sometimes. He doesn't mean to, it's just that he knows so much about politics and everything, and I don't. And I don't mind if he kisses me, or . . . I suppose that's the problem—I don't *want* him to kiss me, particularly, I just *don't mind* when he does. When we had our picnic on Sunday, I was wearing a short-sleeved dress and he remarked on my freckles. We were side by side on the grass, lying on our stomachs, and I said, 'Oh, they come out in the sun,' and he said, 'Perhaps if I look hard enough I'll catch one in the act,' then pounced on my arm and pretended he had, and laughed a lot.

It was nice, but I didn't feel . . . oh, I don't know. Just that I was laughing right along with him, but I didn't feel part of it, somehow. It wasn't *like that*, more as if he were my brother—or at least how I suppose it would be if I had a brother. He said to me afterwards, 'You don't respond much.' I said, 'What do you mean?' and he said, 'Well, you don't wriggle about much.' He meant when he kisses me and all that. I thought, I don't get the urge to wriggle, that's the problem. Perhaps it's because he's too familiar, somehow. I don't mean in the sense that he's not a gentleman, because he is, but because he's always been there. His family used to live in Albion Avenue, which is only a few streets away. We went to different schools; he was at Larkhall—the Larkhall Lunatics, we used to call them—but he's always been around the place, at the tennis club, and . . . I don't know. Everywhere. His parents moved to Gloucester a few years ago, but his mother still writes to Mums, and there's a sort of cosiness about the whole thing that makes me feel as if I'm being pushed into a convenient

26

little box before I've had a chance at life.

I ought to worry about Frank joining the army, but the fact is, I don't. I'd mind if he was killed—I'd mind if *anyone* was killed—but I don't think I'd be heartbroken. At least, I would for his family, but not for myself. The fact that I can even think this shows I can't be in love with him, but I know that, anyway. It's horrible of me to lie here thinking about it in such a cold way, but I don't see what else I can do. I'm certain he's going to propose to me before he leaves, and I'm dreading it. I know it would please Mums no end if I said yes, but I can't. It wouldn't be honest, or right.

When I look at some of the older women at work, who've spent all their days toiling away in offices, typing and tea-making, thinking of spending my entire life like that is almost enough to make me want to fly straight into Frank's arms. I can hardly pretend that working for a company that makes stationery, as I do, is a noble calling, or even very exciting, but then you see some poor woman with five kids and the drudgery of endless housework, and you think, what a terrible thing. It seems unfair if that's all you can expect, but then it's a man's world, isn't it?

Perhaps I'd feel differently about all this if I lost my virginity. I don't mean with Frank, because I'm sure he wouldn't—at least, not unless we were married, because he's so decent and that's one of the reasons Mums likes him so much—I mean with somebody else. I can't deny that I'm curious, but honestly! I can't imagine Minnie ever having a thought like that, and as for Mums . . . perhaps there's something wrong with me.

It's like the thing that happened a couple of

years ago. That's how I think of it, 'the thing'—when I let myself think of it, that is. I can never recall exactly how it happened, which is odd, and makes me wonder if it did happen at all, even though I'm pretty sure I didn't dream it. It was at a picnic with lots of people, and we must have been playing hide-and-seek, or something childish like that, just larking around, really. I dashed off behind one of the trees, and one of the boys was following me, and then I must have tripped over, because I suddenly found myself on the grass, and he fell on top of me and pinned me down and kissed me. I don't remember his name, if I ever knew it, and I suppose it was all pretty innocent, really, but what's stayed with me is the sensation: fear and thrill at the same time, and how much I liked it. And it was all the better, somehow, because I hadn't courted it, it just *happened*. It's all rather hard to explain, really, and even thinking about it makes me want to hide my face, even though it's dark and I'm on my own.

Dear, oh dear . . . Poor old Frank. But one can't think about the future at all, really. It seems so incredible that these air-raids are happening and quite impossible to believe they'll ever stop. Even that sense of excitement you get, almost pleasure, of being right in the middle of it—I don't mean when it's happening, but after—like when I was running an errand for Miss Henderson at work the morning after Holborn got it: heaps of broken bricks and plaster where the buildings had been, and glass and twisted pipes, demolition workers everywhere with picks, or sawing at beams, and some smoking, even though there was a powerful smell of gas. It made me feel exhilarated to see these men at work, and all the Londoners going about their business and *carrying on*, and just as I was thinking this one of the rescue men said, 'You're pleased with yourself, aren't you?' which made me feel dreadful, because there I was indulging in a purple patch when people were dead or wounded. And of course the other thing, which is natural, I suppose, is that although you'd never rejoice if a bomb brought down death or destruction on someone else, you can't help feeling jolly glad to have escaped it yourself.

Actually, that isn't quite true, it isn't just afterwards—I do mean while it's happening, because it *is* exciting. The fires, anyway. Those first weeks, when it was the docks and nowhere near us, Dad and I went out to watch, and there was something extraordinary about it. It was terrible for all the people, of course, but the whole sky was a fiery orange with the roofs against it like silhouettes and not real houses at all, like the reddest, most violent sunset you ever saw, except in the east and not in the west, and then there was a great mushroom of smoke. I could feel the excitement welling inside me, and I think Dad must have felt it, too, because he put his arm round me—unusual enough, because he doesn't go in for all that—and I could feel him shaking, but only a little, and his voice was very firm and clear.

'All right, Smiler?' he said.

I found it hard to speak, but I managed to whisper that I thought so.

He said, 'I never thought it would come, but now it has, we mustn't worry. It'll take them a hell of a time to knock it all down.'

'Mums doesn't like you to say hell.'

He said, 'You wash your mouth out, young lady.'

I said, 'Well, you said it first,' and he gave my shoulder a squeeze.

We went inside after that, because we knew Mums would be worried, and I sat and thought about all those poor little houses and the people inside, and I felt ashamed.

I look in the mirror sometimes and wonder who it is that's staring back, but it must be me because there's no one else there. I suppose it looks like me: twenty-one, pale skin, wavy brown hair, blue eyes—and it doesn't look half bad. Minnie looks like it, too. We're both tall and slim, but other than that we both favour Mums's side of the family, not Dad's—he's lanky and beaky, like Frank. Dad's always saying it's a good job we don't take after him, because of his big nose. I think it's a lovely nose, but I've got to admit it would look pretty funny on a girl. But it's strange, looking at your own face and not feeling any connection with it at all. Maybe it's from not having enough sleep— three whole weeks of interrupted nights is enough to give anyone the jitters. Even if the warning doesn't go, you're waiting for it. You see people all over the place with that strained, listening expression, flinching even if it's just a bus or a car in the next street. Either that, or they're yawning.

I know I'm not the only one: when Vi came into the office this morning she was admiring my swagger coat—a blue wool—saying it was very smart and then, quite suddenly, she began to sob, and couldn't stop. Miss Henderson came in and told her to go home for the day, which was kind, and then she asked me was I all right, and I said yes, but I know exactly how Vi felt. Last week I was

30

walking down the corridor with some papers and I suddenly thought, *I may be killed tonight*, and it was as if everything around me had just dissolved and the walls weren't there any more and I was standing on thin air. I made a dash for the WC and went into a cubicle and just sat there. I put my hands on the walls either side so that both my palms were against the tiles, and then I took my shoes off so I could feel the floor under my stocking feet, and that made me feel a bit better because it was solid. I must have been in there quite a while because Miss H came banging on the door—'Miss Armitage! Are you in there?'—and I pulled the chain so she'd think I'd just been spending a penny, but I'm sure she knew. She didn't ask, though, and I was glad because I'm determined I shan't make a fool of myself.

The sirens went at five o'clock, just as we were about to leave—very annoying. Some people had already started for home and had to come back and go into the shelter, which is horribly stuffy. The raid lasted an hour, me sitting on a hard bench because I hadn't remembered my cushion, and I spent most of it occupied with my knitting. The new people from the accounts department came down. One of them, Mr Bridges—he's about thirty, I suppose—looks like Gary Cooper. No wonder all the girls have been talking about him. Kept finding myself looking at him—hope nobody noticed. Once or twice I caught him looking in my direction, though I don't suppose that means anything. But he is *so* handsome—one of the best-looking men I've ever seen!

The All-Clear came just after six, then a long walk round to the station because most of the

Strand was roped off—a time bomb, I think—yellow Diversion signs everywhere, and of course there was a great crowd waiting for the train and long delays. Dozens of bodies on the platform, as usual—I almost stepped in someone's dinner—and the smell of so much humanity is vile. They don't *look* especially dirty, but perhaps they only wash the bits that show. And then in the morning they have to go straight off to work in the same clothes, poor things.

By the time I got home, eight o'clock, I had the most terrible headache, but just as I'd got into the bath, off went Moaning Minnie—the siren, not my sister, who never seems to complain about anything—so that was that. It would be so nice to enjoy a leisurely bath instead of having to hurry over it. I've heard of one woman who was bombed and sent flying through the window, bath and all! Imagine . . . But it always seems to happen at the most inconvenient times; mostly during dinner and tea. Dad says it's Hitler trying to put us off our grub, but he won't succeed—not at our house, anyway.

Woke at quarter past two from a kind of stupor and suddenly felt as if I was suffocating. There was a lull, so I tiptoed out into the garden and stood looking up at the sky. Full moon—not beautiful any more, just a worry, because it means that *they* can see us all the better. I wondered what would happen if all the gas was blown up and the water mains and sewers, and everyone got ill. How on earth would we manage? The thought terrified me, so I tried to keep the jitters at bay by thinking of Frank—not terribly successful, unfortunately. He said on Sunday that men like wars because they are naturally fighting animals, and I suppose there is some truth in that (found myself wondering what kind of fighting animal Frank would be, which was not at all in the spirit of the conversation, and decided on a stork because of his beaky nose and long legs). Then, suddenly and quite unaccountably, I found myself thinking of Mr Bridges, which improved matters. Or at least it did until a loud explosion sent me scuttling back inside. I tried to sleep under the table without much success, woke up again at four o'clock feeling miserable and shivery, and crawled upstairs for an hour's sleep in my own bed. I heard planes again at around five, but was far too tired to do anything about it.

Half past seven now. I feel irritable and exhausted, but the prospect of seeing *him* when I get to work cheers me up no end . . .

MONDAY 16TH SEPTEMBER
Soho, London

Rene

Nice to take the weight off my feet. I hate these public shelters, but they won't let me use the basement where I live, so I came here to Soho Square, which is better than nothing, specially now they've put the light in and given us somewhere to sit. I'd go down one of the tube stations, but if anything happened you'd be buried alive, and it's full of germs, not to mention the snores echoing all up and down the tunnels, and the *smell*. But it's all a bit too close for comfort, tonight. With the guns, though, you feel they're doing something, at least. More bloody racket, but it makes you feel safer. And I've done well this week. We was worried at first, all us girls, when the raids started, that the men wouldn't come, but it seems to have picked up. And the blackout doesn't matter—just flash your torch on your face and they know you're there. 'Course, it's all short-time now, with the bombing, but it's good business, so I'm not complaining.

I got three pairs of kippers for sixpence in the market today—threepence less than the shops, so that's good. Took them round to my sister Dora's for safekeeping. Can't go to work with a handbag full of kippers, can I? Put the men right off, that would. No cigarettes, though—well, nothing decent. Some strange brands he's got. Brazilian, I think they are. Like smoking a bit of old flannel. Still, it's better than nothing, and he knows me, so if he gets anything decent, he'll put it by.

Mr Mitten, his name is. Shop in Dean Street. He's a funny old chap—got this contraption he wears over his face, with a false nose. Some sort of metal stuck on to a pair of glasses, but there's no glass in them, it's just to hold this nose thing in place. I was told he'd lost his real nose through disease—syphilis—but of course you don't ask. Tommy says it was bitten off by a dog, but that's just kiddies' talk.

You can't help wondering what's underneath, though. It's not the best fit but you can't see anything down the side, just black. It must be all rotted away underneath. I suppose he takes the metal nose off when he goes to bed . . . It's not

34

really something you like to think about, is it? Can't imagine what his missus makes of it. She's a decent-looking woman, as well. I've often wondered if he lost his nose before they were married, or after. Imagine being courted by a man with a tin nose! No kiddies, though. Not that that means anything, of course. Still, it takes all sorts, doesn't it? He's a nice old boy, in spite of it.

Now then, let's see . . . I had two at a pound and ten shillings each—those I take back to my flat, along the way in Frith Street. That reminds me, I've got a dirty mark on the wallpaper near the fireplace. Quite a big one; can't think how it could have got there. I'm always noticing things like that—it's a way of occupying yourself while they're busy doing what they've paid for—and I keep a piece of paper by the bed so I can write down anything that needs seeing to, because I'm as houseproud as the next person. Besides, if you're going to have men friends, it's best to keep the place looking decent, even if it is only two rooms with the kitchenette behind the curtain.

Where were we? Oh, yes. I had another at ten shillings—he just wanted me to use my hands so I said seven shillings if he was quick because it was in the churchyard—St Anne's, that backs onto Wardour Street—and it was getting a bit too lively to be outside. Didn't half take his time, but he gave me another three shillings after, so that was nice. You get a few girls round here that'll do everything outside, but they're not what you'd call the refined sort. Fair enough, some of them haven't a place to go, but with others, they don't want to make the effort, with undressing and the rest of it. But then you can charge a bit more, can't you, if you do

35

that? And if you go in a doorway, it's dirty. Besides, I don't want to be starting with varicose veins, not at my age.

There's quite a few in this shelter, tonight. Mrs McIver, with her crosswords. Brings her alarm clock to time herself—beats me how she can see to read in this light, never mind writing down the answers. A couple of dozen knitting and that. Faces I know, not the names. Lot of them wouldn't talk to me. Oop, a man coming in . . . he's looking round. Obvious what he's after. Not with me, though. No hat—that's a non-payer, for sure. Talking to Edie and Lily, now—Edie's stood up to go with him. *She* can't have done much business tonight. Wants to smarten herself up a bit, if you ask me. You've got to dress up or it's not worth the candle. Stockings and high-heeled shoes, that's what they like. And I've got my new coat—blue wool, very smart. Five guineas, it cost me. Edie looks like the dog's dinner. Scrawny thing—I've seen more meat on a hat-pin. Lily's no better. Seedy, she looks, and that's not like her at all. She's quite a handsome woman: dark hair, like me, and she's got what you'd call a *strong* face, but it's pleasant, not mannish or anything.

It's that ponce of hers making trouble again, I wouldn't be surprised. Lily's a pal; she works round the corner from me. We're always chatting, and we go to the pictures together all the time, but I still say you've got to be soft to stand on the street all night and then go off home and give your takings to some man. The thing is, once he knows you're going out, he gets lazy. He's not bringing anything in so you're giving him the money and then all of a sudden it's 'Oh, it's such-and-such a time, don't you think you'd better be going down the road?' Then there's no gratitude any more, he just expects it. And then you've got to give him extra, if you want him to stay, otherwise some other girl'll come and give him more money, and he'll be off with her. That's what happened with Lily—Ted used to be Eileen's boy, but Lily took him off her. I'd have said, 'Good riddance,' but Eileen was that cut up about it, she'd have scratched Lily's eyes out if she could.

Anything's better than that Maltese lot, mind you. Vicious, that's what they are—no more than a bunch of white slavers. Their girls have a terrible time of it: I've heard they'll beat them, even kill one, just to keep the others in line. I don't know why we let them come over here, making trouble. We're too soft; we ought to ship them off back where they came from.

But you want the companionship, and that's something I miss, to tell you the truth, because it can be a lonely old life, doing this. I did live with a man for a couple of years—Alec Voss, his name was. Merchant seaman—ex-merchant seaman, I should say. He died, poor man. That was from alcohol. We had a big teapot, and every morning he'd make tea and pour half a bottle of rum in it. He'd make himself another one in the afternoon, so he was drinking it, cold, all through the day. I suppose I felt sorry for him, really, that was why I let him stay with me. He was another one with a funny nose. Quite a good-looking man, but he'd got this lump of a nose through drink, a great red thing all spread out across his face . . . and they took him in hospital at the end; he was there for several weeks, and do you know, his nose shrank! Right back to what it was before, the normal colour and everything. They didn't let him have a drink, you see.

I wouldn't have a man again, though—well, not unless I gave it up and married, because I'd like a decent life, same as anyone, with a man to look after me. But I wonder if there's much chance of that, now, being thirty and with the war and everything. Although one thing I will say about the bombing, it don't half take your mind off other things . . .

Sometimes, I used to scare myself half to death thinking about where I'll be when I'm sixty, but since all this started it hasn't crossed my mind once. But as I say, it's a hard thing to get married off the streets. There's plenty who are married, and still do it, but that's not a marriage to my way of thinking. Of course, with someone of your own type, who knows what you are and accepts it, they're likely to be a ponce, aren't they? No decent man's going to like the idea that his wife's been with everybody, is he? You couldn't expect it. But I'd like a family, yes, I would—I've got my boy Tommy, but he's at my sister's, down the road, and . . . well, to be honest, we've never told him. Auntie Rene, he calls me. He wasn't from any of these. See, I used to be a Windmill girl. Show girls, we were called—I thought that was very glamorous and American, like the pictures. That's why I did it, really. There were shorter girls that danced and sang and what-have-you, and us taller ones just stood about with not much on. *Tableaux vivantes*, it was called—where you're not allowed to move because then it's immoral. Well, I met this man and fell in love with him and then I fell pregnant and we were going to

38

be married, but it was the old story. Turned out he was married already, only he hadn't told me, and he wasn't about to leave his wife—she was rich, you see—so that was that.

I had to leave the show, of course, and then Tommy was born at Dora's and he stopped with her. She and Joe have never been blessed with little ones, so she's happy because Tommy calls her Mum. I was working in a café after that, and some of the street girls would come in, and I got talking to them, and that was it, really. The first time I did it, that was peculiar, and I felt a bit funny afterwards, but then I thought, why not? It's a good living—I earned five pounds a week as a Windmill girl, but I do a lot better with this. And I look after my boy, make no mistake about it, I do.

All the old ducks are giving Edie the look. Immorality, that's what they're thinking. I could tell them, it's not us girls encouraging the immorality, it's all those that do it for nothing, and none of them clean. They're the ones who spread disease, not us. That old girl at the end, in the black with the lorgnette—a dirty look on a long stick, if ever I saw one—she's got no call to be looking down her nose, not her. Well known round here, she is. We've all seen her, in the pubs. Ale Mary, they call her. Not to her face, of course. You'll get somebody come up, 'What are you drinking, Ma?' and it's 'Oh, just a whisper of port wine,' so the barman starts pouring, and she says, 'Louder than *that* . . .' and before you know it there's a great big glass full and the man's got to pay for it. Then she gets drunk and starts bawling and singing: the Bible or the music hall, and I don't know which is worse. Some people call her a character—I'd say she's a

39

bloody nuisance.

I've always said I rub along with all sorts, but if I'm honest I feel more comfortable with the rest of the girls than I do with ordinary people, even my sister. It's the life, I suppose.

Woman coming in with her kiddie, that's nice . . . My Tommy was evacuated last year, but it didn't take. The government was paying those people to feed our kids and they treated them like dirt, calling us scroungers, when they were out to grab all the money they could. They had no shelters, either, not like London. Dora went and saw Tommy, and she was so upset that she said, 'That's it, he's coming back with me.' The woman told her she'd be glad to see the back of him because he was dirty and wet the bed, but it was only because he was frightened, poor mite, being in a strange house. And he had scabs on his body because he wasn't getting proper food. We were ever so worried about him, but he soon had roses in his cheeks again. I swear he gets better-looking every time I see him, like his father. I hope that's all it is, the looks, because Vic—that's his dad—he was a rotter, and I don't want Tommy doing the dirty on some poor girl like he did to me. I don't want him in the army, either. Gives me the shivers just thinking about it, all these poor mothers with their sons going off to fight; I don't know how they can bear it. I feel so sorry for them. It'd break my heart if anything happened to Tommy. I can't stand to think of it.

But he's happy enough here. Always making mischief. Couple of weeks ago, Dora told me he'd gone out with his chums, and they'd gone in the dustbins behind all them film companies in

Wardour Street for bits of film cuttings to make stink bombs. Dora said they get the film and wrap it round some newspaper and set it on fire, then when the flame goes out the smoke smells like rotten eggs. Tommy's a mischievous little chap, and he'd lit one in his school, during the prayers, and it got him in trouble. I couldn't stop laughing when Dora told me. She said to him, 'Here's Auntie Rene come to punish you, you little devil!' but I couldn't, I gave him a kiss instead. 'All my kisses are yours,' that's what I tell him. I don't let any of *them* kiss me, not likely.

I'd like a little girl, too. I was thinking about that when I went over to Dora's—they've got a nice flat in Covent Garden from the council—and there's all these girls playing out in the road, all clean and sweet. Singing a rhyme, like this: *Dip, dip, dip/ My little ship/ Sailing on the water/ Like a cup and saucer/ You—are—not—IT!* That's how it goes, and then they have to touch the one that's nearest and they all run off, laughing like anything. And this song stayed in my mind, because I thought, well, that's like the war, really, because you don't know where the bomb will come, and if it's you, that's too bad.

My grandmother used to say to us, *We are all in God's pocket*; that was a great favourite of hers. She was always the optimist in the family. Not like my mother, God bless her, she was one of those where if there's any bad news, she had to be the one to tell you. Not that she was a nasty woman, particularly, she just seemed to take pleasure in that sort of thing. If she didn't want you to do something or have something, even if there was a perfectly good reason for it—we hadn't got it or we

41

couldn't afford it—she'd turn it into something terrible. If we said, 'Mum, can we have an apple?', it'd be, 'No, you can't. I knew a man who ate an apple, and he *died*.' She always said things like that. Dora and I still laugh about it. Mum's dead, now. Shame she missed this, really—what with all the bad news about bombs and what-have-you, she'd be having a whale of a time. I'd say I'm more like my grandmother in that way, looking on the bright side, but it's very hard when there's nothing you can do about it. Just have to hope you'll stay in one piece . . . I do go into the church, sometimes, just to sit and get a bit of quiet. The vicar knows who I am. Knows we use the churchyard, too, but he never bothers.

Now this one's a bit more like it. Clean. Nice suit. Married: he's got that look. That's right, darling, over here . . . sit down . . . Would I like a cigarette? Can't smoke in here, dear, got to be outside. Here we go, then. Seems genuine—not one of the sort that gets themselves worked up asking how much and then insulting you and going away all excited, but you can't always tell, not in this job. No All-Clear, but it's safe enough out here now. Quiet.

'Are you a naughty girl?' he says.

'Very naughty,' I say. 'What's your name, dear?'

'Bernard.'

'That's nice. Mine's Rene.'

'I'd like to kiss you.'

'One pound ten shillings all in,' I say. 'I've got a room.'

Once you've got the money, you tell them what's what. Mind you, I always keep to my side of the deal—give what I'm paid for, fair and square. But

42

this one, it isn't his first time. Knows the drill: doesn't bargain, doesn't bring his money out in the street, lets me go off first, and he follows. He'll be my last, tonight. Five pounds I've taken. Not good, not bad. And threepence off those kippers.

TUESDAY 17TH SEPTEMBER

Jim

That smell. Oil and fuel and hydraulic fluid—same in all aircraft, but each type smells different. Where the stuff is, I suppose. But Spits smell better, somehow. Special.

I sit in the tiny cockpit and watch my hands at work. They know exactly what to do; I don't have to tell them. The airman gives me the thumbs-up: battery disconnected, and I am free.

They guide me out and we taxi across the grass, snaking from side to side. All clear from control to take off. Slowly open up the throttle to maximum power, that beautiful, throaty roar, and she's vibrating, excited, desperate to get into the air. She gains speed, I raise her tail . . . 90 mph, a slight bump, and she takes off almost by herself . . . left hand on throttle and right hand on control stick, then change and right hand on lever to raise the undercarriage—indicator light on—bring pitch and mix back . . . 140 mph. Start to climb through the late-afternoon haze. Change radio frequency. Nobody says much on the way up.

Bandits, twenty plus at Angels One Two. Outnumbered, as usual: we are eight, spaced out

43

across the sky. Thank Christ we've given up all that close formation stuff—great for displays but fuck-all use in a scrap. Red Section is leading, with Prideaux at Red One. I'm flying Yellow One, with one of the new boys . . . Holden-Something . . . as my wingman. Much good he'll do me. He's supposed to protect my arse, but I'm not betting on it. Not much cloud. Sun behind us. We climb to 14,000 feet. Good job Prideaux's got the sense to get us up higher than the angels they give us. Check the dashboard . . . Airspeed indicator, artificial horizon—normal; rate of climb indicator, engine speed indicator, fuel pressure gauge, boost gauge, all fine . . . Gun-sight on, gun-safety off . . . Nothing in sight—for the moment, the sky is ours.

Corky flying alongside me, singing, his voice distorted by the radio transmission: *'I love you in your negligee—'*

'Corky, I didn't know you cared.' Mathy, on the other side.

'I love you in your nightie—'

More instruction, with Corky warbling away in the background.

We quarter the sky, looking out for enemy planes. Extraordinary that one can feel as alert and excited as hell and totally calm at the same time, but it's possible. That overrides the tiredness, somehow, because we've been up three times today already. How you can feel all these sensations at once, I don't know. It might have been Corky's singing, or perhaps the exhaustion, but my mind starts to wander, and I find myself thinking about Webster, how he once said that his first flight was like the first time he had a girl. He was in the RFC in the last war, so I suppose that was in France.

44

Perhaps French girls are different, although I don't see how they can be.

I'm not wearing gloves—never do if I can help it—and the metal is smooth and sensitive under my hands . . . it's all about sensations, flying. I'd thought having a girl would be like that. I'd wanted it. Imagined it. But that first one, in the holidays before my last term at school . . . can't remember her name. Girl from the village. She'd done it before; something of a reputation, in fact. Knew the drill. I'd thought it would be easy, and it should have been, but it wasn't. She was pale, fleshy, big features—our noses bumped when I kissed her, she leant against me and tried to push her tongue into my mouth; it made a wet sound, slimy, it didn't feel right, it wasn't what I wanted . . . then, as I lay on top of her in the grass where she'd led me, she unbuttoned her blouse. Chilly, for July. Cloudy and dull. Slack, goose-pimpled breasts. She put my hands on them and they felt cold and lumpy and I could see blue veins between my fingers . . . I didn't know what to do—what she wanted, and she lay there staring at me, waiting . . .

Up here, none of that matters. She's perfect. You could fly her with your index finger and thumb.

I couldn't do it. She propped herself on her elbows, fumbled at my trousers, and lay down again. 'Go on . . .' Waiting.

But it doesn't matter. Not here. She's happy. Exhilarated. Wants it as much as I do.

Two thick slabs of thighs. Clammy. Damp grass underneath. Useless object. And made me useless, too. I said, 'What do you want?' Not what I'd meant to say, because I knew what she wanted, but

45

she wasn't giving me anything, just lying there, waiting, *knowing* . . . I couldn't do it. I felt sick. She started laughing and suddenly I was in a rage, pummelling her, her bulging, ugly body and her stupid, grinning face. Big red lips and white teeth. I hit her until it was all a mess of smeared lipstick and blotches—'Shut—*up*! Shut—*up*! Shut—*up*!'

'Leave me alone!'

'I hate you!'

'I hate you, too.' She scrambled to her feet and ran across the grass, lumbering from side to side as she tried to do up her buttons.

I adjust the trim; keep nice and level. I can still hear the girl laughing, but I know it's insignificant. *She's* insignificant. Let her think she got the better of me—she knows nothing, and never will. None of them do. Always wanting, pestering, teasing, with their stupid conversation, always at you, wanting *that*, all the same, lying there, holding out their arms, makes me furious . . . I don't even like them and they can't bloody see it. They don't understand anything. They don't know the joy of self-reliance, the elation of the chase and the kill, the extraordinary, exultant sense of triumph when the bullets hit home, the satisfaction of a job well done and the entire *rightness* of kill-or-be-killed—it could so easily be the other way about.

Corky cuts across my thoughts. *'When the moonlight flits—'*

'Shut up, Corky, you're making me feel sick.' Prideaux.

'Across your tits—'

Mathy's voice: 'Blue One to Leader, Bandits below, three o'clock.'

'Buster, buster!' Prideaux. Maximum speed,

46

now. 'Turning right, turning right, go!'

That's good. Half the time we get scrambled too late, vectored too low. Easier with the buggers underneath us, but I still can't see . . . Wait. A dot on the Perspex turns into a cross, a shape . . . shapes . . . And there they are: two dozen silver 109s, skating along at a leisurely pace. They haven't seen us. Prideaux shouts, 'Tally ho!'

The taste of fear floods my mouth, my stomach is sick and hollow, my heart is pounding, my ring twitching, and then suddenly, a jolt of adrenalin like electricity snaps my body into the job and I can feel myself taut against the straps of the harness. My teeth clench, my thumb is on the gun button, there is nothing but the chase, the urge to kill, and we dive towards them, Prideaux leading. 'Pick your own!'

Spots in front of my eyes for a moment, then clear as we hurtle nearer—choose one, and . . . Christ! Too fast, too fast, break right and bank— yellow underbelly on the left—flames, smoke—and the air breaks up, shot through with tracer belting straight towards me—haul on the stick . . . Height, need height . . . Planes dodging and diving everywhere, not yet, not yet . . . three-second burst with full deflection—she shakes, and jolts from the recoil—thumb slips—get a grip, get a grip . . . meaningless racket of voices over the R/T—'Other way, you stupid bastard!'

'Ten o'clock, ten o'clock!'

*　　　*　　　*

A 109 shoots past me, followed by a Spit—Ginger, I think—and a mouthful of Polish is spat into my

47

ear. Balchin bellows, 'Speak fucking English, can't you?'

I can't see Holden-Whatsit anywhere. 'Yellow Two, where are you?'

A Spit streaks straight in front of me with a 109 behind, knocking chunks off it—'Help me, somebody help me!' High, choir-boy voice . . . realise it's my wingman, whatever his fucking name is, trying to get himself killed.

'You stupid bastard!' I charge after the 109—get right up his arse and let him have it, a four-second burst—*Bloody Kraut, I'll give you something to take home*—and again—he breaks left but not fast enough—leaking coolant—I give it another squirt and then all hell breaks loose behind me: an almighty thud and she lurches and bumps—tracer flashing over the starboard wing—*get out of here for Christ's sake get out*—feel my bladder emptying, sweat running into my eyes, and cut the throttle and shove everything into the corner for a sharp turn. For a second I think she's not going to respond and I've had it, but then—*clever girl*—she goes, it's working, and the giant hand pushes my guts to the base of my stomach and presses down on my head, forcing it into my chest, I can feel the blood rush from it, can't see but can feel my way round the turn, not yet . . . further, further . . . she judders—don't stall, don't stall . . . rudder pedals heavy as lead, *don't black out, don't bloody black out* . . . and . . . now! 180 degrees, straighten out and I can see again and two 109s are coming straight at me—hear myself scream and she screams too as I yank her into a half-roll to get out of their way—can't swallow so turn my head aside to get rid of the puke that's coming up my throat, everything vibrating like hell, grey spots in front of my eyes and for a moment I am as weak as a baby, hands and legs helpless and quivering, then the plane seems to right itself and I see that one of the machines is crippled and wallowing, trailing smoke, port aileron shot up, the pilot a red smear against the Perspex, and the other—definitely a 109—is shooting at it, so it must be one of ours. Get off a long-range shot at the Messerschmitt—tracer seems to bounce off his wing, then the Spit is on fire and falling, falling, and there's nothing I can do—out of ammo—I see the 109 start to turn and I pull the tit and shove the throttle through the gate to get away from it and she shrieks and shrieks and I'm trying to stay calm, think, be logical, and then I find myself, miraculously, in empty sky, clammy and shivering with cold sweat, and the smell of fuel and cordite and a wet left leg.

Strange how that happens. One minute all hell's breaking loose, and the next minute, the sky's empty and you're on your own. Quick look round: row of holes in the starboard wing. Doesn't look too bad—there might be damage behind that I can't see, but she's flying all right. Now then, where's Holden-Whatsit?

'Yellow Two, where are you?'

No response.

'Yellow Two . . .'

Nothing. Silly sod must have been jumped.

Oh, well. Time to go home. God, that feels good: to be up here, all alone, the sun just beginning to set. Wonderful sense of contentment. She's happy, too, almost flying herself. I could stay up here for ever.

You couldn't get that from any woman.

49

TUESDAY 17TH SEPTEMBER

Lucy

Miss Crombie told me, in a shocked voice, about a notice she'd seen on the train this morning—*Blinds must be kept down after dark*—only someone had crossed out the word 'Blinds' and written 'Knickers' instead. She was terrifically worked up about it. I agreed that people *shouldn't* write on notices, but secretly wanted to laugh. Thought afterwards that this is clearly what happens to spinsters who spend their lives toiling in offices and never do anything else—to be avoided at all costs. That started me thinking about Frank again, what it would be like if I were to marry him. I got as far as imagining what the children would look like before I realised that the whole business was absurd, embarrassing, and horribly typical of the sort of female turn of mind I thoroughly despise. In any case, the man hasn't proposed to me yet! I wondered how I shall feel if he *doesn't*, and realised with horror that I shall be rather put out . . . Heavens! Vanity, thy name is Lucy Armitage.

Great excitement when Mr Bridges came in to see Miss H, and on the way out stopped at *my* desk. He said he'd seen me in the shelter yesterday, and admired my frock. I managed to stammer out a thank-you, and he said, 'I should thank *you*, Miss Armitage. Gazing at you was a delightful way of passing the time.'

In for a penny, I thought, and I said, 'I saw you looking.'

50

'Oh, you noticed. And I thought I was being so discreet. Ever thought of becoming a spy?'

I said I didn't think I'd be terribly good at it, and he said, 'Well, aren't you at least curious about my knowing your name?' Because we don't have them on the desks—well, Miss Henderson does, but she's in charge. The rest of us don't. I said I was curious, and he said, 'I asked La Belle Henderson.' He leaned forward. 'She's a bit of a dragon, isn't she? But she didn't scare me, because I asked her something else, too—how'd you like to be borrowed for the day, tomorrow? We need a capable pair of hands upstairs, and it's much easier to bring Mohammet to the Mountain than t'other way round. Not that you're a mountain, of course . . . far from it. More of a reed, if I may say so. The old girl puts your price above rubies, you know—it took all my powers of persuasion. I had to bribe her with torch batteries.'

'You didn't, did you?'

'No, but I would have done, in order to secure your services. And I promised faithfully that we'd return you in one piece. What do you say?'

'Well . . . yes.' As if I had any choice in the matter—but it was nice to be asked for a change, instead of ordered about.

'Good. I knew you wouldn't let me down in my hour of need. See you tomorrow, then.'

I was flabbergasted! Afterwards, all the girls crowded round, wanting to know what he'd said to me. Vi and Phyllis are crazy over him, but Miss Henderson overheard and pulled us all up short by saying, 'That's enough nonsense; he's a married man.' She sounded disappointed. Lord knows why—she must be forty-five if she's a day! But I felt

51

a tiny prick of disappointment, too, and Vi and Phyll looked most downcast. Still, Mr Bridges chose *me*, and not them, which certainly says something, although I'm not quite sure what. Probably better not to speculate. Perhaps he's just a flirt. Some men are, and that's harmless enough. I heard Mums's voice in my head, telling me I'm sailing in dangerous waters, and some men go all out to spoil a girl. This expression irritates me no end because it seems to put the entire female species on a par with a fancy tablecloth. Mums managed, with no effort on her part, to needle me all afternoon, no matter how much I tried to ignore her.

Frank met me on the corner after work, and we had a cup of tea and some very forlorn-looking currant buns. At least, the waitress assured us that's what they were, but it was all bun and no currant. I broke mine in pieces and unearthed two tiny ones that looked very sorry for themselves. Probably the shape of things to come.

I found myself making a special effort to be nice to Frank because I felt guilty about having enjoyed the conversation with Mr Bridges quite so much. But I couldn't help comparing the two of them, and Frank seems such a boy, somehow. He's clever and funny and, on the whole, fairly sophisticated, *but* . . . There's something else, and it isn't just the age difference.

He asked me if I'd heard the one about the girl who gave her boyfriend a white feather because he was leaving London to join the army. I hadn't thought of it like that before, but I suppose they will be far safer when they're off doing their training than we are here.

Frank said, 'I wish you were out of it,' and I said, 'Well, I don't. I'm glad I'm here—right in the swim,' because it's true, I am. I tried to explain to Frank that I do get frightened, but I want to be part of it, not stuck out in the country somewhere, missing everything.

He said, 'I didn't think women felt like that.'

I said, 'Well, I don't want to fight anybody, it's just that I want to be on the spot. Anyway, it would feel like running away. Ever since the war started we've been retreating from everywhere in a great hurry . . . someone's got to stay put. And London is my *home*, Frank. I'm not going to be driven out of it by Hitler.'

Frank looked at me for a long time without speaking. Then he said, 'We could just as easily be sitting in a café in Berlin, drinking coffee and eating *kuchen*, and having this conversation.'

'It couldn't be worse than this.' I prodded the bun.

'That's true. But I didn't mean that. I meant we'd be German.'

'But we're not German, we're British.'

'Yes, but that's just chance, isn't it?'

'I don't know. I suppose so. But we're different . . . it's the way they're trained, isn't it? To think that the only good race is the German one.'

'Yes, but we'd think that, too, don't you see?'

'No we—' I was about to say that we couldn't possibly think that, but I stopped because I realised he was right.

'We would, you know. We'd think we were in the right. And of course *we* are, it's just that everyone seems to have swallowed this business about how we're the ones fighting against injustice and

53

oppression, and standing up for peace and democracy, but when you look at our position in India, you wonder how we have the nerve. Our history is all aggression in the name of Empire. Same as the French or Dutch, or even Belgium, taking possessions overseas—and now we're saying the Germans can't do it because it's in Europe. We wouldn't care if it was Africa; look at Somaliland.'

'That was the Italians.'

He shrugged. 'It's no different.'

'Yes, but Europe's different, and as for the Empire, it's . . . well, it's ours.'

'Only because we conquered it.'

'But that doesn't make the Germans right, Frank.'

'I know it doesn't, but . . .' Frank sighed. 'It's just . . . you wonder what it's all *for*. All that King and Country stuff went out in the last war.'

'But we can't just let Hitler invade.'

'Of course not, but . . . I just wish I felt a bit clearer about things, that's all.'

'You mean, why you're fighting?'

'Yes.'

'Well?'

'To get it over with, I suppose.'

'Frank . . . What happens if, well, if we don't? Win, I mean.'

He sighed. 'I don't know.'

'I suppose I shouldn't even be saying that. I haven't said it to anyone else.'

'Good. Best keep it to yourself.' He squeezed my hand. 'We'll get through it, somehow.'

When he said that I thought, yes, but *what then*? I didn't say it, though—even thinking about the future seems a waste of time. All the same, it was an odd conversation, because Frank is usually so certain about things—the way men are, I suppose. It made me feel uneasy all the way home, although I couldn't quite put my finger on why. But that's nothing new; I don't seem to be sure about *anything* these days. The things Frank said about England, and the Empire—I've never heard him talk like that, and, to be honest, I've never really thought about it much.

The whole business made me feel as if I'd done something wrong. Talking to Frank often has that effect on me. I'm sure he doesn't mean it to, but it does. I suppose it's because he's a couple of years older than me, and better educated, but I can't just take on his opinions and pretend that's what I think, too, even if I don't have opinions of my own. I want to look at life through *my* eyes, not his.

We did talk about other things after that—although not about *us*, thank heaven—and then he said he was travelling to Gloucester to see his parents and would see me at the weekend, before he 'goes for a soldier,' as he put it. I meekly agreed to this arrangement and allowed myself to be kissed. Halfway through I was appalled to discover myself thinking about Mr Bridges. I've christened him B—if I am going to think about him, which appears to be the case, *Mr Bridges* is far too cumbersome.

I came back to earth when Frank broke off with a peculiar look on his face and said, 'Lucy, are you all right?'

I gazed at him with what I hoped was a suitably spooney expression, so he shouldn't realise . . . Oh, I'm horrible, horrible, *horrible*! Feelings of guilt and also—most unfairly—irritation with Frank, meant that I allowed him to carry on kissing me for far longer than usual to make up for it, then scuttled off to catch my train before anything more could be said.

The station was packed, as usual, and everyone looked weary and dispirited. I wondered how long we can go on in this state. Frank is certainly right about getting it over. The thought of spending all winter like this fills me with despair, but what choice do we have?

When I got back, Minnie told us about a girl at her office who went to the pictures and came back to find the back blown off the house. Mums was very upset by this, saying that people shouldn't go out. When I pointed out that the girl was safer at the cinema than she would have been at home, she didn't reply, but there was a lot of sighing and fussing and slamming about of tea-things. Being so nervous makes her quite impossible.

I said to Minnie afterwards, when we were washing up, 'You shouldn't tell her things like that, you know what it does to her.'

Minnie said she was sorry, and then she said, 'I suppose it's because I feel we ought to talk to her more—she's at home so much by herself.'

'She goes out to the shops, and she's always popping into the neighbours' for tea.'

'Not any more. It takes her an age to work up the courage just to open the door and get outside, even for shopping, and then she just rushes there and back as fast as she can. She used to stop and talk to everyone, but now she doesn't even want to do that, in case there's a raid, or a gas attack, or—'

'When did she tell you all this?'

'Last week. When we had that really bad one,

she suddenly blurted it all out. She's ashamed of it, Lucy, that's the awful thing. I know it was the wrong thing to tell her, about that girl at work—I could have bitten my tongue—but I feel I've got to say *something*, just . . . you know . . . so she knows we're all right, and . . . I don't know. To be friendly, and just . . . just for the sake of talking, really.'

'Perhaps we should get the doctor to give her something.'

'She won't go.'

'Have you mentioned this to Dad?'

Minnie shook her head. 'He'd only worry. Anyway, I think he sort of knows, but there's nothing he can do, and that makes it worse, because he can't *protect* her.'

'I suppose so.'

I could see what Minnie meant, and resolved to spend more time with Mums and talk to her, if I can bear it. I should have realised how bad her nerves are. The combination of that, and feeling hateful for being bored by Frank's lovemaking, made me not want to talk to anybody, so when we heard the siren I retreated straight under the kitchen table and stayed there with one of Mums's Ethel M. Dells. Terribly old-fashioned, but soothing. I realised, about twenty pages in, that I'd read it before, although not very carefully as I don't have the foggiest idea of what happens next. Dad lifted the tablecloth to see what I was reading, then made a face and said, 'Slop.' Which it undoubtedly is, but I don't care, because it takes my mind off everything else. It was quiet by midnight, so I went upstairs, though I didn't undress until the All-Clear went at three. Then I had four hours of utterly *blissful* sleep.

I tried to be very brisk and efficient all morning, with no flirting (well, not much, anyway). B was in the other office, but came in from time to time with requests for me to make tea and type things. The latter I found a little odd as he has his own secretary, Miss Dale, but she's terribly old, poor thing—nearly retiring—so perhaps she can't manage all of the work. Miss H came up a couple of times as well, 'to see how you're doing,' or—far more likely—to make sure there was no inter-departmental poodlefaking. B contrived to be out of sight on both occasions, which obviously satisfied Miss H, because he told me later that he has secured me 'on permanent loan' for one day every week. I thought this made me sound like a library book, and—very much to my surprise—heard myself saying so out loud. B laughed a great deal and invited me to have a cup of tea with him after work. I said yes, but spent the rest of the day telling myself that *he is married* and that *I must not be taken in by him.* These strictures were only moderately successful—even invoking Mums couldn't stop me looking forward to it, and as for Frank, well . . . here's a dreadful confession: I realised on the way home that I hadn't given him so much as a thought the entire day.

The other girls will be green when they find out. About my one day a week, that is. I shan't tell them about the tea, and certainly not about the kiss afterwards. We were walking to the station and suddenly—I'm really not sure how this happened—found ourselves in a doorway. He said, 'I know I shouldn't, but you're so lovely I can't resist you,' and pulled me into his arms and kissed me. I tried to push him away—well, a little bit—but found myself . . . how to put this? Responding. *Wriggling*, that's Frank's word for it. But it *was* all very discreet, and I don't think that people notice or mind these things so much, nowadays. I wondered afterwards if this was due to moral laxity or because they have other things on their minds, like getting home before the raids start, and decided it must be the latter.

I know I should have been offended by B's behaviour, but it seemed such a little thing, really, in spite of his wife. My goodness, though! I thought I knew what kissing was, at least, but *that* was a revelation. Quite different from Frank. I suppose I am turning into the most awful tart, but B made me lose my head completely, and I suddenly understood what Frank had been talking about. And it does seem unimportant, when you think that we might not be here tomorrow. Mums wouldn't think it unimportant, though, and the way she was looking at me this evening made me think she *knew*, somehow. But in a way, these restrictions only go to make it more exciting . . . what a dreadful thought! It's all very odd. Nothing makes sense or matters much any more, and I don't seem to care what happens to me.

I spent the rest of the evening concentrating jolly hard on Ethel M. Dell, and continued under the table when the raid started.

FRIDAY 20TH SEPTEMBER

Rene

My Tommy's had his heart broken, poor lamb. I went over to see him this morning and he was sitting on the kerb with this pretty curly-headed little thing, and holding a telephone. Not working, of course, because it wasn't attached, but it wasn't cracked or anything.

I said, 'Where did you get that?'

'Bomb site.'

'You shouldn't just take things, you know.'

'Everyone does.'

'I know, but it's naughty. Stealing.'

'But nobody wanted it, Auntie Rene.'

'Well, you don't know that.'

'They didn't! They'd have taken it, wouldn't they?'

'Maybe, but you shouldn't do it.'

I couldn't really blame him; it's a big temptation, stuff left lying about. I suppose it's not as if he'd broken into a bombed house or something, or gone hunting round the West End for bombed shops with wrist-watches and fur coats and what-have-you, but still . . . And he's right, everyone's at it, wardens and rescue men and firemen, and if they just pick up a packet of tea or a pipe, it's a bit much to call that *looting*, but all the same, I don't want him turning into a little thief.

I said, 'Well, now you've got it, what are you going to do with it?'

'It's a present.'

60

'Who's it for?'

'Her,' he whispers, and points at the girl, all shy.

I said to her, 'Is he your boyfriend, then?' and this little madam tosses her head, and says, 'Oh, no, not *him,*' and she grabs hold of the telephone and starts dialling up a number. When I ask what she's doing, she says, 'I'm telephoning my boyfriend.' Heaven knows where she picked that up—all of seven years old!

I said to her, 'Why are you doing that?'

'Oh,' she says, 'I'm making a date with him.' Makes you wonder what the world's coming to, doesn't it, kiddies growing up so quick. A few years' time and she'll be a proper caution.

Tommy snatched the phone. 'You don't even know how to do it. You're using it all wrong.'

'No, I'm not. I know how to do it. You're *silly.*' And she's jumped up and gone flouncing off down the road.

I said, 'Oh, dear. Do you like her a lot?'

'I don't like her *at all*. She's a *pig*. Anyway, I don't want to play with girls. They can't even do wars.'

'Why can't they?'

'Because the war's not for *girls.*' Very scornful. 'It's only for *boys*. Girls are stupid.'

'Never mind, darling. You come home with Auntie Rene and have some cake instead.'

But he wouldn't—he shoved the telephone into my hands and ran off down the street. Oh, well. He'll get over it, bless him. There's plenty more where she came from, after all.

Good business tonight. I started early, and by ten o'clock I'd made eleven pounds, so called it a night. Bumped into Lily on the way back. She'd had a bit of a time with one man who couldn't satisfy himself and threatened to punch her if she didn't give the money back, and of course her ponce isn't there when she needs him, he's off at the pub. I said to Lily, 'I don't know why you put up with it, I really don't.'

She said, 'Oh, you know how it is, Rene. I've got to have someone, I can't get by on my own.'

I thought, well, that's honest, because you get a lot of girls who'll say a ponce is no good and you're better on your own, when all the time they're living with a man and giving him money. But we're only human, same as anybody. I said to Lily, 'You come on and have a drink with me, that'll cheer you up.'

'Oh, no,' she said, 'Ted'll be worried about me.'

I thought, well, he wasn't too worried earlier, was he? But I didn't say it—no point in getting her riled. Instead, I said, 'Oh, where's the harm? You look as if you could do with it.'

*   *   *

We walked over to the Wheatsheaf, hoping for a bit of peace and quiet, but everyone was talking about how Madame Tussaud's got a bomb. Ale Mary's in there, and she's well away—never mind a whisper of port, it must have been the whole Hallelujah Chorus she'd put down her neck.

The barman said, 'All the Kings and Queens of England blown to pieces, but old Hitler never even got a scratch!'

Lily said, 'Well, I suppose they did it on purpose,' and one of the regulars—big drinker, always makes a nuisance of himself—said no, they wanted Baker Street station, but they missed. He told us they'd missed Holborn, too, and got a big scientific place in Lincoln's Inn Fields. His pal had seen the stuff on the road—skulls and skeletons and everything. He said they'd even got men's private parts, pickled in jars, and what did we think of that?

Lily said, 'Best place for them, if you ask me.'

We went and sat down then, because we know that sort, they want a bit of dirty talk with us and not to pay for it. 'Mind you,' I said to Lily, after, 'if they *were* all pickled in jars, we'd be out of a job, wouldn't we?'

Lily said, 'I daresay, but you still couldn't trust them.'

'What, the . . . ?'

'No, the *men*. They're all disgusting. You got your own teeth, Rene?'

'Eh?'

'Them your own teeth?'

'You don't think anyone would pay for this lot, do you? What's that got to do with it?'

'Man tonight asked me to take mine out.'

'You mean . . . ?'

Lily nodded. 'I ask you.'

'Blimey. Did you?'

She shrugged. 'Five bob extra.'

Mr Mitten comes by our table and whispers that he's got some proper cigarettes in, and if we come by the shop tomorrow—because Lily's a regular, too—he'll let us have two packets each. Then he taps his metal nose: 'Don't say anything, or everyone'll be wanting them.'

Lily says, 'Ooh, you are a pet,' which makes him blush.

I say, 'Careful,' because I've noticed that him up

63

at the bar is watching all this, and sure enough, he comes over. 'You ladies seem to be onto something good.'

I say, 'I don't know what you're talking about.' But he won't go away and I can see we're going to have trouble—he's tipsy enough—so we get up to leave, but he comes crowding in and grabs Lily's arm so hard she spills her drink, 'I bet you could tell me a thing or two.'

'I can think of plenty,' I said. 'Come on,' and I get hold of Lily's other arm and give a good tug, but he's not letting go and everyone's looking and I'm thinking we're bound to be turned out at any minute, and then blow me if Ale Mary doesn't appear. She's clawing at this chap's arm, hissing at him, 'Listen! Listen!', and screeching out this song, and he's trying to shake her off and at the same time keep hold of Lily, and Lily's walloping his arm with her gas mask case, trying to make him let go . . . I've pulled Lily right out of the door and into the street, thinking that'd put a stop to it, but all four of us end up out there, lurching along like a conga line with me in front and Mary hanging on at the back. For two pins I'd have left them and gone off back to Frith Street to fetch my things for the night, but Lily's only round the corner from me and I thought, I can't leave her in the blackout with this idiot—anything might happen—I'll get her home and Ted can do some work for once in his miserable life and sort him out.

The man's saying to Lily, 'You come over to the Swiss and have a drink with me,' because they don't close till eleven over there. Lily said, 'Oh, go home,' and I was about to tell him the same when Ale Mary suddenly said, 'I know you,' and she

64

leaned over and gave Lily a great shove in the chest so she fell back against the railings. 'I know you,' she said, 'And I don't *like* you.'

The man pushed Mary away from him and said, 'Come and have a drink, come *on*,' and he must have got hold of Lily again because they were scuffling and I got an elbow in the stomach which knocked the breath out of me, and then Lily said, 'You can go to hell, both of you!' She must have kicked him, because he said, 'Bitch!' and we heard him hopping about on one leg. Lily said, 'That'll teach you, now leave me alone!'

By the time I'd got my breath again—I was doubled over, wheezing away, with Lily rubbing my back—he was off down the street with Mary alongside, quoting from the Bible, no doubt. We could hear her singing and the footsteps getting fainter as they got towards the corner, and he suddenly shouted out, 'Dirty whores!'

I straightened up and Lily and I leant against the railings, side by side. 'Rotten bastard,' she muttered, then, 'You all right?'

'I'll do.'

'Thanks, Rene. You're a pal.'

We didn't say much on the way home. I left Lily at her door and went home to collect my blankets and cushion for the shelter.

I felt a bit fed up so I tried to take my mind off it by looking round at all the people in the shelter. There were one or two I hadn't seen before: a young chap with big eyes and buck teeth, and a couple of soldiers. Then a pilot came in, with a girl. I noticed him first, because he had one of those faces you can't help gazing at: bright blue eyes and golden hair that most women would kill for. Early

65

twenties, I suppose, but he seemed older, not because he looked it, but he had something about him, a sort of presence. Tall, too, and a lovely build, broad shoulders and slim hips—all the women were staring at him, wondering who the lucky girl was, no doubt. He didn't stay long, just got her sat down and went away again. Lovely to look at, but you wouldn't want a man like that. Far too dangerous—women round him like flies on a honey-pot. You'd never get a moment's peace, and that sort usually get above themselves from all the attention. She was quite a bit younger than me, but the same coat—blue wool. Suited her, and it would have been smart if it hadn't been for the marks. Whereas he'd been very tidy, she had all mess, dark, like soot, round the shoulders, and her hat, too. Looked like it was singed. Dirt on her face, all streaky, made me wonder if she'd been crying. Probably been in a raid, poor thing. She looked all in, slumped on the bench with her eyes shut, but she came to after a bit. Looked a bit flustered, like she couldn't remember where she was, but then she pulled a powder compact out of her handbag and opened it, then wetted her hankie—very ladylike—turned away towards the wall and started dabbing at her face. Nice hands. Soft-looking. Not married. She must have seen me in her mirror, because she suddenly turned towards me, and it was a quick up-and-down with the eyes and then . . . oooh, such a look. I don't know if it was the coat—no, I do know, because her face said it all: *I know what you are.*

That really put the lid on it. There I was, ready to give her a smile, but no, she was too stuck up for that. Made me think of that man calling us dirty whores—he'd said it, and there she was, thinking the same. I looked at her, and I thought, you think you know everything, but you'll find out: life's not like the pictures.

Ordinary women never know what men are really like, and I wish I didn't, either. Even married women—we get lots of men that don't want to bother their wives too much, but of course they can do what they like with us. I tell you, some of the wives, if they knew what their husbands were after, they'd be horrified. Beating and chaining up and all kinds of things. Took me a while to cotton on to it myself—the first time a man asked me, I didn't know what he was talking about, and when I got the message, I didn't have anything to beat him with, so in the end I got my umbrella and walloped him with that. Didn't seem much good to me, but he must have liked it, because he gave me five pounds. But sometimes I look at the men and I think, if people only knew . . . and it's taking the money away from their families, isn't it, going with a street girl? When I think how I save every penny I can for my little Tommy, I don't think that's right at all, what they do, but they've got to have a woman. Miss Toffee Nose over there, that's what she doesn't know: a man's got to have a woman or he goes like a wild beast, and that means attacks on decent women—like her.

I caught her staring at me again—seen that look before, too, plenty of times. Curiosity. *How can she do it?* That's what she was thinking. I felt like saying, blimey, dear, want me to draw you a picture? They think we do it because we enjoy it. Men do too; you get some that'll say to you, 'But you must get some pleasure out of it . . .' It's a business, that's all—same as any other.

Then she got up and rushed out of the shelter as if she was afraid she'd catch something off me. That really got on my nerves, and I thought, if I don't think of something else quick, I'll want to go after her and give her a piece of my mind. So I thought about my Tommy, instead, all upset over that girl, poor little lamb. I decided to get him a present to cheer him up. I'll nip down to Hamleys first thing tomorrow. I saw the other day they'd got Red Indian headdresses with all the feathers and that, so I'll buy one of those, only one and eleven, and take it round to him. It's bound to bring a smile to his face.

FRIDAY 20TH SEPTEMBER

Lucy

I felt bad, lying to Mums on Wednesday, but all through supper—gluey grey fish cakes, oh dear—she'd kept on and on about how she'd been to buy wool and there's no more three-ply and two-ply is no good, and even though I was hating myself for not sticking to my resolution to be nicer to her, by the end of the meal I was absolutely fed up to the back teeth. Dad was late, so Minnie tried to cheer her up by telling her about a girl at her work who'd dyed her hair with henna. It was only supposed to be left on for ten minutes, but there'd been an air-raid and she'd had to rush to the shelter with her hair in a towel—four hours later, she had a bright orange head! I thought it was funny, but Mums just

68

pursed her lips and said, 'I didn't know you worked with *that* sort of girl,' then carried on with her pet subject. Minnie's so much more patient than I am. She kept nodding sympathetically and saying, 'What a shame,' when I just wanted to shout, 'It doesn't *matter*!' Because it's so *unimportant* to be worrying about wool when there's everything else.

I said that to Minnie afterwards, when we were washing up, and she said, quietly, 'Well, it matters to her.'

I said, 'I don't know why you have to be so *nice* all the time.' I knew it was childish, even before I said it, and wished I hadn't because she looked so hurt. It wasn't fair to snap at her, because she was doing her best and anyway, she's only seventeen— too young to understand about love, or anything, really.

Seeing her bent over the sink, she looked such a kid that it suddenly made me feel like a woman of the world, which I'm not, but I thought, she can't even imagine the conversation like the one I had with B when we sneaked out to the Corner House this afternoon. Well, I couldn't imagine it, either. If somebody had told me a month ago that was going to happen, I'd never have believed them, because it seemed so impossible that even while we were talking I couldn't quite believe it. The tea room was pretty crowded, but we got a little table behind a pillar where no one could see, and I was telling him about the queer feeling I'd had in the corridor with the world all melting away, because I was sure he'd understand, when he suddenly said, 'You're a lovely girl. I can't believe that some young man hasn't carried you off.'

I thought of Frank, and said, 'I don't want some

young man to *carry me off*, as you put it.'

'You're a virgin, aren't you?'

I was a bit taken aback by that, but determined not to seem shocked, so I said, 'Well . . . yes, since you ask.'

He looked at me with his head on one side as if he was considering a picture, and said, 'Why is that, do you suppose?'

'What do you mean, *why*?'

'Exactly that.'

'I don't know. Because I am. Because . . .' I realised I didn't really know. I suppose the answer is, *Because it's the right thing to be*, or at least, it's what the world and men—or men like Frank, at least—expect of girls like me. But I didn't know how to explain that, and felt that if I tried it might sound rather petty.

'Because?'

'Well, I haven't really wanted to be anything else, and anyway, I don't want to get into trouble.'

He put his hand over mine. 'You don't have to get into trouble.'

'But—'

'No buts, young lady. The question is, do you want to now?'

I knew exactly what he meant, and I couldn't look him in the eye at all. 'I don't know.'

'Will you tell me when you do know?'

I was so flabbergasted, I just said, 'Yes.'

'Good girl. And will you have dinner with me tomorrow?'

'In the evening?'

'I believe that's the usual time for dinner.'

'But—'

'That's all right.' He winked. 'I'm fire-watching.'

70

'I see. And what am I doing?'
'First aid lecture.'

*   *   *

I was thinking about our conversation when Minnie suddenly asked, 'Why are you smiling like that?'

I couldn't tell her, so I dropped my tea-towel and dashed out of the room with the excuse of fetching a new one.

When I went back to kitchen, I occupied myself getting Dad's supper out of the oven, so Minnie couldn't see my expression, which must have been peculiar, to say the least. Mums was still talking about her wretched wool when Dad came in, so he tried to take her mind off it by telling her about the lecture he'd been to for the new wardens. He says they are all as old as Methuselah—the lame, the blind and the halt, he calls them. Of course it didn't work, because after about three minutes Mums was going nineteen to the dozen about how we'd all be murdered in our beds and no one was doing anything about it. When Dad pointed out, quite rightly, that the wardens aren't there to *stop* the bombs, she said, 'It's these blasted aeroplanes. I don't know why we had to go and invent them in the first place, we've had no benefit. Now stop going on about it, you're making me tired.' Honestly, she is *impossible* sometimes.

None of us could think of a thing to say in reply, which wasn't surprising, and after a few minutes of rather stunned silence, Dad said, 'They're late tonight. You'd best go upstairs and change your clothes.'

We hadn't heard the siren, but while I was

71

putting on my slacks there was the most enormous crash, so loud that all the windows rattled and plaster came down from the ceiling and I lost my balance and almost put my foot through the trouser leg. I was trembling so much I had to sit down on the bed, and then there was another crash, and then the most almighty *whomp!* of something exploding. The entire house was shaking like a tree, and I could hear Mums shouting and then the guns opened up. I don't think I've ever got downstairs so fast in my life—I was practically flying, and I shot straight into Dad's arms and almost knocked him off his feet. When he'd got his breath back, he said, 'Still in one piece?'

'Just about.'

'That's the ticket.'

'What was *that*?'

'Gas main, I should think. Good job we've eaten.' Then he said, 'I'd better get down to the post and see what I can do.'

I watched him putting on his helmet and I suddenly thought, what a good person he is, for the way he puts up with Mums and is always so cheerful and calm and brave. I felt so full of gratitude and love that I wanted to tell him, but I didn't want to be melodramatic and silly so I just said, 'Be careful, Dad.'

He smiled at me and I thought, perhaps he knew that wasn't what I meant to say at all, and somehow that made it better than if I'd actually said it—can't explain that properly, but it was something between us that was bigger than words. He said, 'Don't worry, Smiler. We'll pull through. Look after your mother, she's in a bad way. I told Minnie to fetch her some brandy.'

I stood in the passage for a moment after he'd gone and I thought, whatever happens, I'll always remember that. Then there was another huge bang, and I went haring into the kitchen and found Mums and Minnie under the table. Mums had her head in her hands, and was rocking and moaning, really wretched.

Minnie whispered to me, 'The brandy isn't doing any good. I'm afraid she'll go hysterical.'

Mums kept saying, 'Oh, Billy, Billy,' over and over again.

I put my arm round her shoulders and said, 'Dad's going to be fine. He'll be careful. I made him promise.'

'But he's *gone*.'

'Yes, but he'll be back as soon as it's over.'

'He's *gone*. He's not supposed to be on duty, so why did he have to go?'

'To help, Mums.'

'I didn't want him to go. I asked him not to.'

'I know, but he had to.'

Mums started to cry and Minnie put her arm round her, too, and we sat there in a row and listened to the bombs. It seemed to go on for ever—the nearest we've had yet—and every time there was a bang we all jumped. My heart must have missed more beats than it ticked. Minnie and I kept looking at each other over Mums's head. 'That sounded like Union Road,' Minnie whispered.

'At least we've still got our windows.'

Mums jerked her head up. 'Windows? Is the blackout—'

'It's fine, Mums.'

'Oh, *Billy* . . .'

73

After a while there was a lull and we crawled out from under the table and across the passage to the cupboard under the stairs. I just had time to rush into the sitting room and grab the cushions from the sofa before it started again with that awful ripping sound like tearing a sheet, which means a high explosive, and I hurled the cushions into the cupboard and myself after them—right on top of poor Minnie—and we'd just about managed to get ourselves into some sort of order when there was another. The noise went on and on, and so did Mums's whimpering, until I wanted to scream. I don't know how she can stand it in this cupboard, night after night—it's like being buried alive, and so airless I thought I was going to suffocate. For the first time, I felt furious that our family, or any human being, could be reduced to this, huddled like animals, quaking in a dark, squalid hole, robbed of sleep and comfort and unable to defend themselves, or even—which I badly wanted to do—spend a penny, but Mums had forgotten the pot.

Every time there was a lull, I tried to get to the toilet, but Mums grabbed me and pulled me back again, and by the time we'd stopped arguing it would be too late because the next lot was coming over. The All-Clear went at four o'clock, by which time my bladder was ready to burst, my stomach was aching like anything and my legs were completely numb. I staggered off to the lav and then went to find a cigarette to steady myself. Minnie was in the kitchen, making tea on the spirit stove. 'Well,' she said, 'we're still here. Well done, House, for not falling down.' It was a daft thing to say, but I knew exactly what she meant. Then she looked down and started laughing.

74

'What?'

'Your feet—look! You've got your tennis shoes the wrong way round.' She was right. In all the commotion, I hadn't even noticed. They looked so silly that I started to laugh, too—relief, I suppose—and the two of us just roared.

When we'd pulled ourselves together, I said, 'Don't you want to go to bed?'

'I'm not sleepy.'

'Me neither. Fancy a game of dominoes?'

'Why not? I'll just take some tea to Mums, first.'

We sat under the kitchen table, just in case. Neither of us said very much, and I could see from Minnie's face that she was listening out for Dad, same as I was. After about an hour, we heard Mums snoring. Minnie went to look and came back with a half-empty brandy bottle. She rolled her eyes at me. 'Did the trick in the end.'

'As long as she doesn't make a habit of it.'

'Be fair, Lucy, it was very close—and with Dad going out like that . . .' she made a face. 'I offered her some cotton wool to put in her ears when it started, and do you know what she said? "I won't be able to hear what's going on!" I said, "You don't want to hear what's going on," and she said, "Yes, I do." There's no pleasing some people.'

We talked about going upstairs again. I said Minnie ought to, and I'd wait up for Dad, but she wouldn't, and then she said I should, and we were on the point of rowing about it when we heard, 'Hello! Any more tea in the pot?' and it was Dad, covered from head to foot in dust. He almost fell through the door and collapsed on one of the chairs.

'What happened, Dad? You look exhausted.'

75

'Let me get my breath, I'll be all right in a minute.'

Minnie said, 'Let me take your helmet,' but he shook his head.

'Leave it.'

We asked him to tell us what happened, but he didn't say much, except to ask about Mums. I said, 'Aren't you going to drink your tea, Dad?' because he hadn't touched it, but he just said, 'You two get some sleep. I'll have to be off again in a minute.' He sounded so tired and defeated, I knew he just wanted to be on his own. I turned back in the doorway and said goodnight, but he was staring straight ahead and seemed not to have heard me. With the white dust on him, and his eyes like craters in the shadow of his helmet, he looked like a ghost.

We went upstairs in silence, and on the landing, Minnie said quietly, 'He didn't want to see us, did he?'

'No.'

'He was *trying* to be Dad, when he came in—you know, be like he always is—but he couldn't, could he?'

'No.'

'It must have been terrible.'

I said, 'Do you want to come in with me?'

'No, it's all right.' Then she went into her room and closed the door.

I wished she'd said yes. It's frightening how much you rely on people to behave in a certain way, and how unsettling it is when they stop. But it's not just Dad, it's me, too. I looked in the mirror just before I got into bed, and was surprised to see anything there at all. I didn't recognise the reflection behind the plaster dust. That must be what an animal sees when it looks into a mirror, a meaningless shape. I wiped the glass with my handkerchief, but it didn't make any difference. I got into bed determined to pull myself together. It's a bad thing to be too preoccupied with oneself, especially at the moment.

Terribly tired, but it took for ever to drift off and then it was only a half sleep. Gave up at quarter to seven and went out into the back garden in my dressing gown to have a look round. It was light, but everything was grey and damp with drizzle. I could smell gas from the burst main. Not much in the way of damage, except windows blown out a few doors down. Ours look all right, though—must have been just far enough away. I concluded that most of the damage must have been in front of the house, not behind it, and was about to go and see, when I noticed a pair of bird's wings, with soft, downy feathers, spread out in the middle of the lawn. They looked perfect, as if they'd been shed by a tiny angel, but I suppose they must have been torn off a carcass by a cat. Like a sign of some sort. I thought it would be bad luck just to leave them there, so I fetched a trowel and gave them a decent burial underneath a rosebush. They were so light when I picked them up, almost weightless. Strange to think of where they must have been, soaring across the sky—although when I looked up, that was hard to imagine because the sky seemed more like a great metal dustbin lid that had been slammed on top of the world to keep us down here with all this mess and misery, than something bright and clear and infinite. Extraordinary, though, to think that mankind has conquered it

77

with machines. That made me think of what Mums said about aeroplanes. I suppose she's right, in a way, because they *are* only machines—machines for killing. They only *seem* exciting and glamorous, when really they are no different from tanks or battleships. But we owe so much to those pilots . . . they must be the bravest men who ever lived.

Found myself hoping, idiotically, that my dead bird could stand in place of an airman—its life in exchange for a human life. Said a short prayer to that effect over the rosebush, feeling very foolish, and hurried back indoors to get dressed.

Dad was back at breakfast, but he didn't say much. Minnie looked exhausted, and Mums was grumbling about the gas. I told her about the first aid lecture, and she said, 'You won't be too late, will you?' I said I didn't know and not to worry. It felt rotten. I hate lying. I suppose I could have come nearer the truth—said it was a date with Frank, but she'd only fuss and say it was irresponsible, and I really can't stand all that at the moment. Perhaps it *is* irresponsible, but another night under the stairs would just about finish me, and besides, if I was fire-watching at the office I'd have to stay in London, wouldn't I? Along with B, of course—but then it would be quite in order. They haven't asked the women yet, but if they do I shall put my name down as a volunteer. I ought to do something, anyway. It's not as if I'm any use to anyone sitting at home night after night, and Minnie's far better at looking after Mums than I am.

It was raining when I went to the station. I passed the end of Union Road: three houses down, and all that was left was an enormous crater with two great mounds of rubble on either side, bricks and plaster mixed up with bits of floorboards, linoleum, curtains, crocks—all the things that make a home. The rescue men had planks up the side of one of the heaps, and they were passing baskets of debris back down, I suppose to clear the way for a shaft through the top. There was an ambulance backed up, waiting. I tried not to think about who might be at the bottom of the rubble and, worse, what they might look like.

I saw a warden cross the road with a woman's handbag in one hand and a frying pan in the other. I couldn't think where he was taking them. Curiosity got the better of me, and when I went to see, I realised that they were putting belongings from the bombed houses into one of the front gardens opposite. China plates with not a chip on them, a milk jug, saucepans, a man's hat turned upside down . . . all laid out in rows on the muddy grass as if children were playing at a jumble sale. There was an old man standing beside them, looking dazed. When the warden showed him the handbag, I heard him say, 'I don't care about that. Where's Peggy?'

The warden said, 'They're still digging.'

'What about Peggy?'

The warden put down the things he'd been carrying and picked up the hat. 'Is it yours?' he asked. The old man looked at it as if he'd never seen a hat before.

'Put it on,' said the warden. 'Keep the rain off your head,' he explained, gently. 'You'll feel better.'

The old man said nothing, but took the hat and put it on his head, and the warden left. The man stood staring straight ahead, and he suddenly said,

'Thank you,' to no one in particular. It was loud and forceful. '*Thank you.*'

About ten minutes later I suddenly thought, if that pilot had dropped his stick of bombs a few seconds earlier—or later, depending on which way he was flying—our house would have looked like that and I wouldn't be sitting in this train, I'd be part of the rubble, and so would Mums and Minnie, and it would be Dad standing in a neighbour's garden with the warden telling him to put on his hat. But instead, the pilot dropped it over Union Road, so I was able to walk out into the garden this morning and find a pair of bird's wings and bury them under a rosebush. It is all just chance, and we are so helpless.

It was awfully nice to go out in the evening again. I suddenly realised, sitting in the restaurant, that I haven't really been anywhere for several weeks. I'd said goodnight to all the girls in the office then rushed away to the National Gallery to meet B, who hustled me into a taxi straight away, which was rather exciting, like being a spy or something. We said our 'hellos' in the back, and he took me to a restaurant in Charlotte Street where we spent the next two hours getting tight on red wine and laughing a great deal. We heard the siren but nobody moved. I asked B if he didn't think it odd to be eating in an Italian restaurant when our countries are at war with each other, but he said that none of them are fifth columnists, or they'd have been interned by now. And two of the owner's sons were serving in the army—he's put a notice about it on the wall—so I suppose it must be all right. Then he added, 'Besides, they're *Italians*,' which made us both giggle, and then I said, 'We shouldn't really be laughing. I mean, that business over Somaliland made us look pretty silly, giving it up like that after everyone had said what a shame for Hitler having the Italians as allies and how lucky they weren't on our side.'

B said, 'Well, at least they've got plenty of sand.' We were laughing again, when he suddenly stopped. 'Oh, Lord.' His face had gone white.

'What is it?'

'Chap we know. Down there. Just stood up.' He jerked his head towards the back of the restaurant. 'Don't look, you fool!'

'What shall—'

'Get out! Just go. I'll settle the bill and come after you. Meet round the corner.' He stood up, jerked my hat and coat off the stand, and almost threw them at me.

Thirty seconds later I found myself standing on the pavement in the dark, shivering and feeling as if I'd just had a bucket of cold water flung in my face. In the restaurant, it had felt so warm and happy and *right*, and then to be pulled up short like that . . . Chap *we* know, he'd said. Meaning him and his wife. The wife whose existence I'd conveniently forgotten. I've no idea what she looks like, but suddenly I could imagine her, a real, flesh-and-blood woman, sitting in a chair in their house, listening to the wireless and thinking that her husband was out fire-watching. It all seemed so sordid, standing on the street corner in the middle of a raid, putting myself in danger and causing worry to others through my own selfishness, that I suddenly found myself wishing I was back under the stairs with Mums and Minnie.

Then I heard footsteps, and as they grew closer I

81

saw that it was B. As I started towards him I saw him make a quick shooing movement with his hand, then he crossed over to the other side of the road. I didn't understand immediately, and was about to call out to him when I heard another set of footsteps, hurrying towards us. I shrank back into a doorway just as whoever it was must have caught up, because I heard a man's voice say, 'Bridges! I thought it was you. Which way are you going?' I didn't catch B's reply, but they moved off together down the street, and I was left on my own, feeling very cheap and rather frightened. I suddenly thought of the warden this morning, handing the old man his hat, and it made me want to cry. Not because I wanted somebody to hand me a hat—I was wearing one—but the small kindness of it, wishing it for myself. It seemed such a terrible contrast with what had just happened in the restaurant, such a little action from a simple desire to help another human being without thought of gain or favour. It made me feel like the worst person in the world, an outcast from the rest of humanity, and I remembered the bird's wings in the garden and thought, where's *my* angel? If I had my own angel, everything would be all right. Not that I deserve one.

The noise of the guns bucked me up, and I thought I'd better stop feeling sorry for myself and concentrate on getting home before it got any worse. I thought B and his friend must be heading for Tottenham Court Road, and I didn't want to follow in case we met up at the station, so I turned and walked the other way. It was very dark, and pretty soon I was dashing around in a panic, with no idea which way to go. I could hear machine guns and aircraft, far off at first, then nearer, and when I looked up there were flares like exploding chandeliers, breaking up and dropping downwards, and then the sky was lit up in red and orange, turning the pavement pink and making the buildings flicker and glow in a sort of half light, rosy and magical. It was the most extraordinary sight, and for a moment I forgot that I was afraid, because it seemed as if the whole world had turned into a vast display of light, and I was at the centre of it—the strangest feeling, no awareness of danger, or even of myself, just *wonder*. Like being at the very heart of the universe.

A policeman came up—his helmet blood-red in the glow—and asked me for my ID card. He said, 'I'd get along home, miss, if I was you. They're bombing this district.' As if I hadn't noticed!

It was only when he'd gone that I realised I should have asked for directions. I called out to him, but he can't have heard me over the guns, because he didn't come back, so I gave it up and started blundering towards what I hoped was Oxford Circus, but I couldn't recognise a thing. In the distance I could see the searchlights, like great bars of light, criss-crossing in the sky, and tiny white flashes from our guns, and the explosions got closer and closer. It sounded as if it was raining bombs: whistling and tearing noises all round and the loudest bangs I've ever heard, and it wasn't awesome any more, but utterly terrifying and all I wanted to do was curl up into a ball and hide.

Pretty soon I was crunching across broken glass, the gas mask banging up and down on my hip, ducking into a doorway whenever there was a bang, huddling down with my heart thumping like

83

anything, telling myself to keep calm but with the most awful frantic terror building up inside—not just of being blown to pieces but of Mums and Dad knowing why I was there, or worse, never knowing *at all.* I remembered standing with Dad in the hall when he put on his helmet, and the way he looked at me, and I wanted to cry again from sheer despair, but then there was a great *woof!* from somewhere behind me and the whole street flashed up like daylight. I didn't stop to think, just let go of the railings and launched myself into the alley round the corner. I caught a flash of something snaking through the air towards me and then a hot, soft mass enfolded my mouth and chin. I tried to scream, but took in a great, choking mouthful of embers that scalded my throat, and for a second I really did think I was going to die. I tore at the stuff in sheer panic, but it wrapped itself around me, suffocating, clinging to my face and twisting round my neck like something demonic as I tried to beat it off, and then suddenly, miraculously, there were hands tearing it away, and I could see a face in front of me, but in pieces as if I were looking through a cobweb and nothing seemed to join up, and then it was over, and the air was cooling my face, and I was taking in great gulps of it, coughing and spluttering, tears in my eyes, and through them I could see a man standing in front of me. I say 'a man', but at that moment his face and hair—he had no hat—looked blazing and golden, and with the glow all around him he didn't seem human at all.

'Keep still,' he said. 'Close your eyes.'

I did as I was told, and felt him push back my hat, very gently, and pat my hair in the front.

'There. You can open your eyes, now.'

I did as I was told, and for a moment, I was too overcome to speak. Then I croaked out the first thing in my head: 'You must be my angel.'

' 'Fraid not. A mere mortal. For the time being, at least.'

I put my hand up to adjust my hat, felt frizzled ends of hair above my ears, and wondered what on earth I must look like.

'Don't worry,' he said. 'It's fine. Does your face hurt?'

'Not really. It's just a bit hot, that's all.'

'I don't think it's burnt, anyway.'

'No. Thank you. For helping me, I mean.'

He was wearing a uniform. Air force. He was very handsome—tall, with thick, corn-coloured hair and blue eyes—and well spoken.

I said, 'What was it?'

'Look down.'

It was the remains of a stocking, lacy, like an old-fashioned gas mantle where it was burned through, hot and writhing like a snake. 'Must have been a dress shop.' The man laughed. 'The frocks are running away. Quite right too.'

I looked down the alleyway and saw the most extraordinary sight: smouldering frocks, floating through the night air beside a burning shop-front, wispy and disintegrating, but keeping their shapes as they minced across the cobbles, as if they were being worn by very prim invisible women. It can't be real, I thought. I've just been attacked by a stocking, and now I'm watching a disembodied tea-dance with an airman who looks like a film star. If it wasn't for the pain in my throat and the burnt hair, I don't think I would have believed it, because it was exactly like a dream.

He said, 'Do you trust me?'

His voice seemed to come down from somewhere high up and sort of settle on me, as if the words were feathers. Shock, I suppose. I just nodded.

'You'd better let me take you to a shelter.'

I must have nodded again, because he took my arm and led me to Soho Square. We didn't speak, but seemed to step through the whole cacophony of bombs and guns in our own little patch of intimate silence, as if we were sealed off and the rest of the world couldn't touch us. I knew that as long as he was with me, I would be safe. It gave me a cool, calm feeling inside—the oddest thing, like walking through a fire and knowing it can't burn you.

When we reached the shelter he dropped my arm and said, 'Well, here you are.'

Like a fool, I said, 'Aren't you coming in?'

'No.'

'Oh . . .'

I suppose I must have sounded dreadfully disappointed, because he took something out of his pocket and put it into my hand. 'I want you to have this.'

'But—'

'No buts.' He closed my fingers around a small, hard object. The feeling of his hand on mine, the warmth and strength of it, gave me a sudden rush of . . . what? Not happiness, but an intensity of sensation that made me feel hot inside and self-conscious, sure that he must be aware of it. Then his voice came again, as if the words were alighting on me from somewhere far above. 'It'll keep you safe.'

'Safe?' The word jolted me and I suddenly saw the two of us as if from the outside; two people standing outside a shelter in the middle of an air-raid. 'We ought to go in,' I said.

He didn't move. 'Look here,' he said. 'It belonged to my mother.'

'But you . . . You need—'

'I don't need it. Not any more.'

'But you're not . . . not . . .' I faltered, not sure what I'd been going to say.

'You can wear it for me. Now then, let's find you a place to sit down.'

We went in, and I sat down on one of the benches. I was jolly glad he was there, because I'd have been horribly embarrassed going into a shelter full of unknown people, raid or no raid. It was pretty nasty. Dank concrete, water on the floor and a strong smell of stale bodies, but I didn't really notice any of those things—well, apart from the smell—until after he'd gone.

He smiled at me, clicked his heels and made a funny little bow, then said, 'Look after it, won't you?'

'Of course, I—' I started to say, *I promise*, but he turned and walked away and left me staring after him.

I didn't open my hand until he'd left. It was a brooch: a dull, green stone, lozenge-shaped. Cheap-looking, not like an heirloom. Not from *that* sort of family, anyway. But it must be very special for him to carry it about like that. His mother must have been beautiful. I wondered when she'd died— if she knew. She'd have been so proud of him.

He hadn't seemed like a grammar school boy, not like Frank, too . . . *confident*. Not in a horrid,

87

flashy way, swanking and swaggering, but something real and quiet that comes from inside. Perhaps that's how you tell a true hero—sharp and keen-eyed and straight-backed and . . . but that's only looks, comic book stuff. Dad would say it's all slop, but he agreed when Churchill said, what was it? *Turning the tide of the war by their prowess and devotion* . . . His speech about the pilots. Dad made a joke about how we need heroes so badly these days that we'd make them out of cardboard if we had to, but he'd be the first to agree that these men have qualities which set them apart from the common herd.

I'll keep this always, I thought, as long as I live, and wished with all my heart that I had given him a kiss.

I put it in my coat pocket. I shan't let Mums see it—she's bound to say a green stone will bring bad luck. Besides, I can hardly tell her what happened, can I? Thinking that made me remember the business with B in the restaurant, and I realised I hadn't given him a thought, but it all seemed so shabby by comparison, such a trivial, squalid concern when these men are fighting to save our country from Hitler . . . I suddenly saw how small-minded B is, and how foolish I'd been, and wanted nothing more to do with him. It's only when you meet someone like that, someone who's truly brave, that you realise. It seems all wrong for someone like that to sacrifice himself so that men like B can be free to carry on their squalid little intrigues in safety, but I suppose that's only a tiny part of the picture. It's the ideals that matter, not the petty things. Meeting *him* has given me something to live up to, at least, and when I think

88

of how vain and self-centred I've been . . . Well, not any more.

I put my hand in my pocket and touched the brooch, then leaned back and closed my eyes. I only meant to do it for a moment but I must have been exhausted because I fell straight to sleep, and half an hour later I suddenly came to with absolutely no idea of where I was. The first thing I saw was a row of elderly ladies sitting opposite me with rusty black coats and kippered faces, sighing and shuffling and mumbling their jaws to ease their teeth, and a really nasty-looking one on the end in carpet slippers, snoring with her mouth open.

For a moment, I thought I must be dreaming, but then I found myself clutching the brooch in my pocket. The pin pricked me and woke me up, and I remembered what had happened. I thought I'd better tidy myself up a bit before heading for home, but I felt awkward about doing it in full view, so I twisted round towards the wall for a spot of privacy, and got my compact out of my handbag to inspect the damage. I must have picked it up rather awkwardly, because it was on a slant, and suddenly, a pair of eyes very similar to mine stared straight into the mirror from the other side of the shelter, and for a moment, just a moment, it was as if I was looking at myself, as if my body had reproduced itself and walked across the shelter of its own accord and was sitting looking back at me: same build, same coat, same hair style. But when I turned round for a proper look, I saw a woman, quite a bit older than me, plastered with heavy make-up, wearing high-heeled shoes—obviously a prostitute! Well, I thought, it just goes to show—I must be in a queer frame of mind if I can think something like that. Looking for a man, no doubt. I'm sure these people have to go somewhere, but a *public shelter* . . . You'd think the wardens would put a stop to it.

I suppose some of what I was thinking must have shown in my face, because the woman turned her head away quite sharply. I quickly righted the compact and got on with tidying myself up, because the real me was very dishevelled. I was jolly relieved to see that my eyebrows were still in place, but my hair looked a real fright. I tucked in the singed bits as best I could, then I went to work with my handkerchief, which at least got rid of the smuts, but the results weren't terribly satisfactory, and after a bit of scrubbing and rubbing, I gave up. Then I caught the woman looking at me again, and for one awful moment I thought she was going to say something, and wondered if she might be drunk. I don't see how you could do . . . *what she does* . . . unless you were. It's too revolting to think about.

I suddenly thought of B, and what I might have done with him, and felt hot all over. I was sure I was blushing, as if she could read my thoughts, and all I wanted to do was get out of there as quickly as I could, air-raid or no air-raid.

I hadn't heard the All-Clear, but it was fairly quiet outside. The darkness was threatening, and I found myself breathing in, hunching myself up, feeling my way along walls. I just managed to get the last train from Leicester Square and sat, head down, in the carriage, willing myself to stop shaking, desperately wanting to be home and safe and . . . I don't know . . . wishing that none of it was happening—the war, or B, or any of it. Wishing

90

that nothing had *changed*. But it has, and we're not safe any more, none of us. The train was pretty crowded and the platforms heaving and I looked round at all the faces and thought, what are they going home *to*? Then I imagined the house in ruins and Mums and Dad and Minnie trapped underneath and me not there because I'd lied to them.

I put my hand in my coat pocket again and touched the brooch. I found the pin and pressed it against my fingertip so it hurt, and had a silly thought that as long as I did that the house would still be there and my family would be safe. I knew it was nonsense, but I couldn't stop myself, even though my finger was bleeding and staining the pocket and I was worried in case it seeped through the lining and made a mark. I kept thinking of the airman, his face in the flickering light of the burning shop, and I felt as if, in some odd way, I belonged to him. The bird's wings I'd found in the garden and the wings on his shoulder were the same shape, except that the bird's wings were folded, like a resting angel, and the airman's were spread wide as if they were flying. The prayer that I'd gabbled by the rosebush, perhaps it was for *him*, only I hadn't known it then. I decided I'd say it again, and maybe it would keep him safe for another day, because of the connection between us.

A voice in my head, sounding remarkably like Mums, told me sharply that this was romantic tosh, but honestly, I can't see why it isn't as good as anything else, when nobody knows what will happen. I kept the pin against my fingertip for the whole of the journey, but the petty little pain couldn't stop my thoughts going round and round

91

in circles like a dog chasing its tail. Those burning dresses whirling up into the air and the dinner with B and what happened and the airman and the woman in the shelter . . . Especially her. I mean, imagine doing *that* with men who don't respect you—except I don't even know what *that* feels like—and I found myself looking round, as well as I could, at the men nearest to me, the bits of faces I could see, like a jigsaw: wrinkles and shaving cuts and pores and pocks, and hairs on the backs of fingers, dirt under nails, the squared-off shoulders and backs in heavy coats; and I could imagine the greasy insides of their hats, the rims of dirt on their shirt collars, the flakes of scurf in their hair . . . and I thought of being that woman and having them touch you and lie on top of you and squash you and breathe in your face because that's what she lets them do. It could have been any one of those men and she'd have gone with them and taken their money.

I couldn't keep my mind off it, and after a few stops I felt that if any one of those men so much as brushed against me I would be physically sick, so I breathed in and tried to make myself as narrow as possible, but even as I was doing it I couldn't help thinking, what difference does it make what anybody does, if we are all going to die?

It's all so confusing. And dangerous. I didn't want to have those thoughts. They're like 'the thing', only worse, and they can't be right. I'm weak to have been taken in by nothing more than a handsome face and a few compliments. I felt ashamed of myself, but was jolted out of it by the thought that B might secretly despise me for being the sort of girl who would even consider doing what

92

he wanted. The idea of that made me furious. The one he ought to despise is *himself*. And he must know how other people would despise him, which was why I suddenly meant so little to him that he was happy to abandon me in the middle of an air-raid. That made me think of my airman again, how different he was, calm and brave . . . *my* airman! Oh dear, how presumptuous. He isn't my airman at all. But I did wonder if maybe I might see him again. I thought, if I went back to that shelter, I might . . . Who knows?

I got home eventually. Mums launched in immediately. 'My goodness, your hair! And your coat! What's happened to you? You could have been killed! I told you not to go!' I was very tempted to retort that she hadn't told me anything of the kind, but said nothing. Unfortunately, Mums took my silence as a cue for another barrage, this time along the lines of 'Something has happened, and you're not telling us! I knew it! I don't know why you have to be so secretive, Lucy. Minnie always tells me everything, anyone would think you had something to hide,' and so on and so on. Of course, the awful thing is that she's right, I do have something to hide.

Fortunately, Dad stuck up for me, 'Leave her be, she's tired.' When Mums left the room, he said, quietly, 'Don't be hard on her, Lucy. She's worried about you, that's all.'

I said, 'I know. I got caught up in a raid, but I'm fine, honestly. Just a bit shaken.'

'As long as you're still in one piece. She's very fond of you, Lucy. That's why.'

'I know. It's just because I'm tired, and when she starts on at me . . .'

'It's all right, Smiler.' Dad patted my hand. 'I do understand, you know.'

The All-Clear went early, for once—thank you, Hitler. I escaped up to bed leaving Mums under the stairs with Minnie. Didn't get into bed at once, but gave my coat a good brush to get the marks off. I must say, I don't think so much of it since I saw that woman wearing the same model, but I can't possibly afford another. Gas still off, so did my best to clean up with cold water. Ugh! But felt immense pleasure at putting on my nightie, instead of slacks and tennis shoes.

I took the brooch out of the pocket and put it under my pillow. Fell asleep eventually and woke at six after a *very* strange dream . . . not entirely sure that I want to remember it—or that I ought to remember it. There was a man in bed next to me, but not touching. I was most aware of his head. He looked like Robert Taylor, but I knew it wasn't him, just that whoever it was had decided to appear to be like him because he's my favourite film star. He kept asking me to put my hand under the sheets. At first I made excuses, worrying about Mums finding us and how it would look. He was very polite, but he insisted that I should do this, so eventually I did, and—this is the awful part—I touched him, and it felt soft and heavy—ugh—and I wasn't enjoying it, but he said, 'Go on, go on,' and it got bigger and bigger like a balloon and I was scared because I didn't know what to do next, but then he put his hand down under the sheet with mine, and brought out a bunch of flowers, tied up in a bow made out of one of my stockings.

I said, 'How did you do that?' but never got an answer, because after that I woke up, feeling

94

surprised and terribly pleased. I was thoroughly alarmed at the direction my thoughts had taken, and found it quite impossible to meet anyone's eye when I went downstairs. Still, the stocking in the dream reminded me of the ones I need to darn, so I made a start on that at breakfast, much to Mums's disgust.

FRIDAY 20TH SEPTEMBER

Jim

Two a.m. now. What a night! Funny, I ought to be tired after all that. Can't sleep, though. Better try and get some shut-eye: Reilly'll be in with the tea in three hours. Bloody dark getting back across the airfield—had to guess where I was going, then walked straight into the side of one of the hangars. Still, got back in one piece.

Matheson's feet hanging off the end of the bed, as usual. At least he's quiet tonight. Shouts sometimes. No words, just a noise.

A cigarette might help—I've run out. See if Mathy's got some in his jacket. Five left, and his lighter. Better sit down on the bed quietly, so the springs don't creak. Not much chance of disturbing him, though—he's out for the count.

Damn good scrap this afternoon, or rather, yesterday afternoon. Pity about Prideaux. Stupid bastard flew smack into the middle of a bunch of 109s. Didn't stand a chance. Noticed this morning he had the jitters. We were standing by the window in the dispersal hut, drinking tea, and he kept

95

slopping it, couldn't seem to get it in his mouth. Hands weren't steady, face twitching. He didn't seem to be aware of it. Seen that before, so I looked him in the eye and acted it back to him, mouth jerking, tea going all over the shop. After a while, he realised what he was doing, and stopped. He turned away to look up at the sky, clapped me on the shoulder, said, 'Thanks, old boy,' very quietly, and wandered off outside. Last I saw, he was standing with his back to me, looking over at the planes.

If I'd thought about it, I'd have said he might funk it, but he didn't, just yelled, 'Tally ho!' and tore straight into the middle of the whole damn lot. We heard him over the R/T, shouting curses at them, and the next thing we knew, he explodes in a ball of flame, chunks flying in all directions—and that's it.

I remember something I overheard once, something he said. We were in the pub. The gents was full, so I nipped outside, and he was there, with a girl. They didn't see me. He was telling her a story about when he was at school, being called into the headmaster's study and thinking he was going to get a thrashing, but the headmaster told him his father had just telephoned to say that his mother was dead. Said he felt relieved because it meant he wasn't going to be beaten. He remembered walking down the corridor towards the room, the door, the desk, everything. Then, afterwards, he wasn't sad, just relieved. Said he still felt guilty about it. Interesting, the details he remembered, the tiles on the floor, and standing in front of the door, the handle . . . everything . . . as if it was important to him. Good story. And the way

96

he said it. Not like talking to a chap at all. And she loved it, you could tell.

They went off after that, and I went back inside. I'd forgotten all about it, until now. He said another odd thing, once, in the mess. Lot of chaps were shooting a line, and Prideaux suddenly said he thought it was a privilege to fly a Spitfire. Mathy said he didn't see why it was a privilege to go down in flames, but Prideaux was right, in a way, and everyone knew it. Then Prideaux asked Corky why he'd joined the RAF and Corky said, 'Wanted to fly, of course. And I like blowing things up.' Then he shrugged. 'Anyway, they started it.'

Mathy said, 'Better than crawling around some bloody trench.'

It was the only time I've ever heard it discussed. If Prideaux'd asked me, I'd have said the same as Corky and Mathy, but that's not really all of it. It made me think about my first flight again, in the Avro, the amazing joy of it. It's something you can't translate into words.

Everyone was quiet for a bit, then there was a rush for more drinks, and Davy told a joke. There was a lot of laughter, Prideaux the loudest of all, but nobody was looking at each other. I was watching them, and the faces suddenly seemed . . . I don't know, I suppose they might have been thinking the same as I was, but I couldn't tell. I thought of the dials on the instrument panel. I can understand those, how they work. What they register. But faces—sometimes—*often*—not at all. Like not having a map. But I watch, and I remember things, and that helps.

Prideaux had a car. MG. Still there, outside the dispersal hut. Wonder what'll happen to that?

Good little car. Not much point, though, with petrol rationing.

We thought Holden-Thingummybob had bought it, but it turned out he'd been pranged and baled out straight into the drink. Got picked up by a fishing boat. But he's off Ops for a few days while they thaw him out, so I got the other new boy— Sinclair. Flint said, 'We'll give you Gervase to play with.'

'Gervase?'

'Yes. Don't be too rough, or you'll break him.'

'Can't Balchin have him?'

'Haven't you heard? Balchin's at Manston. Landed in a tree. Farmer mistook him for a Jerry and chucked a pitchfork at him. Gave him a bit of a puncture. All cleared up in the end, but I'm afraid he won't be back for a day or two.'

'Well, why can't "B" flight have him?'

'They don't need him. You do.'

'Like a hole in the head.'

Gervase. He did manage to stay with me this afternoon, which was something. When we got back, he said, 'There's no warning . . . it's all so fast . . . I mean, I thought, if someone jumps you, at least there'd be a warning on the R/T, or . . .'

'What do you want? A telegram from Goering?'

'No, but . . . you could just get . . . killed. Just . . . bang.' Tears in his eyes. As if I was a bloody nursemaid.

I said, 'Yes, you could *just get killed*. It's not a picnic. Now piss off.'

'But . . . Look, how do you make yourself stop shaking?'

'You can't. But you can drink your tea through a straw, if you like.'

98

Not the right answer, but there isn't a right answer. He'll have to work it out for himself, like the rest of us.

Overheard Webster asking Flint who's going to lead 'A' flight now Prideaux's gone. 'Not Corky, not Mathy . . .'

'Goldilocks? He's good, isn't he?'

'Bloody good. A natural. But he doesn't fit in, somehow. The others don't seem to like him much. Can't quite put my finger on it.'

'Think he's a bit touched, do you?'

'Do you know a fighter pilot who isn't a bit touched? Half of them are off their rockers. I don't mean that—Goldilocks is different. I've been watching him at the debriefings, when you feel so high you could get pissed on lemonade and everyone's yelling at once, and he's like the rest of us, but he's apart, somehow. Watches people. You can see his mouth moving, sometimes, as if he's repeating what they say, or . . . I don't know. Christ, Adj, I'm not a bloody trick-cyclist.'

'Oh, well. Who's it to be, then? Balchin?'

'Have to be—when we get him back. I'll do it for now, and Ginger can take over "B" flight.'

I knew they wouldn't give it to me—I'm not bloody public school like them—but hearing them talk about me like that made me angry. Told myself I don't give a tuppenny damn who gets 'A' flight, but it kept coming back to me, nagging, all day. We stood down at five, which was a relief. It's usually later, but we don't fly at night any more, thank God—it's a waste of time; there's bugger-all visibility in a Spit and it's well-nigh impossible to bag anything. The others went to the pub. I didn't go with them—better leave it for a bit. That girl

99

looked too dim to kick up a fuss, but I didn't think it worth the risk. Wanted to get off the base, though. Restless. I went for a walk—army truck passing, usual business, 'Thought you lot flew everywhere?' but they gave me a lift to London and I headed for Soho. Don't know why I did it, just needed to get away for a few hours. Kept seeing that plane explode—flashes of it in the corner of my eye, shooting flames, the bits coming towards me, so real I want to duck, or . . . I don't know. But it kept coming at me, suddenly, and I couldn't stop it.

I'd helped Webster with Prideaux's things, packing them up—found three pound-notes tucked away in a drawer and managed to get them into my pocket . . . thought about a girl—don't know why, it's never any good, but I wanted . . . I don't know what I wanted, but something to stop Prideaux's explosion happening inside my head, over and over again. I thought, if I could do something, that would deaden it. But I couldn't work myself up to it, somehow. Just wandered about. Then a raid started—all the sirens like a chorus, picking up the note from each other, echoing . . . Christ, it was worse than anything we've had here. Don't know how they stick it, night after night. I couldn't find a shelter, and it went on and on until I was clammy with sweat and heart pounding. And the helplessness of it, of dying like that without being able to fight back or *do* anything, made me angry. Give me a dogfight, any day. I was angry with myself, as well, for being afraid, and desperate to run for cover, not being able to control it, standing in that doorway with my hands in fists, shaking, eyes tight shut . . . and then, when I opened them, that's when I saw the girl. In that instant, my heart leapt inside my chest, everything focused, and I was calm.

It was only a black shape at first, jerking about like a marionette against a sheet of flame in a grotesque, clumsy dance, the arms flapping up and down, beating at the air. And then I saw the thing round the neck, the ends like streamers, twisting and flapping as the hands clawed at it. As if an invisible man was trying to strangle her. She turned, and I could see that the stuff was across the face, too, a thin material coating that made the head eyeless, noseless—blank—and the mouth an O, sucking it in. It excited me, and I watched it for . . . I don't know how long, and then I ran towards her and began to beat it away and the material began to break apart, like lace, and the head wobbled and jinked . . . I don't know why I did that, because my thought was to push her against the wall and have her; the urge was there and I knew that this time I wouldn't fail, that I could do it, and I felt a wonderful surge of power. I stood there, trembling with the sheer excitement of it, knowing I could do it and that if I did she wouldn't laugh, that no one would ever laugh again, that this thing was an object, a machine, like my Spitfire, and I could make it do whatever I wanted. Then the stocking came away from the face and I saw it was pale and dirty and the hair was singed and she had no lipstick and instantly my mind went back to that other one, where it didn't work, so I didn't touch her—and then she spoke to me, and it was too late.

I don't know why I gave her the brooch I got from the other one. It seemed a nice touch. And she liked it. When I took her back to the shelter she wanted me to stay with her, but I didn't.

I could have pushed her against the wall. I could have . . . with the stocking over the face, before it broke up. That, with some lipstick on it, for the mouth, the shape of it . . . and she wouldn't have laughed at me or struggled like the one at the pub, she would have been mine . . . And all the time, when we were walking back to the air-raid shelter, it was in my mind: I can do this, I can, I must do it—the feeling inside me, I couldn't contain, flashes of the Avro at the flying circus, the Spit, and Prideaux's explosion in my head, the urgency of it, the impulses pounding at me to do it now, because there's no time left . . . Prideaux today, but tomorrow it could be me and there's no time . . . The decision to do it was almost a physical process. Like flicking a switch. Gun sight on, gun safety off.

I walked about a bit and looked at the tarts, and it wasn't long before I found what I wanted. A door opened, and I saw—just for a moment, in the triangle of light—that she had a look about her, cheap and drab, too thin. I could tell she wasn't successful at it. One of nature's victims, I suppose. I knew she was the right one. And I was the right one, too—one of nature's killers. Hunter and hunted, predator and prey. She'd never have lasted long.

I can't remember the conversation—just her saying she didn't usually take men back because her landlady didn't like it, but I insisted, offered her more money, said she'd get a tip if I liked her. When we got there, she wanted a shilling for the gas. Shy—which I hadn't expected, or not to such an extent—but I made her take all her clothes off, and she stood there while I looked, kept trying to cover herself up but I pulled her hands away. I enjoyed that, because she couldn't stop me. I looked at her, and she seemed so worthless, and at that moment, I knew I could do what I wanted and this time, I'd succeed. I picked up something from the chair—clothes, thin stuff, and said I was going to tie her hands so I could look at her properly. She started to struggle then, so I hit her. It must have been harder than I intended, because her teeth came out, the top ones, and landed on the floor. She put her hands up to her face, mumbling, and I could see tears in her eyes. I pushed her onto the bed and she tried to get off to pick up the teeth, but I told her it didn't matter and pulled her back onto the bed and tied her hands, and she was quiet after that.

She'd put her stockings on the back of a chair, near enough to grab, so I got one and put it over the mouth, tied it—said the landlady would come if she made a noise, said I'd be quiet, then put my hands round the neck. The body was thrashing underneath me, then limp, but I still couldn't do it, I needed something more, something . . . walked about a bit, didn't know what I was looking for, but then saw the poker leaning up beside the mantelpiece, and picked it up. It felt good holding it. I undid my fly and touched myself—that was better—then touched her with it, the point tracing down, dragging between the breasts, pulling at the skin . . . see the trace of it, line of soot . . . I could hear a gurgling noise but it seemed to come from far away; it didn't disturb me. Then I drew the poker down the stomach, cold white skin . . . and between the legs, dark there, she wasn't a natural blonde—not natural, and that wasn't right—

cheating—and that made me angry, like a surge, and for a second, she seemed to respond, and I stuck it in, and there was blood—good—and again and again—harder—more—shoved it—twisted it—turned away, because she was too ugly, saw the little mirror on the table and picked it up, stood with my back to her and held it up with one hand so I could see the reflection, just the bits I wanted, just enough—and that was perfect: nipple, throat, the stocking—the stocking stretched across the face—blank and the mouth an O—an O—sucking in—harder—harder—I   did   it—did—it—did diddiddid

It.

Maybe I'll be able to sleep now, after that. I kept the little mirror. Compact. Like that girl in the car with the lipstick; she had one. I'll have it in my pocket tomorrow. Ought to have something: Davy's got that old scarf, Prideaux had some trinket from his girl—fat lot of good that did him—Balchin's got something, too . . . even Corky. And Mathy's got his lighter. Better put it back in his pocket now, while I remember. I'm almost too tired to get up and walk across the room.

There. Sleep now. Gervase, though. What a name . . .

SATURDAY 21ST SEPTEMBER

Fitzrovia

The house was silent, the air heavy and rancid with stale cooking. Elsie the landlady opened the door

104

of the parlour and peered into the hallway. The permanent blackout over the front door skylight made it hard to see, even in daytime. She could just make out the row of stuffed creatures cowering in their glass cases, coats matted and eyes opaque with dust. She padded past them to the bottom of the stairs and stood staring upwards, one plump hand curled round the greasy banister.

Elsie sniffed and looked at the clock. Half past nine. 'Something's not right,' she announced. 'Not right at all.' She turned and marched off to fetch her husband.

'Eh? Eh?' Bert sat up in bed and looked round wildly, hair askew, and turkey-necked in striped pyjamas.

'I *said*, she's gone. Two weeks, she's owing, and I've not had a sight of her since Thursday morning. I've told you I don't want that sort in my house.' Muttering, he cast around for his glasses. 'Here,' she said, dropping them into his lap. 'You can put this on, too.' She held out his mackintosh like a bullfighter. 'And you can just get upstairs and see about it. I've had enough.' She herded him through the parlour and up the stairs, crowding up close behind so he couldn't turn tail and escape. 'I knew she'd be trouble the moment I laid eyes on her.'

On the second landing he stopped, wheezing slightly.

'Go on, then.'

He knocked on the door. 'Miss Parker?' No reply. He coughed and tried again. 'Miss Parker? Edie? Are you in there, dear?'

'Never you mind "dear"!' hissed his wife. 'Try the door.'

'It's no good. She's locked it.'

105

'Break it down, then.'

He hesitated.

'Oh here,' she said, impatiently. She marched across the landing.'Stand back.'

Obediently, he flattened himself against the wall, and she thundered across the lino in a blur of curlers and candlewick, and burst through the door.

'Now then—' She stopped, and lowered her voice. 'There's someone in there.'

Her husband peered over her shoulder. The blinds were drawn, but they could make out a humped shape on the bed, beneath blankets that were pulled up so high that only the top of a head was visible on the pillow.

'Well,' said her husband, more loudly, 'she can't be asleep. Not after that.'

They began to advance on the bed. There was a sharp crack, and the landlady staggered slightly, righting herself on the mantelpiece. 'What's that?'

'Her top set, look. You've trod on it, Else. Broke it right in half.' He thought she was going to make some remark about the floor being no place for a good set of teeth, but she turned and clutched his arm.

'I don't like the look of this, Bert. I don't like it at all.' Her touch was light, like a child's, and fearful. It made him suddenly bold and he took her hand, leaned forwards, and jerked away the bedclothes. He felt the clammy pressure of her fingers against his as they stared through the half-light at the curled white body with its livid face, gagged mouth, and the black thing protruding from the pool of blood between the parted legs like, like—

Elsie shrieked and fell against him and he took her in his arms and bundled her out of the room and down the stairs, while all the time she was screaming the same thing, over and over, 'The poker! The poker!' right out into the street, and she didn't stop and then there were people crowding the door and policemen and everyone was shouting and rushing about and Elsie was shaking against his chest, sobbing and sobbing. And later, at the neighbours', still she kept her hand in his. That was what he remembered most clearly, when the rest had become a terrible blur with the only clear detail being the poker, black and stiff, sticking out of what had been . . . he could not bring himself to think the word for what it had been. The bottom part of her. That's what he'd said to the police, and they'd understood. Men of the world. Not like him, except . . . except . . . that Elsie had turned to him when she was frightened; she'd touched his arm for comfort, before they'd seen the . . . *thing* . . . that was in the bed.

And—God bless her—she'd never once asked him why he'd called Miss Parker 'dear' when he'd shouted through the door. Poor, pathetic Edie Parker, who'd met such a terrible end, and who'd let him kiss her on the landing when no one was there, who'd let him put his hand inside her dress and feel her skinny body. He'd known what she'd done for a living, all right, seen her on the street once, seen the way she was with men, anxious, cringing, not flaunting, so that paying to go with her would almost have been an act of charity, and he knew that that was why she'd stood there, defeated, and let him touch her, perhaps with some dim, pitiful hope that it would lead to something off the rent. He'd often wondered if she'd let him do more—do what his wife would no longer allow—but he'd never dared ask her and he knew that made him as pathetic as she was, so he'd cancelled the memory. Then, turning to Elsie, he'd seen a new look in her eyes, something like respect.

'Don't worry,' he'd said. 'I'll look after you.'

'Thank you, Bert,' she'd said.

Again, he felt the soft, warm pressure of her fingers on his arm, and after a moment's hesitation, he leaned over and gave her a kiss.

MONDAY 23RD SEPTEMBER

Rene

I was watching the boys play cricket when I heard about it. Nothing fancy, just a floorboard for a bat and an old tennis ball up on St Martin's Lane, the bomb site next to the Mitre. It's not at all flat—there's piles of bricks and all sorts—and they're not supposed to be there at all, really; the landlord's always coming and shouting at them, but they've got to go somewhere, haven't they? I'd made a place for myself on a bit of wall that was left, and I'm giving them a bit of a clap every now and then, for encouragement, and then one of the big boys gives the ball a great wallop with the board and it shoots straight into a toilet that's perched up on a heap of rubble! Of course they all start yelling and shouting about who's going to be the one to fish it out again. They've upended one little lad and I can see his head's going to go in there, so I'm trying to

108

pick my way over there to sort it out when Lily and Mollie come rushing up, shrieking their heads off, and almost send me flying.

'Did you hear what happened?'

I said, 'Of course I heard it. I'm not deaf.'

Lily said, 'No, not the bombing. I mean Edie.'

'What about Edie?'

'Got herself killed!'

'I didn't realise it was *that* close.'

'It wasn't a raid. She was murdered.'

Well, you could have heard a pin drop. I looked round and saw all the boys standing there staring at her with eyes like saucers. I took Lily's arm. 'Not *here* . . .' and dragged her off round the corner with them all following a few paces behind, like a game of Grandmother's Footsteps. I told them to clear off, and then I said to Lily, 'Now, pull yourself together and tell me what happened, and for heaven's sake keep your voice down.'

'Edie was murdered.'

Mollie said, 'It's true, Rene. She was strangled, and now they're saying there's a maniac on the loose. It's horrible. I'm not going out tonight; we're not safe. I don't know what I'm going to do.' She lowered her voice to a whisper. 'I heard she had a poker stuck up inside her.'

'Who told you that?'

'Kathleen. Bridget told her. She lives in the same street. One of the neighbours said that Edie's landlady'd been up to her room Saturday morning and found her, and she rushed into the street, screaming her head off. The whole street heard it. As God's my witness, Rene, it's true.'

'It's *horrible*. Who did it?'

'That's what I'm saying, Rene, they don't know.

It could be anyone.'

I said to Lily, 'Remember that one she went with from the shelter? I didn't like the look of him.'

'What, Soho Square?'

'Mm. That one she went out with. Mind you, that was . . . what? Monday? A week ago.'

'Couldn't have been him, then. I've seen her. Anyway, she was only found this morning.'

'He gagged her,' said Mollie. 'So she couldn't scream. Strangled her.'

I said, 'I don't understand. She never took them back. She always went up Rathbone Place—that yard behind the Beer House. The warehouse place.'

'Perhaps he wanted something special—offered more money.'

'Silly girl . . .'

Mollie said, 'But you don't know, do you? One minute it's an ordinary man, and the next minute you've got a maniac on your hands. It's terrible. We'll all be murdered in our beds.'

I said, 'No, we won't. You've just got to watch out for yourself, that's all.'

We talked about it for a while, and then they left and I sat there thinking till Tommy came running over in his Indian headdress I bought him—he's so proud of it, wears it all the time. 'You all right, Auntie Rene?'

'Yes, dear. Right as rain. You go and play.'

But I wasn't all right. I'd planned to go straight to work, but I felt a bit peculiar, so I had a little walk to try and settle myself. I tried to put Edie out of my mind but it didn't work. I kept thinking about how she'd come into the pub once and showed us this doll she'd got. It was a sweet thing, china, good quality, with real hair and a little frock, all lace. She seemed ever so pleased with it, and I thought it was a present for some kiddie, but when Lily asked her where she'd got it, she said there'd been a church hit, and she'd found it lying in the road.

I said to her, 'That's not a dolly, it's Baby Jesus. You can't keep that—what'll they do come Christmas?'

She got all upset and told me she wasn't stealing because it was just there, and when I said she ought to take it back she said, 'Oh, you don't understand, I haven't got *anything*!' and pushed it back in her bag and ran away.

Lily said, 'Oh, she's upset because it's like a baby and she had to have one stopped and it's sent her weak in the head.'

I said, 'Well, she wasn't much before,' which is true, but all the same, I felt that sorry for her.

I was standing there on the pavement like a fool, and I suddenly came to myself and thought, just my luck if I get picked up now. Not that it happens so much these days, what with the blackout and the police being too busy since the raids started, but it used to—you'd be going out for a paper, minding your own business, and it'd be, 'Come on, it's your turn.' This every two or three weeks, mind, but you can't argue, because they're only doing their job, same as we are. And to be fair, they always try and fix the bail quick so's we can get back out and earn the fine.

Mind you, there's girls who work in the brothels up at Mayfair and St James's, and they never get raided. It's because of who goes there—politicians and toffs—so the police have to turn a blind eye to it. Not that it's fair—those girls make a fortune—

111

but it's the way of the world. Course, thinking about that brought me back to Edie again, saying what a lot of dirty so-and-sos they are down at Bow Street; not the coppers, but them at the back of the court, all listening. She had one where she was watching a man fiddling with himself and of course the policemen had to say that he was—you know— *masturbating*—and she'd asked him, before, would he say it quietly so the ones at the back couldn't hear, but of course he got told to speak up and they were all laughing at her . . . they just go in for a bit of fun, and of course they're not paying for it. Poor Edie was in pieces, after. She said to me, 'I just wanted to run away and hide.'

I was thinking about all this, and then I heard a voice behind me: 'Here, what's your game?' and someone grabbed my shoulder. It was Annie—I was standing on her patch. She's a big woman, with what I call Scottish looks, freckles and red hair, and she's got a temper to match, so you want to keep on the right side of her. I said I wasn't working, and when she'd calmed down I told her about Edie, and she said she'd warn Susie and Eileen, because they're in the next street, but it's like she said, what can we do? We've got to earn a living.

That made me think I'd better get to work, but I ended up going for a great long walk past the bombing in Oxford Street. John Lewis is wrecked, and Bourne & Hollingsworth, Selfridges, Peter Robinson . . . all these mannequins lying around, plaster things, bodies and arms and legs stacked up on the pavement. It made me think of Edie again, looking at that, so I thought I'd nip down the road to the Marquess, just to steady myself, but of course when I got there, it was all 'Did you hear

112

about poor Edie?' so that left me feeling worse than before. I bumped into one of my regulars, and we went off round St James's Square in a taxi, so that was a pound from him, and then a couple of others I picked up in Frith Street and took back, so that came to four pounds. But all the time I'm lying on my back I'm thinking of Edie cut up like that. I can't get it out of my mind, and I'm gritting my teeth—*Hurry up and get done before I scream*—and there's the man saying, 'Put a bit of life into it, can't you?' Well, after the second, I thought, that's my lot for tonight, and I took my blanket and cushion and went along to the shelter.

Of course all the old girls have got wind of it, so they're whispering about Edie, too, and I can hear Ale Mary louder than all the others put together: 'The wages of sin is death!' and they're all black coats and hats in a row, nodding their heads, and I'm sitting there thinking, I don't want to listen to this, and wondering if it's quiet enough to go home, when this young chap sort of sidles in and sits down beside me. Nervous. First time, you can always tell. I had half a mind to send him packing, because that sort always needs a fuss making and they don't know what to do, but I could see he'd really screwed up his courage to come and speak to me, and of course you can charge a bit more because they don't know the value. There'll be more of them like that now, with all the young servicemen on leave, first time in London . . . He's stammering away and blushing like a girl, and I'm thinking, this is attracting attention, so I turn to him and say, 'Shall we go somewhere else?'

He's nodded, and we're just about to leave when Ale Mary—I see this out of the corner of my eye—

she gets up and starts towards us, none too steady, and she looks at him and looks at me, and then she puts her face right up to his, hiccupping away with her mouth all wet, and she says, 'He preserveth not the life of the wicked.' Then she falls straight over backwards and cracks her head on the floor.

Of course he's out of there before you can say Jack Robinson and then there's a great to-do, everybody crowding round, 'You all right, Ma?' and the warden comes in and he's fanning her with his helmet, and the old girls are glaring at me as if I'd given her a fourpenny one. It was queer, though, when I thought about it afterwards—I mean, other times, I'd have been angry: I know I said I'd shut up shop, but that was a good two quid she'd cost me. I wasn't angry, though, I just started shaking and couldn't stop—I don't know why. I think it was the shock of seeing old Mary come up to that young man and talk right into his face like that, really brought it home about Edie, somehow, even worse, like something coming in a big rush and swallowing me up. I suddenly had to get out; even if there were bombs outside I couldn't stay there another minute.

I found myself in the street, leaning against the wall with my teeth chattering. I'd got my hands over my face and then there was this hand on my arm and I jumped a mile. It was the warden, I could see from the gleam of the helmet, right up close to me, and I thought, I can't bear it, I can't have any more trouble, and I said, 'I'm going, leave me alone.'

He said, 'No, wait,' and held onto my arm.

I said, 'What are you doing?'

'Come on.'

'You're not taking me down the station! I never touched her. She fell over all by herself!'

'Who said anything about that? A cup of tea, that's what you need. Come round to the post.'

You could have knocked me down with a feather. I was still pretty wobbly, but he kept his hand on my arm all the way. He had a funny stride, sort of a lurch, and he kept bumping up against me, but there didn't seem anything queer in it, just very determined, the way he marched us along, like he thought I was the one going to tip over, not him.

When we got there, he called out, 'Lady here had a bit of an upset. Make some room!' and took me right in.

They've got it nice in there, all painted, with a little table with a cloth on and wooden boxes from the market so they can sit down. There were a few men in there lying on the floor, on top of their coats, dead to the world.

The warden said, 'Don't worry, they've been on duty thirty hours—it'll take a lot more than us to wake them now,' and he was right, we stepped right over them and they didn't move a muscle. 'We've got all types, here,' he said, and pointed at them in turn. 'He's a lawyer, he's a taxi driver, that bloke works at the post office, and that one at the end, he's an opera singer!'

The tea was hot and sweet and very welcome. The warden got me sat down, and pulled up a box for himself. I hadn't really got a look at him before, in all the fuss, but in the light I could see he was a big chap. I don't mean fat, more . . . burly, I suppose you'd call it—middle-aged, black hair with a bit of grey, his nose all flattened like a boxer and cauliflower about the ears, but he'd got nice blue eyes with a smile in them. Then I looked down and saw he'd got one leg stuck out in front of him all awkward. He saw where I was looking, and he said, 'Got it in the last one. Eighteen, I was. Haven't walked straight since.'

'Oh . . . I'm sorry.'

He shrugged. 'It doesn't give me much bother.'

There was a pause, then he lifted his mug and said, 'Cheers!' He winked at me. 'Collapse of stout party, you might say.'

'You mean . . .'

'Old Mary. Don't worry, she'll be right as ninepence.'

By now, the other wardens had cleared off, and it was just the two of us. I said, 'Well, this is cosy, I must say,' but I was thinking, him being friendly like that, perhaps he wants something for nothing. He started looking a bit shifty, and I thought, aye, aye.

He said, 'I heard about your pal. Bad business. You want to be careful.' My heart sank then, because I thought, he's after money, the dirty ponce—protection, you might say.

I said, 'What do you mean, my pal?'

'Edie Parker.' He was staring down at his gammy leg.

I said, 'Look, Mr . . .'

'Nolan. Harry Nolan.'

'Mr Nolan—'

'Harry.'

'Harry. I don't want any trouble, so if it's all right with you, I'll be on my way. I won't be coming in the shelter again, I'll make other arrangements, and—'

'Whoa! No need for that. You've as much right

116

to be in the shelter as anyone else, far as I can see.'

Well, now I was pretty sure which way the wind was blowing, so I looked him straight in the eye. 'Listen, *Mr Nolan*, let's get one thing clear. You're not asking, I'm not offering, and there's an end to it.'

That brought his head up sharp enough. 'What I said—I didn't mean nothing by it. Not like you thought. Rene . . . I'm just saying, you be careful.'

'How do you know my name's Rene?'

He looked surprised. 'Well . . . just . . . one of them in the shelter, it must have been. I've seen you there, before. You're a nice woman, Rene, but there's some wicked people out there, that's all.'

I suddenly remembered the man from the Wheatsheaf calling us all the names as if we were the lowest things in the world.

I said, 'No, I'm not. I'm not a nice woman, and that's—' The words came out before I could stop them. I felt so muddled and upset, and about ready to cry, if you want the truth.

He said, 'Here! No need to go upsetting yourself. You're a very nice woman, and don't let anybody tell you different.' He was looking straight at me and his face was so kind, with so much care in it, I thought, he really does think I'm a nice woman, and I know it sounds daft, but that made me want to cry all the more.

I said, 'Oh, dear, what must you think of me?'

'I think you've had a nasty turn, is what I think. A bit of kip, and you'll be fine. Now, I'm going to take you back to the shelter, and if those old cats start giving you trouble, you just come to me.'

'It's very kind of you.'

'Not at all. Doing my job. Upsy-daisy!' He had to

117

put his hand on the table and push himself up because of his funny leg, and then he held out his elbow for me to put my arm through, very polite, as if he was taking me into dinner at the Dorchester, not back to Soho Square. He didn't talk much on the way back, but when we got to the shelter he said, very quiet, 'Now, you remember what I said. And don't you go out no more tonight, it's not safe.'

He marched me right in, and no one said a word. Ale Mary wasn't there, and when the warden—Harry—asked Mrs McIver, she told him she'd been taken to the first aid post. Then she pursed her lips and said, 'Making the most of it, I'm sure,' which made me smile.

I couldn't get to sleep, though—I couldn't get comfortable. And the worst was, every time I closed my eyes I'd get a picture of Edie lying there strangled, right up close to me with her eyes popping out, and then when I did drift off it was only a half sleep, with Edie's and Mary's faces coming in and out, heads on sticks being pushed in front of me, with the teeth come loose so their top sets were moving up and down but the lips weren't going with them, so it was just the teeth and gums by themselves . . . *horrible*.

I came awake with a jolt, just before midnight—didn't want to go back to sleep again after that, even though I was that tired, I was aching all over. I can just imagine what those old cats would say about Edie: serve her right, she was asking for it—as if anyone could deserve *that*. Like saying they deserve a bomb. Mind you, what me and Lily were saying only this afternoon, Edie was daft, she didn't take enough care . . . but that was true, what we said: if you don't look out for yourself there's no one else to do it for you, not unless they're after something in return.

Mind you, that warden—Harry . . . 'You're a very nice woman, and don't let anybody tell you different.' Fancy saying that! Especially when I'd got him all wrong. Ever so nice of him. And it's worth more when someone like that says it—means something. *You're a very nice woman . . .* Maybe I'm not so bad, after all.

WEDNESDAY 25TH SEPTEMBER

Lucy

I slept through most of Saturday afternoon— glorious, no raids—and felt a whole heap better afterwards. Frank came to see me on Sunday, which I'd been rather dreading, but he did look very good in his battledress, not in the least like a stork, and I felt terrifically proud to be walking down the street with him. Moral snobbism, I suppose, if such a thing exists.

We had tea in the garden with Mums and Minnie, and then took ourselves off for a walk. There was a heaviness about the whole thing, and I couldn't help making comparisons with my airman, which is dreadful. Half listening to Frank, and half my mind on *him* and then remembering how I was thinking about Mr Bridges last time we were together, and hating myself for it. I tried to tell myself afterwards that *that* little episode was because I hadn't known any better, but that's not an excuse. There seem to be different Lucys who take turns in being me and then a big blank space when they all run away and hide, and that's when I find myself looking in the mirror and wondering who's there . . . Oh, dear. That sounds as if I'm going dotty, doesn't it? But I'm not, just trying to examine the bits of my character that I can understand, or at least want to acknowledge. It's like losing your keys on a dark street and looking for them under a lamppost, not because there's more chance they'll be there than anywhere else, but because that's the only place where there's any light. I tried explaining this to Minnie, without mentioning Mr Bridges or my airman, of course, and she said, 'Well, you wouldn't have much luck in the blackout.' I don't think she had a clue what I meant! Decided later, as usual, that this sort of self-examination is morbid, and one shouldn't indulge in it.

The walk with Frank felt like an extended goodbye, as if we were both waiting for him to get on a train—which, in a sense, we were—and it was something to be 'got through' rather than enjoyed. I kept thinking that he might propose, and wondering what on earth I should say if he did. I felt I couldn't let him down because he's going away, but didn't want to make promises to him, either. He kept asking me if I was all right, and I kept saying I was, but it was all very unsatisfactory, and I'm sure he felt that way, too.

It was very awkward at the end, standing in front of the gate and neither of us knowing what to say. Frank kept glancing at the hole in the porch roof and back at me, and I knew he was thinking about me being in danger.

'I want to stay in London, Frank, I've told you.'

'I know.'

'I'll be all right, really. Safe as . . .'

'Houses?' We both laughed, but it was uncomfortable, and I couldn't look him in the eye. 'Lucy, there's not . . . not *another* reason, is there? Someone else?'

'No! No . . .' I could feel myself blushing. 'There's no-one else.' I thought as I was saying it that it was an honest answer, because there isn't an actual *someone else*, at least, not in a real sense.

'Lucy?'

A voice in my head screaming, *Don't ask me to marry you!*

'Will you . . . will you write to me?'

Oh, the relief! 'Course I will, silly!' I threw my arms round his neck. He disengaged me gently and stepped back, shaking his head. I couldn't make out his expression at all.

'You're a funny one.'

'Yes, I suppose I am. It's just . . . you know. Everything,' I finished, rather lamely.

'Oh, well.' He glanced at his watch. 'I'd better be going. Let's say goodbye here, shall we?'

I didn't try to change his mind. 'Give me a kiss, Frank.' I don't really know why I said that. Wanting to end it on the right note, I suppose, even if it was a fraud.

He didn't kiss me properly, just touched his lips to my cheek.

'Let me know where you are,' I said, 'so I can write to you.'

He nodded, and I had the sudden realisation that he wasn't going to—that he'd seen through my reaction, my denial, that I'd given myself away.

'Oh, Frank, I'm sorry . . .'

'Goodbye, Lucy.'

I watched him walk down the road, but he didn't look round. There was something final about it, like a door closing behind me. Not with a bang, just a gentle, firm click.

It would have been easier if he'd been angry. Afterwards, I felt empty and dreadful and wished I'd acted differently, but I couldn't tell if it was because I was sorry for him or because of wanting the feeling of a proper parting. I went and sat by myself in the garden and remembered him pouncing on one of my freckles, saying he'd caught it in the act of coming out. I haven't behaved well, and there's no excuse for it. I'm altogether very miserable and sorry for myself. Minnie, thinking me upset for all the right reasons, didn't ask questions, for which I was grateful, but her kindness made it worse. I'm mean and awful and don't deserve her—or *anyone*.

I thought about pinning the brooch on my frock for work on Monday, but decided to leave it under my pillow. Who knows? Perhaps it will protect our house. I spent the whole journey to the office fretting over Frank, and most of the morning in a turmoil, half the time thinking I never want to see Mr Bridges again, or have anything to do with him, and the other half in a state of fury that he hadn't come down to apologise. I jolly well wasn't going upstairs to look for him, though.

I was on my own in the office just before lunch when he came in—he'd obviously been hanging about in the corridor waiting for everyone to leave. I carried on pounding my typewriter.

'Did you get home safely?'

I glanced up, just for a moment. I hadn't formed any idea of what to say to him—too agitated for that—but he looked so sorry for himself, so wretched, that I despised him utterly, and couldn't believe I'd ever felt any different. I felt disgusted at myself for letting him kiss me, and even more for enjoying it. Now I'd seen him, I just wanted him to leave so I could put it out of my mind. I couldn't bear to look at him, so I kept my eyes on the typing.

'Well, obviously, or I wouldn't be here, would I?'

'I was worried about you, out there all on your own.'

'Were you really?'

'Lucy, don't be like this.'

Thump, thump on the typewriter. Carriage return—ping!

'There was nothing I could do, you must see that.'

'Oh, must I?'

'I was trapped. That man—'

Thump, thump.

'I wanted to come down earlier, but I've been tied up all morning.'

'Well, you didn't try very hard to get untied.'

'*Lucy* . . .'

Thump, thump, thump.

'Can't you stop, just for a moment?'

'I'm busy.'

'I want to talk to you.'

'Oh, really?'

'Yes. I know you're angry, and I don't blame you.'

'I'm delighted to hear it.'

'Lucy, *please*.'

Thump, thump—ping!

'I couldn't help it, really! That man, he knows me, knows . . . I couldn't think, I just panicked.'

'Yes, you did rather, didn't you?' I pulled the papers and carbon up through the rollers, and looked him right in the eye. 'I must say, I'm surprised you don't have a better speech prepared. After all, you must have done this sort of thing before.'

He looked wounded. 'No! Never. But then,' he smiled, weakly, 'I've never met anyone as irresistible as you.'

I thought, that came out pat, all right! I folded my arms. 'Clearly not so irresistible as all that.'

'But you agreed to come.'

'Yes. Yes, I did. That was a mistake. It won't be repeated.' I picked up more paper and fed it into the typewriter.

He walked towards the door, and paused. 'I . . .'

'Yes?'

'Nothing. Never mind. I'll go.' And that was that. Except that I suddenly remembered it wasn't, because of the arrangement we'd made for me to help one day a week, but decided I'd have to cross that bridge when I came to it. I felt rather shaky, but satisfied I'd done the right thing.

I looked up at the sky on the way home and felt that *somebody* was watching over me. I barely said hello to Mums, but rushed to my bedroom—sure enough, the brooch was still there. When I held it in my hand I could see *his* face so clearly, the blue eyes and the golden hair like a blaze around his head. I could almost imagine he was right there in the room. I wondered, suddenly, if he was still alive—the idea that I might never see him again is awful. I clutched the brooch tightly and closed my eyes, hoping for some feeling or intuition about him, but got nothing. Told myself I was being thoroughly idiotic, but the desire to go on thinking about him, imagining what he might be doing, was so strong that I lay down on the bed, closed my eyes, and gave in to it. I can't bear the thought that I may never know what happens to him.

I want so much to believe that the circumstances of our meeting have some significance, that they were meant to happen—finding the bird's wings in the garden like that, burying them and saying a prayer, and then, in the evening, being lost and frightened and wanting an angel and him just appearing like that and taking me into the shelter and giving me the brooch. But I know it's not a pattern at all—at least, it would be in a book, but not in real life. Which this isn't, really. Not *normal* real life, anyway. Hard to imagine anything being normal ever again.

I must have been more tired than I thought, because the next thing I knew, Minnie was shaking me, saying that the siren had gone and supper was ready and she and Mums were going to have theirs under the stairs. Had mine in the usual place and thought how nice it would be to have an evening meal at the table instead of underneath it, as so often seems to be the case at the moment. Nice music on the wireless, until it had a fit of the splutters and died. I felt restless and fed up and wished I was doing something, instead of just sitting about. Resolved to put my name down for the mobile canteen.

Mums went to sleep after a while, and Minnie came over to join me. She said that old Mrs Grout told Mums that her dog can tell the difference between our planes and theirs. Seems pretty unlikely, but at least it's stopped barking during the raids, which is something, because that certainly kept us awake, even if the bombs didn't!

Had another queer dream: I was lying flat on my back on a table, wearing a black frock. The skirt kept riding up at the sides and I was trying to put my hand down to smooth it over my knees because there was someone there, but I couldn't make it stay . . . and then I saw it was a man in a dark suit. It didn't look like anyone particular, but I knew it was Mr Bridges, the way you do in dreams. He had scissors, big ones, and he stood at my feet and bent over and started to cut up the middle of the dress from the hem. The material was parting, showing the tops of my legs, and I wanted to pull the edges together to cover myself up, but I couldn't seem to sit up enough to do it; there was something pressing down on my head, stopping me. I suddenly realised that I didn't have my underclothes on and I wanted to get off the table and find them, and I was about to say this when I saw that my airman was there, watching. I didn't want him to see me like that so I tried to get up but there was something lying across me, pinning me down, and I couldn't move at all. I must have started thrashing around because I banged my head pretty smartly on the underside of one of the chairs, which woke me up, and after a moment I saw that Minnie's arm was flung out across my stomach, and that's what it must have been in the dream that was stopping me from moving.

Minnie woke up a second later, looked round wildly, 'What? What is it?' and banged her head on

126

the table leg.

I said, 'It's all right,' and rubbed it for her, thinking she'd lie down again and go back to sleep, but she didn't.

She whispered, 'You know that brooch you were holding, when I came up to your room . . . did Frank give it to you?'

It was too dark to see her face—or for her to see mine, thank goodness. I didn't want to explain. 'Yes.'

'I just thought . . . It doesn't look like you, somehow.'

'It's more for luck, really. From his mother.'

'Oh.' Minnie sounded puzzled. 'I just thought perhaps you'd—well, it sounds silly, now—but I thought you might have met somebody else.'

'What sort of somebody else?'

'You know. A man.'

'No!' I certainly wasn't going to tell her I'd made a fool of myself over Mr Bridges, and besides, I think she's secretly rather keen on Frank. I remember once when we were both at the bottom of the garden, with our backs to him, and he mistook her for me and gave her a kiss, and she blushed like anything.

'Sssh. I'm sorry, it's just that you've been funny. Secret. You always used to tell me things.'

'There's nothing to tell. I'm just tired, that's all.'

'Me too. I suppose that's why I imagined . . . But everybody is, aren't they? You know, this morning I did the stupidest thing. I was on my way to work, going past a bomb site and I saw a whole pile of glittering things on the pavement, all spilled out, like treasure, and I went over, not to take anything, just to look. It was like little jewels, and I picked one up to see what it was. I had it in my palm and I suddenly realised it was a glass eye. It was an oculist's shop with the window blown out, and his stock lying on the ground, hundreds of glass eyes staring at me. I was dreaming about them just now. It was creepy—I'm glad you woke me up.'

'It sounds horrible. You didn't tell that to Mums, did you?'

' 'Course not.'

'Will you be able to go back to sleep now?'

'I suppose so. I wish the All-Clear would go.'

She sighed and settled herself down, and after a few minutes I could tell she was asleep. I listened to her breathing and thought how lucky I am to have such a nice sister. I felt bad about lying to her, but I couldn't have explained—well, I suppose I could, and just not mentioned about the dinner, but I'm no good at making things up, I can't think fast enough. And anyway, if I told Minnie, it would make it all less *special*, somehow. I felt a twinge of guilt—like toothache—about Frank, but managed to suppress it by remembering Minnie's story about the glass eyes. Found myself wondering if people take them out to sleep. I shouldn't fancy waking up to find my own eye staring back at me from inside a glass of water.

I woke up with an aching head and back, but managed to get through the day without running into Mr Bridges, which I was rather dreading. On the way home, I saw lovers in a doorway, embracing. For some reason, it reminded me of my dream and I felt rather disturbed by it. I bought a newspaper in order to have something else to think about—just as well as the train halted outside Charing Cross and didn't move again for three-quarters of an hour!

There was a small piece about a woman killed in Soho, not far from where I was two nights ago. Miss Edith Parker, twenty-six, blonde dance hostess—and we all know what *that* means! It reminded me of the woman I saw in the shelter. I suppose they rather let themselves in for that sort of thing, but all the same, it isn't very nice. The paper said she was strangled. But I suppose it makes a change from reporting the war as if it were cricket—one man on the train pointed to a piece in his paper about the RAF and said, 'Shades of Don Bradman!' The woman with him said, 'Yes, dear,' and didn't seem at all interested, for which I don't blame her. But it reminded me of 'my' airman, and I couldn't help but wonder about him. Still, it took up the rest of the journey nicely.

Arrived home at half past seven, in the middle of an air-raid—I could hear planes and the crump of bombs falling, but nothing very near, thank goodness. Dad and Minnie were under the kitchen table, and she was helping him mend his bicycle: he'd ridden into a bomb crater and the front wheel was bent. He was in high spirits, and made us laugh a lot with a story about an old lady who was deaf as a post and didn't know there was a raid on. He crawled out from under the table and showed us the pantomime he'd done, swooping round the kitchen pretending to be a plane and miming bombs falling. He seemed to be enjoying himself, and we were, too—at least until Mums emerged from her hidey-hole to say we were giving her a headache with all the thumping about and laughing. Then she saw the bicycle and ticked us off for having it in the kitchen.

Dad had to go on duty after that. The bicycle was still wobbly, but it seemed to work all right when he rode it round the kitchen table—after Mums had gone, of course. The gas was off again, so Minnie and I raced around assembling bread and cheese and salad, then settled down to play Happy Families under the table. She was beating me hands down; my thoughts were going round and round in circles with Mr Bridges and my airman and whether it meant anything and Frank and what to do about him, and I couldn't concentrate at all.

Minnie said, 'Are you sure there's nothing wrong?'

'I'm sorry.' I threw my cards down in disgust.

'I *knew* you'd got Master Bun. And Mrs Flower. Honestly, Lucy . . .'

'Oh, who cares? Minnie, can I ask you something?'

'Why not?'

'Do you believe there's life after death?'

She stopped collecting cards and looked at me. 'What a funny question. I don't know. Why?'

'I was thinking about it. Just trying to make sense of things, I suppose.' I meant about my airman, really, and the bird's wings and wanting it to mean something, but I didn't want to tell her that.

She said, 'Do you mean angels and paradise and all that?'

'I don't know, really. Just some sort of survival.'

'Well, maybe. But not harps and clouds. I mean, people floating about with wings when they'd been bank managers or something, they'd feel pretty silly, wouldn't they? And if it is bank managers and . . . I don't know, dentists, then it must be full of

130

people one wouldn't want to see again. Like those gravestones you see, the huge, heavy ones—it's probably the family making sure that Great Aunt Maud or whoever it is can't possibly get out, because the thought of a reunion is too grim for words. And as for hell . . .' she rolled her eyes. 'Where's Miss Dose the doctor's daughter?'

'You're sitting on her.'

'So I am.' She yawned. 'It's awfully quiet. Do you think we might go upstairs?'

I looked at my watch—quarter to ten—and the idea of being in bed suddenly seemed far more tempting than a serious discussion. 'Come on. But for heaven's sake be *quiet*.'

We tiptoed past Mums's cupboard like naughty children—the door was closed and loud snores issuing from inside—and up the stairs.

Minnie whispered, 'This is mad!'

The first thing I did was to check that the brooch was still under my pillow. I didn't undress, just changed my skirt for slacks and rinsed out my stockings before I got into bed.

I was woken up by planes at two, and was wondering whether I should go downstairs when there was a crash from below. I flew down the stairs in bare feet. Minnie was in her nightdress in the hall, struggling with the front door.

'Incendiary bomb!' she shouted, swinging round, her eyes huge and terrified in a stark white face. 'Out there!'

'Don't open the door, you'll burn the house down!' I grabbed her arm. 'The stirrup pump— where is it?'

'By the—'

'It's gone.'

131

'It was there this morning.' Minnie's voice was shrill with panic. 'And the sand—where's it gone?'

'The kitchen!' We rushed in and looked wildly round—nothing. For a second, we stared at each other. 'Lucy—the house—what are we going to do?'

'Come on!' We raced out of the back door into the garden. No sand, no pump, and we were tripping over things because we couldn't see properly. 'Get some earth!' I grubbed up handfuls from the flowerbed, then realised I didn't have anywhere to put it. I was about to ask Minnie to hold out her nightie, when I spotted two boxes by the shed, full of soil. 'These'll do!' I put my torch between my teeth and we took one each and ran round to the front of the house as fast as we could. The incendiary was on the doormat—the crash we'd heard was when it fell through the porch roof, and it was fizzing and spluttering and flames were coming up in spurts, like giant matches being struck.

'You do this,' Minnie panted, 'I'll get water,' and she raced back round the house.

I tipped on all the earth, which seemed to do the trick pretty well, then hared off to get the dustbin lid, which I clapped over the top, and Minnie charged back and forth with saucepans of water until the mat stopped smouldering.

'Not bad, for our first effort,' Minnie said, afterwards. I could see in the torchlight that she had a huge grin on her face, and I'm sure I did, too.

'There aren't any others, are there?'

We looked round the front garden, but couldn't see anything. Minnie said, 'Do you think we ought to move it?'

132

'I don't know. I mean, we don't know it's out yet, do we?'

I was just about to get some more earth in case it wasn't, when Dad appeared with one of the other ARP men, Mr Fenner. We showed them the incendiary, and Dad told us to go inside while they fetched a shovel and carted it away to safety. When we got to the back door we heard a lot of banging and crashing coming from inside the cupboard under the stairs, and the most peculiar bellowing noises. Minnie pulled the door open and Mums almost fell out on top of her. It took me a moment to realise who—or what—it was, because Mums was wearing her gas mask, and appeared to have been trying to put on her corsets over her dressing gown. We tried to calm her down and make her take the gas mask off, but she was completely hysterical, flailing about and making noises that sounded like something at the bottom of a well. The three of us ended up in a heap on the floor, which is how Dad and Mr Fenner discovered us.

When we finally managed to pull Mums's gas mask off, she took one look at Mr Fenner, uttered a wild shriek and retreated back into her cupboard, and no amount of coaxing by Minnie could make her open the door.

Dad said goodbye to Mr Fenner and told Minnie to go and make some tea. As soon as they'd gone, he said, 'What the hell did you think you were doing?' It was like a slap in the face. I was so elated about putting out the fire that I didn't understand immediately what he was talking about. I was taken aback—I don't think I've ever seen him so angry. 'Where's the stirrup pump?'

'I don't know, Dad. We couldn't find it.'

'What do you mean, *couldn't find it*? It's by the kitchen door.'

'It isn't, honestly. The sand isn't there either.'

'Of course it's there, you stupid girl. I left—' He broke off suddenly, and looked towards the cupboard door. 'Where is it, then?' he asked, more quietly.

'I don't know, Dad. Honestly.'

'I see.' He went into the kitchen and sat at the table, looking grim. He didn't say anything until we'd drunk our tea. Minnie must have heard our exchange in the hall, because she didn't say anything, either.

'Oh, well,' he said, finally. 'I'm proud of you. Even if you did use my seedlings.'

Minnie clapped a hand across her mouth. 'That earth! Oh, no . . . oh, *Dad*!'

I stared at him. 'You mean, those boxes?'

He nodded, and said, 'Still, not much use having a lot of cabbages and no house to eat them in, is it?'

'Oh, Dad, I'm sorry.'

'I know, love. But you did well. Both of you.'

Minnie said, 'Shall I take some tea to Mums?'

Dad shook his head. 'Leave her. The best laid plans of mice and men, eh? I'll explain it to her in the morning. *Again*.' He grimaced. 'The most sensible thing we can do now is get some shut-eye.'

The three of us spent the rest of the night under the kitchen table. When we took down the blackout in the morning, the first thing Minnie said to me was, 'Heavens, Lucy! your face is *filthy*. And your slacks! I didn't notice last night.'

'You look as if you could do with a good scrub yourself.' Her nightdress was covered in dirty marks, and her feet were black.

'Better hope there's some hot water.'

We cleaned ourselves up, and were on our way down to breakfast when we heard Dad say, 'Did you move the pump from the hall?'

Minnie whispered to me, 'Wait till they've finished.'

Then we heard Mums's voice. 'I kept tripping over it. I don't know what you have to have it there for—it ought to be in the garden. It's untidy.' She sounded cross.

Dad said gently, 'It's important, Ethel. The house might have burnt down.'

'Well it didn't, did it?'

'If it weren't for the girls—'

'Oh, stop it, Billy! My head's terrible, and my back. I never get any peace with it.'

'It has to be there, Ethel. And the sand. It's important.'

'I know that!' she snapped.

'Come on,' I said, 'we'd better go down. She'll only start a row.'

When we went into the kitchen, she said, before either of us had a chance to open our mouths, 'And a very good morning to you, too.' Honestly, she's *impossible*! I don't know how Dad puts up with it. I sat through breakfast in a state of suppressed fury, not trusting myself to speak, while Mums talked in a martyred tone about having to clean up the porch. Minnie said, after, 'Anyone would think we'd been making mud pies out there!' She was smiling, but I couldn't see the humour in it. I left the house feeling so frustrated and churned up that by the time I got to the station, I was almost in tears.

135

Everything looked grey and mean and squalid— battered houses and broken windows, the drizzle and heavy sky, the tired, pale people, cats picking their way across scorched gardens, a great plume of smoke rising up in the distance, and the horrible, acrid smell. These are our homes, our lives, yet it all seems so flimsy, so tawdry. But this is normal, now, like the tinkly noise of broken glass being swept up, which one seems to hear all the time. And at the end of Union Road, the old man was standing in front of the rubble that had been his house, staring as if he couldn't believe it was no longer there. He looked like a big, stupefied animal. Again, I thought, this is what we are reduced to, and felt such a wave of hatred towards the Germans that I almost wanted to be sick. I remembered how the old man had asked about a woman—Peggy, I think. But he was alone, so . . . God, it happens so quickly. They can be as jolly as they like on the wireless, but it's a horrible world where people can do this to each other.

I felt hot, headachy and very tired all day. Think I've got a sore throat coming. Took the opportunity to put my head down for a doze while the others were out, and woke suddenly after about ten minutes to find Mr Bridges leaning against the doorway, staring at me. He smiled in that awful ingratiating way he has and said, 'Hello, Sleeping Beauty.'

I said, 'I'm afraid you'll have to excuse me,' snatched my handbag and rushed off to the Ladies' to put water on my face, which I did, but then, standing up straight in front of the mirror with a hairgrip between my teeth, I felt such a strong sense of unreality that I was almost surprised to see any reflection there at all. It could have been any female with brown hair and blue eyes—Minnie, or even that prostitute from the shelter, or anyone at all, really. I thought in a detached way that the person in front of me needed some powder on her nose, and duly provided it, but it didn't make much difference. I still didn't recognise her.

I tried telling myself I was tired, I wasn't feeling well, all sorts of things, but it didn't work. I don't want to be Frank's wife, I certainly don't want to have anything to do with Mr Bridges, I don't want to have to put up with Mums for another minute. I don't know who I am or what I want. In fact, there's only one thing clear in my mind: somehow, I want to meet *him* again. My airman.

Then I heard the siren. I wouldn't have bothered—most people ignore the daytime raids now—but Miss Henderson appeared and herded all of us down to the shelter. The others were talking, but I shut my eyes, thought longingly of my bed and wished with all my heart that I was there, bathed and clean and sound asleep.

WEDNESDAY 25TH SEPTEMBER

Jim

Waiting for a flap. Just stooging around the last couple of days. Pretty uneventful, thank God. I'm feeling bloody tired, though. Everyone is: lounging around in armchairs, dozing behind newspapers. Mathy's staring at Prideaux's car, which is still outside the dispersal hut. I saw him kicking the tyres. 'Can't somebody move the bloody thing?' he asks.

Webster puts a hand on his arm.

'Lay off, Adj.'

The car's getting on Mathy's nerves. He keeps on about it, so now it's getting on everyone else's nerves as well.

I heard Mathy telling Webster about his sister yesterday. Nobody else was in the mess when he said it, and they thought I was asleep. She died years ago, apparently. A car ran into her. She was only sixteen. Mathy sounded cut up about it, said it should have been him. Older brother and all that, should have protected her. God knows how—the way he told it, he wasn't even there. She died in hospital, and he was too late to see her. I don't know why he told Webster that. Interesting, though.

I can hear Gervase pestering Flint, now. He knows he's not going to get any change out of me. 'How do you manage to hit anything? I can't even think, let alone fight.' *Christ Almighty.*

Flint shakes his head. 'Don't worry about that. You'll get the hang of it. Watch your tail, watch the sun—always climb towards it—don't fly straight for more than thirty seconds when you're in a scrap, because if Jerry gets on your tail, you're dead. What else? Oh, yes. Stick to Goldilocks like glue, and then you just might have a chance.'

'What if I lose him?'

'You find somebody else. Got that?'

'Yes. But what about shooting?'

'Don't bother about deflection or any of that fancy stuff. Your best chance is to get right up his jacksie, and wham! Don't ponce about taking pot-shots from miles away. Waste of time.'

*   *   *

Flint's right. We never got taught to shoot, either, apart from taking the odd pop at a drogue, and most of us were just as likely to hit the plane that was towing it. But there's no point stuffing the new boys' heads with technical business—they won't remember it. Up there, it's all instinct and reflexes. You can't do it by numbers. Like going in line astern, so you can see bugger all except the plane in front. Waste of time. We just have to make it up as we go along, but it's no good telling him that. At least it's Flint he's bothering this time, and not me. He keeps bleating out questions there's no answer to. What can we tell him? You can't prepare someone for combat. You've just got to learn to throw the kite about, and hope like hell that when it all starts and you're scared shitless, you can manage to stop yourself freezing up, or panicking and dashing for cover because you're so fucking desperate to stay alive. But then, when the urge to chase and kill overrides the fear, it's the most exciting thing imaginable. And then the first kill— supposing he gets that far—the sheer amazement of watching bits fall off and disintegrate, the plunge down, and then the pleasure, the jubilation, of realising you've done it.

The best thing is not to think about it. Better to be too tired, or too pissed, to start taking it too seriously. But that moment: when you're closing in for the kill, and the Spit's not even a plane any more, it's a gun-platform and you're not even aware that you're flying it. All this business about

139

pilots being heroes is just a load of cock. Being able to fight and kill is something primitive and fundamental.

Dying's not so frightening if you're responsible for your own fate, unlike those poor buggers on the ground, and I don't think I shall mind, much. I'd never thought of it at all before the war started, couldn't take it seriously. Still can't now, that's the odd thing. Strange how you can be terrified and blasé at the same time, but chaps here manage it all right, that's something I do know.

No sense wondering who'll be next—could be me. No reason why it shouldn't be. That puts the wind up the new ones all right, when one of the experienced pilots goes for a Burton. Some of the new ones won't last five minutes anyway. I can't put my finger on it, but there's a particular type—a natural victim, like that tart. You can see it straight off. I don't know about Sinclair, I just know I don't want to talk to him. He wants to have it all down pat. Play by the rules. I said to him, 'There aren't any rules. There used to be, but there aren't any more. It's not a bloody cricket match.'

He blushed like fury, then looked at me all innocent and said, 'It doesn't matter, you know.'

'What doesn't?'

'What school you went to.'

'What do you mean?'

'It's rot. Schools, who your people are, all of it.'

I said, 'What do you know about my people?'

'Nothing. But it doesn't matter.'

'Oh, bugger off.'

Doesn't matter. Of course it bloody matters. He went to a decent school, didn't he?

Like Rodney Bowers. He lived down the road

from us, where the good houses were. I can see him now, standing in front of his big, half-timbered house with the neat garden, his trunk in the driveway beside him, waiting to be driven off to school for another term, and me, squatting in the leaf mould, staring through a gap in the hedge at what I wanted—what I *should have had*—and thinking it should be me, *me*, not him, but instead I went to the local dump and came back day after day to a cramped, shabby life of putting up and making do and no space or time that wasn't filled with my stupid, dribbling cretin of a sister, what she needed, what she wanted, so I couldn't go to a good school or have anything new. And Bowers just took it all for granted, that he should have what I did not, in that easy way those people have as if it's their birthright, when it should have been mine.

We'd go about together in the holidays, and it was easy to make him do things because he was younger than I was . . . the two of us in our garden, up a tree, pelting Maisie with apples. She was about sixteen then, a formless, tented lump on the grass, gazing up with eyes like currants folded in dough, twisting her head round, not understanding what we were doing up there, crying when the apples hit their mark and trying to crawl away. When I tired of that, we went down the lane and found a dog turd on the path and I persuaded Bowers to scrape it up on a seaside spade and creep back to the garden and throw it at Maisie over the hedge. She sat there, shrieking, red-faced, with shit in her hair and Mother came out and caught Bowers and marched him back to his house in disgrace and told his mother what he'd done.

141

That got him in trouble, all right. I remember seeing his face, and knowing that he wouldn't pass the blame to me.

That reminds me: there's a letter from home in my pocket. It came yesterday, but I forgot about it. I almost threw it away—it'll only be news of Maisie. Mother wouldn't write for any other reason, unless it was for money. Either way, I shan't read it. I'm just surprised she could be bothered at all. One of the first things I can remember her saying to me was, 'Oh, you won't have any success in your life.' Even when I joined the RAF, it just made her angry—she'd said I'd never amount to anything, and I'd proved her wrong. She said it was irresponsible. I might 'get myself killed', as she put it, and then who'd look after Maisie when she was gone?

Anyone else would have put her away years go. I asked Dad once, why they didn't, and to hear him talk you'd think Mother was some sort of saint. He said it was her life's work. Not that she ever had any time for him, either.

Maisie can't even recognise her, that's the stupid thing. She can't do anything, except eat. Everything goes in her mouth. Mother was always telling me I was lucky to be so healthy with Maisie like she was. It was just as well. I was always having to do without so she could have some extra treat. Dad didn't have an overcoat for fifteen years, because of her. Probably what did for him. He should have told her. Letting her walk all over him, her and that great lump, feeding her face, gnawing her knuckles if there wasn't anything else, and everything *her, her, her*.

'We must make sacrifices.' She *liked* making

142

sacrifices. Liked being pushed to the side of her own life—made a fetish out of it, and she wanted us the same. She liked going round with her clothes all threadbare, saving money on groceries, cheapest cuts of meat, and always talking about it, drawing attention to it. There was nothing decent in the house. I was ashamed to bring anyone home; school was bad enough. Rushton's sister's a loony, that's what they used to say. And she was always saying, 'It's not Maisie's fault', as if it was *my* fault.

One year we had a wasps' nest at the top of the house. Maisie got stung, and from the way Mother carried on, you'd think she'd been killed. I went up to look at it the next day, and I got stung too, but of course that was my fault and nothing was made of it. Then I heard her tell one of her friends I'd been making up stories and I'd never been stung at all—as if I wasn't entitled to have anything happen to me, not even a wasp sting.

It was always like that. They never wanted to know anything about me, either of them. Don't think I'd have existed if it hadn't been for Maisie. All Mother wanted was someone to help look after her. Even Dad drew the line at that. *She* was disappointed I wasn't a girl—that would have been easier. But Dad never stood up for me. Never. 'You'd better do as she says.' We should have put it on his headstone.

I used to put flour on Maisie's face, for powder. Rub it on all over, except round her mouth where she kept licking it off. She'd try to grab the bag and cram all the flour into her mouth but I wouldn't let her. Then she'd start to scream. Everything in her face would bulge, straining underneath the coating of flour, and the *noise* . . . I wanted to stick my compass in her.

Mother always expected me to fetch and carry for her, clean up after her. Great stupid *lump*. All those years, the dullness of it. It was as if I was standing in a corner, facing the wall, unable to turn round, and the world was a tiny, narrow space, with no interest, no proper life. But when I learned to fly it was as if I was suddenly facing the other way, looking out.

I don't expect that I shall live long, and the reality is, I don't want to. I know there won't be anything for me when this is all over, just a world in which I am always out of step. I'm not going to read this letter. Why should I? I'm throwing it away. I'll look at the paper, instead. It's yesterday's but it'll do. *RAF bag 46 in 5 attacks . . . Boy, 12, Saved Dog, Will Get Medal . . . The Bomb Squad That Saved St Paul's . . . Cathedral Gives Thanks for 5 Heroes . . . Don't put that schoolgirl complexion away 'for the duration'—Palmolive soap still costs only 3 1/2d a tablet . . . Soho Girl Strangled*—What's this? *Police surgeons have established that the blonde Soho dance hostess, Edith Parker, was strangled. Miss Parker, 26, was found murdered in her flat in Gresse Street, London, on Saturday. The killer committed further injuries with a poker.*

I must have read it through three times before I realised. Strangled . . . injuries from a poker. Bit of a jolt, seeing it in the paper like that. It must have been . . . what? Thursday that it happened, but already it seems like a dream I had and can barely remember. Took a while to get reported in the paper—perhaps they didn't find her straight off. It's funny, because I can recall the place, but not her. It's the room that's in focus, the old-fashioned

144

mantelpiece, dark wood, standing in front of it—dust on it—small table beside the bed, the feel of the little mirror in my hand. It all seems more real than she does. And there was an eiderdown—blue—with marks and spots, as if someone had spilt tea or soup or something. I threw it over the bed before I left. Edith Parker. Odd to think of her having a name. It seems far away now, not important. It says here she was blonde. Strange to see it reduced to this, like a combat report: all the intensity of it, the sensation, gone, and it's just words on paper. Funny how you can do something that you can't explain or describe. I don't feel a connection with it, much. As if it happened to someone else. Funny altogether. But I'll keep it, all the same.

Nothing much else in here. Mathy's still sounding off about that bloody car. Nice day today, blitzy weather. I ought to empty my bladder before we get called again . . .

Edie's a blonde, dilly, dilly; My true love was red; But when it gets dark, dilly, dally; She'll do instead . . .

That's better. Too much tea this morning. I don't want to get caught short.

Don't see many redheads. It ought to be a brunette next time, really. For balance. But soon, because there's not much time left.

THURSDAY 26TH SEPTEMBER

Rene

I haven't felt much like going out to work these last few days, to be honest. Lily and I agreed to meet in The Black Horse before we started this evening, to buck ourselves up a bit. All the old girls go in the Ladies' bar, but they don't like us in there, so we go to the public room instead. There's a barman there, Walt. Poor chap had some operation on his face as a nipper and one of the nerves got cut by mistake, and he's got one cheek paralysed, with a droopy eye and his mouth screwed up so he only talks with half of it, but he's nice enough, and he's been sweet on Lily for ever so long. It's a bit pathetic, really, because he never says much, but whenever she comes in his face lights up—well, the part that works does—and he stops whatever he's doing and runs over to serve her. Every time she speaks to him, even if it's just to say 'thank you', he looks that pleased, and he's always got some little present that he pushes over the bar, quick, so no one can see. I did ask Lily once, if she'd ever gone with him—you know, when she's working—and she said he'd never asked, so I suppose he likes to keep it a bit romantic. It's sad, really, but you haven't got a lot of chance with girls if you look like he does.

This time he'd got Lily some artificial flowers to pin on her frock. He said he'd heard about Edie and he was sorry, and then he went and cleared a table for us in the corner so we could sit down. I was joshing Lily about him, trying to cheer us both

146

up because I wasn't exactly relishing the idea of going out to work, and I knew she wasn't, either, when she suddenly opened her bag and pulled out a scrap of newspaper. 'You seen this? It was in Tuesday's paper.'

'Let's have a look. *Police are hunting the killer of Edith Parker, a twenty-six-year-old former dance hostess, who was found strangled in her Soho flat yesterday*. Doesn't say anything about the other business. Perhaps Bridget was making it up.'

Lily shook her head. 'Who'd make up a thing like that? Anyway, they've got it all wrong. Edie was only twenty-three, not twenty-six, and she didn't live in Soho, either. Oh, Rene, it's horrible. I told Ted I didn't want to come out, and he was ever so nice about it, but then he went out and I thought I'd better come. I mean, there's the rent, and . . . you know.'

'Come on, Lily. You know how Edie was. Weak in the head—you said it yourself. I don't like to speak ill of the dead, but it's her own fault if she got into trouble. Look at the way she went off with that chap from the shelter.'

'He offered her three pounds. I heard him.'

'There you are, then. Double the money—you know what that means.'

'No French letter.'

'You wouldn't have gone with him, would you?'

Lily shook her head.

'There you are, then. You've got to know how to handle them, that's all.' She still looked doubtful, so I said, 'Come on, Lil, it's all right. We'll look out for each other, won't we?'

'I suppose so. But Rene—'

She never got any further, because some idiot,

147

stinking like a distillery, plonks himself down at our table. I was about to say, 'Do you mind?' but he cut straight in with, 'How's Henry?'

I said, 'I don't know anyone called Henry.'

'Well you should, he's your husband.'

'Not me, dear, I don't have a husband.'

'Yes you do.' He thumped the table. 'Henry.'

'No, dear. You're thinking of somebody else.'

'Have you divorced him?'

'How could I divorce him when I never had him in the first place?'

'Poor Henry, fancy getting divorced . . .'

This was beginning to get on my nerves, and I was about to tell him so when Lily jumped up, saying, 'Oh, I can't bear it! Bloody men, all the time. Why can't we have some peace and quiet?'

He turned to her and said, 'Are you going to marry him, then?'

'Who?'

'Henry! You couldn't do better. Straight as a die, he is. Don't know what's the matter with *her*,' jerking his head at me, 'divorcing him like that.'

Lily said, 'Oh, get out of my way,' and made to push past him.

He put out a hand to stop her and I thought, *here we go again*, when I heard someone say, 'This gentleman giving you trouble?'

I thought, I know that voice, and sure enough when I turned round there was the warden, Harry Nolan. He took the man by his arm and said, 'Time to go, mate.' Lily and I got behind the table pretty sharpish at that, expecting trouble, because he was a little runt of a man, and with Harry being so big, well, that's when they're usually spoiling for a fight, wanting to prove themselves, but he didn't say a

148

word. Just left, quiet as a lamb. We thanked Harry, then Lily said she ought to be going—despite what she'd said, I reckon she was worried in case Ted came in and saw she wasn't working. I was about to go with her, when Harry asked if he could buy me a drink. I thought, oh, why not? I could do with a bit of Dutch courage, and besides, it's not often I meet a man I actually want to pass the time of day with, free and gratis, so I might as well enjoy a bit of decent company for a change. I told Lily I'd catch up with her, and sat back down again.

'You feeling a bit better now, Rene?'

'I'm not so bad.'

He said, 'I'm glad. That was a bad business, all round.'

I felt a bit awkward, talking about it. I mean, I know he knows, and he knows I know he knows, but all the same. And it was hard to make him out, because there wasn't any sort of . . . *suggestiveness*, if you see what I mean. And he could be married with five kids, for all I know, although I have to say he hasn't got a look of that. There were a lot of people in the pub, and we could hear Ale Mary in the passage outside, singing away over all the racket. To change the subject, I said, 'Bit early for her, isn't it?'

'Be thankful for small mercies. At least it's not the Old Testament.'

'Not unless there's a Book of Marie Lloyd.'

Harry laughed. 'I'll bet she hasn't enjoyed herself so much in years.'

'Wish I could say the same. It's enough to make anyone go off their head, all this.'

'Oh, cheer up, it's not so bad. I heard a good story yesterday. One of the chaps in our ARP is a

149

dentist. He had a man come in for a new set of teeth, and do you know what he'd done? He was a bit quiet about it, but they got it out of him in the end: he's with the AFS and he's on the hose for the first time, the fire's nearly out and he hasn't been home in three days so he thinks it's a good chance to clean his teeth. He takes them out and holds them up in the water, but of course he hadn't reckoned on the pressure, and they shoot out of his hand and go sailing through the air, straight into the fire!'

'No!'

'Honestly. Flying right through the air, snapping away like anything.'

'They never.'

'Well, that's what he said.'

'*Snapping?*' It was such a funny picture, I couldn't stop laughing.

'Well, I don't know if that was strictly true, but it makes a good story, doesn't it?'

'Priceless . . .'

'It's nice to see you laugh, Rene.'

'Snapping . . . oh, dear, you've really cheered me up.'

'You look lovely when you smile.'

There was a bit of a pause after that, with neither of us knowing quite what to say, so I stood up. 'I'd best be going.'

Harry stood, too. 'Yes. I'm glad you're feeling a bit brighter.'

'Well, I've got you to thank for that, haven't I?'

'All part of the service. Take care of yourself, Rene.'

It was just about dark outside. All the way to my patch I kept thinking of Harry saying I look lovely when I smile, then telling myself not to be soft. Being in this business can take you two ways: one where you don't trust men because you see all the bad side, and the other where it makes you want a bit of romance more than ever, to have the contrast with the other thing. That's why so many have ponces, but it's no use if you have to pay a man to stay with you. Except of course that they're your own sort because they understand the life.

But with Harry . . . Well, I don't know, because you do get these types, every so often; they'll give you money and help you out and not want anything for it, but it's all done to make them feel a better person, so even if they don't get the physical satisfaction, they get another sort. There's a lot of men have a fascination with women like us, but with this particular type of person, it takes them in a different way from the usual. I'm not saying there's wrong in it, and I wouldn't refuse the money, why should I? But Harry hasn't offered me anything more than you would an ordinary woman, so I can't make it out. But I like him. Yes, I do. But I'm not getting my hopes up, because even if a man thinks he can forget you've been a tart, I don't reckon that's true—it'll always come back later. First quarrel, and he'll throw it right back in your face how he's picked you up out of the gutter. But then I said to myself, I'm not going to think about Harry any more tonight, because I'm working.

I had an appointment with one of my regulars at my flat—Raymond the Barber, I call him, because he always wants to comb my hair. Puts a towel across my shoulders and calls me 'Madam' and all the rest of it. He comes to see me about once a month. I charge him two pounds for it, being a bit out of the ordinary. Mind you, I have to pretend to tip him. First thing he does, he gives me a couple of shillings and I have to put them in my handbag so I can bring them out after and give him, and he says, 'Oh, *thank* you, Madam.' You get a fair bit of that sort of thing. I've got my button-boot man, too, who comes to see me, he's another one. He's got these boots he brings with him and he likes me to walk up and down in front of him wearing nothing but. They don't half pinch! Still, it makes a change from the usual.

I had a fair bit of business after that, and then I'd just come back out onto the street when a man comes shooting past and nearly knocks me flying. I thought, what's this, I'm being robbed, and I shouted out. Not that he'd get much, mind you, because I keep my money in my shoe, not my handbag, and he'd have a job finding that. Anyway, he wasn't a thief, just a young fellow in a hurry— uniform of some sort, all apologetic, nice manners and the rest of it. Said he was looking for a pal who'd given him the slip. I said, 'Doesn't sound like much of a pal to me.'

'Well, he's not, really, he's a funny chap. But you haven't seen anyone, have you?'

'I've only just got here, dear. I can ask my friend round the corner, if you like.'

'I didn't see anyone.'

'Well you wouldn't, would you, the way you were going?'

'Yes, I'm sorry about that, I—'

'Never mind. I meant the other corner. Where you were heading. Let's have a look, shall we?'

I shone my torch across the pavement, but Lily wasn't there. 'She's busy, dear. I'd give it up, if I were you.'

'Yes . . .' he sighed. 'I suppose you're right. I say . . . are you, I mean, do you . . . could . . . that is, could I buy you a drink?'

Here we go, I thought. 'Oh, you don't have to do that, dear. It'll be two pounds unless you're after something special.' I said two pounds because I had him down for a novice and I thought I might as well take ten shillings more for the extra bother—I'm not a bloody nursemaid, after all.

'*Special?* Heavens, no . . .' He laughed nervously. 'What do, I mean, where . . . ?'

'Come along with me.'

When we got back to my flat I saw he was RAF. Nineteen or twenty, I suppose, with a sort of baby look to him—big dark eyes with long lashes and lovely wavy hair—but as if the face hadn't taken on its proper shape yet, if you know what I mean. Blushing like fury, of course. He said, 'Look here, I don't know the form . . . Name's Gervase.'

Blimey, I thought, you couldn't make it up, could you? 'That's nice, dear. I'm Rene.'

'Pleased to meet you.' He put his hand out for me to shake.

'It's all right, dear, it's not a garden party.'

'Oh. Sorry.' He put both hands behind his back, and looked down at his feet. I thought, I've got my work cut out here.

'Haven't you forgotten something, dear?'

'I'm sorry, I don't—'

'The money.'

'Oh, yes. Of course.'

At least they're quick, the first time. Afterwards, he said he wanted to talk. That's something else you get a lot of, and it's always the same: hard luck

153

stories. The wife's left or the girl won't marry them or they're miserable. Once you've heard one man feeling sorry for himself, you've heard them all.

I mean, I'm not one of these 'Get your trousers off and get on with it' merchants, I like to keep it polite, but you don't want them hanging around afterwards, especially if they're going to come over all moral and try to save you—well! I tell you, I've had clergymen in here giving me a sermon about what a tragedy it is to live like I do and how I ought to repent and all the rest of it, when not five minutes before they've been begging me to talk all manner of filth to get them excited. Funny, you'd think they'd see how ridiculous it is, but they never do. And men say *women* are stupid! Although now I come to think of it, I suppose we must be, because we put up with it, don't we?

Not that I thought I was going to get that from this boy, but I wasn't in the mood, so I said, 'No, you've had what you've paid for,' and he said he'd give me more money. I told him a pound. He gave it to me, then he said, 'Will you put your arms round me?'

'Very well, dear, if that's what you want.' Then blow me if he didn't start to cry! I've got one arm round him and one eye on the clock, I'm patting him on the back like a baby and half-listening, and he talks and talks. He was going on about how he's afraid he'll let down his family and his chums and how it wasn't like he thought it would be—the air force, I suppose he meant—and he didn't know if he could fight, and then he said how ashamed he was at coming to see me. I thought, that's a bit rich, so I said, 'Well, if that's the case, dear, you'd better be going, hadn't you?' He apologised and said

154

something about getting carried away because it was a relief to talk to someone, and then he sort of checked himself, like he'd been about to tell me something else. Then he started on about this pal who'd run out on him and what a good flyer he was, and how he seemed to be fearless, but how he hardly ever spoke to anyone, and how some of the other fellows liked a joke but this one never joined in, and a whole lot more like that, but I wasn't interested to hear it, I was thinking of how soon I could get rid of him and back downstairs, so I'm at the mirror putting on lipstick, nodding away: 'Yes, well, never mind . . .'

'I don't understand,' he kept saying. 'If only I could understand.'

I said, 'Oh, everybody feels like that sometimes. It's a funny old world, after all.'

'Do they really?' He looked at me with these great big wet eyes and just for a moment it reminded me so much of my Tommy that I almost went and gave him a proper cuddle, but then I thought, that won't do. It was touching, though, because some of these boys are *so* young, really, and when you think what they have to do . . . But I hadn't time for any more of it, so I said, 'Come on, dear. Off you go.'

He gave himself a little shake, and said, 'I'm sorry if I've bored you.'

'Oh, don't you worry about that.'

'You've been very kind.'

'Only doing my job, dear. Come back any time. Ta-ta.'

Then he said he'd got to go and find this queer chum of his, and off he went.

I went back out, too. It was pretty quiet, so I

155

thought I'd nip round the corner for a chat to Lily, see if she wanted a cup of tea, but she wasn't there. I stayed on for a bit—a couple more, then nothing for half an hour, and Lily still wasn't back, so I thought, oh, well . . . Then, just as I was about to go in, I heard footsteps, not very steady, and this mournful voice, like a fog-horn: 'Poor old Henry . . .' with a great beery belch that echoed up and down the street and had me chuckling all the way up the stairs. Poor old Henry! I'll tell that to Lily tomorrow, when I see her.

THURSDAY 26TH SEPTEMBER

Lucy

When I woke up yesterday morning I decided it was time to turn over a new leaf. At Minnie's firm they take turns in fire-watching twice a week, but so far, I've done nothing at all, and when I think about her, and Dad, and Frank joining up, it makes me feel pretty useless. I put the green brooch in my handbag as a reminder, and attended a lecture on first aid—a real one, this time—in the evening. I spoke to one of the ladies from the Women's Auxiliary Council of the YMCA about volunteering for the mobile canteen, and she said she'd see if it was possible for me to do service part-time, which bucked me up no end. There's no cooking, thank heavens—unless you count making tea—just playing shop with pies and buns, which suits me down to the ground. Came out feeling that at least it was a step in the right direction, then—

horrors!—I saw Mr Bridges across the road, obviously waiting for someone. Rushed down the nearest side-street so he shouldn't see me, but it was too late, he'd started calling out to me. He caught up and then I *had* to stop because people were turning round to see what the noise was.

'Go away,' I hissed.

'Lucy, please. Let me explain.'

'You don't need to explain. Just go away.'

'Please, Lucy. I know you don't want any more to do with me, you've made that clear, but if you could just listen—'

'All right, I'm listening. Tell me.'

'Not in the middle of the street. Let's sit down, at least. Have a drink. This isn't easy.'

'Well, you don't have to do it on my account.'

'I want to. Don't you understand?'

'No, frankly, I don't.'

'For God's sake, Lucy!' He grabbed hold of my arm, and a man stopped and said, 'This chap bothering you, Miss?'

Flustered, I said, 'No, really, it's fine.'

He looked doubtful. 'If you're sure . . .'

'Yes, really. Thank you.'

The man moved away, and Mr Bridges said, 'Can I take that as a "yes", then? You'll come?'

'I suppose so. But I can't be long.'

We went to a pub in Rathbone Place. Very rowdy. Mr Bridges said that the customers were all artists and intellectuals, but I must say they didn't look it to me. They all smelt strongly of alcohol, and there was a man in the corner telling dirty stories in quite a loud voice, most of it incoherent, thank heavens. One woman was actually staggering, and the man trying to hold her up

157

wasn't much better. What a place! It beats me how people, especially clever people, can behave like that.

I think Mr Bridges must have been in a pub before he'd seen me, because he started pawing at me and being sentimental, saying his wife was ill, a chronic invalid, and dreadfully bad-tempered, and had been that way for years. I didn't believe a word of it, and said so. I was fairly disgusted with the whole thing, and angry at myself for backsliding by agreeing to listen to him at all. I got up to leave as soon as I could. Mr Bridges tried to follow, but I told him not to bother. I know he could make things awkward for me at work if he chose, especially because I jolly well won't go up to his office again, but I felt, for once, that I was *in the right*. I walked down the road with no real sense of where I was going, but by the time I came to Oxford Street I'd cooled down a bit. It was nice to be in the fresh air, and the bangs weren't too close, thank goodness. Decided to try and find my way to Leicester Square. A spur-of-the-moment thing, really, which certainly had something to do with meeting you-know-who, and thinking it must have happened close by, and wondering if by any chance he'd be there again, coupled with exhilaration at getting rid of Mr Bridges and a strong desire to put off another dose of Mums for as long as possible.

I realised, even as I was doing it, that it was silly and pointless, and I'd probably end up getting lost, but I carried on stumbling in what I hoped was the right direction as if something was impelling me— as if my torch wasn't in my hand at all, but the little beam was coming from somewhere else, to guide me. Very strange. Managed to get across Oxford

158

Street and into Soho. Remembering the prostitute who'd been murdered made me nervous, because you do hear these terrible stories about gangs and white slavers and the like. I know it's hardly likely to happen to me, but all the same, I didn't feel very comfortable—kept thinking that some horrible man was going to reach out of the darkness to grab me and bundle me through a doorway or something, and every time someone brushed past me, I imagined I could feel a hand reaching out for my neck. After about five minutes I was starting to wish I'd just gone down Regent Street, and I just about got the fright of my life when someone ran straight into me and I slipped off the curb and sat down hard on my bottom, right in the road. I managed to put my hand on my torch, which by some miracle was still working, and the first thing I saw was a swaying tripod of legs—frayed carpet slippers, varicose veins thick as creepers that seemed to be moving in the torchlight, twisting their way up columns of grey, puckered flesh, and in the centre, the solidness of a man's trouser and shoe.

My first thought was—idiotically—for the man's other leg, but a phlegmy whinnying noise from somewhere above my head made me jump, and a woman's voice cackled, 'The foolish virgins said to the wise, give us your oil, for our lamps are gone out.'

A torch shone into my face, and a man said, 'Rene! Let me give you a hand.'

'Thank you, but you're mistaken. I'm not Rene.'

'Oh no, so you aren't. Sorry, Miss, my mistake. It was your coat, Miss, made me think I knew you. Are you all right down there?'

159

'I think so. I must have tripped.'

'Easy to do in the blackout. Let me help you up.'

' . . . but the wise virgins said no—'

'That's enough sermonising, Ma. Here, Miss, let's get you upright.' As he bent down to help me up his other knee came into view, which was quite a relief. He was a big man with a nice, kind face. All the time, the woman droned in the background,' . . . they said, not likely. That's what they said. Wouldn't let them have it.'

'Come on, Ma. Don't you worry about her, Miss. Now then, if you're fit, I'd best get you both round to the shelter. You shouldn't be out here, it's not safe.'

'Yes, thank you.'

'Don't mention it. You just lean up here and get your breath back for a minute, and then we'll make tracks.'

The old woman was still bawling away, 'He said to them, He said, You know not the day nor the hour! That's what He said . . .'

'I'll give you the day and the hour in a minute, Ma. Now come on! Don't you worry, Miss,' he said to me, 'She's had a drop too much, that's all.' He winked. 'It wouldn't be the first time, either.'

It was nothing to be afraid of, but it took the wind out of my sails, and I began to wish I'd never embarked on such a stupid venture in the first place. My leg was hurting, and when I put my hand down and touched my knee, I realised I'd cut myself. I limped along after the warden until we came to a shelter, which I was pretty sure was the same one I'd been to before, and I sat down to inspect the damage. The warden got the old woman settled in the corner, where she went

160

straight to sleep. 'There you are,' he said to me, 'she won't give you any more trouble.'

'It's very kind of you.'

'Not at all, Miss. Nolan's my name. Harry Nolan. I'm the warden here. I've not seen you before—not local, are you?'

'No, I was just on my way home.'

'Pardon my saying, but you want to be careful, miss, walking round here. You'll have a sit-down before you go off home, won't you? I'll take you over to Mrs McIver, she'll see you're all right.'

'Thank you.'

He ushered me across the shelter to an elderly lady, who was bent almost double over a newspaper, trying to make out the crossword. He leaned over and spoke to her, then waved at me and left. I didn't think she'd heard him, but she must have, because I was dabbing at my knee with my handkerchief when she said, 'You need a plaster for that.'

I looked up, and she was peering at me, her head twisted on one side. It reminded me of Dennis, the tortoise we had until last year. Minnie always said the shock of being at war must have killed him, because he hibernated for the winter and never woke up again.

'You look in there.' She jabbed a finger at a carpet bag by her feet. I hesitated, because it seemed rude, but she said, 'It's all in there. Go on.'

She didn't seem to mind me rooting around amongst her things, just went back to her crossword. She was wearing an ancient horror of a hat with a brim, and flowers, and every so often she'd put her hand up, tug a stub of pencil out of it, lick the end, scribble down a clue, and jab the

161

pencil home, all without straightening her back.

I found a bundle of first aid things, dabbed the cut with some iodine and stuck a plaster over it. My stockings were laddered, as I'd feared, but not too badly to mend. I tidied my hair, which improved things a bit, and brushed the worst of the grit off my skirt and coat. Looking down at the blue wool, I remembered the warden saying, 'It was your coat, Miss, made me think I knew you,' and I thought of the prostitute I'd seen in the shelter who was wearing the same model. She'd looked a bit like me, too. I couldn't imagine that such a nice man would know her in her . . . well, let's say her *working life*, so decided immediately that it must be because she's a regular in the shelter. Anything else would be unthinkable! But slightly disturbing to think I could be mistaken for a woman of that sort, even for a moment—not nice at all.

The elderly lady stowed away her pencil with an air of finality and picked up an alarm clock from the bench beside her. She shook it, peered at it, sniffed loudly, rolled up her newspaper, and turned to me. 'You waiting for someone, dear?'

I shook my head. It was daft, really, because all the time, sitting there, I kept expecting *him* to come in—no earthly reason why he should but . . . Oh, I don't know. Stupid.

'I've seen you before,' she said.

'Have you?'

'Yes, with a young man. I'm sure it was you. Services, he was. That was it. Air force. Yes,' she said. 'I remember. Handsome.'

I could feel myself blushing. 'He's not . . .'

'Not what? Not your brother, at any rate,' she said, sharply. 'Meeting him, are you?'

162

I shook my head. 'Really. I was just seeing someone—well, a man, and we argued, and I came this way, and . . .' I launched into an account of what had happened—no mention of *him*, of course—wondering why on earth I felt the need to explain to a complete stranger, and whether she'd think me mad for telling her, but she didn't seem to. I said, 'That lady over there. She was shouting at me.'

'Oh,' she said. 'Mary. The Bible, was it?'

'I think so. Does she . . . ?'

'Like a drop?' She laughed. 'More than a drop, dear, but she's harmless enough. You don't want to take any notice.' She leaned over. 'Nuns,' she whispered.

'I beg your pardon?'

'Educated by nuns. Then they wouldn't let her join. Took it badly. Doo-lally.' She tapped her forehead, then peered at me, more like Dennis the tortoise than ever, and said, 'That young man. The handsome one. He's the one you favour, isn't he?'

'Well, I don't know. I . . .' The whole thing suddenly seemed farcical, and I felt such a fool I didn't know where to look.

'You be careful, dear. That's all. Don't go looking for trouble. Now then. You'd best be off home.'

'Yes. Yes, I suppose I had. Thank you.'

'Don't mention it, dear. McIver's the name.'

'Lucy. Armitage.'

'Lucy, is it? Well, good night, dear, and good luck.'

I journeyed home in a sort of daze and ate sandwiches with Minnie under the kitchen table. No tea, because there's only enough left for tomorrow morning. Mums was very shirty about this, according to Minnie; apparently it's our fault for making tea in the middle of the night and using up the ration. I thought of pointing out that we're not the ones here all day drinking cups of tea, but felt too preoccupied to get indignant about it.

I tossed and turned all night—planes at one, then again about four. The All-Clear went at five, so I went upstairs to bed. I felt tired and irritable, but couldn't settle. Kept thinking how pathetically transparent I must be if a complete stranger could see through me so easily . . . as I saw through Mr Bridges . . . Oh, dear. Well, that'll teach me. So much for turning over a new leaf. Drifted off to sleep after that.

FRIDAY 27TH SEPTEMBER
Soho

Ted Gerrity woke up with a bastard behind the eyes. His head felt as heavy as a sandbag and ready to burst, and even the action of turning it sideways on the pillow produced such an intense wave of nausea that he thrust his upper body forward to hang over the edge of the bed. Lily'd make a fuss if it got on the sheets. He waited, eyes closed, for the heave, but nothing happened. After a few minutes, he opened his eyes. Even that was painful, although the blackouts kept the room mercifully dim. He concentrated on the floor beside the bed, trying to get it into focus. Pair of scissors down there? He leaned down further and picked them up, but the movement brought another upsurge, so he let them

164

fall, wincing as the *thunk!* hit his cortex, and closed his eyes again.

Lily's curling tongs. Fancy leaving them on the floor like that, where anyone could trip over them. Slowly, he became aware of the other parts of his body. He felt stale, constricted, and . . . damp. Oh, no. Lily really would raise hell about that, if he'd pissed himself again. He was fully clothed, as well. Shoes, and all. Must have been quite a night, he thought, blearily, feeling too grim even for self-disgust. He fumbled with the top button of his trousers until it came undone—that was better—and lay still again, trying to summon up the resolve to get off the bed and sort himself out. How had he got home, anyway? Had Lily been there? Surely not, or she'd have got his clothes off. It wasn't like her to go to the shelter without him, and anyway, last night hadn't been too bad, had it? Unless he'd slept through the lot. Not wanting to turn his head again, Ted put out a hand and felt towards the middle of the bed. His fingers stubbed against the flesh above someone's elbow—Lily's presumably—and he drew his hand back, not wanting to wake her. He couldn't face up to a row, not now. Perhaps they'd had one last night, and that was why she hadn't undressed him. If they had, though, he couldn't remember a thing about it. Best not let on about that, he thought. It would only start her off again.

What time was it, anyway? Perhaps if he made some tea . . . What had happened last night? Oh, yes. Some of it, anyway—the early part. The new girl. Well, maybe. Said she was terrified over that business with Edie Parker and pretty much told him straight out that if he wanted to come and live

165

with her . . . Nice flat. Nice *girl*. Younger than Lily, too. Could be the start of something; bound to be more girls getting nervous, wanting protection.

Nah. Nice idea, but Lily'd never stand for it. Jealous. As long as the girl . . . what was it? Marie, that's right. As long as Marie didn't tell her, he could forget all about it. But there was always the risk. She might get nasty, if . . . He'd been a fool to go back with her, but you don't turn it down when it's offered, do you? Besides, Marie might not be so . . . being younger, and all that. Might be flighty, or lazy. One thing about Lily, she was good, always out bringing in the money. She could do with cleaning up a bit, mind you—the place was a mess. He'd have to have a word with her about that. Not yet, though: Lily had quite a temper on her, and she'd been a bit off with him lately, with the raids getting on her nerves, and then Edie. And then there was the little matter of the call-up. She didn't know he hadn't attended the medical board. He'd heard of a man—an invalid—who'd go in your place if you paid him, but it was seventy pounds, and he'd have a job getting that out of Lily. Maybe she'd got something saved, money he didn't know about, but all the same . . . She'd been all for it at the beginning. It was all right for her, she wasn't the one going off to get killed, was she? But she'd changed her tune pretty quick after Edie, so perhaps he could ask her. She might cough for it, if he put it like that.

Tea first, Ted thought. Got to keep her sweet. He sat up and swung his feet carefully over the side of the bed. Head thudding, he stumbled across the room to the kitchenette and reached across the sink to open the blackout curtains. He rubbed the

166

back of his neck, wincing at the light, then turned to squint at the clock on the mantelpiece: twelve noon. Blimey. But he'd got in late, hadn't he? Early, rather. He reached out a hand and groped behind the clock—Lily usually tucked the money back there so he could take what he needed. Nothing. Must have forgotten. Or perhaps she'd got angry when he hadn't come home, and taken it back again.

He searched his pockets for cigarettes, found nothing, and looked round for Lily's handbag. Not there. He filled the kettle, lit the gas, and called through the doorway, 'Hey, Lily!'

Nothing. Asleep or sulking? Still, he thought, she never stays angry for long. Loves me, doesn't she?

'Where's your bag, Lil?'

He glanced across to the bed. Pillow over her head. All he could see was a few tendrils of dark brown hair curling out at the side. Sulking, by the look of it. Or perhaps she'd had a few as well. That wasn't like Lily, not when she was working, but then she'd not been herself since poor old Edie . . . Looked a bit queer lying there with the eiderdown and blanket pulled back and her vest rolled up over her tits. He moved nearer to cover her up and find her bag while he was at it. Maybe he'd nip out and get himself a pick-me-up. Hair of the dog.

He walked round the end of the bed to Lily's side. Her breasts lolled outwards, pallid and blueish in the poor light. Dark bruises on her ribs. Had a rough customer, poor kid. Still, the extra kip would do her good. He'd make her that tea when he got back from the pub.

Her handbag was on the floor, at the head end.

167

He lowered himself slowly, careful not to disturb the sandbag inside his head, undid the clasp and took out a packet of Players and Lily's battered leather purse. It felt nice and fat. Good old Lily. Treat her to a drink later, he thought. Cheer her up a bit. She deserves it.

He lifted the pillow away from her face, thinking to say, I'll leave you to sleep—but the words never came. Instead of the Lily he'd expected, with soft, sleep-pouched features, there were two viscous, clotted eyes in a swollen mass of dark red, mottled flesh.

Ted gasped and backed away from the bed, holding the pillow in front of him like a shield. His heel knocked something that spun across the floor. Looking round, he saw, as it clattered to rest, that it was a kitchen knife.

He whirled back to the bed. The quick movement made the room dip and spin, and in the middle, Lily's bulging, ruined eyes with their burst blood vessels bobbed like the north point on some hideous compass. He staggered, caught his feet in a trailing blanket, and tripped over backwards, pulling the bedclothes with him.

He gasped and scrambled upright. On the bed, Lily's legs protruded from a bloody, tangled mass, dark, glutinous loops and glistening slabs of flesh that seemed to writhe in the half-light.

One glance was enough. Ted flung the pillow at it and bolted, bellowing and retching, out of the room, down the stairs and into the street. For a moment, he stood on the pavement, gasping and shaking, then weaved his way down the road, towards Fitzrovia.

In the Black Horse, the working half of Walt the

168

barman's face twisted upwards into an expression of surprise as Ted slid Lily's purse across the bar and gestured towards the row of optics. 'Drink,' he croaked. 'Anything.'

Walt poured a whiskey and slid it across the bar, then opened the purse. 'Blimey. You're quids in, aren't you?'

Ted wasn't listening. Slumped on his elbows, head down, he muttered, 'What happened . . . Christ, what happened . . . All night . . . in bed with . . . with *that* . . . all night . . . Give me a drink, for God's sake.'

'There.' The barman nodded towards the glass, and was about to turn away when Ted said, 'Lily . . .'

'What about Lily?'

'Her face . . . She . . . Oh, Christ . . . All night, lying there . . . with, with her *face* . . .'

'What's happened to her face?' said Walt, sharply.

'She . . . I can't go back in there.'

'Where? She at home?'

'Yes.'

Walt leaned forward. 'She in trouble?'

'She . . . she . . .'

'That's it.' Walt wiped his hands. 'I'm coming with you.' He took off his apron, hung it up, and put on his jacket.

'No.' Ted's voice was a whisper. 'I can't go in there again.'

The barman ignored him. He stepped through to the other bar to tell his fellow-worker to mind the shop for a minute, then opened the hatch and walked round to Ted.

'What you done to her?' He caught hold of Ted's

169

jacket, spinning him round, and shouted into his slack, shocked face. 'You show me. Come on. Show me what you done.'

'No . . .' Ted was whimpering now, shaking his head violently, but it was too late. His legs buckled beneath him and his feet scrabbled for purchase as the barman towed him across the room and out of the door.

'Right,' he said. 'Where we going?'

'Bateman Street.'

They walked in silence, Walt gripping Ted's arm.

Ted stopped automatically in front of the door and stood, head down, like a horse in harness. 'Up there,' he whispered. 'Don't . . . I can't . . .'

'You're bloody well going to. Open the door.'

Ted jabbed the key at the lock with shaking hands and dropped it. As the barman bent to pick it up he made to run away, but not quick enough—the barman straightened and threw a punch that sent him reeling into the wall. 'Now open that door before I do you some real damage.'

Ted staggered into the front hall and the barman pushed him up the stairs with a series of jabs, muttering, 'You bastard, what you done to her? Let's see what you done.'

The door stood ajar. Ted reeled back, grabbing the banister for support. 'I can't go in.'

Walt gave the door a shove, and dragged Ted inside.

'What's that smell?'

Ted shook his head.

'Jesus, something's on fire!' Walt flung open the door to the kitchenette, grabbed the handle of the kettle, and dropped it again, gasping. 'Red hot.' Ted stood in the doorway and watched, stupefied,

170

as he twisted off the gas.

'Right. Where is she?'

'In there.' Ted jerked his head towards the bedroom. Walt hesitated on the threshold.

'Lily?' he called, his voice gentle. 'Lily? You all right?'

Ted shook his head. 'She can't . . .' he said, hoarsely. 'She's . . .' He shrank back into the hallway as Walt rounded on him.

'She's *what*?' In the dim light, the moving half of his face looked as if it was trying to tear itself away from its lifeless counterpart. 'You bloody well stay there, or I'll kill you.'

Ted's legs gave way entirely as the barman opened the bedroom door, and he slumped to his knees against the wall. 'Oh, Christ,' he muttered, 'Oh, Christ . . . Lily . . .'

A moment later, the door was slammed shut, and the barman stood over him once more.

'Keys,' he said, 'Give me your keys.'

Ted fumbled at his pocket and handed them over. He heard the door slam, the key turn, then footsteps thundering down the stairs.

'Lily . . . Christ . . . *Lily* . . .'

When Walt arrived back with the police, some ten minutes later, they found Ted curled up in a foetal position on the hall lino. In the days that followed, the police amassed evidence for use at his trial: the fingerprints on the handbag, the bloodstained trousers and curling tongs, which also bore Ted's fingerprints, the theft of Lily's purse, and the evidence of the girl Marie, who, anxious to placate her new and very jealous protector, denied she had ever set eyes on him.

Walt told the police that Ted had said he'd done

171

it. It wasn't a lie. Over and over again they'd prodded him through the sequence of events that led to his discovery of Lily's body, and there always came a moment, after they'd entered the flat and he'd called out to Lily, when Ted said he'd killed her. 'I can hear him now,' he told the officer. 'He said he'd done it. I can see his face as he said it. Clear as day.' His certainty grew each time he said it. The police asked Walt if Ted had confessed to killing Lily when he walked into the pub, but Walt said no, it wasn't then. He remembered Ted giving him Lily's purse and muttering a bit and asking for a drink, but that was all.

As the barman's affection for Lily was common knowledge amongst the regulars at the Black Horse, they were careful not to ask questions or discuss the case in front of him. They knew he was touchy; who wouldn't be with a face like that? What they couldn't understand was why Ted had done it. He wasn't the brightest, and he drank too much on occasion, but he wasn't violent. He'd never laid a finger on Lily as far as anyone knew, and anyway, why kill the goose that laid the golden eggs? Coming so soon after that other poor girl, as well . . .

Walt kept schtum and got on with his work. When the pub closed for the night he went home and sat out the raids under the stairs. Alone, because he was ashamed of the nightmares that woke him, shouting; and besides, the other lodgers preferred the cellar. Afraid of sleep, he fingered the artificial silk slip which he had, on impulse, scooped from the floor of Lily's bedroom and stuffed in his pocket before he'd fetched the police. He didn't know why he'd done it—in fact, he didn't

172

remember he'd done it until he'd pulled it, rumpled and slithery, from his jacket pocket. But he was glad, because it reminded him of her. It still had a faint smell: powder, perfume, and a hint—very slight—of perspiration. Lily when she was alive. By feeling, not thinking, he could banish the terrible image of the corpse that lurked in his mind, seldom out of sight for long. He rationed his imaginings to a single picture of Lily in the slip, waiting for him, warm and soft and kind. Nothing more. Then he would press the garment against his damaged cheek as if it were a relic and he a supplicant, hoping for a miracle.

FRIDAY 27TH SEPTEMBER

Jim

Friday, now. Two a.m. Just got back. No raids, thank God. When I came into my room I found Ginger, stark naked, sitting bolt upright on the edge of the bed. He didn't look when I came in. I said hello, but he didn't hear me, either. Fast asleep with his eyes wide open. He used to share with Prideaux. They took the car away yesterday afternoon—too late for Mathy. He bought it yesterday morning. Found Webster and Reilly packing up his things when I came in after lunch. Webster told me I'd got a new roommate. I'd rather be on my own, but Ginger's decent enough. It could be worse—Corky or Davy.

It must have been Mathy who went down in flames. Must have been trapped in the cockpit.

173

Burnt alive. Heard his screams over the R/T. We all did. Poor bastard. He'd dreamed about it—woke me up once, yelling and beating the bedclothes, trying to put the fire out. Called it the flames of hell . . . *Jesus*. I don't want to go that way. I could be next. This time tomorrow, I might not be here. It's possible. Might as well make the most of it while I am.

I told Webster Mathy'd left me his lighter. Don't know if he believed it, but he gave it to me. Found a photograph of his sister, underneath a pile of shirts, and pocketed it when Webster wasn't looking. Money, too—thirty bob. Not sure why I took the picture. She's a nice-looking girl, and I thought it might be useful.

I wonder if Ginger'll have nightmares like Mathy used to. He's got the jumps, all right; yesterday he threw a boiled egg at a WAAF waitress because it wasn't done enough. Hit the target, too. He's obviously a better shot on the ground than he is in the air. He's shouting in his sleep, now. I flick Mathy's lighter and see that his hands are clawing the air as if he's reaching for the stick, thumb at the ready, then his arms come down and he subsides. I lean over and hold the lighter up to his face: he's staring ahead with a fixed expression, tears on his cheeks. Doesn't know I'm here. I wonder if I should push him down flat on the bed, but decide he's better left as he is.

We flew four sorties yesterday. I haven't felt that tired since I got concussed. I had a nap at six, but it didn't do the trick and I woke up with a headache, very restless. I wandered about outside for a bit. Didn't want to go to the mess, so I decided on a walk. Didn't fancy going anywhere particular, but I

174

knew that finding a brunette would take the edge off it, at least. By the time I'd got across the airfield there was no doubt in my mind: London again. The same feeling that comes with the scramble klaxon: there is nothing else.

I heard someone calling me as I was walking through the wood, but took no notice. Bloody Gervase. He wanted to know where I was going. I told him to piss off but he wouldn't, just kept trotting alongside asking stupid questions. I got to the road, saw an army lorry and flagged it down, but when I turned to say goodbye he was climbing in behind me, and I could hardly pitch him back out again.

All the same, I knew I was going to go through with it. I closed my eyes and pretended to be asleep to stop him talking. I felt better, knowing I was on my way.

They dropped us near a tube station—east, somewhere. Gervase said to me, 'Where are we going?'

I said, 'I'm going into town. I don't know where you're going.'

'I'm coming with you.'

Nothing I could do. He clung to me like a limpet. The thing I'd wanted, first, to be by myself in a crowd of people, I couldn't have, because he was there. I tried to stay calm in the train and was able to forget he was there for a while, then he'd say something, and the irritation would begin all over again. We got off the train at Piccadilly. Soho was more lively than last time. Raids some way off, thank God, although I did laugh when I saw one chap running down the street holding a dustbin lid over his head.

I wanted to enjoy myself, but Gervase was still trailing after me like a lamb that's lost its mother. I said, 'Will you fuck off?' but he trailed me into a pub in Greek Street and insisted on buying half a pint for both of us. When we'd finished, I told him to go and find himself a girl. He turned the colour of a tomato, which annoyed me even more. I said, 'What's the matter with you? Is it a disease or something? There's things I need to do, and I don't want you along.' He was turning the whole thing into a farce.

There were a few likely-looking brown-haired women in the pub, and a couple came up to us, but I couldn't talk to them with him hanging about and watching me, and this irritated me even more, because time was getting on. I told Gervase I'd meet him later, and we arranged it, but he still wouldn't let me alone. Then a dirty-looking man who said he was a poet started pestering us for money. Gervase gave him half a crown, and I slipped off while they were talking.

I didn't have to go far, just a couple of streets before I saw a torch flashing. A woman stepped towards me and asked me if I'd like to go home with her.

I said, 'I want to see you, first.' When she shone the torch at her face I saw the hair was brown. The face and body looked all right as far as I could tell, but I wasn't concerned with that.

She said, 'Like me, do you?'

'I like your hair.'

She said, 'Well, it'll be a pound and ten shillings.'

I followed her down the street, and when we got up to the room and I could see her properly, she looked better than the blonde one, not so thin.

When she asked my name, I told her it was Gervase. I handed over the money and sat in an armchair while she took her clothes off. She didn't mind me looking, not like the other one, but she had a bored expression on her face as if I didn't interest her much. She knelt down and unbuttoned my flies and started to touch me but it wasn't any good with her looking like that, so I said, 'Did you hear about the girl who was murdered near here?'

She carried on, not listening properly, and that made me angry because I wanted her to pay attention, so I said, 'I heard she had a poker stuck up her, inside.'

That brought the head up, all right. 'What?'

'That blonde girl. Right round here, it was.'

'How do you know?' Now she was listening, all right. I could see the eyes widening, beginning to look more how I wanted.

'She was strangled, that's what I read, but I'd say the poker killed her. That's what did it.'

She stood up, then. 'How do you know about that?'

'I told you, it was in the paper. You ought to be more careful. You don't know who you might meet out there. It could be anyone.'

She turned away and went to the other armchair where she'd put her clothes and I saw she was reaching for something—underwear. I said, 'What are you doing?' I stood up, and she started backing away, saying, 'I don't like that sort of talk.' She put on her brassiere and a vest, then she got hold of her handbag from the mantelpiece, and held some money out to me, saying, 'I'm sorry, dear, but you'll have to go. You're making me uncomfortable.'

I said, 'Come on, don't be silly, I was making

177

conversation, that's all. I'll give you another ten shillings, if you like.'

She sniffed and said, 'Funny sort of conversation,' but she took the extra money and put it all back in the bag.

She went and sat on the edge of the bed and fumbled around in her handbag, then pulled out a French letter and held it out to me, but I could see the bored look was on her face again, so I took my trousers off and my shirt because I didn't want them messed up, and put them on the chair on top of her clothes. Then I picked up one of her stockings. She said, 'Here, you be careful with that!'

I told her to lie down, but she wouldn't, just kept telling me to let go of the stocking and saying they cost money and a lot of other stuff like that, and then she jumped up and tried to snatch it from me. That was the last straw—I could see she was going to spoil everything. She was stronger than the other one; she kept pulling at the stocking and shouting, and I had to make her shut up so I hit her, hard, on the face, and she fell back on the bed and twisted onto her side with her hands up, trying to protect herself, but I got on top of her and pulled her head round facing me. The eyes were wide, but not how I wanted. She was angry, and even though I was holding her down she looked at me as if she despised me and did not understand. I couldn't look at her, so I shut my eyes and she said, 'Get out,' and her voice was low and flat, as if she was talking to some ordinary man and she wasn't scared, and she was ruining it all, and then I thought I'd have to leave and I must have relaxed my grip because I felt her head jerk up and something wet landed on my face—spit—and then I was furious she could do that and speak to me like that, and she was thrashing and screeching and clawing at my arms—and it was Mathy I heard, not her, but Mathy, and I tried to block it out. I shouted 'You stupid bitch, it wasn't in the paper,' and I punched her to make her quiet, and she was quiet after that, and still.

I knew what I was going to do, so I went into the kitchen for a knife and then I saw an instrument on the chair, like tongs, metal tongs. They looked good so I rubbed myself with them and as I did I remembered how I'd seen a woman—must have been Mother—use them to make waves in her hair, so I took them back to the bed as well. It wasn't a pretty sight. She was lying on her back with her eyes shut and blood coming from the nose. I wanted to give her face a better appearance, and wished I'd brought the compact from the other one, which had powder, but I saw the handbag where she'd dropped it by the bed so I opened it and looked for some cosmetics. There wasn't powder, only lipstick and a funny little blue bag that I put in my trouser pocket for later. Then I took hold of the lipstick and got on top of her and started to smear it on the mouth. I wanted a lot, but it was hard to get it in the right place, and she started moaning and moving her head, and then it got on her chin and round the mouth, and the blood from her nose was mixed up in it, and it looked a mess.

It took me by surprise when her eyes suddenly opened again and her mouth must have opened, too, because it jogged my hand so the lipstick clicked against her teeth. I could see a red ridge

179

where the tip was squashed against them. Then a scream came up out of her mouth and then another, and I couldn't bear the sound of it, or the look, the open mouth and teeth; I had to stop it so I jammed the whole lipstick into her mouth and put my hands over it, and I was pressing down hard and she was bucking and retching. I got my knee on one arm, pinning it down, but the other was loose and flailing, trying to reach my face, and I had to keep jerking my head out of the way. I could feel her face bulge underneath my hands and her body wracking and heaving underneath me, the chin slick with vomit where it was coming out between my fingers, making my hands slip. I pressed down as hard as I could, but she kept on jolting and thrashing underneath me and all the chords in her neck were taut, the veins almost bursting at the temples and blood was pounding into her face and the eyes turned pink and wet and the whites burst into bloody threads. Her loose arm flapped weakly and fell back on the bed, her legs stopped jerking and I let go.

I was trembling from the effort but there wasn't much time and I wanted to push up the brassiere and vest, but I couldn't with her lying down like that. So I put my hands under her armpits and hitched her into a sitting position, but I didn't like the look of that, the face was spoiling it, so I pushed her down again. The vomit was sticky between my fingers so I wiped my hands on the vest where it was bunched at the top. Her face was too ugly, so I put a pillow over it and then I was ready to do what I wanted.

I don't remember much about getting out of the place afterwards. I know I washed myself at the sink and wiped myself with something I picked up from a chair, then got dressed and came away as fast as I could. As soon as I'd finished, I was desperate to get back to the base, same as the other time. Odd, that: before, I can't wait to get away to do it, and afterwards I can't wait to be back again. Gervase was waiting for me where we'd arranged. Had to do a fair bit of walking—more than last time—but we got a couple of lifts that took us most of the way. Gervase had stopped talking, thank God. Probably been with a whore and felt ashamed of it—his sort always do. He fell asleep in the lorry, but I was too excited. I'd got the stocking in my pocket, and the little blue case, and I wanted to take them out and look at them, but I couldn't in case he woke up and started asking questions.

I got back to the room about ten minutes ago and found Ginger sitting up like that. I still wanted the chance to go over it all properly, but I couldn't enjoy myself with those eyes gleaming at me, so I came back outside. No one was about, and it was very dark and quiet.

I wound the stocking round my hand so it was stretched across my knuckles, and after that it was like re-running a film in my head, faster and faster, especially the end part, the knife and the curling irons I used to finish, and afterwards, when I'd pulled the bedclothes over it and gone across to the big mirror on the wall and stood looking into it so I could see just the reflection of the torso—breasts—the curve with the pillow above, over the face—then I shut my eyes as I had before and there were flashes of the girl in the alley, her blank face behind the stocking, the mouth an O like—that—more—yes—more—yesyesyes—*yes* . . .

181

Funny, remembering it just then, it seemed more real than it did while I was doing it. The excitement's more afterwards; at the time, it's just reflex actions, and the concentration on getting it done. Like debriefing, with everyone jabbering away nineteen to the dozen, shouting and laughing—and then they say we don't remember it right, because if we did the Luftwaffe wouldn't have a single kite left by now.

It was good looking into the big mirror, too. Better than that small compact thing. I didn't like having to hit her. Oh, well. I suppose I'd better go back inside and get to bed. Damn tired.

FRIDAY 27TH SEPTEMBER

Rene

Sweet of Hitler to let me have a decent sleep last night. I decided to risk my own bed for once, and slept right through till nearly eleven, so I must have needed it. The sunshine was lovely when I took down the blackout. There are great cracks across the panes, mind you, after last week . . . Ought to be grateful they're still there, really.

I went down for cigarettes about midday. Asked Mr Mitten if he'd seen Lily because I wanted to tell her about the man last night saying 'Poor old Henry', but he said no. Bridget was in the café, but she hadn't seen Lily, either. I did the shopping and found a nice piece of fish, so I went home and cooked that for tea and tidied up a bit . . . artificial silk flowers I've got, lovely, but they take a lot of

182

dusting, especially when you get all this grit blowing in through the window after the bombing. Nothing feels clean any more.

I'd got an appointment with one of my regular men-friends at half past five, so I got myself ready, then after that I went out and I thought, well, I'm bound to see Lily now, but when I got to my patch I looked round the corner for her and she still wasn't there, so I thought, maybe she's with a regular, too, or she's gone to the cinema, because we do that sometimes, in the afternoon. We always choose romantic films, and if we like something, we'll see it three or four times. We like a good cry. She's crazy about Robert Taylor, got his picture on a cigarette card in her handbag. She even made this little case for it, like an envelope, out of a piece of blue felt, so it won't get damaged. Calls it her lucky charm. No one knows about it except me, not even Ted.

I was standing there thinking about that when I hear someone shouting 'Rene! Rene!' and Kathleen comes haring round the corner with Susie behind her, both of them in a rare old state.

Kathleen said, 'Oh, it's terrible—it's Lily, he's killed her, last night—'

'What?'

'Lily, she's—'

'She's *dead*?'

'Yes, last night, she—'

'Are you sure?'

'She was killed, Rene. That's what I'm trying to tell you. Murdered.'

'*Murdered?* She can't . . . I only saw her . . .' I was too shocked to think straight, and Kathleen and Susie were both talking nineteen to the dozen.

'Wait . . . You mean, like Edie?'

Kathleen said, 'It was her ponce.'

'Ted?'

'Yes, if that's his name. He's been arrested.'

'How do you know?'

'Mollie heard it from French Marie. She's got a friend goes in the Black Horse, and she said Lily's ponce came in and told everyone he'd done for her. Covered in blood, he was.'

'Ted was?'

'Yes, I told you. Marie's friend said he had Lily's purse with him, full of money, and he just threw it down on the bar and said he was going to buy everyone a drink, and then he said he'd killed her. Everyone heard it. Imagine!'

I was that stunned, I couldn't really take in what they were saying, not straight away. Then they said they were going to find Bridget, and went tearing off again, and I just stood there in a daze. I could hear what they'd said in my head, over and over, about Ted killing Lily, but it had all happened so quick I couldn't really believe it. I kept thinking, I'll snap out of it in a minute, and everything will be like before.

It's one of those things where one minute you're going about your business, and the next: boom! And you don't know where you are. I wandered off up the road but I barely noticed where I was going until I found myself in Covent Garden at the end of Dora's street. I knew Tommy'd be having his tea, and I wanted to see him, but I could feel myself welling up inside and I thought it might upset him if he saw me like that. I must have stood there five minutes, and I don't know why, but I had the urge, stronger than I've ever known it, to go and put my arms round him and say, 'She's not your mother,

I'm your mother.' The longing was so fierce it was nearly pulling me down the street, but I stayed where I was. It would only confuse him, and as for Dora . . . Well, it wouldn't be fair. Tommy's hers now, and that's how it should be.

I knew all that, but it didn't stop me wanting to do it, or stop the pain I was feeling in my heart. I just stood there and looked up at the flats for a while, and then I saw there were people coming out, so I came away.

I didn't know what to do. I didn't want to talk to anybody, apart from Tommy, but I didn't want to go home and be on my own, either. I suddenly found myself thinking, I know, I'll go and see Lily. Quite matter of fact, I'll go and see Lily, and I actually got about ten yards down the road before I realised what I was doing, and I thought: I'll never see Lily again. The jolt of it was like running up against a lamppost in the blackout, but more, because it's your emotions, not your face. One minute Lily and I were sitting there having a drink and a chat, and the next minute, she's gone and that's it. The end.

I thought maybe she and Ted might have had a fight, because Lily could be quite sharp on occasion, and if he'd come home drunk . . . well, he must have been if he did it and went straight off to the pub and told them, mustn't he? Or perhaps Lily wanted to take up with another man and he was jealous. She never said, but then you don't, always, not with something like that.

In the end I thought perhaps I should go home. I couldn't face working, and there was no sense in moping about the street. Then it struck me that I might go by the warden's post and see if Harry was there. I don't know why I thought of him, except that I just wanted a bit of comfort, and he'd been so nice.

When I got to the post he wasn't there, but one of the others told me he'd be back soon, so I sat down and waited. When he came in he had a big smile, seeing it was me, then he took another look and said, 'What's happened?'

'Oh, Harry, I'm sorry to bother you, but—'

'No bother. And no sorry, either. Just forget all that and tell me what's up.'

'It's Lily. My friend Lily. She's been killed.'

'When?'

'Last night. I only found out just now.'

'Come on. You don't want to talk about this here. Upsy-daisy.'

He gave me his arm, like before, and we went out and down the road. After a while, I said to him, 'Where are we going?'

'My flat. It's just across here. Don't worry, no funny business.'

'It's all right, Harry, I trust you.'

'Now you do—but you weren't so sure when we first met, were you?'

'No. I'm sorry I thought you—'

'Hey! Stop saying you're sorry. I was only pulling your leg. Now then, it's just up here.'

It was one of the old LCC flats in Bedfordbury, a big, grey tenement block in a yard with wash-houses and a surface shelter. We climbed the stairs—Harry's on the top floor. He opened the front door and we stepped straight into his living room. The first thing I saw was a great big old-fashioned range, all polished up smart with black lead. I didn't take in much, except how tidy it was.

No ornaments, but a nice rag rug in front of the sofa, and a wireless on a wooden table.

In spite of Harry being so kind to me, it felt like a bad dream. He sat me down on the sofa and I tried to tell him about Lily—well, as much as I knew—but it came out all jumbled up and nothing seemed to make sense at all. I remember saying, halfway through, that perhaps I'd just imagined it or it was a horrible joke, because it didn't seem real, somehow, but then it suddenly came back to me like a slap in the face that it was real, and Ted had killed her, and I couldn't help it, I started to cry.

I was sort of perching near the edge of the sofa, and he was next to me, and he moved up so our knees were touching. Then he took my hand and held it. I only cried a little bit—not enough to mess up my face because I hardly ever do, except at the pictures. I felt dreadful about it, but when I apologised, he said, 'You're not allowed to say sorry, remember? Come here.' And he put his arm round me.

'How could he do it, Harry? Lily was good, she looked after him, and he just—'

'Sssh . . .'

'How could he?'

Harry patted my hand. 'I don't know. Sometimes people just lose their temper, or . . . I really don't know. It's dangerous, Rene. A dangerous world.'

'I never liked him, Harry. That's why I feel so bad. He knew I didn't—used to keep well clear of me. But I never said anything to Lily, because . . . well, you don't interfere, do you? And she'd never said anything to me about any trouble, not more than the usual, so . . . but I should have

187

warned her.'

Harry said, 'Warned her about what? You didn't think he was going to kill her, did you?'

'No, nothing like that, I just didn't like him.'

'Well then. You can't warn somebody about something if you've no idea it's going to happen, can you?'

I shook my head. 'It must have been an accident. Ted must have been drunk—wouldn't have been the first time. It's just, coming after that horrible business with Edie . . .'

'Like I said, Rene, it's a dangerous world.'

'Lily thought she was keeping herself safe living with Ted, and look what happened.'

Harry got up. 'I thought you said you trusted me. Look, Rene, I know what you're thinking, and I'll say it again. I'm not interested in anything like that. I'm worried about you, that's all. We can be friends, can't we?'

'Yes . . . yes, of course we can, Harry. I'd like that.'

Then he said he'd make us a cup of tea, so he went out with the kettle. He's not got his own tap like I have; there's a sink and lav outside he shares with the neighbours. I sat and touched up my powder and that made me feel a bit better, so I took a look round. I could just see into the other room because the door was a little bit open, and there was some sort of divan affair for a bed and a shelf with books on it. Quite a lot of them, by the look of it. I was just wondering if I could get up and see what they were—not go into the room, just stand in the doorway and look from there—when I heard this little rustly noise coming from beside the sofa, so I look down and there's this cardboard box

188

like a shoe box, with holes punched in the top. I was bending over it when Harry came back and said, 'Shall I show you?'

'It's not a spider in there, is it?'

'No. Look. You don't have to stand back, it's not going to bite you.' He picked up the box and took the top off, and at first all I could see was cotton wool, but then Harry pulled some of it away and there, right in the middle, was a little baby bird. It must have been very young, because it was all naked and folded up, but its eyes were open. 'I found it in the street. Must have fallen out of a nest.'

'It's sweet. Are you going to keep it as a pet?'

Harry shook his head. 'It can fly away when it's strong enough. Been feeding it with a fountain-pen filler. Have to get it some worms, soon.'

'Ooh, I don't fancy that much. But it's so kind, looking after it like that. Most people wouldn't bother.'

Harry looked embarrassed. 'I don't know why I did it, really. I just thought it deserved a chance.'

'Everyone deserves that.'

We stood there for a moment, looking at this tiny thing, and then Harry said, 'Now, I've got to get back to the post, but first I'm going to take you home.'

When we got to my door, he said, 'Look, I know it's none of my business, but I don't think you should go out tonight.'

'Don't worry, I'm stopping at home. I'm all in.'

'I'll be dropping by the shelter, later. See how you're getting on.'

'Thanks. For the tea and . . . everything.'

I went in and lay down on my bed, but I couldn't

189

settle. Tried to listen to the wireless but they might as well have been talking Japanese for all I understood of it. I kept thinking how I'd have to go back out there tomorrow or there wouldn't be the money for Tommy, or the rent, or anything, but each time I tried to imagine myself talking to the men and bringing them back and all of it, I had this terrible panic come over me, like someone had put a black hood over my face so I couldn't breathe, and my chest got tight. I tried to look at it coldly, I kept telling myself it's just a business like any other, but I felt sick thinking about Lily and I didn't want to be on my own—I hadn't heard the warning but I thought, there's no point to staying here, I'll get down to the shelter now and make myself comfortable.

I took a magazine with me, but I couldn't get interested in it. I sat and watched the people come into the shelter with their blankets and bits and pieces, one pale face after another, all dog-tired, and I thought, it's so hard, and everyone's cold and dirty and frightened, but they're still hanging on like grim death—we all are—and for what? What's the *point*? Why does anyone go on with it? I thought, I bet there's a load of people in Germany right now, all doing the same as us, and they're thinking the exact same thing, except they'd be thinking it in German, not English. You struggle on and you get bombed or you end up like Lily. Oh, I had the blues all right.

Even little Tommy, when I thought of him— well, that usually cheers me up no end, but I thought, Dora's his mum, and she and Joe would manage somehow if anything happened to me, and I suddenly imagined him as a grown man, saying,

'Oh, Aunt Rene, I don't really remember her, she died when I was a kid, and I never realised till years later that she was on the streets . . .' and that would be that. And then remembering that moment when the midwife put him into my arms that first time and I held him, and what it felt like . . . I wasn't going into one of those places for unmarried mothers where they treat you like dirt and work you half to death, not likely, so Dora said I could have the baby at their flat and she'd tell the midwife I was a widow, which she did. But all the way through, she kept coming to the bedroom door and saying, 'Keep the noise down or we'll have the neighbours up,' and I did my best, but it took a long time and the pain was terrible. I thought I'd never get through it. But then when it was over and the midwife gave him to me, and I sat there holding this little thing in a shawl and I thought, now I know what it's all about: love. So much love—overwhelming. But then you forget that, and life goes on, and you don't really know the reason for any of it. So that made it worse, getting sentimental like that, and then the raid started and I thought, I might as well just walk out into the middle of this and have done with it.

I was thinking about it when I heard a noise in front of me, someone clearing their throat, and I looked up and the first thing I saw was Mrs McIver's alarm clock hanging in front of my nose, and her little birdy hand clutching it like a claw. Do you know what my first thought was? Blimey, it's the grim reaper. Like the pictures I've seen in church, except this was a she not a he and it was an alarm clock instead of an hour-glass, and Death's wearing a black hood, not a battered old hat that

191

would disgrace a seaside donkey. Of course, now I say it, it doesn't sound anything like, but that's what I thought at the time.

'Hello, dear.' I was astonished because she'd never spoken to me before, ever. 'I'm sorry about your friend.' I said it was nice of her to say so, and she said, 'It's a terrible business.' Then she pulled this packet out of her bag, wrapped in newspaper, and said, 'Here you are,' and put it down on my lap. 'Go on, open it.' So I unfold the paper, and blow me if it isn't a lamb chop.

I said, 'I can't take this, it's half your meat ration.'

'You have it. Keep your strength up.'

'It's very kind—'

'Oh, don't thank me, dear, it isn't much. You enjoy it. Now then, I've got a message from Harry. He says to tell you he's been called away but he'll be coming round as soon as he can.' Then she went off to her place, just as usual, pulled her pencil out of her hat, licked the end, and got stuck into her crossword.

You could have knocked me down with a feather, and I wasn't the only one. I could see all the old girls' faces, the whole row—I had the parcel with the chop in my lap and they never once took their eyes off it. Like being watched by a lot of hawks. In the end I felt so uncomfortable that I picked it up and shoved it into my handbag. I swear I heard a whimper when I snapped it shut.

I must have dozed off some time after that, because a loud noise woke me up with a jerk, and I saw Harry was there, dealing with a couple of troublemakers—drunks, I think. Seeing as he was occupied, I took the chance to powder my nose and

192

give my hair a bit of a pat, and when he'd sorted out the nuisance he came over and sat down by me. That gave the old girls more to gawp at because they'd all woken up with the racket, except for Ale Mary who was snoring fit to beat the band. I was starting to feel like an animal in a zoo, so I said, 'Would you mind if we went outside? I could do with stretching my legs.'

'Why not? It's been pretty quiet for a while.'

He walked me round to the mobile canteen and got us both mugs of tea. 'It was nice of you to come by, Harry.'

'I said I would, remember? How are you feeling?'

'Oh, I just needed to get away from that lot. Mind you, though . . .' I told him about Mrs McIver and the chop and I opened my handbag to show him. 'Can't let it out of my sight for a minute. But it just shows you, you can't tell what people will do, can you?'

'Oh, she's a good sort,' said Harry. 'She was friends with my mum, way back. Anyone in trouble, she'd be straight round there.'

'With her alarm clock?'

'No, but she had this set of Apostle spoons. Very fancy. Always had them in her bag, and when she came to our house she'd take them out and put them on the table and give them a little polish, and they'd sit there till it was time for her to go home. Never went anywhere without them, not even the shops. She was worried they'd get stolen. First night I saw her in the shelter, I said, "Got your spoons?" and she was ever so flustered, telling me she'd never had any spoons worth the name and she didn't know what I was talking about, and the

193

next day she came by the wardens' shelter and gave me a right ticking off about how I wasn't to mention them because you don't know who's listening.'

'You're having me on!'

Harry shook his head. 'Honestly. But she's right really, because we have had robberies—poor old girl last week, over in Marylebone, she lost all her savings. Had it in her bag and someone walked off with it, so you be careful, won't you? Now, I'd better get off to the post, but I'll walk you back.'

On the way, he told me he'd been to the Black Horse on the excuse of checking the blackout, but they didn't know anything more than I'd told him, except that there were some swearing blind they'd heard Ted tell everyone he'd done away with Lily, and others saying he hadn't said anything of the sort, and nobody knew what to think. But he did tell me that it was Walt, the barman, who'd gone back with Ted and called the police.

'Was he there?'

'No. The police might want to talk to you, Rene.'

'Me? Why?'

'Well, you must have been one of the last people to see her—I mean, that they know about.'

'But if they know it's Ted that's done it, why do they need to bother with me? I can't tell them anything.'

'I'm not saying they will, just that they might, that's all.'

I said, 'I'll never go in the Black Horse again. I couldn't bear it—the idea of Ted standing there, covered in blood, saying he'd killed Lily . . . it's horrible. I honestly don't think I could bring myself to go through the door.'

Harry said, 'I don't think . . . well, nobody said anything about him being covered in blood, and it isn't something you'd forget in a hurry.'

'Well, that's what I heard. They might have been making more of it, but even if it was just a bit of blood, it's still horrible. And they still don't know what happened to Edie. Not that they'll care. They're only bothering with this because Ted was caught red-handed, and that makes it easy for them.'

Harry said, 'Look, Rene. Why don't you come up and have a drink with me, tomorrow? We don't have to go near a pub if you don't want to. We can go to a café.'

'That'd be nice. Shall I come to the post?'

'No, come to my flat. In the afternoon. I'll have a bit of time then. We can have a cup of tea.'

When we were at the shelter, he said, 'Now, you will stay here till the All-Clear, won't you?'

'Oh, don't worry. I'm not going anywhere tonight.'

'Good. You look after yourself, and I'll see you tomorrow. And remember . . .' he put his finger to his lips, 'don't breathe a word about those spoons.'

Despite Lily and everything else, I couldn't help laughing.

SATURDAY 28TH SEPTEMBER

Jim

No chance of going anywhere in this—you can't even see across the airfield. Shame, I'm in a perfect mood to go up and get stuck in. Got stuck into bacon and eggs, instead. Gervase is at the end of the table, pecking at his plate. He looked up and saw me, blushed like fury, then ducked his head again. Ginger wandered in and pulled up a chair. 'You wouldn't be hungry, by any chance?'

'Starving. Get some more coffee, would you?'

He tilted back his chair and signalled a waitress. 'By the way,' he said, 'Where did you get to on Thursday night?'

I shrugged. 'Went for a walk.'

'Bloody long walk. Got a popsy tucked away somewhere?'

I winked. It was enough. Gervase could hear all of it, but I knew he wouldn't say anything. He didn't even look up.

'What about you?' I asked Ginger.

'Popsy.'

'Who's the lucky girl?'

'From the village. Name's Mona. Actually, it wasn't much fun. She was a bit cut up.'

'Why? What did you do to her?'

'Oh, it wasn't me. It's this friend of hers. Got herself attacked a couple of weeks ago, and now she won't leave the house. Mona wouldn't stop talking about it. God knows why—I don't know what she expects me to do.'

'Who attacked her?'

'Some man. Pilot, Mona says.'

'What, from here?'

'Nowhere else, is there?'

'Did he hurt her?'

'Not badly, I don't think. More of a scare than anything.'

'Really? What did he do?'

196

'Not really sure.' Ginger looked uncomfortable.

It was queer. When Ginger said it was a pilot, I thought: *It must have been me*. I knew it had happened, but it hadn't really registered. I couldn't remember what I'd done, or anything. Not details. I'd chalked it up as a failure, and that was that.

I felt excited. I wanted Ginger to talk about it, to know how much the girl had told his girl, but also to have the pleasure of hearing about it, knowing I'd done it, even if it hadn't gone according to plan. 'Well, he might have throttled her, or hit her, or—'

'I don't know. Let's leave it, shall we? I had a bellyful of it last night.'

'But what did he do?'

'Oh, you know . . .' Ginger rolled his eyes. 'Wanted to have his way with her.'

'Did he get it?'

'Not by the sound of it. Megan—'

'Is that her name—Megan?'

'Yes. She told Mona he tried to kill her.'

'Why would he want to do that?'

'Exactly. That's what I said—doesn't make sense. She probably made the whole thing up.'

'Sounds like it.'

'Was she a bit tipsy at the time?'

'Oh, probably.'

'Well, it'll teach her to be more careful in future.'

'Look, I don't know.' Ginger shrugged. 'What I do know is that Mona's worried sick, and I was bored sick, listening to it.'

'So are we.' Davy, sitting backwards on his chair, flicked a spoonful of porridge at him.

'Hey! Cut it out!'

Davy flicked another spoonful. 'Right on target! I knew it was good for *something*.'

197

'Piss off, Dunlop.' Ginger snatched a napkin and mopped at his jacket.

I wondered if Ginger's girl was the one in the car, with the lipstick. I hope it was—if it put the wind up her, all the better. She won't be so cocky any more, will she?

I said, 'I was reading about an attack where a man strangled a woman, in London. I think I've still got it, somewhere.' It was strange. I'm not sure if I meant to say that, but I wanted the conversation to continue, to hear more about Ginger's girl, and the other one, Megan, and I wanted to see Ginger's reaction to my piece of newspaper.

He stopped wiping his jacket, and looked up. 'Don't fancy that much.' A third spoonful of porridge hit his cap. Davy whooped, then slipped off his chair and ducked under the table as Ginger picked up the milk jug and stormed after him.

I decided I'd try and show it to him later. I swung my feet up on his chair, out of the way, and reached for my cigarette case. Wrong pocket—the only thing in there was a scrap of material. When I pulled it out, I could see that it was a very small envelope, made of blue material, with something inside it. It felt like paper. A cigarette card. Robert Taylor. I turned it over—no message on the back, just the usual business. For a moment, I wondered why someone should have slipped it into my pocket, but then I remembered: I had it from the brunette. Who knows, it might be lucky.

A heavy body rolled against the legs of my chair, and then a hand appeared over the side of the table and pitched the now empty milk jug towards me. I managed to duck in time and it sailed over my head and smashed against the wall. Davy's head emerged, on a level with an empty plate— 'Howzat?' and immediately disappeared.

I had another look at the cigarette card. *Robert Taylor* . . . girls like film stars. I thought that if I had a girl, like Ginger, I could give her this—might be rather funny, knowing where I got it. I could make up some story . . . Oh, yes, that sister of mine who died, I could say it was hers. What Mathy said about his sister in the car crash, that'd do. And I've got that photograph, as well. Better slip that in my pocket, next time I go to London. I'll have a look round for something that looks the part—shouldn't be too difficult. What was it that astrologer said in the paper the other day? *Do not hesitate to try something new.* Well, that's what I'm doing. Lots of new things, in fact.

My cigarette case was in the other pocket, empty. No idea I'd smoked so many. I glanced down towards Gervase, but he'd gone. Davy and Ginger were still pummelling each other under the table, but I could see Corky at the other end of the room, with the paper.

'Corky? Corky!'

He didn't answer, so I went and stood in front of him. 'Corky!'

He jumped. 'Oh, sorry. Gone a bit deaf.'

Davy emerged from under the table, with Ginger in an arm-lock. 'Try blowing your nose.'

'What?'

Davy pointed at him, then reached down and pinched Ginger's nose. Ginger blew. 'Bloody hell!' Davy let go of him and he ran out of the room.

'I've tried that,' said Corky. 'Doesn't make any difference.'

'Well, what do you expect?' grumbled Davy, wiping his hands on his trousers. 'Up and down like a whore's drawers all week. Have you tried poking them?' He put his finger in his own ear to demonstrate, and wiggled it about.

'That doesn't work, either.'

Ginger put his head round the door, gave Davy a quick burst with a soda siphon, and made a run for it. Davy dashed off in pursuit. I looked round the room to make sure there was no one else there, then pulled up a chair beside Corky. 'I killed a girl last night,' I said, casually. 'I can recommend it. Quite as much fun as killing Germans. No flying, of course, but it has its compensations. You should try it.'

Corky stared at me. 'Riveting. At least, it would be if I'd heard a bloody word of it. Now bugger off.' He went back to his newspaper.

I wandered back to my room and lay down on the bed, turning the cigarette card over and over between my fingers, thinking. It shouldn't be too difficult to find a girl. Might even kill two birds with one stone, ha, ha. I'm sure I caught sight of a redhead in that pub on Thursday . . . she'd do all right. Perhaps they're not so thin on the ground as I thought.

Ginger banged into the room, cursing and looking as if he'd been dunked in a horse-trough. 'Pass me that towel, will you?'

'I saw something in the paper, a woman attacked—'

'What?'

'A woman. Attacked. What you said, before. I've got it, here.'

Ginger twitched the paper out of my hand and

200

glanced at it. 'Bit morbid, isn't it?' He threw it down on the bed, followed by his wet shirt. 'Have to wear this, I suppose.' He picked up his pyjama jacket and put it on. 'Bloody Davy.'

I leaned over and retrieved the newspaper cutting. It was damp, but you could see the type well enough. 'Did you read it?'

Ginger nodded. 'Chap must be cracked. Don't know why you're hanging round in here, Goldilocks—you're on duty. Yellow section's at available.'

'What, in this?'

'It's clearing.' He nodded in the direction of the window. 'Look.'

He left, and I lay down on the bed again and stared at the newspaper cutting. I suppose the brunette will be in there soon. Don't know why I showed it to Ginger. Don't really know *why* anything, any more.

No point thinking about it, anyway.

WEDNESDAY 2ND OCTOBER

Rene

I had to go round to Dora's on the Saturday morning to give her some money for Tommy, and I thought I'd better warn her that there mightn't be much coming in for the next couple of weeks. I wasn't going to go into details, because . . . well, partly because I didn't have the energy for it, and partly because she knows what I do, but she doesn't like it and she certainly doesn't want to hear about

201

it. If I don't bring up the subject, she can pretend I get the money from a respectable job, and that keeps her happy. Anyway, she'd only worry for me if I told her, and I couldn't see the sense in that.

First thing I noticed when I got there, Dora's eyes were all red, so I said, 'I can see you didn't get a lot of sleep last night.'

'Oh, you know what it's like. I'll be all right when I've had a cup of tea.' So we did that, and I explained about the money. I said I'd been feeling a bit poorly—nothing serious, but I wasn't up to doing much, and she looked a bit down at that, so I was thinking, what can I do to cheer her up? Then I was looking in my handbag for Tommy's sweets—I always bring some for him—and I suddenly realised I'd never taken out that blessed chop Mrs McIver gave me, so I said, 'Joe's not coming back for his dinner, is he?' because I wanted her to have it and I knew she'd only give it to him if he was there.

'Oh, no,' she said, 'he's working.'

'Good.' Then I held up the parcel with the chop and I said, 'Now, I've only got the one, but it's a little treat for you.'

So she opened up the newspaper, and the minute she saw what it was, she burst into tears. Dora's not one for crying, so I didn't know what to make of it. She kept saying, 'Oh, Rene, you're so kind, that's so kind, you shouldn't,' on and on like that, all teary, so I said, 'There's no need for all that; it's only a bit of meat, not the crown jewels.'

'Oh,' she said, 'It's not that. Well, it is, but it's not—and, and, I don't know what it is—oh, I'm lying, I do know—but I don't know what to do, I really don't.' And she sat there, all red in the face

202

and crying, shoulders heaving, the lot. I waited till she'd pulled herself together a bit, then I said, 'What's the matter?'

'It's Joe.'

'He's not been called up, has he?' That was the only thing I could think of, but I thought it couldn't be right because Joe was in the navy when they married, but then he got this tubercular knee, and I was pretty sure they wouldn't have him again, because of that. In any case, they haven't started taking the older ones yet.

'No, nothing like that. I don't like to speak badly of him, Rene, he's a good man, really, but I don't know how I'm going to manage . . .' and off she went again, sobbing.

I said, 'What is it? What's he done?'

'It's the housekeeping. He's been doing it for a time, keeping me short, and I haven't liked to complain, but now it's worse, he's keeping everything back that he can and there isn't enough, I can't make it stretch, and then he shouts at me, and I can't sleep for worrying . . .'

'He's doing all right at the dairy, isn't he?'

Dora nodded. 'Well then,' I said, 'Why don't you ask him for more?'

'I've tried. It's hopeless. He just says I've got to manage, and I'm spending too much. If it wasn't for what you give me, I don't know what I'd do—I can't think about anything else, it's always on top of me, and if there's nothing decent on the table he gets so angry, Rene. I tell you, how it's got to, some days, if I had a shilling for the gas I'd put my head in the oven.'

'What, and help that lot up there? Hitler'd love that, wouldn't he, us all gassing ourselves. He'd be

203

tickled pink.'

She gave me a crooked little smile. 'I know it's silly, Rene, but it's the worry of it, always on me, and I'm doing my best, but Joe doesn't see it, he doesn't seem to understand. If I could just have a bit more money . . .'

'He never used to be like that, did he?'

'No. He was always what you'd call careful—you know, putting it by for a rainy day. He used to grumble if I asked him for a bit extra, but not like this. Now he's saying I can't make it stretch because I'm buying things for myself. I said to him, you show me one thing I've bought for myself, because I've never done that, never. I can't remember the last time I had something new—I make it last till it wears out. Look.' She twisted her arm round to show me her elbow, where the cardigan had worn through and she'd darned on top of the darn. She went quiet then, and stared down at the lino. When I looked where she was looking, I saw there was a hole in that, too. Then she said, very quiet, 'He even said . . . he said I ought to ask you for more money.'

That made me see red, because I give her a lot for Tommy, and there's always extra for new clothes and shoes, but I didn't want to take it out on Dora because it wasn't her fault. I said, 'Oh, he thinks I don't give you enough, does he?'

'No, not that, but he said . . . just . . . oh, it doesn't matter.'

'Yes, it does. What did he say?'

'Well, he said you're always buying Tommy presents. He says you must have money to burn.'

'He's my son, Dora. Why shouldn't I buy him presents?'

204

'No reason—it's just what he said, that's all. But it's like I said, Rene, if it wasn't for what you give me, I don't know how I'd keep the food on the table. I've even pawned my coat, don't know when I'll get it back.'

'For crying out loud. What's he doing with the money, anyway?'

'I'll show you.' She got up and went through to the bedroom, and I followed her.

I don't know what I'd expected, but she bent down and lifted up a corner of the counterpane. 'Look.'

It was a funny old wooden box, like a miniature chest of drawers. 'It's all in there.' She opened one of the drawers, and there were all these sixpences and shillings stacked up. 'He's had this for years,' she said. 'He used to keep his papers in it, and I never interfered, but a few years ago I was doing the spring cleaning and I went to move it, only I couldn't, because it was so heavy, so I looked inside, and there was all this. There's notes in there, too, stuck down the back.'

I said, 'Can't you take a bit?'

Dora shook her head. 'He knows exactly how much is in there, right down to the last farthing. He's turned into a miser, Rene. It's dreadful—he won't even come down the shelter no more. He says somebody'll steal the money while he's away. I've said to him, time and time again, how's anybody going to steal it if they don't know it's there, but he won't listen to me. He says what with all this looting you hear about—he's even accused me of telling people, and I've never told a living soul except you, Rene. I told him, if this place gets bombed, fat lot of use it'll be if you get blown to

205

pieces, but he won't listen.'

Well, if it was me, I'd have taken what I needed and had it out with Joe later, but Dora's not like that—probably why she's married and I'm the way I am, now I think about it. I went and got my handbag and tipped out what I had left in my purse, five shillings, and gave her that.

'There. You go straight round the pawn shop and get your coat back, and I'll be round with some more as soon as I can, but you've got to talk to him, Dora.'

'I've tried, but it's hard. He's so tired, what with all this and then having to go to work. He's just exhausted, and he gets so irritated if I ask him anything about money. Bites my head off.'

'I know, but it's the same for everyone.'

'Yes . . . I'll do my best. Oh, Rene, you are a dear. I don't know what I'd do without you, I really don't.' I knew she wouldn't talk to Joe, though. She's too much for keeping the peace, and I can't say anything—that would be interfering, and besides, there's my little Tommy to think of. Walking back, I was thinking, well, I'll just have to give her a bit more, that's all. Which means earning it. Then I thought of Lily again, and that gave me the shivers, all right. Makes me fairly miserable to think about it, I can tell you, but I don't have a choice. Even if I got war work—if they'd have me—I wouldn't earn half as much, and I wouldn't be suited to it, either. But at least I can go out and earn the money, which is more than Dora can.

I'll just have to put the whole business out of my mind, that's all. I've got enough at home to cover the rent and then a bit over so that's me all right for the next few days, at least. Dora's coat isn't a patch on mine—it's not going to cost the whole five bob to get it back, so the rest of that, along with the other money I gave her, ought to see her through the week, even if Joe doesn't. I was surprised, though. He never seemed that sort, but like I always say, you can't tell.

I had a policeman waiting for me when I got back. 'Are you Miss Rene Tate?'

I didn't recognise him—I know most of them round here, but this was quite a young lad. I said, 'You'd better come in,' because I didn't want him hanging about outside the door, upsetting the neighbours.

So we went inside, and he said, 'We'd like to talk to you about Mrs Franks.'

Well, that threw me. 'I don't know any Mrs Franks. You must have come to the wrong place.'

He had a look at his notebook. 'This would be Mrs Lillian Franks.'

'Oh, Lily.'

'You knew her as Lily?'

'I knew her as Lily Gerrity.' Because she used Ted's surname, you see. 'Everyone did. I don't know about any Franks.'

'You're saying you don't know Mr Franks?'

'I told you, I've never heard of him.'

He asked me a lot of questions about when I'd last seen her and where, and did I know Ted and had I seen him in the pub and had I seen him later and was she soliciting and was I soliciting. I was honest with him, but he didn't seem to believe anything I said and we went round and round in circles until I didn't know if I was mad, or he was. By the time he'd gone, I thought, that's it, I've had enough, and I lay down on my bed and the next thing I knew it was the middle of the afternoon and time to pull myself together and get round to Harry's for tea.

I must say, he'd got it very nice, proper cloth on the table and everything. We had a look at the bird; I swear it's bigger already, and soon as he took the lid off the box it had its beak open, ready for grub. Harry said, 'I've been out for worms, this morning.'

'Ooh, don't show me. I can't bear them. Have you fed it?'

'Oh, yes. Breakfast and dinner.'

'You ought to give it a name. Is it a he or a she?'

'I don't know. How do you tell?'

'I don't suppose you can, unless it lays an egg.'

'Well, what about Albert?'

'Albert . . . that's good. I had an Uncle Albert. Talk the hind leg off a donkey, he could. Always had his mouth open.'

'Albert it is, then. Shall I put the lid back, and we can have tea?'

'Go on, then. Goodbye, Albert.' I gave him a little wave, and Harry said, 'You like him, don't you? That's nice.'

'Well, he's sweet. Now, don't go using all your ration, because I bought this,' and I took out a bit of tea I'd twisted up in paper and put in my bag.

'I can't take that. I invited you, remember?'

'But . . . you must let me give you something.' The words were out of my mouth before I realised what I'd said, and I thought, oh, *no*, now I've done it, because Harry was looking me up and down—not in a nasty way, but still I thought, oh, what's he thinking?

He said, 'Tell you what. How about you give me a kiss, instead? Just there.' And he pointed to his

208

cheek. So I got up on tiptoe and gave him a little peck, right where he said.

'There. Now, this stops in here,' and he took my hand with the tea in it and pushed it back into my bag, 'and I'll make the tea.'

When he came back, he'd got this nice little tray with the things on, but I burst straight out laughing, because he'd got a woman's apron on, with a little frill, tied round his waist, and it did look so funny. 'Oh, look at you!'

He was terribly embarrassed, poor man. He'd obviously forgotten he was wearing it, because he banged the tray down very quick on the table, and then he couldn't get it off, he was all thumbs. Of course I was embarrassed, too, for laughing. 'Here, let me help,' and I went round behind him so he couldn't see my face. I was fumbling away with the knot, but I got it in the end, and held it out to him. 'I'm sorry. It wasn't fair of me.'

He said, 'Oh, it doesn't matter. I should have remembered. It's just a habit I've got into, you know, if I'm doing a bit of cooking, or . . .'

Oh, I felt rotten. I could tell he was uncomfortable, because he didn't say anything after that, just busied about with the tea things, so I started talking to cover it up, saying how hard it was with the ration, being on your own, and how prices had gone up and . . . just a lot of nonsense, really. He wasn't answering back, just saying, 'Hmm, hmm,' and I didn't know what to do. It was on the tip of my tongue to tell him about Dora and Joe, just for something to say, but I thought, that's family, you can't talk about that. So then I thought, well, I ought to tell him about the policeman, because that had gone right out of my head for

209

some reason—the embarrassment, I suppose—but just as I was about to say it, Harry said, 'It belonged to my wife.'

'What's that?'

'The apron. If you were wondering.'

'I wasn't . . . I didn't know you were married.'

'She died.'

'Oh, I'm sorry.'

'It's not, I mean . . . To be honest, it was all a bit of a mistake. We never really got on.'

Immediately when he said that, I thought, oh, dear, here we go. 'That's a shame, but I suppose we can't all be lucky.'

Harry said, 'I don't know if I can tell you. It doesn't seem fair, with all your trouble.'

'Well, if you don't want to, but what I'm saying, if it's something you want to tell me, I don't mind.' And I put my hands in my lap and set myself to listen.

'Well, how it was, we didn't really know each other, you see, not well, and it turned out we didn't have the same ideas. About marriage . . . intimacy.'

When I heard that, I thought, well, Rene, you asked for it, now you'll get it.

He cleared his throat and said, 'I don't say it was her fault, because I was young, I didn't have the experience. I'd have liked some children, but she wasn't interested, even for that, and she made it pretty clear, so after a while I thought, there's no point banging your head against a brick wall, and I suppose I just gave up. I don't mean just with what you'd call the physical side, I mean someone to talk to, have a joke—she didn't have much of a sense of humour—and I was evidently all wrong for her, a disappointment, because she thought her family

210

was a bit above mine, you know. So it wasn't in any way a life *together*, if you see what I mean. At one point I did think of leaving, getting a divorce, but then I thought, well, I married her, I've got to stick with it, and there was all her family, and mine. Well, she died from blood poisoning. 1936, it was. Just a scratch from a rosebush. My roses; I had a little patch down there in the yard. It was only a little cut, but it went bad, you see, and they couldn't do anything. I felt terrible about it, Rene, because they were my roses, and really, you could say I'd spent a happier time down there with them than up here with her, and I didn't love her, and I thought it must be my fault. Afterwards, well, I did want to start again, you know, somebody else, but I couldn't. I felt guilty about Doris—that was my wife—because of the roses, and because I didn't love her. When we were in the hospital, and they came and told me she was dead, and it was like a weight off my back. I hated myself for that. I thought, well, she didn't make you happy, but I hadn't made her happy, either, and perhaps I should have tried harder, or if I'd made more money . . . I don't know. But that's what I thought for a long time, and then I began to think, supposing I did get married again, it might be just the same, all wrong, and I'd rather be on my own than have that, so I couldn't do it.'

'But it wasn't your fault, Harry. You stuck by her, didn't you?'

'Yes, I did that. You know, Rene . . . I hope you don't mind if I say this, but how it was, she'd go to bed first, go into the bedroom and she'd shut the door while she was getting undressed and then she'd say, "You can come in now," and I'd go in,

211

and the room was dark and she'd be lying in her bed, and I'd get undressed and get into my bed, quite separate, with the strip of carpet between, and I'd say to her, "Sleep well, goodnight," but she never answered, never said "goodnight". I'd lie there, thinking, tomorrow it'll be another day, just the same, and the day after, on and on, keeping up the appearance of this marriage, and that's my life . . .'

All the time he was talking, he'd been fiddling with his cup and saucer, not looking at me, but then when he did, oh, it went straight to my heart. I felt so sorry for him, and before I knew it, I was crying, because it was so sad, everything was sad, and I didn't know whether I was crying for him or Lily or Dora or the whole bloody world.

'Rene! I'm sorry, I didn't mean to upset you, I'm so sorry.'

'No, Harry, it's not . . . you didn't. I'm just being silly.'

'Look, if you want to go, or . . . Rene, I feel terrible, I honestly didn't mean to upset you—'

'Harry, it's all right. I'll be fine in a minute. Just let me get fixed up, that's all.'

He picked up the apron and retreated into the bedroom while I blew my nose and powdered it. After a few minutes, he put his head round the door. 'All right now?'

'Yes, thanks. Much better.'

'Are you . . . do you want to go now?'

'What, without eating this cake? Not likely! Don't know when I last saw a Victoria sponge. How did you get it?'

'I made it.'

'You *made* it? But how did you get the . . . I

mean, that's your whole sugar ration.'

'Not quite.' Harry tapped the side of his nose. 'Ways and means, you know.'

'I won't ask. It's perfect. Much better than I could do.'

Harry blushed.

'There I go, embarrassing you again. I don't mean to. But you shouldn't think badly of yourself. You're a good man, Harry. Anyone can make a mistake. Look at me.'

Harry opened his mouth, then shut it again, and I thought, oh, well, in for a penny, and I said, 'There's no point denying I've made mistakes, Harry, or I wouldn't be where I am now. I don't do it because I enjoy it.' It came out more harsh than I meant. Harry looked a bit awkward again, so I said, 'I'm sorry if I spoke out of turn, but you said, before, well, you said I was a nice woman, and I just wanted you to know . . .' He didn't reply, and I thought, oh, I've really gone and done it now, so I said, 'Look, perhaps I should be going, I'm sure you're busy, and—' I'd got up out of my chair, but he took my hand and pulled me down again.

'No, there's something else, something I want to say. My grandmother, she . . . well, she was . . . like you. Her husband died, you see—an accident—and she'd got seven children and no money and she didn't want them all in the workhouse, so . . . . I didn't know any of this, but my mother told me, oh, years later, after my grandmother'd died. She said that one day she was out in the street with her and a neighbour started abusing her, calling her names. My mother didn't know how my grandmother was making ends meet—none of them did—so she didn't understand why this woman was saying such terrible things. But when she was grown up she was talking to her cousin, about the old days, and when she mentioned this the cousin said, "Oh, that must have been when your mother . . ." you know, when she'd gone on the streets, to keep the family together. So I do know how it happens. It's odd, though, because I've got a photograph of her, and she doesn't look particularly . . .'

'Like a prostitute?'

Harry looked taken aback. 'I didn't mean that, exactly, just not very . . . Well, a bit stern. I wouldn't have said she was very . . . appealing, that's all.'

'Do you think I look like one?'

'No! I didn't mean—'

'Oh, ignore me. I don't know why I said that. I didn't mean to put you on the spot.'

'I think you look lovely. Especially when you do that.'

'What?'

'When you smile like that.'

'Well,' I said, 'it's been quite an afternoon for confidences, hasn't it?'

'It has a bit. Now, I've got a suggestion. How about some fish and chips before I go back to the post?'

I said I'd like that, and on the way to the place I told Harry about the policeman who'd come in the morning, and after we'd eaten, he walked me home, arm in arm, like before. When we got to my door, I said, 'We did it the wrong way round, didn't we?'

'What do you mean?'

'Well, it should have been the cake *after* the fish and chips. What a pair we are!'

Harry said, 'Yes, aren't we?' Then, after a

214

moment, he said, 'What I said this afternoon . . . I hope you didn't mind.'

'Not at all. I'm glad you told me.'

'Would you mind . . . if I kissed you?'

'Oh, Harry, I'd love it if you kissed me. But not in the street—don't want to get into trouble.' I opened the door and we went into the hall, and he kissed me. I could have gone on like it all evening, just standing there with our arms round each other—it was lovely. He broke off once, and touched my face and asked, 'Do you do this when . . . ?'

'With them? No. Never. This is special.'

'Yes,' he said. 'It's special.' And he kissed me again, and I wanted it never to stop. But he had to get off to the post, so I saw him out and went upstairs to my rooms.

I sat down on my bed for a moment, just to remember it, but then I came back to myself—what with all the talk and the fish and chips, I was late to start work. And thinking of that, all the warm, safe feeling I'd had from Harry seemed to melt away and instead I felt frightened. Sick, almost, thinking about going out, and I found myself dawdling about when I should have been changing my clothes, spending twice as long on the make-up when all it needed was a quick once-over, fiddling with my hair. Making excuses for myself about why I wasn't already out there.

I kept thinking, it'll get better, it'll wear off, but the next few days were dreadful like that, and I never saw Harry, even in the shelter, and I was starting to think, well, he's thought better of it, and I couldn't blame him for that. After all, there's plenty of decent women out there, so what does he

215

want with me? And sometimes I'd be angry, thinking, oh, he's like all the rest, just after something for nothing. But then I'd remember our kiss, and how nice it was, and it made me want to cry, remembering how lovely it was to be in his arms like that, and then I'd get impatient with myself for being soft.

Last night when I went down, I looked round the corner the way I always do, just out of habit, and there was a dark-haired woman standing there, in the dusk, with a look of Lily, and for a moment, I thought . . . I almost called out, but then she turned and of course it wasn't Lily, but a stranger, and it brought tears rushing into my eyes. I had to go and stand in a doorway and count to ten, all sorts I did, to try and stop the feeling.

I didn't recognise the woman. She must have thought she'd get in quick or someone else would have it. Not that I blame her entirely, a good beat is hard to come by, and if you don't go out regular someone'll take it off you, and then you're in trouble.

Not much business at first. It's funny, sometimes you can stand for three hours and get nothing, then you'll make ten or twelve pounds in the next two. But I've got so I can't bear to take any of them back—it's a knee-trembler or nothing, if they want the full business. Which I don't like, mind you. It's harder to spot if they're diseased in the dark, and I won't touch anyone who's bad like that . . . and if you end up bargaining with them, you've got to drop the price. I had one wanted to give me ten shillings! He was with his chum, tipsy, the pair of them: 'I want to rent it, not buy it!' and they both laughed fit to burst.

I said, 'Well, you can rent it somewhere else, can't you?'

He said, 'Oh, we can suit ourselves, there's better than you.'

It was nothing out of the ordinary, really, because you get these characters all the time and think nothing of it, but my stomach was churning something rotten, and when I'd flash my torch and a man would come up, well, usually, I'm seeing them as a job, you know. Don't really look at them as people, just as a way of getting money. But now I was looking right at them, at their faces, their eyes, thinking if they could be a maniac. I mean, if Ted turned out a murderer, who can you trust? And as for poor Edie . . . It seemed like everyone I saw, I thought, you could be that man, with a rope in your pocket, or a knife. And seeing these shadowy faces, parts of faces that seem to come at you—stained teeth crammed up inside a mouth, grime on a collar, hooded eyes that don't blink, hair sprouting inside ears and noses, and others that seem like corpses, collapsed jaws and cheeks and grey skin. Everything seemed distorted by the torchlight and the sky flaring up at intervals—the sirens went at eight—so that the faces seemed to jerk and jump at you. I kept telling myself not to be foolish, they're just *men*, but after a while I began to think, if any of them so much as lays a finger on me, I'll scream, and I knew I wouldn't be able to carry on.

It's not like me to be frightened, but I tell you, I was standing there doing everything I could just to keep myself on the spot, thinking about Tommy, Dora, Joe . . . I can't have words with Joe about hoarding the money, it isn't my business, and besides, he is looking after Tommy, giving him a

217

name and putting a roof over his head. If he and Dora weren't there I don't know what I'd do, because he couldn't live with me.

The bombers started getting louder around eleven, and that made me even more nervous, but I said to myself, I'll see if I can get another ten shillings, at least. Then a man came up, and I thought, here we go, because he didn't look too bad, but he gave me the once-over and said, 'I don't want you, I feel like a blonde tonight.'

I said, 'Well, please yourself,' and I was just thinking I might go back after all, when I heard a swoosh and a whistle, and then a crash and the pavement started to tremble, so I rushed to the nearest doorway and stayed there. I was shaking so much I couldn't tell if it was me or the building, but I heard windows crack above, and the panes dropped straight down in front of me. When I finally plucked up the courage to make a run for it, there was smashed glass everywhere, glittering like snow on the pavement, and crunching under my feet. I pelted back to my flat to collect a few bits and pieces and made for the shelter before anything else happened.

The place was packed to bursting, more than I've ever seen it. You couldn't see the floor for people. It was like a human carpet, with arms and legs sticking out all over the place so it was a job to walk between them. There were prams, people on deckchairs taking up far too much room, and all the old girls wrapped in shawls and blankets as if they were in burial clothes and someone had propped them against the wall in a row, mouths still open like black, gaping holes. Men dozing, with hats tipped over their faces, or playing cards, and the noise going on and on, swishing and droning and then that awful r-i-i-p of a high explosive every so often, and inside, the woman next to me clattering away with knitting needles all night, and people arguing, and Ale Mary, drunk as a fiddler's bitch, telling everyone who'd listen about how she'd been praying for Hitler, that he'd see the error of his ways and come to the right path.

Well, I thought, if she's been doing that, we haven't got a hope. But all the same, I've never been so glad just to be with other people, even if they did pong a bit. I got settled eventually, and managed a couple of hours' sleep. Just before I got off, I heard this little voice saying, 'Mum, my arse is numb,' which gave me a chuckle. I woke at nearly six, very stiff and uncomfortable, and decided to get along home even though the All-Clear hadn't gone. A lot of others were doing the same, everyone pale, red-eyed and moving slowly as if they were dazed with tiredness. I suppose I must have looked like that, too.

Outside, everything smelled of smoke, and there were lots of rescue squad men about, and ambulances. Someone said there were a couple of houses down in Dean Street, so I thought I'd walk round to have a look. One of them must have taken all the force of the blast, because it was just a lot of debris, all smashed and splintered, with a sort of cave in the middle and men digging their way into it, passing out baskets of rubble. The next door was just a shell with no roof or windows, and the top storey had smashed down into the one below it.

I picked my way across the rubble to see if it was anyone I knew, but apart from the rescue men there was only a woman in a nightdress, hunched between two wardens, small and frail, covered in dust so she looked like a lost little ghost. I suppose they must have dug her out of the ruins. She had her back to me but I could see she was clasping a hat to her head with one hand, and there was blood trickling from underneath it, down the side of her neck. I felt bad for staring, so I turned to go, but then I noticed a bit of metal, what looked like a pair of spectacles, sticking out of a little pile of debris. I thought they might belong to the woman, and I picked them up but when I pulled them free, I saw there was a metal piece sticking out from the middle.

It was almost flattened, but I knew right away what it was: Mr Mitten's false nose.

I stood there for a moment, just staring at this thing in my hand, and then there was a terrible cry behind me, a howl like a wounded animal. The woman in the nightdress came staggering towards me, and I realised it was Mrs Mitten, still clutching on to her hat. She grabbed the nose away from me with her other hand and clutched it against her chest, and her eyes, the anguish in her eyes was more than . . . oh, anything. That look of pain—I can't describe it. Then a nurse came with a blanket to put round her, and the wardens started to lead her away to the ambulance, but she suddenly stopped and turned back to me. Her voice was barely more than a whisper, but she said, 'Him on the corner . . . The man . . . Tell him I shan't be needing a paper. Will you tell him?'

'Yes . . . yes, of course. I'll tell him.'

I stood there staring after her, like an idiot. The things people think of! Then one of the rescue men came out from the next door house, so I asked him what happened.

'What, the man in here? We found him—well, what was left. Proper jigsaw for someone. There's a girl in there—' he pointed to the house he'd just come out of—' she's trapped by the legs, and the mother underneath her.' He sat down on a heap of bricks and pulled out a packet of cigarettes. 'Want one? I got plenty, now—we got a fair few out of the shop here.'

'Thanks. Will they be all right?'

He shook his head. 'Can't say. We got the dog out, though. Pekinese, it was.'

'The dog. Well, that's something, isn't it? The dog.'

'Something. I'd go home if I were you, miss. You look all in. Take these with you.' He pressed the cigarettes into my hand. 'Like I said, I've got plenty.'

I was turning to go when this little woman scuttled past me and started scrabbling at the debris like a dog after a bone. The rescue man said, 'Hold on, missus, what are you up to?'

She didn't seem to hear, so he went and tapped her on the shoulder, and when she stood up, I realised she was one of Mr Mitten's regulars, a neighbour of Annie's.

'It's my husband's cigarettes,' she said. 'His nerves are that bad, he can't do without. He's an invalid and he can't leave the house. I've been coming here for years.'

I said, 'So have I, but it makes no odds with the shop gone, does it?'

The rescue man said, 'You'd best take these, then,' and brought a packet out of his jacket.

She looked at them suspiciously for a moment,

221

then snatched them out of his hand. She looked at me and sniffed again. 'It's all on account, you know,' and then she shot off, muttering, 'We're good customers . . .'

The rescue man rolled his eyes at me. I said, 'Ledbetter, her name is. Friend of mine lives in the flat above. She says the husband's not an invalid at all—he's too fat, that's his problem. Never goes out.'

'Let's hope he don't get bombed, then. I can do without lugging fat people—my back's playing me up something chronic as it is.'

I started to walk back. I thought, I'll have to find another place to buy my cigs, now, too. And Mrs Mitten, poor woman . . . have to tell Lily—*No*. Lily's not here any more. Mr Mitten wouldn't come to the shelter, because of his stock. He was afraid the place'd be robbed if he was away. Funny to think I won't see him again. It's like buildings—here one minute, gone the next, except they can't have had time to go away, it happens so quick. In your mind, it's the same street, with the dead people still walking about, so you feel you might walk round a corner and see them, like I did last night with Lily.

A few windows were out in Frith Street, but my flat was still in one piece, which is something, at any rate. Fairly dragged myself up the stairs. I was putting things away—I keep the blanket and whatnot ready in a pile by the door—when I noticed my head felt itchy, so I undid my hair and brushed it out. Well, you never know what you might pick up in those places, but there was nothing that I could see. Not that I could see much with the great clouds of dust coming out of it. I'd

222

like to wash it, but I can't make one basin of water do for hair and smalls and stockings, so it'll just have to wait. Thought I'd better look in on Dora when I've done the washing, make sure my Tommy's all right. Just sit down and close my eyes for ten minutes, first . . . get the shoes off . . . Ooooh, that's good. Then I'll have a cup of tea . . .

FRIDAY 4TH OCTOBER

Lucy

What a week! Ab-so-lutely fed up to the back teeth with everything, including myself. The only bright spot on the horizon was a letter saying they've accepted my offer of help on the Mobile Canteens and will I start next Friday, but apart from that, I've spent the last week listless, irritable, and jolly sick of creeping around at work trying to avoid Mr Bridges. I've been telling myself it's my own fault, but it doesn't help much, and Frank's been popping into my mind every so often—he just seems to wash up there on a tide of guilt. I should like to attach some other emotion to him, but I can't.

I came into work yesterday morning and found a packet on my desk, wrapped in brown paper. Whisked it into my handbag so that the others shouldn't see, and then excused myself to spend a penny so that I could open it in private. It was twenty Players, with a scribbled note: 'I'm sorry' signed Donald Bridges. It's impossible to think of smoking them—they'd choke me. I should like to throw them away if it wasn't so wasteful. I decided

223

to give them to Mums as a 'make up' present. She's been as infuriating as ever; seems to see bad in everyone, especially me.

She's been going on and on about the Anderson shelter, insisting that if we stay in the house we'll be buried alive, crushed, suffocated, decapitated and heaven knows what else. The awful thing is, I've imagined all these things myself, and hearing them spoken aloud does *not* make things any better. I tried to make her understand that she's in the safest possible place, under the stairs, but it makes no difference. A couple of days ago I just snapped, and found myself shouting, 'Oh, shut up, you get on my nerves!' I apologised afterwards, but of course the damage was done.

But it wasn't only that. Last night, she was awful to Dad. He'd come in with Mr Fenner, and they were in the kitchen, deep in questions of cricket and football, and Minnie and I were making supper. We thought it would be nice to ask Mr Fenner to stay, because he's a widower and doesn't get much chance of a home-cooked meal, and because it's nice for Dad to have some male company. When I suggested it, Dad looked pleased as Punch, but then Mums rushed in, obviously furious about the amount of tea they'd consumed, and made it very clear to Mr Fenner that he wasn't *at all* welcome. Dad was very quiet after that, but I was boiling inside—how dare she begrudge him a bit of fun? And as for speaking to Mr Fenner like that . . . I was angry with Dad, too, for sitting there and saying nothing, when it's *his* house. I whirled about the kitchen, slamming things all over the place, ignoring Mums completely and not bothering to conceal my disgust for the whole thing. Quite by mistake I knocked into Minnie—she was carrying an egg and dropped it, and Mums instantly screeched, 'Now look what you've done! Can't you be more careful? You never think of anyone but yourself!' Mayhem. Minnie started crying, although none of it was directed at her, and Mums and I made for the cloth at the same time, 'For heaven's sake, I'll do it!'

'No, let me, give it here, you're all thumbs—'

'I've said I'll do it!' I got a firm purchase on the cloth and tugged it away from her. During all this chaos, Dad sat looking down at the table and didn't say a word, and I caught sight of his face, which looked so weary that I was instantly sorry and felt very ashamed of myself. It must be dreadful for him, being surrounded by this awful gaggle of women who are constantly at each other's throats or in hysterics.

Supper was conducted in complete, but very loaded silence, apart from Minnie's sniffing. The siren went halfway through and we took our plates and retreated: Mums and Minnie under the stairs; Dad and I under the table. My anger, apart from a niggling indignation that none of it was my fault, had left me, and I felt about an inch high and couldn't bring myself to look at him or say anything. Couldn't eat anything, either, but pushed the food around my plate, wondering how to get rid of it without anyone noticing.

I saw, out of the corner of my eye, that Dad had finished his meal and was looking at me.

'Lucy?'

'What?' I could hear how ungracious this sounded, but couldn't help it.

'I know it's not much fun for you youngsters,

225

with all this, but try not to be too hard on your mother. She can't help it. She worries about you, you know.'

'But she's *impossible*! What she said to Mr Fenner, when she could see you were having a perfectly nice time, and it wouldn't have hurt to—'

'I know, Lucy. But you've got to make allowances. She's not herself these days.'

'But that doesn't give her the right to speak to people—'

'It doesn't give you the right, either. She was very upset last night . . . it won't do.'

'No. I'm sorry.'

'I'm glad to hear it. Just don't do it again, that's all. Now . . .' he pointed to my plate. 'Are you going to eat that, young lady?'

'I don't think so. I'm not very hungry.'

'Well, hand it over. Can't have it going to waste.'

'Thanks, Dad.'

'Think nothing of it.' He finished my supper, then said, 'Now, you stay put here, and I'll clear the dishes.'

I sat under the table watching his feet and legs move about, and had the odd thought that this is the view a dog would see all the time. 'Dad?'

'Yes?'

'Did you know that Mrs Grout reckons her dog can tell the difference between our planes and theirs?'

'What, old Blackie? Perhaps he ought to join the ARP. Mind you, we'd have a job finding him a tin hat . . . Does that little accident mean we're out of eggs?'

'I'm afraid it does.'

'Eggless in Gaza.'

'*Da-ad!* That's awful.'

'Eggless in Clapham, then.'

'That's even worse.'

He stuck his head under the table and grinned at me. 'I thought it was one of my better efforts. I'm just going to check on the stirrup pump. You'll be all right here, won't you? It's pretty quiet.'

'I'm fine, Dad. Honestly.'

'Good.' He reached awkwardly under the table and gave my shoulder a pat.

It suddenly occurred to me that when Dad was my age, he was in the trenches. That must have been terrible—I've never heard him talk about it, ever. The one time I asked him, all he said was, 'Some things are best forgotten.' I remember him sighing when we heard Chamberlain on the wireless, saying we were at war. I suppose it must have seemed that everything they'd been through then was for nothing. Mums was in the armchair opposite, crying and peeling potatoes at the same time, and afterwards, we all stood up, very self-conscious, staring down at the rug while they played the National Anthem, Mums still clutching her basin of spuds.

To be honest, I didn't really know how to react to the announcement. I remember watching Dad to see how he was taking it. He seemed so weary and disappointed. I suppose I was . . . what? Afraid? Yes, a bit. Excited . . . yes . . . and curious about what would happen. That seems a lifetime ago, but it's barely more than a year. Dad always looks worn out, nowadays, yet he's so kind and forgiving. Like Minnie. It's a shocking realisation that in this respect, at least, I am more like Mums—a horrible thought, but probably a true one. Perhaps that's why Dad, without saying much, seems to understand me so well: he's had a lot of practice, poor man. And I think he does love Mums. She doesn't strike me as being the lovable type— perhaps I'm not, either. Or maybe Dad sees something else there, that we—or at least, I— don't. In my room this morning, getting dressed, I took the green brooch from under the pillow and put it in my bag. Silly, perhaps, but it reassured me a little, and anything's better than nothing.

I came downstairs in the morning to find that the water was off, again. Had to use the contents of Mums's hot water bottle to make our tea. This won full marks for initiative from Dad, and pursed lips from Mums—through which she drank two cups. Decided it was time to present my peace offering of cigarettes, and did so, to be met with a suspicious look, and asked if I'd got them on the black market! I could feel Dad's eyes boring into the back of my head, so bit back a sarcastic retort and exited, hurriedly, to work.

I spent four hours in the shelter today, at Miss Henderson's insistence, and got very little done, but Mr Bridges didn't seem to be about, thank goodness. In any case, when it comes to running errands upstairs, Vi and Phyll are only too happy to oblige, which lets me off the hook. I could feel Miss H's eyes on me all the time, but no one else seemed to notice, so perhaps it is only imagination. Found myself looking at the brooch in my handbag several times for comfort. Came out later with a terrible headache—it's stuffy enough in there and people will insist on smoking, even though they aren't supposed to.

I was exhausted by the end of the day, but didn't

want to go home. Two stations were closed and most of the streets around roped off and deserted. Precious few buses, and all bursting with people, with a lot more milling about, waiting. I felt very tired and gloomy, and started to wonder if perhaps I've got a cold coming. If so, I probably caught it from Miss Henderson sitting beside me in the shelter, because she's got an absolute beast—nose bright red and streaming, and eyes smaller and more gimlet-like than ever.

The thought of another evening listening to Mums's endless complaints was more than I could bear, and the sheer effort of getting home suddenly seemed too much. I did wonder, afterwards, if I'd already made the decision to go to Soho before I'd seen the transport situation. I'm not sure, but I can't deny it might have been at the back of my mind. I found myself taking the brooch out of my handbag and holding it in my hand like a talisman, and then, after a while, I started to walk.

I had a strangely disembodied feeling, probably a consequence of having cut breakfast and picked at lunch. People were jostling to get home, all walking very fast with their heads down. I noticed how shabby it all looks—windows everywhere have been replaced with cardboard, and the whole place is grimier than ever. I saw peculiar reflections in broken panes—myself split into halves, or cracked down the middle, or flowing from side to side like a pantomime genie appearing from a bottle.

There were a lot of women standing on street corners and in doorways, and odd splashes of bright colour, dulling as the blackouts started to go up and the dusk greyed everything. The sharp edges of the buildings began to blur. It looked nicer like that, less harsh, as everything seemed to soften and settle. A woman bumped into me—'Look where you're going, dear!'—our eyes met, and, just for a moment, I thought I knew her, and then I remembered: it was the woman from the shelter. The prostitute. The one who looks like me. I had an odd, fleeting impulse to speak to her—I couldn't think why, or what I would say if I did speak—but then she walked past me.

I remembered to check my bag and pockets, just in case, but everything was still there. I felt ashamed of myself for my suspicion, and turned to make sure she hadn't looked back and seen me do it. That was when I caught sight of *him*, through the window of a café. Wearing his greatcoat over his uniform, head bowed, the smudgy, greasy window softening his hair, making it seem almost like a halo. A cup of tea stood on the table in front of him. I thought, stupidly, that angels don't drink tea. Then the brooch seemed to jump against my palm and I heard Dad's voice from very far away, 'You youngsters don't have much fun, nowadays . . .'

The moment—it must have been only a moment—seemed to last a long time, and then he looked up at me, and smiled. I put my hand on the window, feeling as if it would just melt away and I could step through it, like Alice did through the looking glass. My heart was thumping like mad, and I seemed to have forgotten how to breathe.

I got a rude shock when a slovenly-looking girl with a broom appeared at the door. 'We're closing, Miss.'

'Oh, I don't want anything, I just . . . I've got something for this gentleman.' I don't know why I

230

said that. It just popped into my head.

'It's like I said, Miss, we're closing.' She was blocking the doorway, greasy, moon-faced, one hand on her hip. I could just see my airman through the crook of her arm. He'd bowed his head again and was tracing a pattern with one finger on the table-top. He didn't seem to be noticing either of us.

'Please,' I said, 'just for a moment. It's important. I won't trouble you.'

'Oh, please yourself.' She stood aside, grudgingly, giving me just enough space to squeeze past.

A warden poked his head round the door, and when he took his helmet off, I recognised the man who'd helped me up and taken me to the shelter. He must have remembered me, too, because he said, 'Good evening, miss. Nice to see you again. Just doing my rounds for the blackouts.'

The girl grunted. 'I was just about to do them when *she* came in.'

'Glad to hear it,' said the warden. He turned back to me. 'You keeping well, miss?'

'Fine, thank you.'

'Jolly good. Well, I shan't keep you.' He looked past me, towards my airman, who was still sitting at the table, and smiled. 'I can see you'll be well looked after, so I'll bid you goodnight.' He turned and left, and I could hear the wretched girl huffing and clattering behind me as I made my way across the room to the table. My airman hadn't looked up, and I suddenly felt very awkward indeed, because I hadn't thought what I might say to him—hadn't thought of talking at all, just imagined the two of us together, somehow. Words hadn't seemed important. I decided not to try to speak, but simply unclenched my fingers and put the brooch down, very gently, on the table. After a second, his head jerked up and he stared at me, blank and shocked at the same time, as if I'd just woken him from a dream.

'Hello.'

He frowned at me. 'Hello.'

'I thought perhaps . . . the brooch. I thought you might want it back. My name's Lucy.' My voice didn't sound like mine at all. He didn't speak, just looked at me. 'I thought you might not like to be without it.'

'Oh . . . I don't mind. I gave it to you, didn't I?'

'Yes, but . . .' His face was even more handsome than I remembered it. I knew I was staring at him, but I couldn't help it. 'When I looked through the window . . . I knew it was you.' I was aware of the girl watching us. She'd put up all the blackouts and was leaning against the wall, arms folded.

'I want you to have it,' he said. He pushed it across the table with his fingertips, and as I reached for it, our hands touched with a tiny electric shock. He drew back his hand quickly, and put it in his pocket.

'I'm sorry, I didn't mean—'

'Look,' he said, 'take it. I don't want it.' He slumped in his chair, free hand tapping on the table-top as if he was waiting for something. I should go, I thought. He doesn't want me here. But I couldn't leave. I felt paralysed. I was so aware of my nearness to him that it felt as if my skin was on fire, and I stood there holding the brooch, trying to think of something to say and feeling like some silly schoolgirl with a 'pash' on the games mistress.

232

Suddenly, he looked up. 'She wants us to leave,' he said, jerking his head at the waitress. He pulled some coins out of his pocket, tossed them on the table, and stood up. 'Can I take you somewhere?'

'I don't know . . . I . . .'

'I'm sure you need to get home. Before the raids.'

'Oh. Yes. Well, thank you. The station. That would be very kind. I mean, I can manage on my own, if you'd rather . . .'

'It's not safe round here. Women have been murdered—strangled and cut up. You shouldn't be wandering about by yourself; you don't know what might happen.'

'Oh . . . it's very kind of you.'

'One of them was attacked with a knife. Had her insides cut out.' His eyes seemed to lock onto mine, and I didn't know what to say.

'Ooh . . . that's horrible! Don't tell me any more.' I heard myself laugh, stupidly.

'I didn't mean to scare you.'

'Well,' I gave him my brightest smile to show I wasn't afraid, 'I certainly shan't be frightened with you.'

'Of course not. I'll look after you. Where's the nearest station?'

'Leicester Square. It was closed, before, but perhaps—'

'Let's go.'

It was dark outside. He turned left instead of right. I followed him for a moment, afraid to touch him or stop him, then said, 'Actually, it's the other way. I mean, that's quicker.'

'Is it?' He laughed. 'I don't know my way around. Not in the blackout, anyway. Haven't been

233

round here, much.'

'You're not from London?'

'Coventry. I went away to school, of course.'

'Yes . . . Is it nice, Coventry?'

'All right, I suppose. Same as anywhere.'

'Where are you based?'

'Hornchurch.'

'So you don't get much chance to go back there. Back home, I mean.'

'No. But I don't miss it, much. Not now.'

'Because of your mother?'

'Mother?'

'I'm sorry, I didn't mean to . . . but you said, the brooch, you said it belonged to her, and I thought—'

'Yes, it did. Belong to her. It would have gone to my sister.'

'But surely—'

'No. She died. Years ago. Car crash.'

'That's terrible . . . I'm sorry, I don't know your name.'

'Tom. Tom Matheson.'

'My name's Lucy.'

'Lucy. Look, the raid hasn't started yet, so . . . would you fancy a drink, or do you have to get home?'

'Yes . . . I mean, yes, I'd like a drink.'

I wondered, briefly, if such behaviour could be viewed as delinquent, but pushed the thought quickly to the back of my mind: after all, we have met before, if only in a manner of speaking, and in any case, I was a whole lot safer with him than I would be on my own.

He took me to a quiet bar. Not many people, but they all seemed respectable types—no signs of

234

drunkenness, at any rate. As soon as he saw the uniform, the waiter was straight over to serve us, and said the manager had told him the drinks were on the house! 'Your money's no good here, sir,' and *lots* of admiring glances from the other customers. I felt disgusted with myself for revelling in this reflected glory, but all the same, it was rather nice. Tom, on the other hand, seemed slightly embarrassed by the man's effusiveness, although it can't be the first time it's happened; after all, the pilots are our heroes. But it was a bit awkward after that, fumbling for conversation and avoiding each other's eyes. I was very conscious that we were being watched, and wouldn't have minded betting that every single woman in that bar was wishing she could be in my shoes.

I said, 'I'm sorry . . .'

'What for?'

'In the café. Arriving like that. I didn't mean to startle you.'

'I don't mind.'

'It is a coincidence, though, meeting again.'

'Yes. Coincidence.' And suddenly, he was staring at me as if he wanted to memorise every detail of my face. 'Coincidence,' he repeated, vaguely, and started patting at his pockets for a cigarette as if his mind was elsewhere. 'Sometimes it's difficult,' he said, 'knowing what to say, I mean. When you're with a lot of chaps all day.'

'Must be better than being with a lot of girls. My office is like that—they can be the most frightful cats. What do you talk about? When you're not . . .' I jerked my head upwards.

'Talk about? Oh . . . flying, I suppose. Aeroplanes. Very dull.'

235

'Not if you understand it.'

'I suppose not. But you don't want to hear about all that.' He smiled. 'What do you do when you're not in your office full of frightful cats—go to the movies?'

'Sometimes. Not recently, because of the raids. But I like them.'

'I want to show you something.' He pulled a little piece of blue cloth, like an envelope, out of his pocket and laid it on the table between us.

'Very mysterious. What is it?'

'Open it and see.'

It was a cigarette card. 'Robert Taylor! He's my favourite.'

'There's another coincidence. I'd like you to have it.'

'Are you sure?'

'Why not? Now if it was Betty Grable . . .' He laughed, then looked serious again. 'I only keep it because it belonged to my sister.'

'You mean, your sister who . . .'

'Died. That's right. I only had the one.'

'Then you ought to keep it. It's special.'

'It's that all right. That's why I'd like you to have it. You'll look after it, won't you?'

'Yes, but—'

'She'd want it to be appreciated.'

'But why? I mean, why me? There must be dozens of girls who—'

'No. There aren't. And you remind me of her, a bit. I've got a picture, somewhere.' He pulled a small, rather crumpled photograph out of the top pocket of his jacket and placed it in front of me—a studio portrait of a rather nice-looking girl in a gym-slip.

236

'She's . . . She was . . . very pretty.' To be honest, I couldn't see that she looked much like me, apart from the hair, but then I suppose photographs don't always tell the truth about a person. 'She's written something. "To Tom, with love from . . ." What's that?'

'Maisie.'

'But that's a Y . . . Yvonne?'

'Oh, yes, well, that was her real name. We always called her Maisie. She preferred it.'

'That's like my sister—her name's Margaret, but she hates it. Everyone calls her Minnie, even my parents.'

Tom put the photograph back in his pocket, and said, 'The thing is . . . that cigarette card . . . I don't deserve to have it, really.'

'What do you mean?'

'Well, it was very quick. The car crash, I mean. Head-on. There wouldn't have been . . . she wouldn't have suffered. But I never had time to . . . What I mean is, I was away at school when it happened, and we'd had an argument before I left. It was my fault we'd had the row, and I'd meant to write her a letter to say I was sorry, but somehow I didn't get round to it, and the day she died, I'd been with some other boys and we'd been, you know, playing tricks. Ragging. Anyway, we were caught, and we knew we were in trouble, so when I was summoned to the headmaster's study, I thought I was going to get a thrashing—for what we'd done, I mean—and then, when he told me there'd been a telephone call from my father, saying my sister . . . saying what had happened . . . and the awful thing was, I was relieved. Because I wasn't going to be beaten, you see. And it was only afterwards, walking down the corridor, that it really came home to me, and then I realised. I'm sorry. I don't know why I'm telling you all this. I suppose it's because you remind me of her, and I've always wanted to say I was sorry. Being her older brother, I should have protected her somehow, when the stupid thing was, she ended up protecting me, in a way. All the others got a thrashing, but I didn't. Because of her. And I'd meant to write to her, and I didn't.'

'Nobody can see the future, Tom. And you couldn't have stopped her dying if you weren't there.'

'I know, but . . . Look, you don't want to hear about all this.'

I held up the cigarette card. 'Are you sure you want me to have this?'

'I've said so, haven't I? Take it.'

He seemed angry—with me as well as himself—for saying too much, and pushed back his chair as if he was withdrawing from the conversation. It was so strange; when he was telling me the story about his sister, we'd seemed so much together, so intimate, as if we'd known each other for years, and yet when he stopped it was like sitting with a complete stranger, an unreachable stranger, with this strange sense of . . . isolation, I suppose. Yet I wanted so badly to comfort him. I put out my hand, across the table, but he didn't take it, just leaned back and stared at me with a peculiar sort of intensity that I couldn't fathom.

'Tom, I'm sorry.'

'About what?'

'Your sister, what hap—'

'It wasn't your fault.'

'No, but—'

'Will you do something for me?'

'What?'

'Will you let me see you again?'

'Yes, of course.'

'I want to see you soon. I don't know how much longer I've got.' He said it quite bluntly, and then continued before I could say anything, 'Will you write to me? I'd like it if you did that. I'll give you my address. Have you got a pen?'

'Here.'

'Paper?'

I didn't have any, but the waiter brought some, and he wrote down his address, then tore the paper in two and asked me to write mine on the other half, which he pocketed. 'Good. Now, I think I should escort you to the station.'

'Yes . . . thank you.'

I suppose it must be the strain that makes him like that—battle fatigue. He's obviously a much more *complicated* person than Frank, but that's attractive in itself. Mysterious. And interesting, too. Makes me want to try to understand, or at least meet him halfway. I never really did with poor Frank. But I've never believed in it before, when people say they meet someone and they just *know*. I've always thought it was romantic nonsense, but now . . . I wonder if it was like that for Dad and Mums? Did they feel as if they were walking on air? Because that's how I felt, when we went back to the station. We didn't talk much, but I was so aware of him, as if . . . sounds like nonsense, even to think it, but: as if I could be him and he could be me. Yet I know that's not possible. He didn't kiss me, just shook my hand and said, 'Goodnight,' and

239

I felt the shock again, all the way up my arm, and then, on the train—in operation again, thank heavens—I felt it all the way back home, as if he were holding my hand.

I really was exhausted by the time I got home, back aching and thighs with that horrible dissolving feeling, like having the curse, except it wasn't that, it was Miss Henderson sniffing over me for hours, landing me with her wretched germs. Was met with a barrage of questions from Mums—'Where were you? I've been so worried'—repeated *ad nauseam*. I must have told her at least five times that the station was closed, but she still didn't stop.

I didn't have the energy to explain I wasn't feeling well. I must have looked all right, though, because Mums didn't say anything. The odd thing was, it didn't annoy me in the slightest; I simply sat there and let it all wash over me. Minnie said, when we were on our own, 'You are in a strange mood— are you sure you're feeling quite well?' I told her I was fine, just tired, but really I wanted to be by myself and relive the evening and enjoy the lovely, special feeling that comes from knowing that you are *in love* . . . I reflected afterwards that there must be more romantic ways of doing this than lying under the kitchen table, aching all over, with a series of bangs and thumps and crashes going on all round you, but I don't care. Right now, I feel I'm the luckiest girl in the world!

Dennis Ledbetter sat on the floor of the basement flat he shared with his wife Betty. His back, broad as a table and solid as a pig, was buttressed by the front of his favourite armchair, his splayed buttocks overspread the cushion beneath them by a good margin of lino, and his stomach sprawled across his thighs. He lifted his glass from its convenient place on the pile of books by his left elbow, took another swallow of brandy, then bent over, as far as he was able, to peer at the level in the bottle that stood at his right elbow. One-third down. He checked his watch: half past eight. Jerry was late tonight. Still, the more he could get down his neck before the bastards got going, the better, and sitting on the floor meant there was no chance of falling when he was blotto. The floor had been Betty's idea—stroke of genius, he'd thought. Pity she'd taken to going to her sister's when he could do with her here, but at least she always made sure he had everything he wanted, and she'd be back in the morning to help him up into his chair again. He looked round—torch, blanket, pot—everything in order. He grunted with satisfaction, extracted *No Orchids for Miss Blandish* from under the brandy glass, cupped a pudgy hand over one eye in order to aid his focus, and began to read.

Not a bad book, this, if only the words didn't slide around so much. Especially the part where the chap had thrashed the girl with a hosepipe, that was rather good. That big sow upstairs, always banging about—she could do with a taste of that. Might even shut her up a bit. She'd been at it again

241

this evening, thumping and crashing.

The siren went. Here we go, thought Ledbetter. He drained his glass and poured himself another generous measure. A loud crack, just above his head, made him jump and the brandy sloshed out of the glass and splashed on the front of his shirt. He cursed. Bloody woman, she'd have the plaster off the ceiling if she didn't look out. Never mind the Luftwaffe, he thought, she's enough to smash the place up by herself. Not to mention lowering the tone: it wasn't right that a decent woman like Betty should have to live under the same roof as some dirty tart with dyed hair. Annie, her name was. Great brassy redhead—he'd caught a look at her a few times from his armchair, when Betty'd had the door open—and he'd heard her, too, bringing men back at all hours. Yes, he'd take a hosepipe to her all right, given half a chance. No more than she deserved.

Ledbetter sighed and went back to his book. He could hear the heavy drone of bombers in the distance, punctuated by gunfire and the odd swishing noise, followed by the crump of an explosion and the clatter of falling incendiaries. He carried on reading, more slowly now, as the brandy took hold and the words began to rearrange themselves before his uncovered eye, sliding together and slipping slyly apart again as he traced them laboriously across the page.

A crash from above made him jump. Not a bomb, this time, just her upstairs again. What was she *doing*? Then more bombers, lower this time, angrier, and in the middle of them, from somewhere above his head, raised voices, hers, mostly, a single word. It sounded like . . . yes, it was

242

. . . 'Don't!', first shrieking, then lower, more plaintive. Then came a scream, followed by another, then another and another, ending on a wild, terrified top-note that seemed to slash through the top of his head like a knife.

Shuddering, he took a long swig of brandy, and looked blearily up at the ceiling. Were they hit? They couldn't be. He'd know about it, wouldn't he? There was another scream, abruptly silenced by a sharp crack and the sound of something heavy crawling—or possibly being dragged—across the floor. It couldn't be a direct hit, he thought. Couldn't be, or I'd have her in my lap by now. Then I'd give her something to scream about, all right. Mind you, judging from the sound of that little lot, somebody'd managed that already. About bloody time, too. The way she carried on, she was asking for it. The landlord had no business renting rooms to a woman like that; not that Ledbetter didn't know full well why he did it—he could charge more, couldn't he? And she could afford it, the money she earned up there on her back, night after night.

Ledbetter raised his glass in a toast and tilted his head back to address the ceiling. 'Good for you, son!' He drained the glass, refilled it, then picked up the book again. Now then, where was he? Fuddled, he opened it at random and stared at the page for some time before the letters ceased jigging about long enough for him to realise that he'd lost the thread—not only that, but he couldn't remember the characters, either. There seemed to be a whole new set, with different names, doing different things. Moistening a forefinger and thumb, Ledbetter grubbed up the edges of the pages to turn them back, and discovered that these people had been there all along. Funny. He didn't remember reading about them. Baffled, he flipped the book over, and stared at the cover: *Dames Don't Care*. Well, that explained it. It wasn't the hosepipe one at all, that was called something else ... something about ... couldn't remember.

A bang from upstairs jerked him out of his reverie. A door slamming. Sounded like quite a hiding he'd given her, whoever he was. Perhaps I ought to send Betty up there in the morning, thought Ledbetter, make sure the woman's all right. He glanced at the level in the bottle. It wouldn't hurt to be neighbourly. He'd laid in a good stock of brandy before the raids started, but it was going down fast, and a woman like that was bound to know someone . . . a pal in the black market. Yes, send Betty up there, that's what he'd do. He reached for the glass again.

The bombers were quieter now. The glass fell sideways as Ledbetter's hand slipped down to the floor, where the pages of *No Orchids for Miss Blandish* soaked up the last of its contents. He inclined his head and watched them for a moment, and then, after a single, soft belch, he fell asleep.

SATURDAY 5TH OCTOBER

Jim

I'd forgotten her face. What do I need the face for? No bloody good to me. It gave me a jolt, seeing her like that. Buggered up the evening. She thought

244

she'd get the better of me, sneaking up and putting that brooch down on the table in front of me. Thought she was being clever, catching me out. She said she'd been watching me, asked me if I wanted the brooch back. Damn stupid question—if I'd wanted it, I wouldn't have given it to her in the first place, would I? But I know what her game is, coming after me like a bloody predator.

It gave me a laugh the way she swallowed that story about the cigarette card. Mathy's sister's picture came in handy too—nearly came a cropper over the name, mind you—should have thought to look what it was. But they're all the bloody same. Thinking she could get one over on me . . . in that café, standing so close, unsettling me like that, teasing . . . crafty bitch. But I showed her, all right. She'll write to old Mathy, and the letter'll come back marked 'Deceased'. That'll shake her up. But I'll write first. Make a date. Have to do something about it, or it'll spoil things.

I'd decided on a redhead, but after the girl had gone I saw a brown-haired tart who looked a bit like her and wondered if I ought to have that, instead, but I didn't see why I should change my plans just because of that stupid woman. She thought she could confuse me, put me off my stroke, but I showed her. I kept seeing the face, all the same.

I couldn't think straight, and went and had a drink, then another, trying to decide what to do. My hands were shaking. *Lucy*. Bitch. I'll teach her a lesson she won't forget in a hurry.

I was so disgusted with the whole business, it was in my mind to pack it in and go back to Hornchurch there and then, when I saw the redhead coming towards me. If it had been any other colour hair I wouldn't have been interested, but that made me think I ought to stick to my original plan. Brassy—obviously a tart—face glistening with paint, big red mouth, cheap perfume. She came and sat down beside me.

'Are you lonely, dear? I'm lonely. I'd like a bit of company.'

I bought her a drink, and she told me she had a room, so off we went. She tried to tell me it was two pounds—thought I was born yesterday. Got her down to a pound and ten shillings, but the whole thing was a washout, right from the first: walking behind her up the stairs, I saw she had no stockings on, so that was no good. I hadn't seen it before: white, floury legs, with freckles, great flanks under the clothes, thumping up the stairs like a carthorse. Made me think of Maisie, and I knew already that it wasn't going to work, but I carried on—not sure why, I suppose by that time it seemed as good as anything else.

It was a dirty, stale room, all cluttered up with pictures of film stars in frames. She told me she knew them all.

I said, 'Brought them back here, have you?'

She said it was in America—a likely story. When the siren went, she said, 'You staying, or going?'

I said I'd stay, but I wanted to see her stockings.

She took her coat off, and her frock; standing under the bare bulb, doughy flesh hanging out of the underwear, hands—big and red, like a docker's—on the hips. 'Never mind that, let's get on with it.' She was tugging at my clothes as if I was some piece of meat, yanking off my greatcoat and jacket: 'Come on, put a spurt on.'

246

I said, 'Don't you tell me what to do.'

'Look, dear, we're here for one thing, so let's do it.' Great blowsy thing, ordering me about.

I said, 'Leave me alone, I don't want this.'

'Your choice, dear.'

She wouldn't give the money back. I said, 'Well, I'm not going without it.'

'Too late now, dear. If you're not interested, clear off and stop wasting my time.'

'Don't you talk to me like that!'

'Oh, suit yourself.' She just shrugged and picked up her frock. Turned her back on me as if I didn't exist and started getting dressed.

I was damned if I was going to let her get away with it, so I said, 'I'll show you what's what,' and got hold of her round the neck. I must have got a handful of her hair, as well, because she screamed and clutched at it, and then she kicked me, hard, and her elbow jabbed into my stomach and I lost my grip and fell backwards on top of a table. It was a spindly thing, covered in these photographs, and when it broke they all crashed onto the floor. I landed on top of them, and when I looked up the woman was standing there staring down at me with her hands on top of her head and shouting, and then I looked at my hand and saw it was full of orange hair. For a moment, I thought I must have pulled it out, but then I saw it was rolled up in a pad and realised it wasn't her hair at all, but some sort of piece she'd put on, to look like a redhead when she wasn't anything of the kind. Her own hair was brown—thin, downy stuff, all uneven at the ends. I jumped up then, shouting that she was nothing but a cheat and a swindler, but she wouldn't shut up, just kept on yelling back at me, calling me names, over and over . . .

I don't remember much of how it happened after that, just making a grab for her legs. She must have lost her balance because she fell on the floor and I was on top of her. I had a piece of broken glass in my hand from one of the photographs and I was stabbing her with it and she kept on screaming, I could hear it over the noise of the bombers, and there was blood. I could see the blood, but I wasn't really registering any of it; it was black and white, like a film, as if a part of my brain had just shut down. The drone of the bombers was getting louder and louder and her screams further and further away, and at some point I must have got up because I remember blundering round the room, knocking into things, and suddenly I couldn't think why I was there or what I'd been doing, and still I could see no colour, but I could hear the bombers as if they were talking to me—*Where are you, where are you, where are you* . . . I shut my eyes and put my fingers in my ears to stop it, stop them coming to find me and kill me, and in my head I could hear Mathy screaming over the R/T, again and again.

When I came to, I found myself curled in the armchair with a cushion over my head, trying to block it out. I opened my eyes and the room flared up in front of me, in colour again, and I could see blood spattered across the wallpaper and the lino, and pooling out from underneath the body, which was splayed out on the floor on a bed of splintered wood and shards of glass. The dress was shredded, there were great gouges in the chest and belly, and blood lacing the arms and legs. It made me sick to look at it, so I caught up the bedspread and threw

248

that on top of it, then I put on my jacket and greatcoat. I knew there must be some blood on my trousers, but I thought the coat would cover it well enough in the blackout, so I didn't worry about that. The main thought in my mind was to get out of there as fast as I could and back to the base so I could forget it ever happened. It was safe outside in the dark, where no one could see, but the noise of the bombers was driving me mad; I had to get away from it . . .

The next part's a bit of a blank. I know I walked a long way, then I was in a truck, then stumbling through the wood towards the edge of the base. I didn't meet anyone. Numb with exhaustion, I only just managed to remember to take my clothes off in the bathroom, because of Ginger. Tiptoed back to the room and stuffed them into the back of my cupboard. No one'll find them there. I'm down to one uniform, now. I'll have to get another, which won't be cheap.

Ginger was asleep. I wanted to sleep, too, but everything was whirling inside my head. All just bits: Mathy, the bombers, the girl, the redhead . . . my brain was snatching at thoughts but I couldn't seem to keep hold of any of them; I kept dropping off and then jerking awake. If only there was a switch to flick and I could turn off the images inside my head, but every time I shut my eyes it was there, waiting.

I don't know how long I lay there like that, but I must have fallen asleep at some point because I was dreaming. It was only on the surface of sleep, because I could remember it all: I'd lost control of the plane and we were falling, the stick was useless, she wouldn't respond and I knew I had to bale out.

I'd got the hood back and suddenly I found myself in the air and I couldn't find the ripcord, I was falling and falling and the bloody thing just wasn't there and then when I finally got it and I thought, that's it, now I'll be safe, I tried to tug it but my arm was too weak, it wouldn't work, and all the time I was going through the air with the wind roaring in my ears and the ground getting closer and closer and I knew I was going to die—and then I jerked awake and Ginger was shouting at me, slapping me, trying to get me to wake up. I was clutching him in a total funk, shaking, so terrified I thought I was going to faint. I knew Ginger was talking to me but I couldn't hear it, all I could hear was the wind rushing past my head and still, in my mind, I had flashes of the ground coming up towards me and it wouldn't stop. Then something came up hard against my face—the impact like meeting the ground—and I realised it was Ginger, he'd hit me. His face was opposite mine and he was holding up his flask to my mouth—brandy—and it made me cough when I tried to swallow. I suppose that's when I finally came to, and he was thumping me on the back, saying, 'It's a dream, only a dream . . .'

* * *

'All right now?'

 'I think so. Thanks.'

 Ginger shrugged. 'Happens to everyone. What can't you do, anyway?'

 'What do you mean?'

 'What you were shouting—"I can't".'

 'Oh . . . the ripcord. Couldn't find it.'

 'Nasty. But like I said, happens to everyone.

250

Better not to think about it.'

I never used to have dreams like that. Marvellous, before. I used to look forward to them. I could do anything. Not at the mercy of it, like . . . like . . . *Jesus, what's happening to me?* I went to the bathroom and splashed my face with cold water, trying to pull myself together.

I went back to the room after that. Ginger was asleep again. I sat on the edge of the bed till Reilly came in with the tea. Couldn't find a clean shirt so I thought I might as well put on my Irvine jacket over my pyjama top. My clothes were still bundled up in the cupboard where I left them last night, but I know they'll be all right for a while—Reilly never looks in there. I'll have to get rid of them eventually, though, in case they're found. Got a clean pair of trousers, so that's all right.

I sat down on the side of the bed again. Couldn't seem to find the energy to stand up. When Ginger asked me how I was, I couldn't reply—thought I'd burst into tears if I so much as opened my mouth. He didn't press it, just emptied his flask of brandy into my tea.

When he left the room, I lay down again, but I couldn't close my eyes. How long can anyone stay awake? Can I stay awake till the end? It can't be long, now, I know that. It doesn't feel so bad, just staring into the half-darkness. Maybe oblivion is like this: everything just draining away. Like a plane leaking coolant: knowing you're in trouble, with nothing to do but pancake, if you can. I feel curiously detached from it. Like watching one of theirs go down. No emotions. No feeling at all.

251

SATURDAY 5TH OCTOBER

Rene

Ten minutes, my foot! I must have been tired, because there I was in the armchair, flat out till mid-afternoon. First thing I remembered when I woke up was that I had to tell the newspaper man about poor Mrs Mitten not wanting her paper, so I went straight out to do that. I don't know how I'm going to manage about cigarettes. Got some funny foreign things from another place, but the woman there didn't seem too friendly. I can't see myself chumming up with her, and they'll only save you the good ones if you're a regular. Have to make some enquiries—somebody's bound to know something I don't, provided they'll tell me, of course.

I did some shopping, but when I got back home I couldn't fancy a bit of it—finding that nose really turned me up, and what that rescue man said about poor Mr Mitten all blown to pieces . . . I tried to take my mind off it, but after a bit I thought, well, I've got to do something, so I decided I'd go round to Eileen's to ask her about cigarettes. I'd go to Bridget, but she'd touch me for money, like as not, and Annie's not the sort you ask for favours. Eileen's never had a good word to say about Lily since the business over Ted, but she and I get along all right. Besides, with all this going on, we've got to stick together, haven't we?

I was just getting my coat on when somebody came charging up the stairs and started pounding

252

on the door. 'Rene! Rene! Quick!' When I open up, it's only Eileen, looking like she's been through a hedge backwards, puffing and panting fit to burst.

'Whatever is it? You look terrible.'

'Rene . . . it's awful, it's happened again . . .'

I got her in the armchair but it was about ten minutes before I could get anything out of her. She was rocking backwards and forwards like a madwoman, crying and moaning, and all the time I had this horrible feeling I knew what she was going to say, and my stomach was churning something dreadful.

I managed to get some tea down her in the end, with a drop of brandy in it, and I said, 'Now then, I'm going to hold your hand, and you tell me all about it.'

'Annie was killed, Rene, last night. Like Lily, all carved up.'

'Annie? Never! You're having me on.'

'She was; the woman downstairs found her this morning. I went round to see Annie—she'd borrowed two pounds off me and she told me she'd have it this morning—so I go in and there's policemen there and everything, and I can hear this woman crying and sobbing, and they've told me I can't go in, and they won't tell me what's going on. And then all these others go up, and there's this copper, he's white as a sheet, he comes rushing downstairs and sicks up in the gutter and it's gone everywhere. And the other one asks him if he's all right, and he says, "Oh, it's bad . . . I've never seen anything so bad . . ." He was shaking, Rene, shaking all over, he couldn't hardly speak. So then I said, "I've come to see the woman upstairs, Annie Burgess," and he says, "No, you can't," and I say, "I want to see she's all right," and I've rushed up them stairs before they can stop me, and there's Annie's door wide open, so in I go and there's men everywhere, and the room's all over blood, it's everywhere, on the walls and everywhere, and Annie's on the floor covered in a blanket, and then one of them grabs me and takes me out and . . . Oh, Rene, it was horrible, you can't imagine . . .'

I just stared at her.

She said, 'It's a madman, Rene, a maniac. He's going to kill us all. First Edie, then Lily, now Annie—'

'But with Lily, that was Ted. They arrested him, didn't they?'

'That's rubbish. He never did that.'

'How do you know?'

'I know *Ted*. Anyway, I saw him.'

'What, you saw him the night he . . . I mean, the night Lily was killed?'

'Yes. I was finished for the night, on my way home, and he bumped right into me. He'd had that much he could hardly walk, never mind murdering anyone. You should have seen him, Rene, he'd had a skinful. I didn't think he'd be able to get home so I asked him, did he want to come along with me, but he said Lily'd be angry. He never drank like that when he was with me—she drove him to it, Rene, and now look what's happened. Oh, it's horrible. I told him he should have stayed with me, I'd have looked after him . . .' Eileen started crying again.

I said, 'Well, if that's true—'

'It is, I swear it, I saw it with my own eyes!'

'He might have been that drunk he didn't know what he was doing.'

'No, he couldn't . . . he wouldn't do a thing like that.'

'So you mean he went back home and Lily was dead and he didn't . . . Well, I suppose it's possible, if he was as drunk as you've said.'

'Oh, he was, you should have seen him. He was never that bad with me, never! That cow Lily, she took him off me. I said to her, "What did I ever do to you?" And she said, "Oh, I can give him this, I can give him that . . ." Making out she's better than me. She was a bitch, Rene, she deserved it!'

Well, I thought, button it, Rene, because that was a load of rubbish about Ted not drinking when he was her boy, but I wasn't going to have her speaking ill of my pal. Mind you, I could never understand what Lily saw in Ted, because he's a useless article at the best of times, though I have to admit I never thought he'd murder anyone.

I said to Eileen, 'Did you tell the police?'

'Oh, and I suppose they'd believe me, wouldn't they?'

Well, she had a point there. They don't believe anything we say, and of course once they knew that Ted had been Eileen's ponce and Lily'd got him off her, well . . .

Eileen said, 'I don't know what I'm going to do. It's not safe out there with this madman on the loose.'

'No, I know. Poor Annie . . .'

'Oh, Rene, it was dreadful, you can't imagine.'

We had a drop more tea with the brandy in it, but it didn't help. I didn't know what to do. If I'm honest, I didn't want to be with Eileen, because she kept harping on about Lily and what a bitch she was and how it was her fault Ted was arrested, and

255

it was getting on my nerves; but I felt too shaken up to be on my own, and when you're that way, any company's better than none. In the end I said, 'Well, there's nothing we can do, so let's go to the pictures and try to take our minds off it.'

So that's what we did. We went to the Dominion Cinema, where Lily and me always used to go, because it's cheaper there—one and nine each. The film was *Night Train to Munich* with Rex Harrison and Margaret Lockwood. I can't remember much about it—I was too pre-occupied with everything else to pay attention—so it was a waste of money, really. But it passed the afternoon, so I suppose I shouldn't complain.

We sat through it twice—there was an air-raid halfway through and the manager came and said we could take shelter if we liked, but no one took any notice. All the time, at the back of my mind, I was thinking, I've got to go out tonight. If this goes on much longer I shan't have two pennies to rub together, and there's Tommy and Dora to think of besides myself. I even started thinking about having it out with Joe about him hoarding money, but then I thought, what if he gets nasty? I rely on them to look after Tommy, and if he said they wouldn't look after him no more I don't know what I'd do.

I'd all this in my mind, going round and round in circles, and I kept thinking of what Eileen said about Annie, blood all over the room, and what it must of looked like, and then about Lily and Edie . . . I'm sitting there with my fists all clenched up, nails digging into the palms, thinking, *I've got to go out there, I've got to, got to, got to* . . . and totting up in my mind how much I'd get if I just stuck to my regulars, but even as I was doing it I knew it

256

wouldn't work because I don't have enough of them. None of us do, round here, except maybe French Marie, and she's got a telephone. Mind you, that's probably not much good at the moment, with all the disruption—takes all day to get a call through, that's what I've heard. But what it boils down to, is: I've got to go out, or I can't survive, and neither can my Tommy—and that's what matters.

On the way back, Eileen suddenly said, 'You know them pictures Annie had? The film stars?'

'Yes?'

'They were smashed. Every last one. Smashed to pieces. Glass everywhere, and the frames all broken. That was more sad than anything, seeing them all like that. She was so proud of them.'

'Yes, wasn't she?'

Those photographs, well . . . we used to joke about them behind Annie's back, her saying she'd been to America and she'd met them and been with them and all the rest of it. They all had these little messages written on them—'To Annie, with fondest memories from Ronald Colman,' or Clark Gable or whoever it was—but the thing was, these film stars, if you looked closely, they all seemed to have the same handwriting! And it wasn't proper photos at all, just stuff she'd cut out of papers and magazines. But I knew what Eileen meant about being sad, because Annie was that proud of them. It was just her way of trying to make herself seem that bit more important. I suppose it's something everybody does, a little, but with her, it was so . . . childish, I suppose, especially from this big, strapping woman who'd take no nonsense from anybody. And that was the awful thing: if anyone

257

could take care of herself, it was Annie. I thought, if Annie couldn't protect herself, what chance is there for the rest of us?

I felt Eileen give a little shiver, beside me, and wondered if she was thinking the same. She said, 'What are you going to do?'

'Same as usual. Not a lot of choice, really.'

'No. Look, Rene, take care, all right? I shan't take them back home no more . . .'

'Nor me.'

'Well, then. Good luck.'

'Thanks, Eileen. Be careful.'

Then she went off home, and so did I. I got dressed, and painted my face and did my hair, and all the time there was this resolve inside me, a big, cold lump, like something settled on my stomach. I was thinking: *You won't get me, you bastard. You won't get me, because I won't let you.*

I went marching downstairs holding my handbag like it was a weapon, and out into the street. Well, being brave was all very well as long as it lasted, but once it got dark, that was another story—it was even worse than before: all the time, in the back of my mind, I was thinking, *is it you?*

I kept nipping round the corner to see if I could catch the new girl—wanted to see if we could look out for each other, you know, keep a check. She never showed up. Probably terrified, and I don't blame her.

Not a lot of business. I kept saying to myself, another ten shillings, then I'll go. I got two pound ten in the end, and I was just about to call it a night when I heard footsteps. It sounded like a man, so I shone the torch, and then I heard, 'Rene? That you?' and before I know it, there's Harry standing

258

in front of me.

He said, 'I came as soon as I could. Had to see if you were all right. I've just heard—your friend . . .'

'Well, I'm still here.'

'I was worried about you, Rene. I thought . . . well . . . I'm glad you're here, anyway.' And it's true, he did sound pleased, and I was so pleased to see *him* I could have flung my arms round his neck there and then, but I didn't, because it felt a bit peculiar, me standing there as if . . . you know . . . and him coming up to me like that, on the street. He said, 'Look, I can't stay long, but I can walk you round to the shelter, if you like. That is, if you're . . . if . . . you know . . .'

'Yes, I've . . . I'd like that.'

'Come on then, take my arm. We'll get your things, shall we?'

As we walked, he said, 'I'm sorry I've not been to see you, but the last couple of nights . . . and then that business in Dean Street . . .'

'I know, the tobacconist—I used to go there. Terrible. And his poor wife!'

'The house next door, as well. They were still digging this afternoon. Only just got the last one out.'

I thought, what can you say? It's terrible, but it keeps happening, all the time. And who's going to worry about some madman killing a few street girls when there's all that going on? With everybody in so much danger already, why should they care about us?

Harry came upstairs with me and waited while I gathered up my bits and pieces for the shelter. Seeing him under the light, he looked so tired and strained, I said, 'You look as if you could do with a

259

good night's sleep.'

He shrugged. 'Couldn't everyone? You've got more to worry about than me, Rene. You've got to be careful.'

'Oh, Harry . . .' I was determined I wouldn't cry again—not in front of him, at least—but I felt like all the heart had gone out of me. I must have looked it, too, because he said, 'Come here.'

Being in his arms felt like the most natural thing in the world. He didn't kiss me, just held me for a long time. 'We'll get through this, you'll see,' he said.

'Will we?'

'Yes. We'll come out on top.'

I said, 'You know something, Harry . . .'

'Not until you tell me.'

'My friend Eileen, this morning . . . she said she thought Ted—that's Lily's ponce—she never thought he did it. Killed her, I mean. And she'd know, because she was with him before Lily, see. Said she'd seen him, too, that same night, and he was dead drunk and couldn't hardly walk. And if that's true, that means there's someone out there, a madman, because it has to be the same man, doesn't it? And he's going round—'

'The police'll get him, Rene. You'll see, they—'

'They don't care about us, Harry!' I broke away from him. 'No one does. They think we're asking for it.'

'That's not true, Rene.'

'Of course it's true. D'you think they'd help us, any more than those old peelers, or whatever they were called, would have helped your grandmother? They don't give a monkey's, they just—'

'Rene, listen! I *do* care about you, and I don't think you should go out, I mean, go to work . . . any

260

more. I've got a bit of money, and I—'

'I'm not taking your money, Harry.'

'You can pay me back, when—'

'When what? When the police find him and it's safe to go back out again? They're not going to find him, Harry. I told you, if it's us, they're not interested. They didn't find Jack the Ripper, did they?'

'No, but that was years ago. They've got modern methods now. They'll find him.'

'It's not their methods, Harry, it's the way they think. That's just how it is, and it's not going to change. Not ever.'

Harry sighed. 'I know you're brave, Rene, the way you've gone on working with the blackout, the raids, but—'

'We've all done that. No choice.'

'I know, but now—'

'I'm not taking your money, Harry, and there's an end to it.' And I turned my back on him and picked up my things. 'Let's go.'

He shrugged. 'Fair enough.'

We walked round to the shelter in silence, and I was thinking, I shouldn't have been so sharp with him when he's trying to help me, but all the same, I can't put myself in his debt like that. I've got some pride left, whatever anyone thinks. You get some girls, they'll go to a man and tell him some pathetic story and get money out of him: there's a baby coming, or the child's under the doctor, or they've got to get a divorce . . . I've known girls who've had as much as fifty pounds from a man that way, but I wouldn't do it. I thought of telling that to Harry, but he wouldn't understand. He'd say it's different, and I suppose it is, in a way, but all the same . . .

261

Besides, I felt angry with him for offering, and angry with myself, too, for being rude, but I thought, if I try and explain, I won't be able to say it right.

Outside the shelter, he said, 'Well, goodnight then,' and he was off before I'd even opened my mouth.

I went in—crowded again—and sat down. I thought, Well, Rene, whatever daft ideas you had about a decent life for you and Tommy—when Harry don't know Tommy even exists—you can just forget them, because it ain't going to happen. Shows you, though, how impossible it is, someone like me and a decent man like that. There's some things you do in your life that can't be undone, and whatever happened, Harry'd never forget what I'd been and nor would I, and that's the truth of it. There'd always be that between us, like a wall. And then I thought, you're making it all up, Rene, because he's never said to me about anything like that, has he? Just that he liked me, and kissed me once, and that's all. Talk about mountains out of molehills!

But I shouldn't have been so sharp with him, when he was only trying to help. I don't know why I'm bothering about any of this, really. Perhaps I'm better off with the girls, after all: like should keep to like, makes things easier all round. And the way things are going I won't be here tomorrow to worry about it, never mind the future. I'd rather have a bomb than wind up like Annie, any day. They say you don't hear the one that gets you, so at least you wouldn't know about it, would you? But you'd know if someone was choking the life out of you, all right. Poor old Annie . . .

THURSDAY 10TH OCTOBER

Jim

This week's been bloody terrible, each day worse
than the one before. This morning was the worst of
the lot. I kept telling myself that once I'd been up,
I'd be fine, but the dread was worse than it's ever
been. I gripped the edge of the deckchair, planted
my feet firmly on the grass, looked down . . .
Nothing worked. Thank God nobody says much,
first thing: tired, hungover, or scared shitless. It's
the same for everybody: came through yesterday,
but then it starts all over again, and you wonder
how long you can keep it up.

Balchin looked bad, swilling down tea to get the
taste of last night's beer out of his mouth. I don't
suppose I looked much better. Corky was
pretending to read, and Flint was trying to talk to
Davy, who fell asleep in mid-sentence.

My insides started clenching and loosening, each
spasm getting stronger. No good—I had to run,
doubled-over, for the latrine. I got my trousers
down just in time before my bowels emptied
themselves like a high-pressure hose. I felt as weak
as a kitten; I could have sat for ever above the pan
full of vile-smelling liquid and never moved again.
Hadn't even got the energy to pull the string and
flush it away.

I couldn't make myself go out there. I couldn't
even move. But I knew I had to, I bloody well had
to. I thought, if all of them can do it—if bloody
Gervase can do it—then so can I. I can't stay in

263

here and shit myself while they . . . Then Mathy's scream cut into my mind like a knife and the pain of it was so sharp that I banged my head repeatedly against the side of the wooden hut, but it wouldn't stop, just got higher and higher until it wasn't Mathy any more but the tart and suddenly she was there in front of me, twisting from side to side on the floor, her neck a red gash and lips peeled back from her teeth in a snarl. I could see the greasy scalp through the sparse brown tufts of hair as her head thrashed back and forth and her eyes were staring and she was screaming and screaming and suddenly I felt my bowels constrict and give way. My back ached. Slowly, like an old man, I pulled myself upright, searching for paper.

I imagined Webster packing up my possessions, finding the stocking in the drawer, the compact from that first one, and the photograph of Mathy's sister—*To Tom, with love*—which was in the uniform jacket, the bloodstained one that I put in the cupboard . . . I wondered what he'd do. Would he tell the police? Or would he pack it all up and send it back to my mother? Not that she'd want it. My whole stomach felt scalded and empty, and all I wanted was to be left alone.

A bang on the door made the little hut shudder. 'Goldilocks! Get a move on, we've got customers!'

I stumbled outside, fumbling at my fly, legs as weak as water. I stooped to pick up my parachute and helmet and someone cannoned into me from behind—'Move, for Christ's sake!'—Balchin sprinted past me, tailed by Corky and Davy. I followed as best I could, heart pounding, a voice in my head saying, *I can't do this* . . . I've got to do this: I haven't got a choice.

264

The planes gleamed dully in the thin, early morning sun and for the first time in my life I saw them not as beautiful, but monstrous. I didn't want to approach them. The fear was almost paralysing, and for a moment I thought I might shit myself again but then something in my stomach hardened and I was able to move forward. The fitter jumped down from the wing. Parachute on. He put a hand under my arm to help me up and I was shaking like hell—he must have felt it, but he said nothing. Right foot planted on the wing, then the other, and I swung into the cockpit. And I thought, what the hell happens next? I couldn't remember what I was supposed to do. There was a voice in my head saying, 'Instinct, trust your instinct.' But what instinct? My only bloody instinct was to stay on the ground and not get killed.

Instructions came, muffled, as if someone was shouting through a dense fog. A voice from inside me was saying strap in, switch on, check oxygen . . . My hands seemed to scuttle about of their own accord—over the throttle, the magneto, then doping the engine—but there was no part of me that had instructed them or given them the signals; my mind wasn't part of the loop, and the fear was metallic and sour in my mouth, rancid in my armpits and I could feel sweat running down my back and face. I wanted to shout 'Stop!' but I couldn't, I was trapped in the cockpit and I could see the airman giving me the thumbs up . . . turn the dial . . . thumbs up again for disconnect—they were standing by the wings to guide me out. *Oh, Jesus* . . .

I managed to get into the air but it was ham-fisted and I couldn't seem to connect with the plane. She was like an alien thing, jerking and bucketing all over the place as I over-corrected and twice nearly sent her into a spin. Instructions came over the R/T, but I couldn't follow them. I concentrated on staying with the others, but I could barely keep level. I couldn't *feel* her . . . My beautiful Spitfire was just an unresponsive lump of metal.

Then I heard Corky's voice: 'Blue One to Leader, Bandits at three o'clock.'

I saw them, a swarm of insects. Had they seen us? My brain was jammed. All I wanted was to turn tail and flee. I knew I couldn't claim engine trouble—as soon as I landed they'd spot that nothing was wrong. What was I supposed to be doing? Reflector sight . . . range . . . What then?

They were above us. We climbed. More instructions. Gibberish—couldn't seem to understand it—all going too fast—even the first time wasn't like that, the stark, raw, petrifying *fear*. I was straying out of formation, but my hands were shaking, and they wouldn't let me correct it. I could hear Gervase's voice over the R/T, anxious, 'Yellow One, Yellow One . . .' Tracer seemed to float towards me like a silent firework display, only it wasn't fireworks, it picked up speed and whipped past my starboard wing, and suddenly, a 109 was slap in front of me, sparks coming out of it. He was shooting at me, I knew that, but I just sat there, my brain racing but my hands wouldn't move, and then I threw the stick forward and put the plane into a dive to get away because that's all I could think of: *Get out of here, just get out . . .*

I don't remember much about getting home, just tumbling out of the kite and sitting on the grass, soaked in sweat, thinking I'd never be able to get up again. I got across to the mess somehow and got a cup of tea. Then Flint was there, standing in front of me.

'What the bloody hell happened up there?'

I couldn't answer him. I couldn't even look at him.

'Well, whatever it was, you'd be at the bottom of the sea by now, if Sinclair hadn't taken care of that Hun.'

'Gervase?'

'Yes, Gervase. Your wingman, remember? The one you're always binding about. And then you just buggered off and left us to it. The CO wants to see you.'

'Now?'

'Yes.'

*   *   *

Webster ushered me into the office. 'Flying Officer Rushton to see you, sir.'

The CO told me to sit down, then said, 'Flight Lieutenant Flint tells me you packed up and pissed off in the middle of a dogfight. Is that correct?'

'Yes, sir.'

'What happened?'

'I . . . I don't know, sir.'

'Well, try.'

'I just couldn't . . . I couldn't . . .' It was no good, I couldn't get the words out. The worst thing was knowing I'd failed myself—him, Flint, all of them. And then finding I couldn't even explain.

'Look, Goldilocks, you're a bloody good pilot, and what's more you're one of the only decent

267

shots we've got, and I don't want to lose you. I'm sending you to the MO. Perhaps he can give you something to pep you up. And I'm taking you off ops for the time being. Can't risk any more stunts like that one.'

I went back to my room and lay down on the bed. I've got to sort myself out—if I can't fly, it's hopeless. I might as well not be alive. If they take me off ops permanently, there's no point to anything. It's that woman. She's a jinx, that's what it is. I'm not coming off ops for some bloody popsy, and, what's more, if I'm going to die I'll do it on my terms, not because of some bitch sticking her oar in, I'll make damn sure of that.

There was a knock on the door. Webster was standing there.

'I've come to sort out Ginger's bits and pieces.'

'Ginger bought it?'

'I'm afraid so. Now then . . .' He started making an inventory of Ginger's things, laying out brushes and photographs and clothes on the bed. I rolled over and stared at the wall.

'Five pairs of socks, black wallet with two photos. Pretty girl . . . Letter from his mother . . . another letter . . . Mona . . . I say, this is a bit spicy, better get rid of it, I think . . . two pairs of shoes, one tennis racket—'

'I'm going for a walk, Adj.'

Poor old Ginger. Still, at least it gave me an idea about what to say to the MO. I wondered if I'd get the room to myself. Ginger's girl, Mona, and that letter Webster picked up . . . she was that other one's pal, the one with the funny name. Still, I suppose if she was going to say anything, she'd have done it by now, wouldn't she? Anyway, it's only her word against mine.

*   *   *

It was all pretty clear-cut with the MO. One of those sympathetic types. 'The CO told me what happened. Well, in so far as he could. I'd like you to put me in the picture.'

'I don't know if I can, sir.'

'Take your time.'

'Well, I just sort of . . . froze. Couldn't do it any more. Couldn't think straight. I was bloody terrified, sir.'

'This freezing—is this the first time it's happened?'

'Yes, sir.'

'You've been at it for quite a while now, haven't you?'

'Yes, sir.'

'Have you been sleeping?'

'Not very much, sir, no.'

'Is there anything bothering you?'

'To be honest, I'm beginning to think I might be a bit of a jinx. I keep losing my wingmen, and I've had three roommates in two weeks. I know that doesn't sound . . . I mean, we're all in the same boat, aren't we? But I keep wondering if it's me that's doing it, and I can't . . . well, I don't really know how to put it into words, sir.'

'I see. The CO's taken you off Ops, hasn't he?'

'Yes, sir.'

'Good. What about a spot of leave? Would that do the trick?'

'Well, perhaps . . . If I could go next weekend. I'd like to see my mother and sister, you see. My father's dead, and I've been worried about them. My sister's crippled, sir, and with things the way they are, it hasn't been easy for them.'

'I see. Well, I'll recommend you for a forty-eight-hour pass, and you'll be knocking around here for the next week . . . These things are bound to happen, on and off. I'm sure you'll be fine after a bit of a break.'

So there it was—piece of cake. A few days off Ops and forty-eight hours to sort that bitch out then I'll be fine. That's what it comes down to: her or me, and there's only one way to fix it. Need to see Uncle for the pass, and as soon as I've done that, I'll write her a nice little letter . . . Get rid of those clothes, too.

I'm starting to feel better already.

THURSDAY 10TH OCTOBER

Lucy

I'm in a quandary. Despite the fact I've spent the whole week floating on air, I have managed to pull my head out of the clouds for long enough to realise that my erstwhile fellow-typist, Phyllis, who has been sent upstairs in place of me—for which I'm profoundly grateful—is utterly smitten with Mr Bridges, and he, apparently, with her. They've been carrying on dreadfully—even Miss H has noticed! It's too awful for words. I'm sure I was never that silly. At least, I jolly well hope not. I'd hate to think anyone was talking about me like that.

Yesterday, I caught them canoodling—that's the

270

only word for it—in the store room. I pretended I hadn't noticed what they were doing, which isn't easy when two people are standing quite so close and one of them is scarlet with blushes. I said, 'Good morning,' very politely, and disappeared back upstairs as fast as I could. When Miss H asked me why I hadn't got the fresh carbons, I told her I'd forgotten to take the key with me. She wasn't pleased, but honestly, I couldn't have stayed down there a moment longer. Phyll came into our office about ten minutes later on some pretext, wearing a look on her face that I can only describe as defiant triumph. She hovered about my desk, obviously hoping that I'd make some remark, but I'm afraid she was disappointed, because I bent over my typewriter and affected not to notice her at all.

I found myself wondering, on the train home, if Phyll has conveniently forgotten, as I did, that Mr Bridges is married. She certainly knows it, because she was there when Miss H told us. I've been wondering if I should warn her about him, but she'd probably think it was jealousy. I don't know what, if anything, Mr Bridges has said about me, but obviously she knows we didn't 'click'. I wonder if he's fed her that line about his wife being a chronic invalid and all the rest of it. But then the truth is, I might have swallowed all that myself, if it hadn't been for that awful business in the restaurant, and what happened after . . .

I feel rather sorry for Phyll, but I'm pretty sure she wouldn't listen to me if I did say anything. But then, if I hadn't met Tom, perhaps I wouldn't be able to see the difference between something real and meaningful and a sordid little intrigue, either. What she's up to seems so tawdry by comparison,

271

and I simply can't believe Mr Bridges could ever be capable of the kind of raw *honesty* of the conversation I had with Tom, which really was a meeting of minds. All Mr Bridges' talk about virginity and so on is simply a veneer of sophistication, done with an intent to shock, and would only impress somebody who didn't know better—as I didn't, not then.

It sounds as if I think I know everything. I don't, it's just a matter of seeing things from a different viewpoint. But I don't think it's something which can be *learned*—not without experience, anyway.

I should like to put some of this in my letter to Tom, but it's jolly difficult, and I'd hate to give him the impression that I'm foolish, or weak. I've spent the last few nights under the kitchen table, trying to write something, but I keep tearing it up in disgust. I found one of my school exercise books which wasn't used up and took pages out of the back of that to scribble on. I'd decided that using up our whole stock of notepaper would make me even less popular with Mums than I am already.

I thought that perhaps I ought to write a nice, gossipy letter about Mums and Dad and Minnie, and what happens at the office, but it seems so inadequate, after our conversation. Tom would be bound to despise it, and rightly so! But I mustn't descend into purple patchiness, either. I suppose that's why there are poets who can say these things for the rest of us, and then we can point to this or that verse and say, that's how I feel, or, that's what I think. But this seems rather lazy, and in any case, I don't know any poems, apart from the ones I had to learn at school, and verses like *The boy stood on the burning deck* and *How horatius kept the bridge* don't fit the bill at all. I asked Minnie on Sunday evening if she could think of any poetry, and she immediately screwed up her face and recited, like a child doing a party piece: *Glad days, sad days; Are all the brighter made; In the happy knowledge; That our friendship will never fade.* This made us both giggle, because it's painted on a hideous plate that Aunt Norma sent Mums from Eastbourne. It's probably the only poem in our entire house, and it's *awful*.

When we'd stopped laughing, Minnie asked if I was writing to Frank, and I said yes, and immediately felt bad for lying about it.

She said, 'You haven't written to him since he went, have you?'

'No.'

'Are you going to make it up with him?'

'What do you mean?'

'Well, I know you had a quarrel, that's all. Before he left. I'm sorry, I wasn't spying or anything, but I saw you at the gate, and he didn't come in to say goodbye. You didn't seem to want to talk about it, so . . .' She made a face. 'Well, anyway, it's none of my business.'

'No,' I said, 'it isn't.'

'I've said I'm sorry, Lucy. Look, I'll leave you in peace. I ought to see how Mums is doing, anyway.' Part of me wanted to call Minnie back and to say that I was the one who ought to be sorry, and explain everything, because we *have* always talked about things. But I just couldn't. Minnie'd be upset—she did like Frank a great deal—and also, I suppose I was rather ashamed of how I'd behaved, and no one likes to say things that reflect badly on them. And if I'm honest, there is a certain guilty pleasure about all this secrecy. That 'special' feeling, inside . . . I can't pretend I'm not enjoying it.

I came home on Wednesday determined to complete my letter to Tom. The house was empty except for Minnie, who was making supper. When I asked her where Mums was, she said, 'She's with Mrs Dorn.'

'Why?'

'She's expecting a baby. Mums has been going out to sit with her.'

'Oh, yes. Her husband's away, isn't he?'

Minnie nodded.

I said, 'Well, good for Mums.'

'It's been a few days now, she's done it. The baby's supposed to come any time.'

'I didn't know. Mums must be feeling much better if she's doing that.'

'Yes, she is . . . I'm surprised you haven't noticed. But then, you've had other things on your mind, haven't you?'

That surprised me, because Minnie isn't usually catty like that, but I felt I'd deserved it for being selfishly interested in my own affairs and not noticing what was happening at home. I said, 'Do you think one of us ought to go round there?'

Minnie shook her head. 'Mums said not to. She said she had a feeling that the baby might come tonight and she wants to stay put in case the midwife can't get there.'

'Heavens . . .'

Dad was at the post, so it was just the two of us at dinner. For the first time in my life, I felt uncomfortable being alone with Minnie. I couldn't think of a thing to say that wouldn't prompt a

274

question about Frank, and I could see she was burning to ask me. We ate and washed up the plates in silence, and finally, she said, 'You ought to tell Frank.'

'Tell Frank what?'

'If there's someone else. It isn't fair, Lucy.'

I felt my face burning, and heard myself say, 'It isn't like that.'

'It's still leading him up the garden path, isn't it?'

I couldn't look her in the face. 'Look, Minnie, I don't want to talk about it. You wouldn't understand.'

She threw down her tea-towel. 'I'm not a complete baby, you know!'

'I know that, but it's just . . . complicated, that's all.'

'Complicated. I see. Look, there's no earthly reason why you should tell me, but it's not fair on Frank, that's all.'

There wasn't any answer to that, at least, not without admitting everything, and I couldn't bear to do that. I hate, hate, hate this feeling of separation between us, but it's my own fault, I suppose, so I'll just have to put up with it.

Nothing more was said. Minnie retreated under the stairs with a detective story. I stayed in the kitchen, trying to write my letter, but I couldn't settle down to it, and in the end I gave up. I could hear the drone of planes, but not near us, thank God, so I crawled out from under the table and found Mums's newspaper to take my mind off everything. Another wretched woman found murdered in the West End. I vaguely remembered Tom saying something about it, and realised, when I looked at the date, that the paper was several days old.

The planes got louder at about eleven, and I began to worry about Mums. The bangs and crashes got nearer and nearer, and by half past I was starting to panic, and was just about to go and find Minnie when she crawled in under the table and said, 'I know Mums said not to, but don't you think we ought to go to Mrs Dorn's and make sure they're all right?'

'Definitely. I was just about to come and say the same to you.'

Just as I said that, there was a very loud crash—couldn't have been more than a couple of roads away—that made the house shake. Minnie and I exchanged glances, then she shot out from under the table and started rummaging in one of the cupboards. I scrambled after her. 'What are you doing?'

She turned round, and I saw she had a big saucepan in each hand. 'Tin hats,' she said. 'Come on!'

We got ready in double-quick time, because the bangs seemed to be getting louder by the minute, then she clapped her saucepan over her head, and I did the same, and we rushed out of the house and groped our way into the street. It was almost pitch dark—just a couple of hooded lampposts with a circle of weak light at their bases—and we could hear planes and the whine and swoosh of shells, and—further off, thank goodness—the most terrific explosions. Every now and then the sky would flare up in light, and then go dark again, so that an orange afterglow seemed to imprint itself on my vision for several minutes afterwards.

We stumbled along holding the saucepans on

276

our heads with one hand and our torches in the other, then Minnie fell into someone's hedge, and I had to pull her out and banged my knee rather badly—thank heavens for slacks—and by the time we got to the corner of Mrs Dorn's road, we were panting like anything. I said, 'Do you know what number it is?'

'Oh . . . twelve, I think.'

I said, 'Well, they're going to get a shock if it isn't.'

We found the number on the gate, but when we knocked, nobody answered. After a minute or so, Minnie said, 'Of course, they'll be in the Anderson,' and made her way around the side of the house with me following. I'm ashamed to say that it flashed through my mind, most uncharitably, that the Anderson shelter might be the real reason for Mums's attendance on Mrs Dorn.

The garden was even darker than the street. I would have bashed my brains out tripping over the mangle if it hadn't been for the saucepan, and Mums must have heard the clang it made against the side of the house because we heard her calling out, 'Who's there?'

'It's us, Mums!'

I thought she'd shriek, but she just shouted out, 'Good! We could do with a bit of help!'

We climbed down into the shelter. It wasn't too bad in there, quite cheerful with the lantern, but the floor was wet and very slippery. Mums said, 'The midwife's not arrived yet, and the baby's well on the way, but there's no need to worry; we can manage.' I was amazed because she didn't sound like her normal self at all, but somebody much calmer and stronger, and not at all afraid.

277

Mr Dorn had put up bunk beds on one side of the shelter, with little curtains drawn across them for privacy. I heard a voice from behind, 'Oh, is that Minnie?' and a woman's hand pulled the curtain on the lower bunk back and we saw Mrs Dorn there in her dressing-gown, lying on her side with a mackintosh spread out underneath her. Then the curtain on the top bunk twitched, and a sweet little face appeared—Mrs Dorn's eldest— 'I'm Bella. I'm six.' She pointed at Mums. 'Is that your Mummy?'

'Yes,' I said.

'*My* mummy's having a baby.'

I raised my eyebrows at this, but Mums just said, 'Yes, dear. You pull the curtain now, and leave us in peace.'

'Only if I can see the baby when it comes, like you promised.'

'Yes, dear, of course you can.' Then she turned back to us. 'I want you to go into the house and get some hot water and towels.'

Mrs Dorn's head appeared again. 'I'm very sorry, dear, but all my nice things are upstairs, and you're not to go and fetch them, it isn't safe.'

Mums bent down and took her hand. 'Now don't you worry, they won't do anything silly.'

'Well, I don't want them putting themselves at risk on my account.' Then she looked at us and laughed. 'Nice hats, girls. You'll start a fashion.'

We went into the house and got the water going. I only managed to find one towel, but there was plenty of newspaper, so I took that instead, and some galoshes for Mums that I found by the kitchen door. The noise outside was as bad as ever, but inside the Anderson it was all calm and rather

278

lovely, somehow, in spite of the muddy floor and the lack of space. Mrs Dorn was very quiet. I'd always thought people screamed when they were having a baby. Mums was calmer than I've ever seen her, holding Mrs Dorn's hand and giving her encouragement. She seemed so kind and wise; a different person, in fact.

I said this to Minnie when we went back to the kitchen. Mrs Dorn's got a good, big table, like ours, so we pushed it against the wall and settled ourselves underneath to wait for further instructions. I could well have done with a cup of tea, but it seemed a bit rotten to take Mrs Dorn's ration, so I didn't suggest it.

Minnie said, 'She's extraordinary, but I suppose it's from having babies herself. She loves all that, you know. She told me once it was the happiest time of her life, when we were small. She wanted more—more than just the two of us, I mean—but Dad said they couldn't afford it.'

'Oh.' I was a bit shocked by that. It made me think how little I really know about Mums. As a mother, she's the most maddening person in the world, but I don't have much idea of her as an individual. I suppose I've never been close enough, or interested enough, to ask.

'Just imagine,' Minnie said, 'bringing a baby into all this.'

'It seems crazy, doesn't it?'

'But people go on with their lives, don't they? War or no war.' She seemed so calm about it, rather like Mums, that I didn't want to show her how shaken I felt. I suppose it's this business of people not acting how you expect them to, although in this case, it was just as well! Minnie

279

said, 'I've got a cig in my bag—just the one. Do you want to share it?' Then, rather sheepishly, 'I pinched it from Mums. Don't tell, will you?'

' 'Course I won't, silly.'

We'd smoked about half when I noticed it was a Players and it suddenly dawned on me that it must be one of Mr Bridges' cigarettes. That made me feel a bit peculiar, but when I turned to give it back to Minnie, she'd nodded off. I didn't want to disturb her, so I put the cigarette out, and after a while I dropped off too.

Mums put her head round the back door at quarter past three to tell us that the baby, a boy, had arrived, and we traipsed over to the Anderson to see it. It was wrapped in a blanket, and all we could see was its face, which looked very squashed. Minnie held it up to show Bella, while Mums looked after Mrs Dorn and made her comfortable. There wasn't really room for me to fit inside, so I stood at the entrance and watched, and there was something so wonderful about it—miraculous, almost, that this new life had come into the world in the middle of so much death and destruction— that I suddenly felt sure I was going to cry. Fortunately, at that point Mums looked up and said, 'I'm sure we could all do with a cup of tea, Lucy, if you'd like to make one.' I said yes, of course, and fled back to the house before anyone noticed what a fool I was.

Just as I was filling the pot, Dad turned up with the midwife in tow. She was most displeased when I told her she was too late, as if the baby ought to have waited, and bustled straight out to the Anderson to see Mrs Dorn.

Dad said, 'I'm glad to see you're still in

280

one piece.'

'Don't be angry, Dad. We were worried, and I think Mums was pretty pleased to see us.'

'I'm sure she was. Is everything all right?'

'I think so. It's a boy, and Mums was marvellous. She didn't panic, just stayed there with Mrs Dorn, all the time, and helped her, and . . . you know.'

'Yes, I know. And I'm sure you were a great help, too.'

'Yes, but we just fetched things. Mums was the one who was *there*. She was wonderful.'

'She does get it right sometimes, you know.'

'Oh, Dad, I didn't mean . . .'

'It's all right, Smiler, I know. Now then, let's see to that tea, shall we?'

Minnie came back then, and started rummaging about in Mrs Dorn's dresser. I asked her what she was looking for, and she said, 'Brown paper.'

I said, 'What on earth for?'

Minnie looked uncomfortable, and whispered, 'I think it's for . . . you know . . . the *afterbirth*. To wrap it in.'

I wished I hadn't asked!

It was much quieter when I took the tray out, and after a while Minnie and Mums came back to the kitchen. Dad said, 'Here's the heroine of the hour,' and Mums went pink and said, 'Oh, nonsense,' but I could see she was smiling. Dad held out his arms and said, 'I can't give you a medal, but I'll give you a kiss, anyway,'—and she let him!

I thought, I've never seen them embrace before, and suddenly they became not Mums and Dad, but Ethel and Billy, two individuals with a relationship that had nothing to do with Minnie and me, and

281

the thought of their life before we existed and the love that had brought us into being made me oddly sentimental about them, in a way I don't ever remember being before. I couldn't have voiced it, and anyway, it wasn't necessary. As a family we're not given to displays of feeling, unless you count bad temper on the part of Mums and me, but when they turned back to us, their faces seemed to shine with happiness, and the room was full of love, with all the petty irritations and annoyances forgotten. But it was embarrassing, too, because you could see from the faces that everyone was full of these emotions, but nobody quite knew how to express them.

Mums laughed and said, 'Well, I don't know what I'd have done if you two hadn't turned up. I know I told you not to, but I'm glad you did, and Mrs Dorn says to thank you, too. Oh, Billy, you should have seen them. Go on, show Dad your hats.'

So we put the saucepans on our heads and paraded across the kitchen pretending we were mannequins, while Dad laughed and clapped. 'Oh, very smart—full marks for initiative!'

After that, he said he had to get back to the post, and that we ought to go home and get some sleep. The All-Clear hadn't gone, but it was pretty quiet, so Minnie and I went up to our rooms. I caught sight of us in the bathroom mirror while we were washing our faces, both hanging on to the basin with one hand, leaning shoulder to shoulder to keep upright. 'Oh, dear, look at us! I'm so tired I could sleep for a week.'

'Me, too.' Minnie yawned. 'But it was lovely, wasn't it?'

'Yes. Yes, it was.'

'I'm glad we went. Well done you, for suggesting it.'

Minnie mumbled something, but I couldn't hear it because her face was covered over with her flannel.

I said, 'I'm sorry we argued.'

Minnie pulled the flannel off her face and hung it on the rail. 'So am I.'

'That silly poem . . . our friendship won't fade, will it?'

Minnie rolled her eyes at me. ' 'Course not. Come on.' She put her hands on my hips and pointed me towards the door, and we did a very feeble version of the conga across the landing to our rooms.

' 'Night, Lucy.' She closed her door.

' 'Night, Minnie.'

I stared for a moment at the saucepan, which for some reason I'd brought upstairs, then went into my room. I shut the door, fell on the bed, and was instantly asleep.

*　　　*　　　*

I was too tired in the morning to think sensibly about anything. I'd have been excited about my first shift on the mobile canteen if I wasn't so jolly tired. I just hope I don't make a complete hash of it. Told Mums, so she shouldn't worry, and—to my surprise—she seemed to think it was a good idea. Minnie looked rather jealous, and said it sounded heaps more fun than fire-watching.

*　　　*　　　*

I yawned my way to work and back, and was asleep by half past eight, and so were Mums and Minnie. I don't think anything short of a direct hit would have woken us. A month ago, that would have been out of the question, so it just shows that you can get used to anything, given time. I am looking forward to the mobile canteen tonight, but even more to the weekend—more sleep—and to a letter from dear, dear Tom: short of the war ending, I can't think of a better recipe for happiness. I do hope he's safe. I don't think I could bear it if anything happened to him. Said a prayer for him, as I do every night, now. I go into the garden with the excuse of checking the blackouts and stand by the rosebush where I buried the bird's wings. I know it sounds silly, but it makes me feel closer to him, somehow.

FRIDAY 11TH OCTOBER

Rene

Every night this week I've tried everything to put it out of my mind, but every time I look at the clock, I think, three more hours, two more hours, and I've got to go out there . . . Tonight was no different. I tried to get dressed, picking things up and putting them down again, putting on stockings—that was as far as I got, because my hands were shaking so much I could hardly fasten the suspenders. I had a cigarette to calm my nerves, then another, and I thought, I won't have any left at this rate; I'll have to go out for those, at least, try to get some more.

I've been thinking, suppose something does happen to me, I ought to write a letter for Tommy to read when he's older. Not to say . . . not that I'm—not that I do what I do—but just to tell him I love him, really. No one'd want to discover that their mother was a prostitute, would they?

I wasn't doing this when he was born, of course, only later, but I don't want him to think it was his fault, you know, that I did it for the money because he came along, although I suppose that's true, in a way. Mind you, there's plenty of women in my situation that don't go on the streets, but it came easy to me, and it was good money, so I did it.

My first idea was, if I'm going to write this letter, I ought to put something about his father. But then I realised, I can hardly write that Vic was a bastard who lied to me and left me in the lurch, and the more I thought about it, the more I thought that, sometimes, it's better not to tell the truth. Then I thought, well, if I'd known the truth about Vic being married, I wouldn't have gone with him. But that was a lie, really, because I was head over heels in love with him, and when you're like that you'll do anything they ask, won't you? And if I hadn't, Tommy wouldn't have been born, and then . . . well, it's no use trying to change history. Heavens, if we could do that, we'd never have a war, would we? If I were to tell Tommy that I'm his mother, not Dora, I'd be doing it for myself, not for him. And I want him to have a good life. Respectable. I don't want him to think badly of himself. Suppose when he's older he finds a nice girl and wants to marry her, and if he feels he's got to tell her about me, she might not want any more to do with him. No one could blame her for that. Mind you, it's not my name on the certificate—we agreed it before: Joe would go and register the birth and put Dora down as the mother. That's against the law, of course, but she is his aunt, so it wasn't like putting down just anyone.

We made a promise, the three of us, and it wouldn't be right to break it. Mind you, when we said that, I didn't reckon on Joe turning into a miser, and I don't suppose Dora did, either. The more I think about that, the more I see I will have to have it out with him—interference between a man and wife is one thing, but when it's affecting my boy . . . and I've always kept my side of the bargain, so Tommy's never wanted for anything. But it's set me wondering—I always give the money to Dora, but if Joe's been taking it off her and putting it in that chest of his, under the bed . . . She told me he wouldn't go down the shelter with them during the raids, so I thought, I suppose he must sit at home counting out his money.

In the end, I just wrote a few words to Tommy— *Dear Tommy, You mean a great deal to me. I wish you a long and happy life. Your loving Auntie Rene xxx*—then I put it in an envelope with a photo of me and Vic on the pier at Brighton. Nothing special, just strolling along together, arm in arm, all done up in our best. There was nothing written on the back, and I didn't put anything.

Perhaps I should have written a longer letter, but I decided I'd never be able to explain, not properly. And I'd never be able to tell him that, however he came about, the first time I held him I felt so much love for him that I could have just about burst— more than anything I've ever felt in my entire life . . .

I wrote on the envelope:

Dear Dora. If I'm no longer around, I hope you will give this to Tommy on his twenty-first birthday. I have broken no confidences, but if he should ask any questions, tell him as you think fit. Thank you for all your kindness to him and to me, from Rene. One more thing I will say, I couldn't have wished for a better sister.

I'd say Dora'd recognise Vic all right, and Tommy's got a look of him, so perhaps he'll guess . . . but she could always tell him it was a relative, a cousin or something. Then I thought, right: now I've done that, I'll go and see Joe. I wasn't going to let on that I know about the chest with the money in it, only to say how I'm frightened because of the murders and I can't go out and earn for a while. I'd got it planned for him to tell Dora that I was still feeling poorly, but nothing serious, so she wouldn't start worrying about me.

I was just crossing Drury Lane when the siren went, but I thought, no time like the present, I'm damned if I'll stop now, and I knew Joe'd be at home with his precious money, while Dora's always in the shelter by half past six, warning or no warning. They've got one they share with some of the other blocks, not in their yard, but further down. It's a good one, too—iron bunk beds they've got, and two Elsan toilets—a lot more comfortable than Soho Square. But you can't just go and park yourself in there because it's only meant for the residents.

I thought I'd better get a move on, so I went

pelting across the junction and down to Dora's building, and just as I got there, I heard this great load of planes, hundreds of them by the sound of it, all droning, and then the guns started up and the noise was enough to deafen you. Fortunately, Dora and Joe's flat's on the nearest staircase—it's one of these arrangements where the stairs are outside, but they're covered, if you see what I mean, and you've got three floors with one flat on each, and then there's the courtyard outside with the washhouses and a place to hang the washing and all the rest of it.

Dora and Joe are up on the top floor, but I never got there. The whole building's shaking and I'm huddled under the stairs, eyes tight shut, fingers in my ears—fat lot of good that did—when suddenly there was this tapping on my shoulder, so I look round and it's Mrs Everley, their neighbour from downstairs, and she's making signs at me, come in, come in . . . so I follow her, and we run through her front room and into the bedroom and we both crawl in under the bed, which is one of those old-fashioned affairs, big high iron bedstead, and she's got the eiderdown underneath, so we're both lying on that, fairly screaming at each other over this racket. 'It's Mrs Nicholls's sister, isn't it?'

I said, 'That's right. Rene Tate. Kind of you to take me in like this.'

'I'm Mrs Everley. Honestly, this is the worst yet. I hope we're giving them a taste of their own medicine, I really do, because this is murder, no other word for it. I'd be in the shelter now only I was looking for my cat, because he's expecting— Oh, I've done it again, said "he"—it's a "she" really, but that's what I thought at the beginning you see, that it was a boy, so I called it George. He's out there somewhere and I'm worried sick.'

I said, 'They can take care of themselves, can't they, cats?'

'I suppose so, but with all this . . . Oh, I do hope he's all right—'

At that moment everything went black and there was this sound of smashing and crashing, tearing paper, crackling and ripping, not a bomb but more like a building being knocked down, and it was right over our heads. I suddenly thought, it's true what they say, you don't hear the one that gets you, and then all my nose and throat were filled with dust, thick white stuff, choking me so I thought I'd suffocate. I could hear this sort of croaking noise coming from my left, and I thought, it's Mrs Everley, I've got to get to her, and then that was drowned in this great rumbling—more collapsing brickwork—like an avalanche, the whole building crashing down on our heads. After that, there was a bit of quiet. I couldn't hear anything from Mrs Everley because my ears were still ringing like anything, and I didn't know if I ought to move, but I started feeling towards her with my fingers, inching along this eiderdown, and then suddenly I couldn't get any further so I felt around a bit and it was the bottom of the bed, the springs—and I realised that her side of it must have collapsed from the weight of the ceiling and everything coming down, and she was trapped underneath it.

My first thought was to find my torch, which was in my pocket, not my bag, or I'd never have got it out, so I slid my hand down, very carefully, and got hold of it. It was all gritty with dust, but it still worked, thank God. When I shone it about, it was like looking into a thick fog, but I could see bricks and bits of cornicing and what have you on the floor in front of me, and I started inching out, little by little, because I didn't want anything coming down on me. When I looked over to my right I could see Mrs Everley's head, twisted to one side, just one eye and the corner of her mouth, and this bedstead right across her neck, squashing it. I think I must have called out her name, because I saw the eye move to look at me, and then she made a little noise like she was trying to clear her throat. I said, 'It's all right, the rescue men'll be here soon.'

She said, 'I'm only sorry I couldn't offer you a cup of tea.'

I said, 'Oh, never mind about that, I'm sure we'll be out of here in a minute.' She didn't answer, and after a few minutes I realised that she was dead, poor woman.

I thought I ought to try and move the other way, but when I looked towards the door, it was all blocked with bricks and mortar and heaven knows what, but I thought there might be a way through and anyway, I wasn't going to get very far stuck under the blasted bed, which might have collapsed on *me* at any moment, so I started wriggling out, very slowly, on my stomach, so as not to disturb anything, until I found myself on my hands and knees in the middle of a lot of rubble. I started inching forwards, but then more stuff came raining down, great lumps of debris, and I hunched right over to make myself as small as I could and put my arms over my head to protect myself.

There was complete silence—at least, I think it was silence, or perhaps I was still a bit deaf from all the din—and I stayed like that for a while because I was a bit frightened to move in case I dislodged anything. When I looked through my fingers I could make out laths and bricks through the dust, and what looked like bits of smashed furniture, and I was just wondering if I could manage to get over to the door before anything else came down when I realised there was something lying across my shoulders. I put out one of my hands to feel it, and it was fingers: a hand. You know my first thought? That's nice, someone's got their arm round me. I wondered for a moment if it was Mrs Everley, that she wasn't dead like I'd thought, and she had managed to crawl out from under the bed somehow and get to me, but when I clasped the fingers I knew it couldn't be a woman's hand because they were hairy, and thick, and I thought, it can't be the rescue, not yet . . . and then it fell down on the floor in front of me. It was still attached to an arm, but where it should have been joined to the shoulder, it was just a bloody, sticky mess. I was too shocked to scream, just stared at it, and I saw this mark on the forearm, dark blue, and even through the dust I could see it was a tattoo, an anchor, and letters underneath.

It was Joe's. He'd got the tattoo when he was in the navy. Dora always said it looked common. She never liked him to roll up his shirt sleeves in case someone saw. Even when I came round, if he'd been doing something in the house, because he was good that way, she'd say to him, 'Put yourself straight, we've got company.' I could see him in my mind's eye, whole, with a hammer in his hand and a mouthful of nails, and I thought: where's the rest of him? Could he still be alive with his arm ripped away like that? There wasn't no material on it, no shirt or anything. I suppose it must have been blasted off him when the bomb came down. It sounds stupid now, but I thought, Dora wouldn't like people to see that, I ought to cover it with something, but of course there wasn't anything, and the next minute the noise started again, and I curled tight into a ball on the floor with this stuff—bricks and plaster and wood—raining down on me. I can tell you, I've never prayed harder in my life than I did then.

When it stopped it was all pitch black again, and I couldn't find the torch, so I felt about a bit with my hands, very gently, and it seemed to me I was underneath this sort of criss-cross arrangement of floorboards and beams like a tent, but flatter, with not even enough space to sit up. I couldn't see Mrs Everley any more, or Joe's arm, which was a blessing, but then it dawned on me that the whole block was directly above my head, two storeys' worth perched on top of my little wooden tent, and it could all come down on me at any moment. And of course I was in the bedroom, so if the rescue wanted to come through where the door had been, there was the front room to get through first, and from what I'd seen in the doorway, that wasn't going to happen for a while. I started thinking, supposing it all falls in before they come? I'll be crushed.

I thought, it's like a grave I'm in, a tomb, because it was, just like it, so I said to myself, pull yourself together you silly cow, they've got to have the rescue men out there, looking. But I'd got all these thoughts running through my head: what if it's just my legs or my chest that get crushed? What if I don't die quick? What if there's gas? I had a sniff, but I couldn't smell anything, and then I suddenly thought: what if the whole street's been hit? The shelter? Tommy and Dora? I said, 'Dear God, I'll give my life willingly if you'll only save my Tommy. Let him live, let him not be hurt, and you can do what you like with me.' And in the back of my mind, all the time, I'm waiting for it to happen, but then I'm calling out, 'Help!' and 'Down here!' just in case, you know . . . but at the same time I'm imagining these bricks falling down on me, smashing my arms and legs, and praying, 'Let it be quick, please God, let it be quick,' and all these pictures were going through my mind: Mrs Everley, and Joe's arm, and poor Mrs Mitten clutching Mr Mitten's metal nose, and the rescue man telling me how he was all in pieces like a jigsaw, and imagining this whole heap of stuff on top of me, toppling over, just ready to come crashing down . . .

Well, after a while—I couldn't tell you how long, because I think I was in a daze—an old hymn suddenly came into my mind, one of those we used to sing at school. So I thought, let's see if I can remember it, and I'm warbling away to myself, very quiet, just to try and raise my spirits a bit: *The Lord's my shepherd, I'll not want, He maketh me down to lie, In pa-a-stures green, He lea-ea-deth me, The qui-i-et waters by* . . . but then I got to the bit about death's dark vale and I thought, blimey, this is no good, I've got to think of something a bit more cheerful than this. So then I tried 'Onward Christian Soldiers', and that was a bit jollier, except I could only remember one verse and the chorus. 'Lead, kindly light, amidst the encircling gloom' didn't do me a lot of good, and then 'Rock of Ages'—well, the only words I could remember for that was the bit about *While I draw this fleeting breath, When my eyelids close in death, When I soar through tracts unknown, See Thee on Thy judgement throne* . . . So that wasn't much comfort, either, and as for the bit about judgement, well!

I suppose I'd never thought about it much before. I mean, you don't when you're a child, you just sing the words, la, la, la, and never stop to think about what they mean, do you? So I lay there racking my brains in the pitch dark, and every so often, I called out 'Help!' but the only hymns I could think of had words about death and darkness and judgement and all the rest of it, and in the end I said to myself, this is no bloody good, so I started off: *Joe brought his concertina, and Nobby brought the beer; And all the little nippers swung upon the chandelier; A blackout warden passing yelled, 'Ma, pull down that blind; Just look at what you're showing' and we shouted 'Never mind'; Ooh! Knees up Mother Brown, knees up Mother Brown; Come along dearie, let it go, ee-i, ee-i, ee-i-o* . . .

You hear about these shelters in the east end where they do all that, singing, and I don't think I'd take to that at all, but it was a bit of comfort, and certainly better than nothing, so I carried on a bit—not loud, because I couldn't, but sort of half-singing, half-muttering to myself, *It's your blooming birthday, let's wake up all the town.*

And that's when I heard tapping. Very soft, but different from any noise I'd heard before, so I'm shouting out, 'Help! Down here! Help!' at the top of my voice. Well, nobody answered, so I shouted again, and I'm thinking, *please, let there be somebody there*, because I'd got my hopes right up, you know, as soon as I'd heard the tapping, and I thought, what if I've imagined it, and there's nobody there, or they can't hear me and they just leave me to die? So I'm yelling my head off, and every so often I stop and listen, and then I hear a man's voice, very faint, 'Hello?'

'I'm here! Down here! Come and get me, for God's sake!'

More tapping. I thought, right, Rene, don't panic. You'll be out of here, girl, you'll be all right, just keep calm . . . and I'm telling myself this, but then I'm thinking, what if they're going the wrong way, because it didn't seem to come any nearer, or what if they do the wrong thing and it all falls down? Then I hear, still very faint, 'Who are you? What's your name?'

'Tate! Rene Tate!'

'Are you hurt?'

'No, I'm all right! Just hurry up!'

'Do you live here?'

'No, that's Mrs Everley!'

'What's that?'

'Mrs Everley!'

'Is she with you?'

'She's here, but she's dead.'

'What's that?'

'Dead!'

'Anyone else?'

'No!'

'We're coming for you . . . Can you still hear me?'

'Yes!'

'Don't move!'

'I can't move, I'm trapped!'

'Right—just stay there!'

I thought, I can hardly go anywhere, can I, you

295

silly bugger? But I felt a lot better after that, or at least I did until I started hearing the planes again, and the guns, and then I just—oh, I can't explain. It about finished me, I can tell you, hearing that and thinking, that's it, the house'll come down and the shelter and Tommy and Dora . . . it's no good, I can't begin to tell you what that felt like, but I'll never forget it, never, lying down there in that tomb and thinking, that's it, I'm finished. And I'm screaming, I can hear myself, this noise coming out of me, screaming and wailing, and it was like . . . well, you're just so *alone* . . . I was in such a panic I could hardly breathe, and then there was more dust, a great choking fall of it, coming down between the planks, and I thought, next it'll be the bricks and that'll be it, and I couldn't think any more, not about songs or Tommy or Mrs Everley or anything, just that I was going to die, shut up in this tiny little place, all alone in the dark. If there is such a thing as hell, that's what it must be like, how I felt then.

Then there was silence for a bit, and more tapping, and eventually I could see a little bit of light through the wood, and after a while, I started to hear voices—not the words, just men talking to each other, and then I started to make out the odd word and I realised they weren't coming in from the top, as I'd thought, but from the side. And then I realised that they were sawing wood and taking out the bits and pieces to make a sort of tunnel, but from what I could see it was getting darker, not lighter, and there was more and more plaster dust trickling down on top of me—they couldn't help that, I suppose, but it felt like I was breathing it in, and it was choking me. So I turned my face as

296

much to the ground as I could, but it was hard because the space was so little I was terrified I'd dislodge something, and that would be that.

I heard this odd sort of flapping noise, like heavy material, and I couldn't think what it was. I was getting these terrible cramps in my legs from being all screwed up in such a tiny space and more than anything else I wanted to straighten them out, but I knew I couldn't, so I was trying to get the singing going again, only this time in my head: *Knees up, Mother Brown, knees up, Mother Brown*, over and over, like that, but to be honest, this time it was all more like a dream—well, a nightmare, really—than anything else, and I thought, I'm going mad, they've left me here to go off my head . . . then suddenly I could see this little light coming from the planks beside my head, and there was a face there—a girl's face. She must have had a torch because I could just see her out of the corner of my eye, and it was the girl from the shelter, the one that gave me the look—the one with the airman, the handsome one—and I thought, this is it, I'm dead and she's dead too, and it's the judgement, like the hymns. This is what it's like, she's come to tell me I have to stay here for ever, and I've closed my eyes tight, and I'm waiting, but then I heard her say, 'Hello, I'm Lucy. What's your name?'

I must have said something back, because then she says, 'It's all right. The doctor wants you to have this tablet.'

'Why aren't you in the shelter?'

'I've been working in the canteen. The mobile one. If I can put my arm through this gap here, can you take the tablet in your hand?'

'I'll try . . .'

297

'Wait a minute . . . I'll shine the torch on my hand, so you can see. Can you put your hand out?' Then the light was dazzling me, and the next moment, I could feel the warmth of her hand on mine, through the grit, and I knew she must be real and not dead like I'd thought she was.

I said, 'I don't know if I can swallow it,' because my throat was that dry.

She said, 'They didn't give me any water. Do you want me to ask for some?'

'No, don't go . . . I'll try.'

'See if you can do it. It's ever so little.'

I did manage after a few tries, but it wasn't easy.

'What was it?'

'Morphia, I think. Just a little. It shouldn't be long, now. It's just . . . well, it's hard for them to make the hole any bigger without . . . you know . . . and none of the men could get through, so I said I'd come.'

'You're very kind. I'd like it if . . . I mean, if you don't mind, but please, would you hold my hand?'

'Of course I will. It's Miss Tate, isn't it? That's what they said.'

'Yes, but don't call me Miss Tate; my name's Rene.'

'Well, Rene, pleased to meet you.'

'You too, dear. Shame it had to be like this.'

'Yes, it is, rather.'

Then we had another great fall of plaster dust, and neither of us said anything for a couple of minutes because we had our heads down.

After a while, she said, 'Are you all right?'

'Yes.'

'I must say, I'm jolly glad I didn't wash my hair last night.'

298

It was funny, really, her stretched out on the ground, and me all curled up, just with our hands touching through this little space, but so reassuring, it made me feel quite peaceful, really. I said to her, 'Oh, it is nice, having someone to talk to. I've been down here ever such a long time.'

She said, 'Yes, but it'll soon be over.'

'People keep saying that, but no one's come.'

'I'm here.'

'Yes, dear. And I'm ever so grateful.'

All the time, I could feel her hand in mine, and she never let go, she just kept saying, 'You'll be all right. They'll have you out.'

Then the tablet must have taken hold, because I started to feel a bit better, and I said, 'Oh, thank you, thank you for staying with me.'

She said, 'Now listen, Rene, if I can come in, you can come out. I can see you, with my torch, and you're slim, like me.'

I said, 'Well, I don't know how you can make that out, with me all hunched up like this.'

She said, 'I remember you, I've seen you before . . .' and I thought, oh, dear . . . but then she said, 'I'm sorry if I . . . well, in the shelter, it was a bit of a night, you know.'

I said, 'Don't you worry about that, dear, we're all human. You know there's a body down here, don't you? It's the woman who rents this flat. Behind me.'

'Gosh . . .' She took a deep breath and said, 'I'm rather glad they didn't tell me that.'

'Well, it was very brave of you to come.'

'Oh, nonsense.'

I must have drifted a bit then, I think, but after a while, we heard the man's voice, louder than

299

before. 'All right, miss?'

We both shouted, 'Yes!'

'Soon have you out, now. You better come back now, miss.'

I said, 'Oh, you're not going?'

'Well, I've got to. But they must have made the hole wide enough to fetch you out, so it can't be long. Tell you what, I'll be waiting with a cup of tea. How does that sound?'

'It sounds like heaven. And you're an angel.' I gave her hand a squeeze before I let go, and I said, 'Thank you.'

'I'll see you in a minute. Now I've got to crawl out backwards . . .' She gave a little laugh. 'Thank goodness for slacks, that's all I can say.'

There was more talk after that, and then it was a man on the other side of the planks, sawing, then hands reaching for me, and the man got his hands under my armpits and dragged me out through this sort of tunnel, and at the top I saw they'd covered up a great section with a tarpaulin, so that must have been the flapping noise I heard.

It was pretty dark, apart from the torches, but half the block was gone. There was just a heap of rubble with odd shapes sticking up here and there. The centre staircase was still in place, and as I looked, a searchlight beam went across and I saw the wall of what had been the top flat in the middle of the block, green patterned wallpaper and little table with barley-sugar legs standing up there all by itself. There looked to be something on top, as well, an ornament of some sort, but it was too far away and the beam passed before I could take in any more.

There were people everywhere, passing out

baskets of debris, ambulances backed up, ARP, but I was too tired and dazed to take much of it in, really. A bossy woman—a nurse, judging by her uniform—came and was all for getting me to the first aid post, but I told her, 'There's nothing wrong with me, and I'm not going anywhere until I know about my family.' She said the Wild Street shelter hadn't been hit, but I told her that wasn't good enough, and I wasn't going nowhere until I'd seen them because I'd got to tell Dora about Joe. Then of course she's asked me who Joe is, and I've explained, and I suppose she must have reckoned I was all right after that, because she didn't press it, just said she'd go and have a word with the warden about the records, whatever they are.

I could hardly stand, so the rescue man carried me over to sit on the kerb by the mobile canteen because there wasn't any glass back there. When he put me down on the ground I could suddenly feel my legs again, very cold, and I looked down and saw my skirt and slip were ripped right down the side and you could see the tops of my stockings. That was pretty much all that was left of them. The rest was torn to shreds.

I was shivering all over, so somebody fetched a couple of blankets, and next time I looked up, there was the girl with a cup of tea.

I said, 'Oh, you kept your promise.'

'Of course I did. It's hot, and there's plenty of sugar.'

'I'm sorry, dear, what did you say your name was?'

'Lucy. Lucy Armitage.'

'Thank you, Lucy.'

She tried to put the mug into my hands but I

301

couldn't hold it, so she said she'd sit down beside me on the kerb and hold the cup so I could have a sip whenever I liked. That was too much, her kindness, and I'm afraid I made a fool of myself then, and started to cry a bit, and she said, 'Here,' and took her handkerchief out of her pocket and held it out to me. 'I'm afraid it's a bit crumpled, but it's quite clean.'

So I had a bit of a mop-up, and the hankie, after, was stiff with plaster and grime. I said, 'I'm ever so sorry, I've ruined it.'

Lucy said, 'Oh, it'll wash off. Now then. I'll just put this tea down, and I'll go and fetch my handbag. I've got another hankie, so you can tidy up a bit more before you see your little boy.'

'What did you say?'

'Tommy. Your little boy. You were talking about him. You know, down there.'

'Oh. Well, I . . . He's not *mine*, of course, he's my sister's, but . . . but . . . I . . .'

'But I thought . . .' She frowned for a moment and said, 'Oh, dear, I'm sorry. You were saying you love him as if he was your own, weren't you? That's what you said, and I misunderstood you.'

'Yes . . . yes, that's right . . . as if he was . . . I do . . . yes . . .'

'Of course. How silly of me. Now, I'll just be a minute.'

What a nice girl! When she'd gone, I thought, where's *my* handbag? And then I remembered it was still down under the bed with poor Mrs Everley. I tried to remember what was in there—keys, purse . . . not that there was much in that . . . identity card, lighter, a photograph of Tommy, compact, lipstick . . .

Not much chance of getting any of it back. At least I always leave my ration book at home unless I'm shopping, so that was one thing I didn't have to worry about.

'Here we are.' Lucy came back with her handbag. 'I expect you'd like a cigarette, wouldn't you? It always helps.'

'I can't take that, it's your last.'

'I insist.' She lit it and handed it over. 'Now you'll have to have it.' She watched me for a moment, then said, 'That's better, isn't it?'

'Lovely. Just what I needed. You are a dear.'

Lucy gave me another hankie, all neatly folded, and said, 'Take this.'

'It's no good, dear, without soap and water.'

'Well, you keep it anyway. You might need it later.'

An ARP warden came up then, with a lot of papers in his hand. 'Are you Miss Tate?'

'That's right.'

'This Joe you mentioned . . . We've got a Mr J. Nicholls listed for Flat Three; would that be the person?'

'Joe Nicholls, yes. Do you know . . . ?'

'We've dug him out, yes, but—'

'He's dead, isn't he?'

'I'm afraid so, miss. Are you a relative?'

'He's married to my sister. Have you told her?'

'No one's been notified, as far as I know, but—'

I said, 'Right. I want to see them—her and the boy. I'd like to be the one to tell them, if you don't mind. They're in the shelter down the street.'

'Well, miss, they can't come up here. You shouldn't be here yourself, now.'

'I tell you, I'm going nowhere until I've seen

303

Dora and Tommy.'

Lucy said, 'I can take you down to the shelter, if you think you can manage it.'

The warden said, 'She ought to go to the first aid post.'

I said, 'Who's "she"? The cat's mother? I'm fine. I'll do all that later. Give us a hand up, Lucy, and we'll go down there now.'

She said, 'Are you sure you can manage?'

I said, 'Well, we won't be beating any greyhounds, but we'll get there,' because I was determined I was going to tell Dora and Tommy myself. I was a bit shaky when I got up—it didn't help that I'd lost a heel off one of my shoes, but I couldn't take them off because of all the glass. I said to Lucy, 'I can't bear that type. Bloody little Hitler.'

'He's only doing his job, Rene.'

'So were those up there that bombed us. Everyone's only doing their bloody job . . .'

By the time we got to the shelter my knees were buckling, so Lucy found me a place to sit, and said, 'Right, I'll go and speak to the warden about your sister, then I'd better be off.'

'Thank you, dear. For all you've done. I'm very grateful. And if there's anything I can do for you . . .'

Lucy gave me a lovely smile. 'It's nothing, really. Goodbye, Rene.'

When Dora and Tommy came over with the warden, they just stood and stared at me. I wanted to get up and give Tommy a hug, but I didn't think I'd manage it, so I said, 'Don't you recognise your Auntie?'

Dora said, 'Blimey, Rene, *I* wouldn't have recognised you! What happened?'

I said, 'I was in the block.'

'Oh.'

I didn't know how to tell her, but before I could start, she said, very quietly, 'It's Joe, isn't it?'

'Oh, Dora, I'm so sorry . . .'

'Are you sure? I mean, there's not . . . there's no . . . ?'

I shook my head. 'The warden up there, he told me.'

'But what . . . I mean, why are you . . . I don't understand. Oh, I knew, I knew this would happen. I said to him, "Joe, you've got to come to the shelter." I kept telling him, but he wouldn't listen. Why didn't he listen, Rene? I told him . . .'

'I'm sorry, Dora.'

'Did you see him, Rene? That's why you were there, wasn't it, to see him?'

'I didn't see him. I was there just when it started—never even got up the stairs.'

'Oh, I'm glad. I'm glad you didn't fight. I wouldn't have wanted him to die angry. It was bad enough us having words before, but if . . . if . . .'

She stood there with tears streaming down her face, and I felt so helpless, I couldn't even get up. All I had was this handkerchief Lucy'd given me, so I held it out and said, 'Come on, Dora, sit down.'

I don't remember much after that, just Tommy in Dora's lap with his arms round her neck saying, 'Mum, where's Daddy? Where's Daddy?' and Dora like a block of wood staring straight ahead, muttering, 'I told him, I told him . . .' over and over, and Tommy shouting louder and louder, drowning her out, and then it all seemed to fall away from me like a wave and that was the last I knew.

Lucy

Talk about a baptism of fire—what an adventure! I went to the centre for my first shift, very nervous in case I didn't measure up, and was summoned to the office to meet the van driver, who turned out to be a woman! Her name was Mrs Large, and she looked as if she'd made quite an effort to live up to it, which was rather unfortunate. Hennaed hair—not a very becoming shade—but very jolly and nice. The van was duly loaded with tea and meat pies and some rather nasty-looking cake on trays, and then we set off. It was a difficult route, terribly bumpy, but I must say, Mrs L was terrifically calm and rather good at it.

Two stops at bomb sites, and lots of banter with the demolition workers, who seem a merry lot, and then back to the centre to pick up more food, and—thank goodness—the chance to spend a penny. I'd just come out of the lavatory when the woman in charge rushed up, very flustered, and said there was an emergency and we were wanted immediately and why weren't we on our way already? Felt like retorting, because nobody's told us where to go, and I could see from Mrs L's expression that she was thinking the same, but neither of us said anything.

It took us quite a time to get there—diversions everywhere—but Mrs L was marvellous. Even with the light failing, I could see that it was much worse than the previous two—half a block was down, with beams and bricks and odd things strewn all over the place, and it was very obvious that there must be people trapped underneath, because there was so much activity.

We'd only been there about twenty minutes—very busy—when Mrs L was called away by one of the ARP men. Another man came to join them, and they went into a sort of huddle just outside the van. I seized the chance for some much-needed tidying up, but every time I glanced through the hatch, they seemed to be looking in my direction. Eventually, Mrs L poked her head in and said, 'Could you go outside for a minute, dear, and speak to the gentlemen?'

I said 'Of course,' and went out, Mrs L following. 'This is Dr Royce, dear. He'd like to ask you something.'

Dr Royce took a step back and looked me up and down, then turned to the ARP man beside him and said, 'What do you think?'

'I'd say so.'

Dr Royce asked my name, and then, to my utter astonishment, he asked what was my hip measurement! I thought I must be imagining things, but he repeated the question, so I said, 'Thirty-four inches.'

The ARP man said, 'We've got a problem, you see. There's a party down there, and we're digging her out, but it's going to take time and she's getting rather hysterical. We don't think she's badly hurt, but the doctor says she could do with having morphia. The way the stuff's fallen, there's a bit of a tunnel to where she is, but none of us can fit through and we're afraid she'll start thrashing around and bring the lot down, so we wondered if you'd be willing . . .'

'To take it to her?' I looked at Mrs L.

'I've said I can spare you, dear. I'd do it myself, only I'm too big.'

'Well, I suppose . . . I mean, yes, of course I will.'

The ARP man produced a tin hat—like a magician, I thought—and clapped it on my head, and they walked me round to the entrance of the tunnel, with tarpaulin over the top weighed down at each side by bricks. It seemed to lead right into the middle of a great mound of rubble. 'She's underneath that lot, see,' said one of the workers. 'This is the only way we can get to her.' He handed me a torch, and Dr Royce gave me the tablet to put in my pocket. 'This won't work immediately,' he said, 'but see if you can wait with her and keep her calm. Her name's Miss Tate.'

'Good luck, miss,' said the man who'd given me the torch, 'and remember, keep low and try not to knock anything.' It was easy at first—you could stand under the tarpaulin—but then it flattened down to a tunnel through the rubble, with bits of wood and pipe sticking across it. I couldn't see much in front of me, despite the torch, but I was aware that all the time I was shuffling forward, the tunnel was growing lower and narrower until I was right down on my stomach, scrabbling forward using my hands, with about an inch to spare on either side of my shoulders. I could feel myself starting to sweat, because I was frightened—it was very eerie, like crawling into a tomb, and then this wailing noise burst out from the end of the tunnel, almost inhuman, so that I had visions of meeting Boris Karloff or Bela Lugosi at the other end, as well as this horrible, sick fear inside that there would be another raid and I'd be trapped and crushed.

After a few minutes I was trembling so badly I could hardly move, but I knew I had to do it, because there was no one else who could. Then the wailing stopped, and I thought, I've got to prepare myself for the worst, because no one had actually *seen* the woman and they didn't know what sort of state she'd be in. So I had visions of finding a dead body, but all the time I was saying to myself, *I must not fail, I've got to get there* . . .

Then the space widened out into something like a small cave. The ceiling wasn't any higher, and I couldn't have turned round, but at least there was a bit more room. There were a few planks standing upright at the end, with gaps like a badly made fence, and when I crawled forward and shone the torch through, there she was. At first I couldn't tell which end was which, because the small beam didn't illuminate the whole of her body and she was buff-coloured from dust and seemed, in a strange way, to have merged with the other rubble, but then I realised she was curled up on her side with her face pressed into the ground. She didn't seem to be breathing, and I thought: *I'm too late, she's dead.*

I heard a slight scratching noise and sensed a movement just out of the range of my torch beam—my first thought was, it can't be a rat, not already, and for one awful moment I thought I was going to be sick. I moved the torch over to see, and saw a slight movement of her head towards me, and one eye begin to open, and I realised I couldn't remember her name, and, worse, I couldn't think of anything to say. Something came out—I'm sure

309

it was perfectly idiotic, but the woman muttered something in return, so I thought, well, at least she can hear me. I dug the tablet out of my pocket, found a gap just wide enough for my hand and wrist to fit through without disturbing anything, and asked if she would take it.

When she put out her hand, she turned her head to face me, and for a moment, with her eyes closed, and the plaster-white face and hair matted with dust, she looked like a corpse, and I almost pulled my hand away—but when she opened her eyes, there was something so . . . I don't know . . . human? The human spirit, I suppose. If I was given to flights of fancy, I'd say I was seeing her soul.

She wanted me to hold her hand, so I did, and we stayed like that until they called to me to come out. I just listened, mostly. She told me that she had a son, Tommy—she was rambling, and I don't think she knew what she was saying half the time. I certainly don't think she meant to tell me about her son, because afterwards she said he was her sister's boy, and seemed so worried about my knowing that I had to lie and tell her I'd misunderstood.

Tate, her name was. Rene Tate. About halfway through, I suddenly realised who she was: the prostitute from the shelter. Then she told me there was a body down there: the woman whose flat it was. I thought afterwards: if I'd known both—or even one—of those things, would I have gone? It wasn't a comfortable moment. I'd like to say the answer was absolutely yes, but I can't put my hand on my heart and swear it, which is awful. All I can say is, I'm jolly glad I did go because it was the right thing to do, and I'm glad I met Rene, because let's be honest, in normal circumstances I'd never

310

meet anyone like that, let alone have a conversation. I mean, she didn't tell me she was . . . you know . . . what she *does* . . . but with the child and everything . . . It only goes to show, the ideas one gets about certain people aren't always right, because she seemed just like anybody else. Rather common in her speech, of course—that's the snob in me coming out, I'm afraid—but perfectly nice, and none of that really mattered. Lying there like that, we were just two women, and I don't think I've ever felt so close to anyone in my life. I don't mean close in the way that I'm close to Minnie or Dad, or even Mums, but that I've never had such a strong feeling of shared humanity. There was no difference between us: I could have been her, and she me, because the life force that was inside us both was the same. And if that tunnel had fallen in, it would have been extinguished and we'd just have been two bodies, wouldn't we? Ashes to ashes, dust to dust—no difference at all.

Rene'd called me an angel, and I thought afterwards, you'd never have said that if you knew what I was really like! But it made me think of Tom being my angel, because that's how it ought to be, everyone helping everyone else, and it shouldn't matter who they are or what they do. It's sad, really, that it should take a war to bring out those qualities in people, like Mums going to Mrs Dorn when she had the baby, even though she's so frightened of the bombs. It doesn't say much for the human race as a whole, that it takes something so dreadful. But it's taught me a lesson about judging people, at any rate. It was like the business afterwards with the air raid warden, when they'd brought Rene out and I'd taken her down to the shelter. That was *very* strange.

When I came out Mrs L and the men said how sporting I was to do it, and lots of other nice things that left me blushing like fury. But later on, a warden who hadn't been there before came up to the van and said, 'Excuse me, miss, are you the one who went down to Miss Tate?'

When I said I was, he said, 'I'm Harry. Harry Nolan.'

'Oh. We've met before, haven't we?'

He smiled. 'I rather think we have, miss. They told me what you did tonight and I wanted to say thank you.' He stuck his hand through the hatch for me to shake. 'May I ask your name?'

'Armitage. Lucy.'

'Well, Miss Armitage, what you did . . . bless you for that.'

It struck me as strange, because he didn't sound like an official at all, more like a relative or . . . I suddenly found myself wondering, again, if he was . . . you know . . . a *customer* of Rene's, and I couldn't look him in the eye at all.

He said, 'I don't suppose . . . well, you wouldn't happen to know where she's gone, would you? The nurse here said she wouldn't go to the first aid post.'

'No, that's right. She's at the shelter. The one at the other end.' I leaned over and pointed. 'At least, that's where I took her. She wanted to see her sister, because her brother-in-law died, you see. He was in there, too.'

'Oh, I see. That's dreadful. But Rene . . . Miss Tate . . . she wasn't hurt, was she?'

'More shocked, I think. She'd been down there for some time, you know, but she was terribly brave about it.'

'Oh, she would be, miss. And so were you. There's not many would do it.'

'Oh, anyone would. I was the only one that could fit, that's all.'

'Well, bless you for it. I can't thank you enough.' And he shook my hand again, and hurried off down Wild Street.

I kept puzzling over it afterwards. You could tell from his eyes and the way he spoke that he really cared about Rene, but she hadn't mentioned a brother, only her sister, and anyway, he didn't look anything like her. But you know who he reminded me of? This is going to sound very odd, given what I've said, but he made me think of Dad. Not the way he looked, because Dad's thin and beaky, and Mr Nolan's big and broad and looks like he might have been a boxer once, but the way he was. Decent. You could trust him, I thought. Although how one can pick these things up from less than five minutes' conversation, I don't know. But that's what made me think he couldn't be one of Rene's men-friends, because I know Dad would never do anything like that.

But what a lot I shall have to tell Minnie and Mums! Have decided I will tell Mums—she seems a changed person after the business over Mrs Dorn and the baby. She was singing along to the wireless last night, and that's something she hasn't done for *weeks*. She must have told the neighbours about Minnie and I wearing the saucepans on our heads, too, because this morning when I was on my way to work, Mrs Milne called out, 'Where's your tin hat?' I told her Mums was making breakfast in it! But that's good, because it means Mums must be going

313

out and about again. I'm not going to tell them what Rene *does*, though. They'd be horrified.

The only cloud on the horizon was that I discovered, after a couple of hours' much-needed sleep on a camp bed at the centre, that Tom's cigarette card is no longer in my handbag. I'm pretty sure I had it with me this morning, and I've tipped the bag up and turned everything out, but it isn't there. It can't have been in the van, or we'd have noticed it when we were tidying up. I suppose it could have fallen out when I gave Rene the handkerchief, but I'm sure I would have noticed. If it did fall out in Wild Street I don't suppose I'll ever find it again because the place is such a mess, and in any case, it's probably been roped off by now.

As I walk back to the station, I'm hoping against hope that I did leave the card under my pillow, after all: must check as soon as I get home. I don't know what I shall do if it is lost: I hate the thought of lying to Tom, but the truth would be too awful. However, I shan't put it in the letter, and I needn't bring it up unless he asks, which I don't think he will. I got the feeling it was rather a shock for him to see the brooch again, like a reminder of something he'd rather forget. He certainly didn't want it back, and I think it'll be the same with the card. It's rather odd, now I come to think of it: it's as if he's been entrusting his memories to me because they're too painful for him to keep himself.

That, combined with a perfectly horrible smell of sewage from somewhere near the river, rather take the edge off my feeling of satisfaction at a job well done, but one can't have everything. At least I've got the brooch safe.

Rene

I was pretty groggy when I came round. First thing that happened was I tried to sit up, but hit something, and for a horrible moment I thought I was still trapped underground. Then I realised I was on a lower bunk and I'd thumped my head on the bottom of the one above it. Then I saw a pair of big yellow eyes staring at me, and it was a black cat, sitting at the end of my bed. There was a lot of shouting in the background—a ring of women, all yelling at once, with this little ratty-looking warden in the middle, trying to reason with them.

'You can't turn the poor beast out in this!'

'The rules state—'

'Bugger the rules! That's Mrs Everley's cat, and you're not throwing it out!'

'I'm sorry, but animals aren't—'

'You lay one finger on that cat, and you'll have us to deal with!'

I got off the bed and tottered towards them, then tapped one of the women on the shoulder and pointed at the cat. 'Is that George?'

'Yes, that's right. This bastard wants it out.'

'Mrs Everley's dead.'

'Yes love, I know. Here . . .' She looked down at my tattered skirt. 'Were you the one with her?'

'Yes.'

'Blimey, dear, you didn't ought to be standing up, not after that. Come on.' She led me back to the bunk, helped me lie down, and covered me with

315

a blanket.

'Have you seen my sister?'

'Who's that, then?'

'Nicholls. Dora Nicholls.'

'Oh, yes. Down the other end, poor woman. You heard about Joe?'

'Yes, I know . . . I told her.'

'Dreadful business. Dora's having a lie-down. Best not to disturb her, I think.'

'Where's Tommy?'

'Oh, he's being looked after, don't worry.'

'All her things . . .'

'I don't know about that, dear, but she'll be lucky . . . Looters everywhere. You hear these stories, don't you? No respect for other people's property any more, though from what I've heard, there wasn't a whole lot left to pinch.'

'No, there wasn't.'

'She'll have to go to the Assistance Board, tomorrow. They'll sort it out.'

'The cat . . . it's expecting—Mrs Everley told me.'

'I don't think so, dear, its name's George.'

'I know. She said she made a mistake.'

'It does look a bit big round the middle, come to think of it. All the more reason for it to stay put. I'd lie down again, if I were you. You look done in.'

She went off and got stuck into the argument again, and I closed my eyes. I was exhausted, but I couldn't sleep. Everything was spinning round inside my head: Joe, and how Dora was going to manage, and the chest with the money, and Mrs Everley and her blasted cat, and how I'd lost my identity card, but I felt too tired and numb to be worried about any of it. Perhaps it was the shock, I

316

don't know—or that tablet—but I couldn't seem to get a grip on my thoughts, somehow. It was like being on the outside of my own mind. Then I heard someone say, 'Rene,' but it seemed to take a long time between hearing and understanding, sort of like a pebble being dropped into the middle of a pond when you're standing on the edge and the ripples come out wider and wider until they reach you.

'Rene.'

When I opened my eyes, there was Harry, sitting on the floor beside the bed. 'How are you doing?'

'Oh, Harry, am I glad to see you . . .'

'Are you all right? Nothing broken? You should be at the first aid post, you know.'

'I'm all right, Harry, really. Just a bit . . . you know. What's the time?'

He grimaced and glanced at his watch. 'Half past one. You'd think they'd be asleep by now.' He gestured at the gaggle of women. 'Now, come on, have a bit of this.' He held up a little flask. 'You look as if you need it.'

'What is it?'

'Brandy. Only for emergencies.'

I swallowed some. It felt like fire going down my throat, but certainly helped. 'Lovely. Thanks, Harry.' Then I looked at the end of the bed.

'It's gone.'

'What has?'

'The cat. They were arguing about it. Oh, well.'

Harry looked worried. 'Have a drop more.'

'Well, if you've got some.' I held out the cup. 'But there really was a cat in here. It was Mrs Everley's. I was in her flat when we were hit. Ground floor. She was worried about it, Harry. She

317

said it was called George and it was expecting and she'd lost it and that's why she wasn't in the shelter. Then she said she was sorry she never offered me a cup of tea and then she just died, Harry. Like Joe. That's my brother-in-law; he's dead, too . . . his arm, it was there . . . I didn't tell Dora about it, but his arm fell on me, it just—'

'Come on, don't upset yourself. You don't have to talk if you don't want to. But I am taking you to the first aid post, as soon as you can move, Rene. You've got to let a doctor have a look at you, at least.'

'I'll be all right in a minute. Let me just pull myself together . . . get my legs over the side . . . Ooooh . . . Better keep the blanket, for decency's sake.'

'A-a-a-untie Re-e-n-e-e!' Tommy came barrelling across the shelter, bawling his head off, and buried his face in my stomach.

'There, there, pet, it's all right, it's all right . . .' I'm stroking his head, thinking what a stupid thing to say, it's not all right at all, but you've got to say something, and kids don't really understand, do they?

'Come on, let's mop you up a bit, shall we? Have you got a handkerchief, Harry? That nice girl did give me one, only I gave it to Dora.'

Harry pulled out his handkerchief, and I gave Tommy's face a wipe and got him to blow his nose, but the poor little lad was crying and shaking, and I could see it wasn't doing much good. I said, 'Come on, you sit up here beside me. You've got to be a man now, look after your mum, because she's very upset over your dad.'

'What . . . what are we going to do?'

318

'I don't know, darling, but we'll sort something out.'

'Can we come and live with you?'

'Yes, dear, if you like. This is Mr Nolan. Are you going to say thank you for the handkerchief?'

Tommy looked at Harry, and hiccupped. 'Th-thank you,' he whispered.

Harry said, 'What's your name, son?'

Another whisper. 'Tommy.'

'Well, Tommy, I'm going to take your auntie to the first aid post. She's had a nasty shock, and I think she needs to see the doctor. Do you want to come with us?'

I said, 'Wait a minute, what about Dora?'

'I'll go and see who's looking after her, and I'll tell them he's coming with us. It's probably better if she doesn't have the worry of him, not now.'

So the three of us went off to the first aid post, and Harry got Tommy and me sat down with mugs of tea and said he'd see me later. I did have a fair bit of blood on me—most of it was Joe's, from his arm, but I couldn't explain that in front of Tommy, so the nurse insisted on undressing me to check, when all I wanted was to be left alone. You can't blame them for that, I suppose, but all the same . . .

We spent the rest of the night dozing on a camp bed, and left when the All-Clear went at seven. We saw Mr Bernstein, my landlord, for a spare key, then went home. I was completely filthy, but far too tired to do anything about it, and poor Tommy was as exhausted as I was, so I got his shoes off and put him on the bed, and then I did the same, and he put his little arm round me and we both went straight off to sleep. We only woke up when Dora came at midday.

She looked stunned, like she didn't know where she was. She sat on the bed with Tommy and they had a cuddle and a bit of a cry while I made a pot of tea. I told her, 'You can stay here as long as you want.'

She looked at me over Tommy's head and said, 'It's very kind of you, Rene, but we can't stay here, not with . . . well, you know. Mrs Lord, she's from the next block—ours was evacuated, what was left of it—she's said we can go there, and she's got a camp bed so it'll be easier. I've been back to our block, but it's hopeless. I kept picking things up and throwing them away again. There's nothing worth keeping. I didn't even recognise half of it. I was looking for that chest of Joe's, with the money in, but I don't suppose we'll get it back, not now— it's all the savings that he was keeping for us, all lost . . .'

I said, 'Look, Dora, you'd best forget about that money. It's not going to bring Joe back, is it? Let me take you down to the Assistance Board. They didn't find my handbag, or not that I know of, so I'll have to get a new identity card.' I remembered as I said it that the letter for Tommy had been in my bag, too, and the photo—the only one I had of Vic—and they were well and truly buried. I felt a bit sorry to start with, but after a while I thought, well, maybe it's for the best, all things considered.

I couldn't believe it when I looked in the bathroom mirror. For a moment I thought I'd gone white, because you do hear about that sometimes, when people have a shock, but then I realised my hair was one solid great lump of plaster dust. It took me ten minutes just to get out all the pins, and then I had a dreadful tussle brushing it out, and

320

even when I'd finished it looked so terrible that I had to wash it. The hot water ran out halfway through, and the basin looked as if it was full of thick black soup by the time I'd got done.

I had a wash after that, then I dried my hair in front of the fire and felt ever so much better. Dora was sitting in the armchair with Tommy in her lap, and I couldn't help feeling jealous, even then, that it's Dora he goes to when he's upset and not me. It's daft, but with that sort of thing, you can't help it, even when you've only got yourself to blame in the first place.

The town hall's right down the bottom of Charing Cross Road, by Trafalgar Square. They'd got a list of people killed or missing stuck up on the door. Joe's name was on it, and Mrs Everley, with nine or ten others. There was four there with the same surname, which really upset Dora, because they'd been neighbours, a family with twin girls Tommy's age.

There was a lot of hanging about and waiting, but in the end Dora managed to fill in a war damage claim for the flat and they gave her twelve pounds for food and what have you, to tide her over, and I sorted out my identity card. Dora kept asking me, all the time we were waiting, 'Do you think they'll find Joe's money?' and I didn't know what to say. Afterwards she said, 'I suppose they don't bother, do they, once they've got the people out. I'll go and have a look again tomorrow . . . Oh, Rene, I'd rather have him back than any money, but I don't know how we're going to manage, I really don't. All that money he was saving, and now it's gone, and I don't know what I'm going to do. he'd have wanted us to have it, wouldn't he? He

321

was saving it for us.'

I looked at her poor face, all white with grief and shock, and I thought, well, that's it, Rene my girl, she's convinced herself she's lost a good breadwinner, and you'll have to take his place, for Tommy's sake. I said, 'We'll manage. We're a family, aren't we? We'll stick together.'

'Oh, Rene, I don't know what I'd do without you, honestly I don't.' And she starts sobbing her heart out, right in the middle of the street, and Tommy's tugging at her hand, going, 'Mu-um, Mu-um . . .' and his lip's trembling, and I can see it's all he can do not to join in, and I'm thinking, I've got to look after them, I don't care what happens or how frightened I am, I've just got to pull myself together and look after them . . .

I said to Dora, 'You'll be all right. You'll get your pension, won't you? Widow's pension?'

'I suppose there'll be something, but I don't know, and it'll take time to sort out, won't it? At least I'd got my handbag with me, with our ration books and whatnot.' She'd opened it and she was fishing inside for a hanky, when she suddenly looked up and sniffed and said, 'Oh, I forgot, there's this . . .' and she held up this little blue thing. It took me a minute to recognise it, but then, well . . . my heart almost stopped. It was Lily's blue felt case.

'Where did you get this?'

'It's yours, isn't it? It was in your hanky.'

'What hanky?'

'You gave it to me, remember? In the shelter at Wild Street. When I unfolded it, this thing fell out. Must have got caught up in there. Rene, why are you looking at me like that? It *is* yours, isn't it?'

'I . . .'

' 'Cos if it isn't, we can always throw it away. It's only a cigarette card inside. Robert Taylor.'

'I know.'

'Let's see, let's see.' Tommy's hopping up and down, holding out his hand.

'Are you sure that's where it came from? The hanky?'

'Yes, I told you, it fell out on my lap. Stop looking at me like that, Rene, it's only a cigarette card, for heaven's sake.'

'Let's see!'

Dora gave the little case to Tommy, who immediately started pulling at it so the card dropped out on the pavement. I said, 'Oh, don't do that, dear, give it to your auntie. Look, it's just a silly old cigarette card.'

'Oh.' He lost interest after that, and I put it in my pocket.

'I don't understand. When I showed you, you looked like you were going to have a heart attack.'

'Oh, it's nothing. Just . . . I lost it ages ago, and I was a bit surprised, that's all.'

'I thought you liked Clark Gable.'

'Yes, I do, but it's nice to have a change, isn't it? Anyway, let's get you round to that neighbour, shall we?'

We had to walk past the wreckage that was Dora's flats, and I hurried the two of them along as fast as I could, because it was a forlorn sight. A great big heap of rubble, with a few people scrabbling about on it, and others standing around listlessly, as if they couldn't believe what had happened, and a couple of kids playing tag. I saw the top of a mangle sticking out, and what looked

323

to be half of a basin, and there was the odd bit of material and broken china here and there, but mostly, it seemed to have turned into one big brown and grey lump. Hard to believe that it had been the same as the other half of the building not twenty-four hours before.

Dora was a bit tearful when I left, but Mrs Lord seemed a good sort, very welcoming and friendly. I told them I'd be back tomorrow to see how they were doing, and went off feeling like I'd got a lump of lead in my stomach, with my heart banging away like there was no tomorrow. Soon as I got back round the corner into Long Acre, I stopped and pulled Lily's little blue case out of my pocket.

Dora said it had come out of the handkerchief the girl had given me, which didn't make sense. Why should *she* have it? There couldn't be two of them . . . unless she knew Lily, which wasn't very likely. I mean, she'd been in the air-raid shelter, and if Lily'd lost it, if it had fallen out of her bag, or . . . but Lily would have *said*, because she told me, she always used to kiss Robert Taylor goodnight, and the girl, Lucy, wasn't a regular. But *she* couldn't be . . . I mean, Jack the Ripper was a man, wasn't he? So far as we know. No, that's ridiculous. Women don't do things like that, and if they did it would be some crazy old maid, or a mannish sort that's gone a bit funny in the head, not a nice kid like her. I suddenly thought, perhaps someone gave it to her. Father? Brother? She hadn't said anything about a boyfriend, not as far as I could remember, but I'd seen her in the shelter with that airman, the handsome one. Maybe he wasn't a boyfriend, just a pal. I couldn't remember her surname, either. Lucy what? All I knew was, she came from the mobile

324

canteen.

I went over to the post but Harry wasn't there and no one seemed to know when he'd be back, so I left a message for him, just to say we were doing all right, and then I rushed round to Eileen's. She was at home, thank God, and by the time I got through telling her, and I'd showed her the cigarette card, she was as puzzled as I was, but she kept saying, 'It means Ted's innocent. We've got to take it to the police. They'll have to let him go.'

'But I don't know the girl's name—well, I know it's Lucy, and I know she was on the canteen, but that's all.'

'But they can find out, can't they?'

'And I was the only one who knew Lily had this card. Ted didn't know.'

'He must have.'

'No. Lily thought he'd be jealous.'

Eileen thought for a moment, then said, 'Yes. He could be a bit funny like that. But still, Rene . . .'

'It's only my word, isn't it?'

'Yes, but they'd investigate, wouldn't they? They'd have to.'

We argued for a bit, but in the end we went down to the police station at Tottenham Court Road, and Eileen waited outside while I went in and talked to the sergeant. I wasn't very happy about that, but as she said, it wouldn't look good if they found out she used to be Ted's girl.

I recognised the sergeant immediately—I've seen him a good few times over the years—and I think he probably knew me, too, although he didn't say so, just, 'What can I do for you, miss?'

So there I am explaining about the cigarette card, and he's listening, but I can see from his face that he thinks it's a lot of rubbish, and the more I say, the dafter it sounds.

'You say this girl gave it to you, miss?'

'No, she gave me the handkerchief, and it fell out. I'd know it anywhere.'

'But you don't know this girl.'

'No, but I know that her name is Lucy, and—'

'Did you see the paper today, miss?'

'No.'

'Well, if you did, miss, you'd know we weren't investigating any further. He's been charged, miss.'

'What?'

'Charged. Today. At Bow Street.'

'So . . . that's it, is it?'

'That's all I can tell you, miss. Now, if there's nothing else . . .'

Well, that was that. Eileen was waiting for me round the corner. 'Well?'

'It's no good. He's been charged.'

'When?'

'Today. Didn't you get a paper?'

'No, I never bother with them.'

We bought a paper, and sure enough there it was: *Man Charged With West End Murder*. 'It says Ted's appeared today at Bow Street, charged with the murder of Mrs Lily Franks who was found dead recently in the West End. It says she was suffocated and slashed with a sharp instrument. Doesn't seem possible, does it?'

'I'm telling you,' Eileen said, 'he didn't do it!'

'Well, that's what it says. It's hopeless. You did say he'd had a skinful. I mean, perhaps it wasn't the same as Edie or Annie, perhaps Ted was so drunk he just didn't know what he was doing, or . . . oh, I don't know. Like I said, it's hopeless.'

326

'I don't believe it.'

'Well, they must have some evidence, or—'

'I'm telling you, Ted didn't do it! There's another one out there doing the killing, and this lot—' she jerked her head towards the police station, '—want him to get on with it and see us all off. That'd save them a heap of trouble, wouldn't it?'

'Come off it, Eileen, they're only doing their job.'

'No they bloody well aren't! If they were, they'd have caught the bastard, wouldn't they?'

'Well, there's not a lot we can do, is there? Come on. I don't know about you, but I could do with a drink.'

We went across to the Swiss on Old Compton Street and had a couple of Gin and Its, but it didn't help. Eileen was grumbling on about the police, and I knew she was as scared about going out as I was, only we'd got to the point where it wasn't worth talking about it. Seeing it like that, in black and white, *suffocated and slashed*, made me feel really sick. I sat and thought about it for a while, and then I said, 'Well, as I see it, there's only one thing we can do.'

'What's that?'

'I suppose we ought to have done it before, but . . .'

'What?'

'Find Lucy. Talk to her.'

'The girl who helped you? How can we?'

'Well, there's this warden I know, and I think he might help us if I ask him right. I know it's not like the police, but he might be able to find out where the canteen came from. It's got to be better than us

327

asking, hasn't it? Then, if we find her, we can ask her how come she's got Lily's card. I mean, it might be something or nothing, but at least we'd know, wouldn't we?'

'I suppose. It's got to be better than nothing. This warden, when will you see him?'

'He usually comes round the shelters, so I'll have a word then. But right now, I'd better get off home and do myself up.'

'You're never going out, Rene?'

'No choice.'

It wasn't too lively, which was a blessing, because another big raid would have just about finished me. As it was, I don't know how I got through it, but by midnight I'd managed to make six pounds. I saw one regular that I took back. He always wants a little scene where he pretends I've caught him stealing and goes down on his knees and begs my forgiveness. In some ways it's money for old rope, because you don't have to take your clothes off and you can charge the full amount for it, but it does mean you have to do the play-acting, getting angry and the rest of it, so you've got to put your mind to it, and it took far longer than it should have done because I was all over the place.

By the time I knocked off and went to collect my things for the shelter, I was too exhausted to think about Harry, or Lucy, or Dora, or anything, except sleep. I tottered round to Soho Square, found a place to sit, and that was the end of that until the All-Clear went at six thirty.

It was lovely to take off my clothes and slip into bed, and as I drifted back to sleep, I remembered how nice and cosy it was, lying there with Tommy's little arm round me, being able to stroke his hair

. . . I slept until eleven, when Harry knocked on the door. I was a bit embarrassed at being all untidy, but Harry didn't seem to mind, just said he'd wait on the landing while I got dressed.

When I opened the door, he said, 'Good. Now then, let's start again, shall we?' and he took me in his arms and gave me a kiss. It was just as nice as the first time, especially when he stroked my hair and said, 'You don't know how glad I was to see you in that shelter, Rene. I really thought . . . well, I thought . . . that was it.'

I laughed and said, 'You don't need to worry about me, I'm as tough as old boots.'

'Well, it's lovely to see you anyway. Let's do that again, shall we?'

So we had another kiss, and when we came apart he said, 'I'm getting very fond of you, you stubborn old thing.'

'Less of the old, if you don't mind. I'm very fond of you, too.' I took his hand and led him over to the armchair. 'Now then, you sit down here while I make us a pot of tea, and then there's something I've got to tell you.'

When I brought the tray through, Harry said, 'They gave me your note at the post, but before you say anything—if you won't take my money, at least let me give you these.' And he held up a packet of Players.

'Harry! You are a dear. I was getting desperate. But you can't give me all these; what are you going to do?'

He waved a finger at me and shook his head.

'You've got a contact, haven't you?'

'Ask me no questions, and I'll tell you no lies. Perks of the job, you might say.'

329

'Fair enough. I won't pry. But you've got to have one, at least.' I lit two and passed one over, and then I got stuck into the story about Lucy and the handkerchief and Lily's cigarette card in the blue case and getting the bum's rush from the copper at Tottenham Court Road.

Harry thought for a moment and said, 'I spoke to that girl—the one who helped you. Lucy, her name was, I remember that, but . . . Armstrong? No, that's not right. It'll come to me in a minute.'

'I wondered if you'd be able to find out where she came from. Which centre, I mean.'

'I don't see why not. I can ask, anyway. But it's all a bit complicated—nobody knows what anyone else is doing, most of the time . . . Armitage. That's it! Lucy Armitage.'

'It sounds right.'

'I'm sure it is. I've met her before, you know. In Soho. She was meeting her young man. RAF, if I remember rightly.'

'Yes, he was. I've seen her too, Harry, in the shelter at Soho Square. Only the once, but he was there with her.'

Harry said, 'Supposing I do find her, what are you going to do, Rene? I agree it couldn't be her doing this, but if whoever gave her this thing is . . . who you think he is . . . it could be dangerous. It could even be him, you know. The boyfriend.'

'That's why I need to talk to her. She could be in danger too, couldn't she?'

'Well, not necessarily. He might only be interested in . . . in . . .'

'Tarts? Then what's he doing with her?'

'I don't know, but . . . yes, that's what I meant.' Harry looked embarrassed. 'Rene, I'm sorry. It's just that there are some queer people out there, and I'm worried about your safety, that's all. Come here.' He held out his arms.

'I warn you, I'm not as light as I look.'

'I don't mind. Come on.' He tapped his knee and I went over and sat on it and we had a cuddle.

'I'll be fine, Harry.'

'Well . . .' he stroked my face with the back of his hand. 'If you only want to talk to her, I suppose it's all right. It's possible that Lily might have dropped it, or something, and she just picked it up off the street.'

'I expect that's what happened, Harry, but I've got to find out, because if it isn't—'

'If it isn't, you will be careful, won't you? I mean, you won't do anything without telling me first?'

'I promise.'

'Really?'

'Yes.' I leaned over and kissed him on the lips. 'A real promise. Signed, sealed, and delivered.'

'Good. I'll see what I can do, then. If I find out, what do you want to do next?'

'I could write her a note. Just saying I'd like to return the handkerchief and thank her properly. I won't mention the cigarette card. I thought I could ask her to come round here. I don't know. Normally, I'd never . . . not a girl like that, and she might think it isn't respectable, but I've got to do *something*, Harry, and she seemed . . . for one thing, she came crawling down all that way with that tablet for me, when she didn't have a clue who I was and she could easily have been killed.'

Harry looked a bit doubtful, but in the end he said, 'I suppose it's worth a try. But if I do manage to find the centre, I think I ought to take the note.

331

The volunteers aren't there all the time, and it might be a day or two. Besides . . .'

'Besides what?'

'Well, it'd look better, wouldn't it? My being a warden. More official.'

'Yes. Yes, you're right. And you're a darling. I'll write it now, shall I?'

'In a minute.' He gave me another kiss, and we cuddled for a bit. I must say, Harry's the perfect gentleman, he didn't try to do anything else. I was sitting there enjoying it, when I suddenly realised how easy I could really fall for him, if I let myself, but I can't let him get any funny ideas about trying to 'rescue' me, because it wouldn't work.

In the end, I said, 'Come on, let me up, I've got to get this letter written, and then I'd better get round to Dora, so I can get that handkerchief back and give it a good wash.'

Harry laughed and said, 'There's romance for you,' but he let me get on with it, then he pocketed the letter and we had a nice farewell on the landing before he went back to the post and I went round to Mrs Lord's.

Dora was very quiet. I said hello, but she didn't seem to notice I was there. It would have been better if she'd cried or done something, but she didn't, just sat there. I sat down next to her and held her hand for a while, and then she said, 'They've told me that Joe's at the mortuary. They've said they'll tell me when I can have him back.'

I could imagine why it might take time—what that other warden had said about Mr Mitten being like a jigsaw puzzle, it would be the same with Joe: some poor person having to put enough bits together to make a complete body. I said, 'I suppose they've got a lot to do, but I'm sure you'll get him back soon.' Just so long as she doesn't want to see him, I thought.

She gave me back Lucy's handkerchief, and I gave her some bits I'd bought the day before—chocolate for Tommy, and a tin of cocoa and a few other things. She didn't thank me, just sat there turning them over and over in her hands. Mrs Lord came out onto the landing with me afterwards, and said, 'I'm that worried about her. She won't eat, just keeps going back to the . . . you know . . .' she jerked her thumb in the direction of where Dora's flat had been. 'She keeps talking about money, too, saying Joe had a pile of it hidden in the flat and she's got to find it. Look at this.' They've got this sink on the landing that they share with the others, and she pulled a basket out from underneath it, full of broken china and scraps of material and whatnot. 'She brings it back. It's all rubbish, but she won't let me throw it away. I keep telling her there's no money there, but she seems to think it's valuable. She keeps coming out to check it's where she left it.'

'Oh, dear. I suppose it's the shock. How's Tommy?'

'Out playing. He seems fine, but you never know with kiddies, do you?'

'No. But I'm ever so grateful, Mrs Lord, you looking after them like this.'

She shrugged and said, 'Well, you do what you can . . .'

'You are good. I've left a few bits and pieces with Dora, and I'll be back round tomorrow—if you don't mind, that is.'

' 'Course not, dear. You're very welcome.'

It was queer how I felt after that. Thinking of Joe in the mortuary made me angry, the idea that human beings can do that to each other, but then Mrs Lord being so kind made me think there is good in the world, after all. But I suppose wars bring out the best as well as the worst in people, don't they?

What with worrying over Dora, and fretting about whether Harry'd be able to find Lucy Armitage, I'd got myself into quite a state, so this afternoon I thought I'd go to the pictures to see if I could take my mind off it all. There was a comedy at the Tivoli, with Arthur Askey, and I thought that might cheer me up a bit, but the minute I got inside the actual cinema, and it was dark and all I could see was the beam from the usherette's torch, I just froze. It was like being buried all over again. I kept telling myself, just go in and sit down, you'll be fine, but I couldn't. No matter what I did, I couldn't make myself walk into the dark.

In the end I went home and gave Lucy's handkerchief a good old boil up on the stove, then I got dressed up for work. Just as I was going out, I remembered Lily's little blue felt envelope was in my pocket, and put it on the mantelpiece for safekeeping. Harry told me he'll come round the shelter tonight and tell me how he'd got on with tracking Lucy down, so all I can do now is wait.

SATURDAY 19TH OCTOBER

Lucy

Finally completed my letter to Tom and posted it on Wednesday, although heaven knows when it'll reach him—letters take such ages, now. Told him all about Mrs Dorn's baby—well, most of it—and about the mobile canteen and the 'incident'. Such a nondescript word for a matter of life or death, isn't it? Hope it didn't sound too much like boasting, because I know it's nothing, really, when you compare it to what the RAF do every day. However, I shouldn't like Tom to think I'm doing nothing while he's risking his life.

I arrived home from the office yesterday—only half an hour's delay, hallelujah!—and Minnie handed me a letter. She looked very reproachful, and I saw why when I turned it over: it was from Tom! Tried to be nonchalant, asking what was for dinner and whether she'd done all the blackouts, but fear I didn't succeed too well; it must have been blindingly obvious that I couldn't wait to read it. I tore upstairs the minute I could, flung myself down on my bed and ripped it open. It's dated Monday— five days ago!

It was short and very sweet. Old-fashioned. He hoped it wasn't a liberty, but he likes me very much and wants to see me again. He's got some leave coming up, a forty-eight hour pass, and he wants to meet me in London *this evening*—it only just reached me in time! At the bottom he put, *You needn't write back if this suits, because I may not get*

335

the letter in time. I had to stuff my knuckles into my mouth not to shout out loud from sheer happiness.

I was worried about Minnie coming up and finding me reading Tom's letter, so I put it back in its envelope and pushed it under my pillow, but a minute later I felt I just had to get it out again for another look, to reassure myself that it *was* real and I hadn't just imagined the whole thing. In the end I simply lay there on my back with the letter pressed flat against my heart and only went back downstairs when I heard the siren.

I've told Mums and Minnie about my escapade at the bomb site last week, but I didn't mention it to anyone at work. Everyone's heartily sick of bomb stories, and besides, Phyllis and Vi keep going into huddles and whispering about Mr Bridges, which is very off-putting, especially as they keep glancing at me while they're doing it. I still haven't plucked up the courage to say anything to Phyll, and probably won't—the atmosphere is quite bad enough without my adding to it. As Mums would undoubtedly say, Don't make trouble for yourself. Not that I've told her, of course!

At the centre this afternoon, Mrs L and I were loading up the van when the woman in charge appeared and said, 'Somebody's been asking for you,' and handed me a note. Then she pursed her lips and said, 'I hope you're not going to make a habit of this,'—obviously thinking it was a boyfriend—and I was so flustered I didn't know what to say. Mrs L obviously had the same thought, because she just laughed when I said I'd got no idea who it was from and said, 'It's all right, dear, I shan't pry,' and tactfully removed herself to the front of the van while I opened it.

Dear Miss Armitage,
I hope you will not mind if I take the liberty of
writing to say thank you for helping me. I
would like it if you could come and see me
soonest, I would like to thank you properly
and give back the hanky that you were so kind
as to lend to me. I do hope that you will be
able to call on me at my address which is 14B
Frith Street, Soho, WI. I am usually at home
in the afternoon.
  Yours sincerely,
  Rene Tate (Miss)

Well! I was astonished, and showed the note to Mrs
L. 'It's the lady from those bombed flats in Wild
Street, last week, the one in the tunnel. Saying
thank you.'

'That's nice.'

'She wants me to go and see her. Look.'

Mrs L read the letter, and her eyebrows went up.
'Soho. And, judging by the address, a *flat*.' She gave
me a meaningful look.

'Yes, I suppose so.'

'Well, I don't think you ought to go on your own,
dear. I'm sure this Miss . . . Tate . . . is a perfectly
nice person, but there's a lot of nasty business in
that area, and you do hear these dreadful stories
about the white slave trade. I do think it would be a
good idea if you took somebody with you, just in
case.'

'I'm meeting a friend later, near Piccadilly, and
I'm sure he'd come along if I asked him.'

'I suppose you'll be all right if there's a man
there, but you will be careful, won't you? I mean,

with the blackout and everything, I'm sure they—'

'Don't worry, Mrs L. Tom'll look after me.'

'Tom . . . is that your young man, then?'

'Well, yes.' It was funny hearing him described like that, especially when I haven't even told Minnie or Mums. 'Yes, I suppose he is.'

I thought about it on and off during the shift, and by the time we were finished and I'd smartened myself up, I'd decided that Mrs L is right and it's a good idea not to be on my own. I read in the paper last week that the police have caught the West End murderer—as the press call him—but nevertheless, one does hear of awful things happening to girls in those sorts of places. I'm sure Tom won't mind, not once I've explained, anyway.

I can't wait to see him!

SATURDAY 19TH OCTOBER

Rene

This last week's not been so bad, except that I didn't see Harry at all and I went nearly mad wondering what was happening. The other warden kept coming to the shelter instead of him, and I thought, well, Harry can't have any news, or he'd have told me. At least wondering if Harry'd found the right centre to leave my note for Lucy helped to keep my mind off other things. When he finally did come into the shelter, on Friday, I fairly flew at him. He said, 'Sssh, you'll wake everyone,' and took me outside. He said he'd spent his afternoons off

338

trudging round to all the local centres to find the right one, and eventually he'd managed it. I threw my arms round his neck and gave him a big kiss. He said, 'I can't stay long, Rene, but just remember— *be careful.*'

'I've promised, haven't I?'

'Yes, but all the same . . . How are you, anyway?'

I found myself telling him about the silly business with the cinema, and not wanting to go in, and he said, 'I suppose it's natural. It's bound to be a bit difficult for a while. I tell you what, why don't I take you to the pictures next week?'

'It's sweet of you, but you'll never get the time.'

Harry shrugged. 'Depends on Hitler, but I can try. I can always have a snooze while you watch the picture.'

'Charming.'

'Well, you know . . . But apart from that . . .'

'I'm not having nightmares, if that's what you mean. I told you, Harry, I'm tough that way.'

'I know. How's your sister?'

'Not very good, really. I'm worried about her, Harry. The neighbour—the one she's staying with—she says Tommy's doing all right, which is something, I suppose.'

'Rene . . . About Tommy. You're very fond of him, aren't you?'

'Well, yes, he's—'

'He looks a lot like you, Rene.'

'That's because, you know, family resemblance . . . Can't see it myself, though.'

'He's yours, isn't he?'

You could have knocked me down with a feather. I meant to say 'no', but what came out was, 'How did you know?'

'Watching you with him . . . something about how you were, how you looked at him. And when you said you'd got no choice but to carry on working . . . I was thinking about it yesterday, and I put two and two together, that's all.' Harry paused, then said, 'He's a nice little boy, Rene. You must be very proud of him.'

'He doesn't know. No one does, except Dora. And Joe, of course, he knew.'

'I won't tell anyone.'

'Please don't. I want him to have the best chance, and . . . Please, Harry. It's important—for both of us.'

'I know. It's all right, Rene. I understand.'

'Good. How's Albert?'

'Getting greedier by the day. Be time to let him go, soon.'

We had another nice kiss after that, and then Harry had to go. Sitting in the shelter afterwards, I thought, maybe he does understand. I suppose I shouldn't have said I'd go to the pictures with him, but he's so nice . . . Mind you, I might not be able to get into the cinema, even with Harry there. Gives me the shivers just thinking about it. Silly, really, but there you are. I got quite a decent night's sleep after that. It's easier with other people there, I think. I never thought I'd get used to it, with all the snoring, and people coming and going, and the smell, but you do. It's better than spending the night in a bomb crater with a house on top of you, anyway.

I'd no idea if Lucy would come. I thought the address might put her off, for one thing, because with a nice girl like that, well, they hear all these stories, don't they? It was in my mind all through today that she might just ignore my letter, or write and tell me to keep the handkerchief, and of course I didn't know if she'd actually got the letter or not, or when she might get it, or anything, and it was getting on my nerves something rotten, so when the knock on the door came at about seven o'clock I fairly jumped out of my skin. And when I saw her standing there, well, that was marvellous—at least, it was for a second, until I saw *him*.

That was like . . . as if everything suddenly went into jerks, like one of those old pictures, where they walk funny, and I heard her say, 'I hope you don't mind, but I've brought a friend. This is Tom,' but it came all in snatches, and I heard myself say, 'Oh, yes, how do you do?' as if it wasn't me at all, because I recognised him immediately, the one from the shelter, the handsome one, and I'm thinking, *is it you?*

Because you don't know what they'll look like, do you? There's no reason why a murderer should be an ugly man, and that's all going round in my mind, and at the same time I'm thinking, don't be ridiculous, it can't be him, a man who looks like that would never . . . I mean, why should he? He can get a girl any time he likes, and I told myself not to be so stupid, because he seemed nice enough, but standing there with his face coming at me in flashes—eyes, hair, mouth, cheekbones—I didn't know what to think. Normally, I can judge a man—well, with my experience, I ought to be able to—but this was like lots of little pieces, and I couldn't make them fit together. All the time I'm remembering when I've had men who couldn't satisfy themselves, and how some of them get nasty. I've never had one I couldn't deal with, but this is a different thing all together, knives and pokers . . . you don't expect it with a young man, or a man who looks like that—and a fighter pilot, too—but that doesn't mean it never happens, and a nice girl like Lucy wouldn't have a clue about that sort of thing.

My mind was whirling, and the girl was talking away but I wasn't hearing half of it. It crossed my mind just to bring out the hanky and give it to her and say thank you, and then they'd go away and that'd be the end of it, but at the same time I was thinking of Lily and Edie and Annie and I just couldn't do it, because I had to know. That makes it sound noble, but it wasn't; it was all happening so fast I didn't know what I was doing at all, really, and I heard myself say, 'Oh, do come in,' and there I was, taking them through to my big room, and the minute we've got past the curtain in the doorway I see the blue felt case where I've left it on the mantelpiece, in front of the clock. But they're right behind me and it's too late to go over and hide it, because they'd notice, and I'm thinking, what am I going to do, oh dear God, what am I going to do?

Then the girl, Lucy, sits down in front of the mantelpiece and I'm thinking, that's all right, she can't see it, but he's not sitting down, he's looking around, and I'm thinking, any minute, he'll see it, and if it's him . . . Then I think, I've got to distract them, and I'm talking about tea and all sorts, but when the girl says yes, that means I've got to go through to the kitchen. And I'm standing there waiting for the kettle to boil with my heart going like the clappers and I'm praying, praying it isn't him. So then I'm making this tea, thinking, *calm down, Rene, get hold of yourself*, and trying to think about what I'm doing: now I'm getting the cups, now I'm opening a tin of milk, now I'm filling the teapot, but it's like a nightmare, and I can hear them in the other room, whispering, and then I think, maybe it's a trick, they're in this together, they're going to kill me. But at the same time I know it can't be true, and if it's either of them it must be him, but I can't be sure . . .

I go in with the tray, and there's the girl sitting there with the blue coat, and for a moment I think, *she's wearing my coat*, but then I remember, we've got the same model, and she's talking and I'm talking and he's looking round, looking round, and then he says he'd like a glass of water so I go back to the kitchen because I've got a cold tap, and he follows me, and of course I have to stand with my back to him, filling the glass. I'm chattering away— God knows what I'm saying—but I can feel his eyes on me, and I've got my shoulders hunched up and I'm thinking, he's going to come for me any minute now, if I can only smash this glass in time and get it in his face, I've got a chance, at least . . . Then I hear a movement behind me and I whip round and the glass crashes against the edge of the sink and breaks. There's shards of it all over and blood trickling down my arm, and he's there by the door still, staring at me. We look at each other and then I notice his eyes on the jagged bit of glass that's in my hand and the blood, and that's when I know for sure. I'm certain it's him from his eyes, the look in his eyes . . . and he takes a step towards me, and I take a step back, but there's nowhere to go because the sink is in the way and I'm pressed right up against it, and he opens his mouth to speak and a voice behind him says, 'Oh, you've cut your hand!

343

Are you all right? Can I help?' and it's Lucy. She sounds so normal and relaxed that I know she's nothing to do with it and she's a good kid, so I tell her not to worry and I'll sort it out myself. She goes back out again, but he's still in the doorway, watching me, so I say, *Yes?'*

'The water.'

'Oh, yes. Water, of course.' I take another glass off the shelf and fill it and hand it to him and he says, 'Thank you,' and follows Lucy into the other room. I run my cut hand under the tap and when I turn round for a tea-cloth to dry it, I catch sight of the table and it looks different, somehow, not the table itself but the things on it. For a moment I can't think why, but then I realise it's the tin-opener that I used for the milk, it's gone, and I think, no, that's mad, I'm going mad, I must have put it back in the drawer. But when I look it isn't there, and my hands are shaking, going through all this cutlery, and there's blood falling on it, from my hand, but the tin-opener's not there, and it's not on the floor, either, or in the sink, and I'm thinking, no, you're imagining it, you're dreaming, pull yourself together . . . I rinse my hand again and put a plaster on it, then take a deep breath and go through to the other room.

I glance at the tea tray, but the tin-opener isn't there, either. Lucy's still in the chair in front of the mantelpiece, but he's standing up, and the other armchair is facing the mantelpiece, so I sit down quickly, and the girl is talking away and I'm talking back, and I hear myself telling her all about the cat called George that they thought was a he-cat and turned out a she-cat and I'm thinking, for God's sake, Rene, these could be your last words, and you're talking about some bloody old fleabag of a cat. She's smiling and nodding, and I can see him out of the corner of my eye, standing there watching us, and when the siren goes I nearly jump out of my skin, but it's a relief because it's the perfect excuse to get them out and then I'll go straight round to Harry. Without thinking I look over at the clock and make some silly remark about how it's late tonight . . . Even as I'm saying it I realise I've made a terrible mistake because now he's looking at the clock and she's looking at the clock but I know they're not seeing it, they're seeing the blue felt case underneath, Lily's case, and the siren's going and he looks at her and sees where she's looking, and then she looks at him and looks at me and then *he* looks at me and the siren stops. There's silence and I know it's him, I can see it from his face, and I'm trying to work out if she knows and if she knows I know, and I'm trying to think what to do, but it's as if my brain has got stuck. Then she opens her mouth to speak and he cuts across her and says, 'Where's the lavatory?'

SATURDAY 19TH OCTOBER

Jim

After a week sitting in the Ops room doing sweet FA, it was a relief to get away this afternoon. I sat on the train into London, watching the faces. My brain still felt like cotton wool. These last few days, everything's looked like it does when you fly through cloud, and all the sounds seem muffled.

345

Must be that stuff the MO gave me. It's an odd feeling, but probably just as well. I thought I'd enjoy looking at the WAAFs in the Ops room, but all they did was remind me of that stupid bitch Lucy, and then the anger built up inside me—the only feeling I've had that penetrates the cloud inside my head like a sharp point—jabbing at me, goading me until I wanted to grab hold of one of those girls and squeeze the life out of her.

I haven't been going into the mess much. Even if the others don't say anything, I could see it in their eyes. I knew they were thinking 'that could be me' but they've got no idea—it's like a barrier, and if I could just get across it, I could be one of them again, be with them. And I will. I'll do it. Because it's all I've ever wanted, but it was that bitch, stopping me. She thought she could trap me, make me weak, but she got what was coming to her, I made sure of that. I wouldn't let her take it away. I knew I could make it all right. Had to be done. Because the planes didn't look the same. I'd stand on the airfield for hours, staring at them, but it wasn't the same—as if I couldn't see them clearly any more, see them as they really *are* . . . the most beautiful things in the world. The bitch reduced them to nothing, lumps of metal, and the thrill was gone. But I knew I could sort her out. I knew she'd be there, just so long as my letter arrived, I knew she'd be waiting for me, and she was.

And I was prepared. I'd got a knife from the kitchen, a big one, and I took the bloodstained clothes out of the cupboard and got rid of them in the wood. I'd planned it, managed to nip into the mess and pinch the coal-shovel when no one was looking. They'll think it's someone playing silly buggers again. It was hard work digging the hole, but I managed it. No one was about.

I'd arrived in London a couple of hours early and wandered around Piccadilly in the dusk. Eros is boarded up now, just a pyramid shape, and the failing light gave the buildings soft edges, and the bodies, rushing past, seemed fuzzy. I suddenly realised I haven't seen London in the daytime since the bombing started. There are white marks where they've painted the kerbs with stripes.

The odd thing was, the haziness from the pills made it better. When Lucy arrived, I felt quite calm. The idea of what I had to do was fixed in my mind, the only thing that stood out with clarity. When I looked at her, her face seemed blurred as it had the first time, when I saw it through the stocking. We were standing on the corner of Regent Street, and the noises kept coming and going in flashes through the fog in my head: a bus, or high heels on the pavement, very loud, as if isolated from all the other noises, and then it would all merge back, and I'd hear her voice again, talking . . . like switching frequencies on the R/T . . . and she kept calling me Tom.

She thought she was clever, all right. Tried to trick me with some cock-and-bull story about having to go and see a woman in Soho to collect a handkerchief, talking about how they'd met on a bomb site and this woman wanted to see her. I didn't believe it—I could sense that it might be a trap—but she kept insisting, saying she was afraid to go alone. I asked her who the woman was, and she got silly then, giggling and pretending she didn't know—gave me some name she'd made up—and then she started saying Soho was

347

dangerous, which was why she didn't want to go there on her own. I said, 'But you've been before,' and then she started talking about how she'd never visited anyone and some woman she knew had said it might be the white slave trade. I wanted to get on with the job in hand, but she was irritating me with her yapping wearing me down, so I said I'd go just to get some peace, and we began walking towards the place. She took my arm and started giggling again, and it made my skin crawl. I wanted to shut her up there and then, get hold of her and shake her and shake her until she stopped, but there were too many people around, so I stopped listening to her and concentrated on staying ahead of the game, touching the knife inside my jacket and preparing myself for what might happen when we got there.

The front door of the place, alongside a shop, was open, and I followed the bitch into a dingy front hall and up some stairs. She made a great pretence of not knowing which floor this woman was on, which I didn't believe. It was the second floor, I think, and a brown-haired tart came to the door and said, 'I was hoping you'd come, dear,' to the bitch. I was standing back, but I could see she'd got her eyes fixed on me the whole time. I couldn't see the face too well in the hall, but once we got inside I was sure it was a trap and that the two of them were in it together, trying to confuse me, because the tart had the same hair and eyes as the bitch—older, and with heavy make-up, but apart from that, almost identical.

The bitch said, 'I've brought someone with me. I hope you don't mind.'

'Not at all, dear, not at all. I'm Rene, how do you

do?' Then she went straight on, without waiting for me to introduce myself. 'Now, would you like some tea, or something stronger? I've got some beer, if you'd like.'

I thought, you must think I'm stupid if I'm falling for that one, because she seemed very nervous, as if she was up to something, so I said, 'No, thank you,' but the bitch said she'd like a cup of tea. The tart held up a curtain and said, 'Now, you two make yourselves comfortable. I'll be right through.'

It was a room with armchairs and a bed. The bitch looked a bit uncomfortable when she saw that, and sat down quickly and stared at the floor.

I said, very quietly, 'You know what she is, don't you?'

'Well, yes . . . but she's still a human being, isn't she? Though what my mother would say, I don't know. I'm glad you're here, Tom.'

I saw she was undoing her coat buttons and said, 'Let's keep it short, shall we?'

'Yes.' She gave a nervous giggle. 'Don't worry, I'll keep my coat on. Don't want to make ourselves too much at home, do we?'

She laughed and went on talking, but I wasn't listening, because I'd seen how the bed was reflected in the mirror over the mantelpiece—I knew it was done on purpose, because I kept looking at it, then away, and each time I thought I saw, out of the corner of my eye, the body of a woman, one of the tarts, with her stomach and between her legs gouged and bloody. I couldn't see which one because it changed every time I looked—it was making me feel ill and I knew this was what they'd intended, to get me all unsettled, but the bitch was pretending to be concerned.

349

'What is it, Tom? What's the matter? Are you all right?' She was sitting with her back to the mirror and I saw she wanted me to sit opposite, but I wasn't going to do that because of the mirror, and there wasn't another chair, so I went to sit beside her, and just as I stepped on the rug I saw it, in front of the clock: the blue felt case I'd given to the bitch, with the cigarette card in it. The one that belonged to the brunette. She couldn't have put it there—I'd have seen her. She must have given it to the other one . . .

I was trying to figure it out but my head was spinning; everything was getting out of control and I didn't know what to do next. I thought of making a run for it but then the bitch would have won and I'd have nothing. I knew I had to see it through: it was them against me, and whatever they did, *I had to see it through.*

The tart came in with a tray of tea. 'You look like you ought to sit down, dear. Are you sure I can't get you anything?'

'May I have a glass of water?'

'Of course, dear.' She turned to go into the kitchenette and I thought, I know what you're up to, you'll slip something in it, so I followed her to make sure. The room was untidy, how you'd imagine with a woman like that: dirty, with drawers not closed and a lot of clutter everywhere. I noticed a tin-opener on the table, half-hidden by a newspaper, and when the tart had her back to me, rinsing the glass, I slid it out from underneath and slipped it into my pocket. Something extra, as well as the knife. It made me feel better, stronger.

The tart had been chattering away: 'Such a nice girl, Miss Armitage, and so brave. I'm sure she's told you all about it. You must be very proud of her. I'm sure she's proud of you, too,' but she must have heard me moving about because she whipped round suddenly to face me and the glass she was holding smashed against the edge of the sink and cut her hand. She held it up and I could see a gash between the forefinger and thumb, blood running across her palm, and that made me want to pick up a piece of the glass and stab her with it, and I went to move towards her—she was all I could see, nothing else in the room but her face, the fear in her eyes and her hand with the blood . . . And then I heard the bitch's voice and it all seemed to break up, and I didn't want to do it any more.

I knew the tart was frightened. When she gave me the water and I went into the other room I heard her clattering about with the cutlery, dropping things on the floor, and I thought she might be looking for the tin-opener. I wondered if she was going to say anything. The bitch was chattering away, but I wasn't listening. I managed to swallow some of the water, but I could feel myself sweating. The stuffy little room seemed to be closing in on me until I thought I was going to choke, and when the tart came back the two of them pretended not to notice, just carried on talking, glancing at me out of the corners of their eyes like horrible birds, beady brown eyes darting at me, their heads swivelling round when they thought I wasn't looking, talking as if I wasn't there, and I kept catching sight of dead women in the mirror; sometimes the blonde, sometimes the brunette, lying on the bed, so vivid I couldn't believe they weren't actually there, but each time I turned, there was nothing. Then I realised the women had stopped talking—they were looking at me and I didn't know what to do.

The bitch said, 'Tom—' but I didn't hear the rest because it was drowned out by the siren, and the tart glanced at the mantelpiece and said, 'One thing you can say, they're good time-keepers,' but I knew she wasn't really looking at the clock, but at the thing underneath it, the little blue case, and I saw the bitch's head turn in the same direction, and her eyes widen, and I could tell she was about to speak, so I said, 'Where's the lavatory?'

The tart stood up and said, 'Out here, dear. I'll show you,' and she took me onto the landing and pointed down the stairs. My bowels felt molten, ready to explode, and I just got there in time. I knew she couldn't have put anything in the water, because I'd have seen her, and besides, I'd only had a couple of sips. But I knew I had to be quick—I couldn't leave them alone together. The tart wasn't important, just a distraction; it was the bitch. I had to deal with her as soon as possible.

She was standing at the top of the stairs when I came out. Just her, no sign of the tart. She had the blue thing in her hand, holding it out towards me. 'Tom? What's going on? I don't understand . . .' She started to come towards me, down the stairs. 'You said . . . you told me . . . this was your sister's . . .' She stopped in front of me and glanced upwards. 'She said it was her friend's, and she died, and then she said—'

I hit her, and she staggered backwards, one hand on her face. 'Tom!'

'Listen, you stupid—' I reached out to grab her, but she was too quick. She pushed me away and then I was off balance and reeling as she bolted down the stairs. I heard her wrench the door open and then she was gone. I followed, as fast as I could—I had to catch up with her, stop her—and as I left I heard the tart's voice, shouting after us, but I thought, it doesn't matter, she doesn't know who I am, and anyway, she's insignificant, it's the other one I want, the bitch. It took a moment to pull out my torch, but then I saw her near the end of the street. I thought she'd go straight ahead, and I knew I had to catch her before she got to Soho Square, to the shelter, but she turned a corner and then ducked into an alleyway, and I followed. I picked out her feet and ankles in the beam of my torch, then she must have tripped because she was sprawled out in front of me, face down, and I could see all along the length of her stockings, where her coat and skirt had gone up as she fell. She twisted round and tried to get up, and I heard her panting. She was saying, 'Please, Tom, I'm sure it's a mistake, please don't hurt me, let me go, please—'

I made a grab for her but she clawed at me and knocked the torch out of my hand and then she was on her knees in front of me and I had my hands round her neck, but I couldn't get a grip on her— the coat was in the way, and the hair, and she was thrashing back and forth and I couldn't hold on to her. The next moment I heard footsteps come up beside me—a woman—and there was a light shining in my eyes, blinding me. I lunged for it, knocked it away and fell forward and heard a grunt underneath me and one of them scrambling to their feet, but I couldn't see anything, just a flurry of arms and legs and hoarse breath and voices. I don't know how long it lasted, but I managed to get hold of a hand; it was balled into a tight fist and when I prised back the fingers there was a crack and a scream and I knew I'd got the bitch because the blue felt thing was there. She was holding it, trying to keep it from me, but she had it all right . . . I got on top of her and hit out at her face and pulled out the knife. It was hard at first, with the clothes and the way she was flailing about, but I did it, did it to her with the knife and the tin-opener, and then she stopped moving and I knew I'd beaten her and I'd won and I felt alive again, with all the sensation coming back to my body and the excitement and the thrill of it, it was there, and I didn't need to look back, even for the torch. I just ran and ran with no idea of where I was going, but it didn't matter, I'd done it, and I knew I could fly again and everything was marvellous and I was free . . .

On Saturday 19th October, I met the man I
believed to be Tom Matheson at Piccadilly Circus.
He had written to me in order to arrange this
meeting. He was wearing an RAF uniform with a
greatcoat and a respirator. I told him that I wanted
to visit Miss Rene Tate of 14B Frith Street, WI,
and he agreed that he would accompany me to this
address. I believed that Miss Tate earned her
living by soliciting and that is why I asked Mr
Matheson to come with me. We arrived there at
about 7.15 p.m. While Miss Tate prepared some
tea, I noticed that Mr Matheson was behaving
strangely. He asked Miss Tate for a glass of water
and accompanied her to the kitchen to fetch it. I
heard a glass breaking and went into the kitchen
where Miss Tate had cut her hand. She told me
not to worry, then we returned to the other room
and talked until we heard the air-raid warning.
During this time, Mr Matheson appeared very
nervous and walked about the room. I believe the
air-raid warning was at about 8 p.m. but I cannot be
certain of this.

When I looked at the clock on Miss Tate's
mantelpiece I saw in front of it a small felt
envelope very similar in type to an envelope given
to me previously by Mr Matheson. He had claimed
it belonged to his deceased sister. At this point Mr
Matheson left the room. I looked at the envelope
and found it contained a cigarette card with the

355

picture of the film actor Robert Taylor. I asked Miss Tate where she had obtained the envelope and she replied that it belonged to her friend Mrs Lillian Franks, who was a prostitute. I said, 'I do not understand.' Miss Tate then asked me who had given me the envelope and I replied that Mr Matheson had given it to me. I explained that it had belonged to his sister. Miss Tate then repeated that the envelope was the property of Mrs Franks, and that she thought Mr Matheson was responsible for her murder and also for the murder of two other prostitutes. I took the envelope and left the room.

Mr Matheson was waiting on the stairs outside. I showed him the envelope. I was very confused at this point and cannot remember what happened exactly, but Mr Matheson hit me, and after that I ran out of the house and into Frith Street. I went to one of the turnings off Frith Street and then into an alleyway. I believe I dropped the envelope at the entrance to this alley. Mr Matheson followed me. He got hold of me by the throat. I remember a woman coming to my assistance. She had a torch at that time, but it went out quite quickly when she came to help me. I believe that this woman was Miss Tate, but I could not see what happened to her. Mr Matheson had previously had a torch, but it fell to the ground. I did not remove my torch from my handbag. I next remember running to Old Compton Street, where I requested the assistance of PC Skinner.

I have been told that Miss Tate picked up the envelope and was holding it in her hand at the time she was killed, and it is my belief that she was mistaken for me.

I have read the statement given above and everything that is in it is true.

Lucy Armitage

On Saturday 19th October, about 8.45 p.m. I was on duty at the top of Old Compton Street and was approached by a man I now know to be Harold Nolan, ARP warden, Post D. I accompanied him to Bateman's Buildings, where I found the body of a woman lying on the pavement. Mr G. Callaghan and Mr R. Gillespie were also present. Both denied any knowledge of the deceased previous to this time. Mr Nolan, who was in a distressed state, informed me that the woman was known to him and that her name was Miss Rene Tate, resident at 14B Frith Street, WI. I telephoned for assistance and waited the arrival of senior officers.

John Halpern, PC 113, 'C' Division

STATEMENTS GIVEN TO CHIEF INSPECTOR PALMER,
'C' DIVISION BY SQUADRON LEADER A.C. MAXWELL,
NO. 603 Squadron, RAF Hornchurch

(i) 21st October 1940
Flying Officer Thomas Matheson has been missing, presumed killed, since 26th September.

(ii) 23rd October 1940
The description which has been given to me by Detective Inspector Walsh, 'C' Division, matches that of 78252 Flying Officer James Rushton. Flying Officer Rushton was recently found to be suffering from battle fatigue, and as a consequence was given a forty-eight-hour leave starting at 0700 hours on 19th October. I have been told that he intended spending this leave with his family in Coventry. He returned to RAF Hornchurch at 2000 hours on 20th October. I spoke to him at that time and would describe him as being in good spirits. He resumed operational flying duties on the morning of 21st October, having been passed fit to return to his duties by the Station Medical Officer, Sqn Ldr F.J. Gregson. His flight was scrambled at 1100 hours. He has not returned. His spitfire received a direct hit from an enemy aircraft while engaged in a dogfight over the Channel. This was witnessed by 72550 Flying Officer N. Balchin and 90294 Pilot Officer G. R. Sinclair. They reported that Flying Officer Rushton's aircraft was on fire. They did not see Flying Officer Rushton bale out and messages received by them over the R/T indicate that he was having difficulty in doing so. Both officers state
359

that Rushton is unlikely to have survived, and he is currently listed as missing, presumed killed. His family have been informed.

The trial of Edward 'Ted' Gerrity began at the Old Bailey on 9th December 1940, before Mr Justice Milne. It ended on the following day, when the jury took just twenty-five minutes to find him guilty of the murder of Lillian Franks.

Gerrity was hanged in Wandsworth prison on 18th February 1941.